GRILLED ARMAGEDDON

COOKING WITH DISASTER
BOOK 1

DAKOTA KROUT

MOUNTAINDALE
PRESS

ACKNOWLEDGMENTS

First, as always, to my wonderful wife, thank you for the support, and specifically making me focus on writing above all else in my career.

Next, to my amazing friends, especially Aaron Michael Ritchey. Thank you for sharing your ideas, comments, and time to help shape this into the series it was meant to be.

Lastly, for everyone out there who wishes they had a second chance with people they have lost, this book is for you.

May your future be delicious.

PROLOGUE

"It's time to go."

On the last night of his life, Nacho stood perfectly still, wrists manacled as his eyes roved one of the few overgrown green spaces of the camp. At that moment, he was doing his best to smell the roses that had bloomed in the area.

He snarled deep in his chest as he looked at his 'captors'. They didn't *need* to lock him up, but even knowing that he couldn't do anything against them—guaranteed by the magical contract that he had signed the second week after meeting the Guild Master in this new world—his own guild members were terrified of what he *might* do.

The reputation he had made for himself after the apocalypse made sure of that.

They'd already taken his assassin leathers, which he'd bought with an exchange of a month's worth of food. Now, he stood in clean jeans and a hoodie, which he'd bought specially from the Store to force people to see how far they had fallen. A person could get anything from the Store.

"Anything except redemption." The best assassin in the world breathed the words softly as he looked at a trio of roses that had grown to be several feet taller than the rest. The flowers were supporting each other, allowing for growth unmatched by those around them.

"*Silence*, prisoner."

Eli 'Nacho' Naches was flanked by Hogan and Whitney, Guild Master Crave's heavy hitters. As the moon began to rise, all three stood on the outskirts of his guild's compound, the muddy camp inside the walls cluttered with a mixture of tents, huts, and stone houses. On the other side of the barrier, the night was filled with howling and chittering monsters. They'd grown so large, powerful, and numerous that it was all humanity could do to hold off the few that came to investigate the fragrance of cooking fires coming from their area. It was autumn on the Starter World, though sometimes it still smelled exactly like Kansas City, Kansas had in the fall… before.

"Thanks for letting me take a few minutes to collect my emotions. I was going a little wild there," Nacho deadpanned; he had been a stone-hearted killer for years now. His emotions were dead and buried in the empty graves he had dug for his friends. His utter lack of empathy—as well as any positive emotion—was part of why he was so feared even by those who were supposed to be his teammates. He figured it had happened thanks to a mix of the terrible conditions, lack of proper food, loss of his friends, and getting hit in the head a *lot*.

The manacled assassin sniffed at the air. "Smells good. Someone found some proper oak. What's for dinner?"

"You are." Hogan's laugh caused the tiny bit of extra flesh beneath his chin to wobble, and Nacho stared at that movement *hungrily*. The mirth vanished quickly, replaced by awkward silence. The goon was a monster of a man; well-fed, his muscles strained his magical plate mail, yet he couldn't hide his fear when Nacho's dead eyes landed on him. The correct response, by all available data.

Crave's heavies were Body Players, and they'd been with the Guild Master since the very beginning of the Juxtaposition, three years ago, when life on Earth had changed forever.

Whitney was shorter than Hogan, though with a mop of bright yellow hair. Like his counterpart, he wore a giant sword at his hip, and he'd paid through the nose for his impressive white lacquer armor. The coloration didn't go well with his pale complexion—it brought out the pink in his rampant acne.

He wasn't alone in his dermatological state: three years of having to choose between getting enough calories to survive or spending credits on a bit of hygiene had been an easy decision for anyone that had managed to make it to this point. Despite the unfortunate state that he was in, his sneer only a few moments prior had been full of smug contempt as he pointed his weapon at Nacho's neck. The huge Tier two man had claimed he'd been a prison guard before the Juxtaposition, but those tattoos seemed a little *too* messy to have been done by a professional. As with all things before the end of the world, what they'd done in their previous lives didn't matter.

The only things that mattered these days were filling food and drinkable water. Those things didn't come cheap. Not anymore.

The assassin had just been returning from his most recent—and apparently final—mission for the guild when Hogan had slapped on the manacles and let him know he was about to be walking to the butcher block; the guild's only method of execution. Waste not, want not.

Nacho inhaled deeply, letting the smell of campfires and Putrid Mana-filled meat cooking fill his nostrils. Even after having lived in this reality for so long, it was still easier to pretend he was just at a backyard barbecue. Normally after a mission, he would've wanted to eat, chase a pretty face that wasn't *too* mud-caked, or seek any other distractions that kept his mind off what he had been forced to do.

Right now, his eyes held a glint of hope. The hope that all of this horror would be over soon. Best not to fight it. He had long since learned that panicking would only waste valuable calories.

Various eyes followed Hogan and Whitney as they escorted

DAKOTA KROUT

Nacho through the squalor. Dirty, gaunt men appraised them, some wearing inexpensive metal armor, others garbed in hardened leather skins. It was easy to tell the Body Players from the Mind Players, generally by how much meat they had on their bones. The Body Players had to be thick to wield their melee weapons; even the archers had to be overly muscular on their arms and shoulders to fire those massive longbows that required a ton of strength just to pull back the string.

The Mind Players were thinner, practically skeletons in comparison, but their skin was clear and well-hydrated. They all wore oversized packs that had once upon a time reminded Nacho of the tanks that flamethrowers required. Their mana pool was directly reliant on the volume of clean water they drank, so no one in their right mind was willing to leave access to a water source to chance.

"Earth is gone. Humanity is on its way out as well, if things don't change." Nacho chatted serenely as they walked. He knew he was correct: he had access to the highest levels of information available, whether legally or not so much. Even the most generous prediction only gave humans another eight months of survival. Not just because of the lack of food and presence of monsters. No... they were actively being hunted.

Monster attacks, rampant cannibalism, not to mention their main opponent in the Juxtaposition: the CrossHumans. They were so far ahead of humans that the competition was a joke, and they were sowing mischief, murder, and mayhem in equal parts.

As for himself, Nacho had done well. He'd kept himself and a lot of the people in the camp fed and safe because of the credits he'd brought in from his staggeringly numerous kills. He was Richard Crave's number one contracted assassin: the famed Shadow Killer. Nacho was the merciless dagger which the Final Victory Guild sent to end the threat of their enemies.

In the end, it appeared that Nacho had been *too* good at keeping himself alive and making his enemies dead. There was one last little question about his final fate, but he wasn't going to

4

waste his time wondering when he could just ask the two goons. Nacho's monotone chuckle made his escorts shiver. "Tell me, gentlemen… is Crave going to buy some tortilla chips, cheese, and jalapeno peppers for me? 'Last meal' sorta thing?"

"Why would he do that?" Whitney questioned his charge seriously. "Seems a waste to spend credits on a dead man."

"You tool, he's making a joke." Hogan slapped his partner, then settled a thick hand on Nacho's neck and squeezed it: a threat he assumed that the assassin couldn't do anything about beyond glare. "It's 'cause his name is Nacho. Why *do* they call you that, anyway?"

"You should be careful where you touch." Nacho deftly twisted away from Hogan, who gaped at his hand in horror upon realizing it was completely numb, and the numbness was spreading. "I'm named after a river. Back on Earth, I was Eli Michael Naches. My friends called me Nacho. Crave thought it was funny and ordered me to tell everyone that my name *is* Nacho. Now I can only tell you what the rest of it *was*. Also… those guys aren't from around here. They shouldn't be guarding the area, no matter if they *will* be allies."

A few warriors stood with pikes near the drawbridge of the keep, staring at Nacho with disturbing glares. Two parts hate, one part *hunger*.

"Always looking out for the guild, even after you found out that they're gonna spit-roast you for peace. You know, we do appreciate your sacrifice." Hogan's lips curled into a disgusting grin as he looked Nacho up and down. He licked his lips, and Nacho had to suppress his internal shiver.

"Not my choice, so it's not *my* sacrifice," the assassin growled in a low tone as they passed the unknown sentinels. "You're fools to think that allowing me to be killed is going to help you. All it does is take one of Crave's chips off the negotiation table."

"*Chips!* Because you're Nacho!" Whitney laughed uproariously, garnering scathing glances from the people around him. The outburst nevertheless succeeded in drawing rapt attention as the prisoner was led through Crave's crowded throne room, gliding like a ghost as the spectators stomped around on the ground hard enough to create tremors. Nacho had to wonder if he actually *was* some kind of dead creature already, and this was just going to be his body accepting that fact. "This place has been a living death since Reuben and Brie died. I'm just glad to-"

Hogan shoved him hard enough that he stumbled and fell to his knees. "Quiet down, meat. On your feet!"

"*Someone's* trying to get a promotion, using their big-boy brain to make rhyming threats and orders." Nacho muttered as he effortlessly regained his standing position, like a snake coiling up to strike. He was briskly marched from the throne room, through a corridor, and into an enclosed courtyard. There he found Guild Masters Crave and Kala waiting, along with their Warriors, Mages, and Healers. "Quite a collection to see little ol' me off."

That was where Nacho would die. Winking his left eye, then his right eye, and finishing with a light shrug, he pulled up his Stat Sheet one last time, just to measure how far he'd come over the years.

Eli 'Nacho' Naches
Patron Boon—0/1 used.
(Prerequisites for boon use: Unknown.)
Class: Shadow Killer
Level: 28 (Tier 2, level 8)
Experience Points: 166,408,000 to Level 29!
Current Credits: 50,897

Build choice: Self-Applied
Body:

- *Fitness: 40*
- *Metabolic efficiency: 19*

Mind:

- *Mental energy: 20*
- *Circuit: 17*

Satiation:

- *Hunger: 100*
- *Thirst: 100*

Total Health Points: 90
Total Mana Pool: 40

Skill Slots (4/4 used)

- *Gamer Reflex (Passive) Level 29: Gain first strike in 58% of all circumstances.*

  No Mana, Hydration, or Metabolic Cost

- *Shadow Speed (Active) Level 29: Enhanced speed on the first 6 attacks when attacking unaware targets, or 3 attacks on aware opponents.*

  Tier 1 Enhancement: Darkness Dash.
  Tier 2 Enhancement: Umbral Stab.

  Mana Cost = 0%
  Hydration Cost = 0%
  Metabolic Cost = 15%

- *Ninja Hush (Active) Level 29: Walk silently 116% of the time on normal surfaces and 58% on loud or annoying surfaces, including squeaky boards.*

  Tier 1 Enhancement: Throw Noise.

Tier 2 Enhancement: Shush Hush.

Mana Cost = 5%
Hydration Cost = 5%
Metabolic Cost = 15%

- *Midnight Blend (Active) Level 29: Hide in shadows 116%*
  effectively at night, 82% in a shadowy environment, and
  58% effectively in daylight or other bright conditions.

Tier 1 Enhancement: Blending Backstab.
Tier 2 Enhancement: Shadow Teleportation.

Mana Cost = 5%
Hydration Cost = 5%
Metabolic Cost = 15%

Nacho couldn't help but be disappointed in the fact that he'd never been able to increase his mana pool; he'd never guessed that his sneakier skills would use so abyssal *much* of it. If only he'd known to choose a different Build Type, all of his stats, skills, and every waking moment would've been so much *better*. Alas, gaining knowledge of the System was just on the edge of impossible, so expensive that only the most foolish or desperate bought the information packs offered within the Store.

He still wondered about his Patron's boon, from a Patron without a name listed. It was common knowledge that the Patrons ran the Juxtaposition, but no one knew why or how; not even the few Warlocks, who received their power *directly* from their Patrons. Some players had managed to receive a boon without being a Warlock—people like Crave. He had confided in Nacho, back when they were friendly to each other, that he had something called 'Dope or Nope' Intuition.

Nacho only had a basic idea regarding what that boon granted. When Crave realized that he had mentioned it out loud, well, that was when their friendliness had dried up. Even so, from what Nacho could gather, Crave could tell if someone, something, or some place was dangerous—the 'Nope'—or if it was 'Dope'. As in, whether it was a hidden treasure for him to interact with.

Upon seeing how beneficial even such a ridiculous-sounding boon had been for the Guild Master, Nacho had tried everything he could think of to trigger his own mystery boon, but it was all for naught. When he finally did manage to snag a boon, it had come with some kind of hidden requirement for use that he had yet to find. Unfortunately, he didn't have much time left.

Kala, the so-called Death Knight, was the Guild Master of the Gorged Guild. She was a big, broad woman, imposing in her black plate armor with her helmet's visor closed. She had been lucky to acquire a rare artifact early on, a colossal black sword nearly as hefty as she was. The weapon had helped her level up faster than anyone around her, and her personal power was one of the reasons her guild had survived the first calamity-class monster that had appeared.

Crave had survived as well, thanks to Nacho. That fact still irked the assassin, moreso now that his good deed was about to go on to be punished.

While Kala had embraced her Death Knight persona with full-on roleplay enthusiasm, Crave had chosen a three-piece suit from the more modern outfit selections in the Store. He'd earned an assassin class, like Nacho, but no one looking at him would have ever known it. Crave didn't talk about his class very much, but he'd been quite stabby in his time—even if he wasn't all that great at fighting. He'd had to go out of his way to kill people in their sleep, thanks mostly to his lack of variety in powerful magic items. That is, until he enlisted people like Nacho to do the dirty work for him.

In his breast pocket lay a fluffy black feather—his best magical item—and while everyone knew it was there, few knew what it actually did. Beneath his suit coat, in a shoulder holster, was his black dagger: the Onyx Tooth. It was a nice magical item, but it wasn't even the best small blade in the room. Abyss, it was barely in the top five. No, the best knives in close proximity belonged to Kala's master assassin, Myron.

Nacho *hated* Myron.

The man had zero professional standards; he was just a too-sneaky thug. Even more irritating, he had lucked into a greater artifact: the MurderSong Blades, which were a linked pair of very powerful daggers. The rumors about the twinned weapons indicated that the MurderSong Blades could cut through *anything*, but the only thing Nacho knew for certain was that their every attack came with a variety of bonuses.

Myron, dressed in red leather armor, carried the knives sheathed at his sides. One was as short and as fat as an actual cleaver, while the other was long and slender. Nacho nodded dismissively at him. "Hey, Myron. Fancy seeing you here."

"Fancy *feast*, Nacho. All you're good for now is cat food." The rival assassin appeared well-fed, his cheeks tinted with a healthy pink glow. It was the unibrow and the bad haircut that wasn't doing him any favors. He licked his hand and wiped at his own face. "Meow. Doesn't look like you were expecting that… haa. Yeah, you're not the only one with jokes. I gotta admit, I'm sorry to see someone with your talent going down. You were too good, Nacho, and you know it."

"No, you're not sad." Nacho scoffed at Myron, who simply shrugged and smiled back at him, highlighting his missing teeth.

The unfortunate fact of the matter was that Crave didn't *need* exceedingly powerful armor or weapons to intimidate other humans. He had the ultimate power: ten *thousand* guild members working for him. Most were Tier one, but some few were Tier two like Nacho. Feeding people at that level was a full-time job, and in the end, the Tier twos were the reason Crave had made this despicable deal that was costing Nacho everything.

The reality of this situation was starting to hit him, and despite his typical propensity to be unemotional, his hands began to display a slight tremble. Taking a deep breath and slowly releasing it, he went over the facts of why he had been betrayed.

Kala would join up with Final Victory, becoming subservient to Crave, and bring along something special that would alleviate some of Final Victory's issues. All Kala wanted in return was Nacho served up on a silver platter—literally. Crave, tall and handsome, had been a Vice President of Sales before the Juxtaposition. Or he'd been a guard at a prison. The story changed, depending on his mood and level of sobriety.

"Oh, hello there!" Nacho snapped out of his despondent mood and cheerily waved toward Kala. He could see her blue eyes drilling into him through her visor. "Did you finally get tired of me killing your Tier ones? Stealing their credits is just the way the world works, isn't it? Last thing; you *do* understand that I could only do that if I was *ordered* to do it, right?"

"Don't be dramatic." Kala's voice was weary. "You know why I want you dead."

"Yup. I killed your dad. Stab, stab. Right through the clavicle and into the trachea. Poor guy had no chance at getting *that* healed." Nacho shrugged and clapped, the manacles clinking together harshly enough to make the observers clench their teeth and reach for their weapons. "Didn't know. Didn't much care. Frankly, didn't have any choice. You're a Guild *Master*; you know exactly what I mean. Crave knew he had that juicy Tier two steak in his Storage Slots. We ate steak au poivre for days. Peppery yum-yum. It was a nice break from, you know, eating each other."

"All this rampant cannibalism does suck pretty hard," Myron chimed in, only to have Kala silence him with a glare, barely able to stop herself killing Nacho herself.

Unyielding, she once again fixed those blue eyes on Nacho. "At the end of the day, *you* were the person holding the knife, so you're the one that dies. Then the Gorged joins the Final Victory, and we have a chance against Arriod and the CrossHumans. They're coming for us, and they're not holding back anymore."

Nacho's shoulders managed to get lifted a tiny fraction before dropping once more, as though the weight of the world was holding them down. "The Gorged lucked into that magic oven, which kinda changed everything for your guild. Answer one thing for me: is it true? Does it *really* take the Putrid Mana out of monster meat?"

"Yes. It does," the Death Knight informed him firmly. "We can eat what we kill now."

"Then my guild members might get an actual meal. Good enough. I just wanted this to be worth something real." That fact made Nacho feel better, and it was time to die before he lost his nerve. "Now, who is going to be doing the actual execution here?"

Myron raised his hand and waved it like an excited child. "That would be me."

"Ugh. *No.* You're the worst, Myron." Nacho stuck his tongue out, then looked over at his Guild Master. "How about you, Crave?"

"I can do it. Gotta preserve any credits you've been hoarding, after all. For the good of the guild, of course." Crave took the black feather out of the pocket in his suit, and Nacho's eyes followed it in confusion. "Thank you, Nacho, for your sacrifice."

"You can thank me by winning whatever messed-up game the Juxtaposition turns out to be. Keep our people safe." Nacho kept his eyes on the feather. He didn't know for sure, but he had a feeling that when Crave had ordered him to kill the party that had included Kala's father, he had known *exactly* how valuable they were to Kala. It was messed up, but if it was true... the bait had been masterfully set.

Nacho closed his eyes and relaxed. Life had given him a putrid deal, but he could finally be done with it. He could see Reuben and Brie again. That realization brought a real smile to his lips for the first time in months.

Crave nodded at Hogan.

Hogan grabbed at Nacho to force him onto the table that had been ritualistically prepared for the event. At that moment,

Nacho triggered his Shadow Speed and dodged the hand easily, then swept around before anyone could react, easily plucking the keys off of Whitney's belt. He had the manacles unlocked in an instant.

His Shadow Speed ability gave him three attacks against surprised targets. He had found loopholes in his skills over the years, which was the only reason he was able to do this all so quickly. He had 'attacked' the keys, then 'attacked' the keyhole with them. Finally, he used the last strike on Myron.

"Nacho, I order you to stop attacking!" Crave called as soon as he realized that the man was moving.

"Are you hiding a delicious secret, Myron? Something right under the skin, if you know what I mean?" Nacho trailed the flat of his blade down the man's stomach, forced by his magical guild contract not to hurt the morally filthy man. Baring teeth blackened by one of the *many* debuffs that came from having to eat other people, Nacho reached out and gently squeezed his target's nose. "*Honk, honk*. Just wanted to prove one last time that you were *always*... second-best."

Kala got all huffy and had unsheathed her weapon in the same second that Nacho began taunting his rival, roaring at her counterpart, "What's the meaning of this, Crave? We had a deal!"

"Getting betrayed by his superior, about to be eaten, and he couldn't do anything about it. I love it." Even with a 'honked' nose, Myron grinned like the unibrowed weasel he was. "I agree you were better, but this just makes me number one."

"Nah, I'm fine with all... *this*." Nacho dropped his hands and hopped onto the table on his own. "I just wanted to make it clear that I decided to do this of my own free will. If I were able to actually *fight* the compulsion, this would've turned into a bloodbath before the charter reduced me to a burned-out husk. I bet I could have taken out all your top rankers... but guess we'll never know now, huh? Don't worry. I'll be quiet and die like a good boy."

He unzipped his hoodie and let it drop, then shivered at the cold wood of the table against his back, relaxing as well as he could. Three years of being alone. Three years of killing other people. Three years of struggling to get food and water…well, food hadn't been a problem at first. Not until he'd Tiered up. Then it had become his *only* problem.

Crave stood over him with the feather in one hand and the Onyx Tooth in the other. "Any last words, Nacho?"

The assassin laughed despite the cold sweat dripping down his face and the colder fear in his belly. "Cook me face down, so you can kiss my butt."

Crave chuckled, then touched Nacho with the black feather. Nacho fell asleep instantly, missing his chance to learn what the feather did. He never even felt Crave's knife plunge into his chest.

One second—or an eternity—later, on Earth, May eleventh, two thousand and twenty-three, six months before the Juxtaposition… a notification appeared in Eli Naches' vision as he sat at his kitchen table, a bite of succulent omelet halfway to his mouth, and his eyes wide open in horror at the terrible vision he had just experienced.

Kronos Boon—Probability Vision—1/1 used.

Weirdest. Thursday. Ever.

CHAPTER ONE

"Crave!" Nacho snarled as he yanked himself away from the table, staggered into his bedroom, stumbled across the dirty clothes littering the floor, and crashed into his closet door. He was back in his apartment? Impossible! He would've thought it was a hallucination, or some kind of simulation, but no, he could smell his roommate's dirty socks. This… this was real? He was back in the apartment that he shared with Reuben, within walking distance of the University of Missouri-Kansas City, Volker campus.

He blinked as one particular detail resonated down to his soul. *"Reuben!"*

"What?" Getting an answer brought on another bout of blinking from Nacho.

That voice, somewhat annoyed, drew a smile on his face that a knife to the heart could never erase. He threw open his door, screaming, *"Reuben!"*

The concerned response echoed in the small space they shared. "What? Come on, Nach-man, are you okay? What happened?"

Nacho stumbled through their apartment, his eyes roving

over the strangest things. There was the couch they had held a party for after they'd pulled it off the street and finally had something to put in the living room. Its cushions were sunken from years of too much use, and it still faced the oversized TV and the PlayStation of questionable ownership.

His muscles seemed to be fighting him, as though he were wading through deep water. He was painfully weak and completely out of shape. Not only that, but all of the assassin skills he had spent hundreds of other people's lives to acquire were just… gone. Before the Juxtaposition, he had just been a twenty-two-year-old college student heavily into gaming. At the same time, just a few minutes ago, he had been *lethal*. Fast, strong, invincible to people at his own Tier. Hadn't he been able to *toy* with the second-best assassin in the world? Yes. Yes, he had.

"You're alive!" Nacho yanked open the door to Reuben's room. "*What day is it?*"

"It's May eleventh?" Still in bed, Reuben threw an arm over his eyes. "I see we're no longer knocking? You play a dangerous game, sir. I happen to have a fresh pair of socks and an untapped bottle of lotion right here."

"Excuse *you*." Brie, Reuben's fiancée and Nacho's second-best friend in the universe lifted her head from her pillow, smacking at the man she was lying next to as he chuckled. Her eyes flicked to Nacho, and she whipped her pillow at him. "No. This is not happening. There should be far less yelling and far more knocking. What's going on, Eli?"

"Probability Vision." Nacho laughed like a crazy man as he dodged the pillow with ease. "It was only a prophecy! I never had to eat people to survive! Guys. *Guys*. I was shown the next three years… ah, three years and six months. I know what's going to happen! We need to get ready!"

"He's lost it." Brie pulled the blanket up and covered her head.

"I'll help him find it again." Reuben heaved himself to his feet. His Sonic the Bedhog t-shirt barely covered his gut, and even then only when he actively pulled it down. "Nacho, if you need help regaining your sanity, I'm your guy. But first, you saw the future? Prove it. What grade do I get in my econ class?"

"A solid C," Nacho replied instantly, his eyes zeroing in on Reuben's with an intensity that made his friend flinch. "Your paper is good. Your final isn't. Also, November eleventh is the worst *possible* day for your wedding. Believe me. You'll want to change that date."

That got Brie motivated and moving. She squirmed upright, keeping the blankets pulled up to her chin. Her blue eyes blazed with fire. "We are *not* moving that date. Do you realize the raw planning it took to get on everyone's calendar? No. You don't. Don't mess with this, Nacho. Don't joke about my wedding."

Both of his best friends in the world were eyeing him with concern on their faces. Right then, Nacho realized that he'd been given a gift, the ultimate gift, but he had to be smart about how he handled things—not only for himself, but for his friends. Best friends.

People that were dead until just now.

He would make sure that never happened again, but he was starting to realize how insane he was sounding. Nacho threw up his hands with a groan. "You're right. November eleventh is *fine*. It's not like the world is going to end *exactly* at noon Central Standard Time. It's not like, for example, we're all going to be finding ourselves in a video game world, with strict rules about food and water, run by psychotic gods. Yeah. Ha. Like *that's* gonna happen."

"You need to stop playing games until five in the morning." Brie shoved Reuben out of the bed with her foot. "Go deal with him. If you made me coffee at the same time, I'd love you forever."

Reuben kissed her head. "You're gonna love me forever anyway, sugar."

"Don't press your luck." There was a long pause, and she eventually waved dramatically at her blanket to indicate her state of undress. "Get *out!*"

Nacho wanted to give them the chance at eternal love. Yet, the reality was, if they all didn't get their act together... 'forever' meant only another six months. He turned and ran from the room, grabbed his laptop, and migrated to the table. In the kitchen, Reuben started brewing the best, most college-affordable coffee they had.

By the time the pot was a quarter full, Nacho was already making notes on everything he could remember. He had to make two to-do lists: one for things he had to do before the Juxtaposition, and one for things to accomplish after they transitioned into the Starter World. The afterward list was critical. Nacho scrambled to catalog the brief history of the Starter World. The post-Evaluation chaos. The rise of the Cataclysm-ranked monster, the overwhelming might of the guilds led by Kala and Crave, and yes, Myron finding the MurderSong Blades.

He typed furiously and ceaselessly.

Reuben ambled over as the coffee pot finished percolating, concern writ large after noticing his friend working so intently. "Are you finally starting on the paper for your marketing class? What was your topic? The social impact of the Twitter sale or something equally 'earth-shattering'?"

Nacho stopped typing and considered his best friend in the world; his *alive* best friend. He knew that he wasn't going to bother pursuing his degree; it truly meant nothing to him anymore. But how could he tell Reuben that? How could he convince his friends that most of the people on Earth would be dead in six months?

No one died right away, though that would've been a kindness. Not until *after* the Evaluation... that was the problem, but Nacho had a solution. However, he had to be careful, or his plan would come unraveled. The foundation of his plan, his entire life, relied on the survival of his two best friends. Without them, he had no plan. He had seen where that kind of life took him.

In some ways, the trio of Nacho, Reuben Colby, and Brie

McCurdy had been completely random. They'd all come from rough beginnings; some rougher than others. Reuben had lost his parents early, and then his grandparents in his teens. For Nacho, who hadn't had actual parents for as far back as he could remember, Reuben's Nana and Papa had been like his parents as well. Then there was Brie, who had her own tragic backstory of a controlling family with an incredible pedigree.

Bottom line, the three were tight; as close-knit as any biological family. Losing the other two had broken Nacho, and subsequently losing himself in the skills of an assassin had been easy. Killing had become effortless.

Reuben took the pot and poured three cups of coffee, adding mocha creamer into his cup as he waited for an answer. "You're not saying anything, Nacho. Still wondering what the date is? The year? How's time traveling treating you?"

Brie popped out of the bedroom wearing her running gear and a scowl. Out of the three, she was in the best shape. It wasn't even close. When it was lacrosse season, she played lacrosse, and all other seasons were lacrosse training seasons. She scooped up her black coffee and drained it, then gave Reuben a peck on the cheek.

Normally, Nacho would have joined in on the mocha creamer, but he intended to start his training right this minute. "Hold up, Brie, I'll go running with you."

Brie had retrieved a huge cup from the cupboard and was filling it with water. She froze, as did her fiancé. She slowly turned to face Nacho. "What did you just say?"

"I want to go running with you. I mean, we'll start off together. You'll run way ahead of me, and I'll probably puke. But hey, I want to get into shape." He turned his focus to Reuben, his eyes full of a killing intent he had been honing for years. It had no effect on his friend whatsoever, bouncing off the steady-minded man without leaving a mark. "You should come with us as well. We both need to take our health seriously."

"Good lord, he was telling the truth about time traveling!

Either that, or he was swapped out with an alien." Reuben slammed a box of Lucky Charms on the table along with a jug of whole milk. "I'm *extremely* healthy. My outlook on life is very positive. My cardiovascular system *glows* with my positivity."

"Your arteries shouldn't glow. That's radiation," Nacho deadpanned as cereal clattered into the bowl in a sprinkle of marshmallowy goodness.

"He's right." Brie caught Reuben's arm before he could pour the milk. "Don't eat. Come with us."

"Don't you love me for who I am?" Reuben turned puppy-dog eyes to his future bride. "I'm already so handsome."

He had a mop of curly brown hair, dimples in his cheeks, and a charismatic affability. Reuben was the big guy everyone adored. Nacho had always liked that about his friend. Brie had been the driven, ambitious rich girl with a hateful family that tried to dictate her every move. They did *not* like that Reuben and Nacho had grown up in Wyandotte County. How Brie had met them, let alone managed to maintain friendship despite their social differences, was as mysterious as anything else in life.

Since he was pondering mysterious things, Nacho's eyes wandered over to the notification still hovering in the bottom right corner of his vision. The boon from Kronos, a Patron named after... the god of time? Probability Vision, time... yeah, that tracked. Unless he was actually crazy, Nacho had been given a window into the future. He had to run that possibility by his friends, but subtly.

First, he couldn't pass up Lucky Charms; actual cereal with actual milk. It had been a long, *long* time, and he'd spent so many days hungry. He dove in, crunching and loving every bite.

Brie scowled at him as her hands jumped to her hips. "I thought we were going running!"

Reuben joined Nacho in the cereal feast. "Don't worry, babe. I can run with a full stomach. That'll be the least of my worries."

Nacho took a minute, eyes closed, to really savor the sweet, milky goodness. Then he presented his friends with a very important question. "Hey, guys. What if one day, you woke up crazy? How would you know you were crazy?"

"Aluminum foil hats would be one way. Tell us, Nacho," Reuben replied lightly, narrowing his eyes as he leaned in closer and lowered his voice, "are *they* listening right now?"

That was a troubling thought. *Were* the Patrons watching? Was Kronos? They… well, they might be. Nacho winced as he realized that he couldn't admit that; he might be a touch paranoid, but they would think he was off his rocker. Brie sipped her coffee, wrinkling her forehead in concentration. "Let's look at this logically. If, objectively, you couldn't determine what was real and what wasn't, I would think that'd be the definition of mental illness—the inability to discern agreed-upon reality."

Brie, as usual, was the brilliant and rational person in his friends' relationship. That wasn't to say that Reuben was dim, but he reacted to things with emotions first, jokes second, and seriousness *only* when the situation had already begun to devolve.

"Objective reality. Sure." Nacho drank the rest of his coffee, keeping his grimace hidden behind the mug. "I'm going to be doing a little thought experiment for the next few months. If I act weird, it's only an experiment. I had this… *dream* about the future. You guys have known me for years, right? Can I ask that you give me a few months of weirdness?"

"How weird?" Reuben polished off his mocha and slowly pushed back from the table, doing his best to procrastinate long enough that a run wouldn't be feasible. "Are we talking 'making a mask out of other people's faces' strange, or 'bonus workouts and diet shift' strange? On that note, why is it so hard to decide which one I'd *rather* you do…?"

"Nothing dangerous to other people," Nacho promised as he pushed away as well, though he also remained in his seat. "I'm just trying to figure out what's real, and… okay, I'll probably have a tiny obsession with knives."

"Well, *that's* not worrying." Brie stood up, prompting the other two to get on their feet and move. After Nacho and

Reuben got into better gear, they went out into the streets and trotted down the sidewalk on their way to the Bush Creek Trail.

Brie zoomed away in no time flat, leaving the two men to huff and puff on their own. The run was *terrible*, and both were sick to their stomachs in no time flat, but it was a start. Thanks to the message that was still available for him to call up, Nacho knew for a fact that the Probability Vision was real, the Juxtaposition would happen, and that Kronos had given him the ultimate gift of knowledge.

The run was just the start. For the next few weeks, he kept things as normal as possible, until his friends were no longer questioning his sanity. Not about his 'dream', at least. Reuben still wiped away false tears when he saw that Nacho was working out every day. Soon, he started doing the absolute minimum for school. Publicly dropping out now, with less than a month until he graduated, would raise red flags with Reuben and Brie, and he couldn't have that. Their lives depended on them trusting him, and his sanity depended on their lives.

There were a few things that might have created issues for him if anyone looked too deeply. First, he began applying for credit cards and maxing them out like a madman. Second, Reuben got a C in his economics class in the exact way Nacho had predicted; but by then, the memory of his outburst had faded. Third and finally, Nacho started wearing baggy clothing to hide the fact that he was starting to coat his body in dense muscle.

He had been given six months to get fast, strong, and build up his endurance. Not only was he rigorously working out and eating an *ideal* combination of macros, but he was also focused on martial arts and knife-fighting to the point that he was sure to wind up on a watch list in the near future… or he would have been, if the government had survived moving to a new world.

Silver linings, and all that.

There were still a few major points of frustration for him; namely, the fact that all of the muscle memory he'd established as the elite assassin of the Final Victory Guild had just…

vanished. He could remember moves and attacks perfectly, yet he couldn't perform them. That realization had forced him to start from the beginning once more, making basic motions hundreds of times to carve out a proper receptacle for the skills he needed.

It had been well-established that real-world skills translated into the Juxtaposition's gaming system. There was one major caveat: only one real-life skill would be turned into a *Skill*, something recognized by the system. It selected whatever it saw as an individual's highest proficiency that was viable for translating into use in the new world. That meant that if Nacho generated *excellent* skills in small blades, then he'd do well during the Evaluation, and he'd do well after it. He already had his sights set on completing the quest for the MurderSong blades.

Myron would start off clueless in the game. Nacho wouldn't. Even now, months ahead of the evaluation, and years before his rival would become well-known, the thought of messing with the smarmy little creep brought a cheesy grin to Nacho's face.

Though he focused almost all his efforts into knife work, he did buy a small bow and arrow, then took archery lessons. Having a ranged weapon was a nice option, and while he'd done most of his killing up close, he'd put an arrow through a neck or two during the game. It wasn't a skill to ignore if at all possible, and he had at least a *little* time to spare.

Eventually, he was caught by his friends and no longer needed to hide his activities as thoroughly. After their initial shock, Reuben and Brie managed to be *tolerant* of Nacho's newfound interest in arrows and knives, even if they taunted him by calling him 'Legolost-his-mind', or 'knife boy'. Luckily for the burgeoning assassin, the pair had more important things to do. Specifically, finding careers and planning their wedding.

Nacho, knowing the entire system was about to fail, lived off credit cards, drained his bank account to pay rent, and forced Reuben to keep running. Nacho also bought a high-end weight training set and started lifting weights in the apartment, convincing his friend to join him by continuously mentioning how good he would look during his wedding.

While Reuben got in shape, Nacho got thicker; his dedication began to pay off. Soon he was able to keep up with Brie while running long distances and could even outpace her in wind sprints one out of every three attempts. While the others were training to look or feel good, the returnee had the ultimate motivation—survival. Having trouble due to overworking himself was nothing compared to the fact that in six months, the three of them would be fighting for their lives against any number of nightmares right in broad daylight.

As time began to run out, Nacho started taking loans from anyone—federal, private, or illegal—that would let him, accepting terrible deals and massive penalties in order to afford the survival gear that would keep his trio alive for at least the first few days of the Juxtaposition.

There were times that he doubted himself or yearned to take a long rest, but every time something notable happened, like a political snafu, or outrage over the stock market, Nacho remembered those events unfolding *exactly* as they had before. That made him feel better and helped him push through: reality was matching his memories.

Finally, the dreaded day that would change everything was approaching. A week before that fateful Saturday in November, Nacho called Reuben and Brie, letting them know that he had gone all-out on a special wedding present for them. After a fair bit of begging and calling in every favor from them that he had —or would *ever* gather, according to the bride—the couple agreed to meet him at the apartment at eleven-thirty a.m.

They had to be there, *together*, at noon. That had been the problem in the simulation. They'd been split up.

Reuben and Brie had died from that mistake.

Nacho took a deep breath, slowly letting it out as he forced his thoughts to the fact that he wasn't going to *let* that happen again. He knew that this one change would make their lives better, and even though things might suck for a while, they could tackle anything as a team.

A grin appeared on his face as the minutes ticked past: Now that the trial was almost here and he was fairly ready... he could barely wait for it. It felt like replaying a level after playing the game to the end once before. Even though he had experienced a bad ending the first time, now he knew where things were, how to access the system properly, and what sorts of dangers to avoid.

"Practice makes better."

CHAPTER TWO

Nacho watched his friends closely, doing everything he could to delay their departure to the wedding venue. As the time to leave slowly became the time to panic and start running, his eyes flicked to Reuben just as his larger friend tugged on the collar of his tuxedo. Slightly to the left, Brie was looking uncharacteristically uncomfortable and trying *not* to see her soon-to-be husband. Nacho suppressed a wince as the pretty lady in her wedding dress glared at him more furiously with each passing moment.

Brie was *not* happy that they'd taken this detour on her wedding day. "Enough of this, Nacho! We have pictures at one, and we need to eat before then because I don't want to faint. Can we get on with this?"

"Wait, one sec." Reuben pointed at Nacho's side, where his suit coat was barely hiding a bulge. "Do the thing with the knife!"

Nacho had dressed in his own tuxedo and was happy to do anything to stall for just another moment. He smoothly produced a Gerber Mark II fixed blade knife from his knife holster and made it dance across his fingers, then shoved it back into the ballistic nylon sheath and concealed it with a single swift movement. "Glad you like it, buddy. I've got one for you, as well."

That brought their attention to the three backpacks lying on the floor, one for each of them. One had an unstrung bow in a tube strapped to the back, along with a quiver of hunting arrows. Nacho reached over and secured a buckle, ignoring Brie's fuming. "At eleven fifty-five, we'll put these on. I'm sorry you aren't going to get your wedding pictures. Or your wedding."

Brie furrowed her brow and took a deep breath, about to go full bridezilla, but Reuben swooped in just in time. "Nacho. Bro. We're worried about you. You haven't worked since before school ended, and all this stuff...? What are you doing for money?"

"I maxed out seven credit cards and took out a loan from, ah... everyone." Nacho chuckled nervously. "My credit is gonna suck unless the world ends in the next few minutes. My knees are gonna hurt a lot as well, getting broken and all that."

"You're out of your-"

Reuben forced a laugh and spoke quickly as Brie sprang to her feet in a flash. "Look, man, if it's the end of the world as we know it, and you feel fine-"

"I feel *nervous.*" Nacho sat his friend down on the edge of the table. They were now arranged in a triangle, waiting in their little apartment, which held so many memories. "This will all make sense in about twenty minutes, or most of it will. I need to tell you a few things. We're going to start an Evaluation for the Juxtaposition—"

Brie cut him off with a wave of her hand. "What is being juxtaposed with what?"

Reuben wasn't planning to be getting any more serious. "Hey, I know this one! Crazy-ville and cuckoo banana-pants, juxtaposed together. Nacho, you're freaking us out, and... I think it's time for us to go."

"Dang right, it is." Brie was practically vibrating in her lacy shoes from sheer rage. "I do *not* want to be playing 'Armageddon prepper' on my wedding day."

"Neither of you are going *anywhere.*" Both of them went very still when Nacho's voice went gravelly and his hand shifted slightly toward the shoulder holster holding the knife they had just seen flipping around. He didn't directly make a threat, as he would *never* hurt his friends, but Brie still sank down into her chair and reached for Reuben's hand with her own, shaky one. "Sorry to say, the apocalypse *is* happening, and I'm not going to lose you two like I did last time."

"Yeah, that sounds great man. Juxtaposition." Reuben's hand that wasn't holding his bride's was hidden below the table, and he was clearly starting to call for help on his phone. Nacho didn't mind; no one would be able to get here before they were all scooped out. "So what does that actually mean? I don't think you told us the whole story before."

"Juxtaposition is just what we call it. That's a word that means 'to compare side-by-side', and… listen. Time's almost up. I'm *begging* you, listen to me carefully, and at noon and one *second*, I'll walk out the door if I'm wrong." Nacho intently continued his instructions. "In just a moment, Earth is going to be replaced with the 'Starter World', and we're given an interface. You'll need to blink once with your left eye, once with your right, then shrug to open it. That'll be really important to know."

"Left, right, shrug." Reuben nodded as he calmly repeated after his friend. Brie's eye twitched.

"The reason it's a Juxtaposition is that it's not just the Earth; there's also the CrossWorld, and both get connected to the Starter World through portals. We were just getting to the point where we were fighting the CrossHumans when I was killed. At the moment I died, I was given a boon. You might get one as well; I don't know. They're godlike entities, these Patrons, and they're messing with the game. They give people gifts, but rumor has it, some of the Patrons are actively trying to kill us off. Others are helpful, or seem to be, but be careful."

Brie and Reuben exchanged worried glances, and Nacho watched a tear fall down his best lady-friend's face. He felt tears try to form in his own eyes and gritted his teeth. He felt sick that he needed to force them to listen, and it certainly didn't look great for his trustworthiness.

He gulped back a sob as the memories of the Probability Vision hit him like a hammer. He remembered being in the apartment, getting ready for the wedding by himself. Because, yes, even though pictures had started at one pm, Nacho had been running late. He'd just rushed out of the door, car keys in hand, in this very tuxedo, when the Juxtaposition had pulled away every soul on Earth.

Nacho had done well in enduring the Evaluation, almost entirely because his gamer side had kicked in. He played the scenario, thinking it was all fun and games like the books he used to read… until the gecko bear had ripped him apart. By then, he was on the verge of exhaustion from hunger and sleep deprivation, and it had only been day two. He'd thought that was the end, but the result was only that he'd done fairly poorly in the Evaluation.

He'd blinked and appeared in a surreal mall that offered anything from food to superhuman abilities. Once more a gamer, he'd bought his character class and then exited. In the next few seconds, he'd appeared in a meadow, holding his car keys, finding himself with everything he'd had on him before being whisked away, except for his cell phone. Technology that required electricity wasn't a part of the Starter World's ecosystem, and *none* of it was allowed.

Nacho's neighbors had been standing around him, those between the ages of fifteen and fifty-five: one man with a pacemaker had dropped in the next second, since a chunk of his heart had been ripped away with the life-saving tech. The ex-assassin's hands shook as he remembered the screams of terror as the nightmare Oscreech birds flew in—talons sharp, and beaks sharper. When the birds hit the ground, the humans had found out that the creatures could run just as fast as they could fly.

He had sprinted for the church where Reuben and Brie were getting married as his neighbors were being torn apart, but it had been five miles, and he was in terrible shape. It had taken him *hours* to try to find the location, but the church was gone... and so were his friends. He'd heard later from survivors that a semi-blind mole creature, later identified as a Dirt Devourer, had come to the surface and wiped out most of the neighborhood around the church. Some of those first monsters had been tough right off the bat. If there was someone controlling the Juxtaposition, they had been playing too much Melden Ring.

Nacho forced himself to relax his jaw muscles before he broke his teeth. "I can save you this time. We have a definite advantage, and we're going to abuse the heck out of it. This is the most important thing. Whatever else happens, choose 'Balanced, Instant' for your Build type. *Any* of the other options are a trap. Do you hear me? *Balanced, Instant.* The next thing... you're going to get a class choice. Brie, you're a natural Body Player. You'll want to choose that."

"That sounds a little PG-thirteen." Reuben's fake work laugh really highlighted how tense the man was. "I mean, it's like a pick-up line. 'Hey there, pretty lady, if I said you were a Body Player, would you hold it against me?' Why do I hear saxophone music?"

Nacho wasn't laughing. Brie either. "My friend, you're going to want to be a Mind Player. You're good with resource management, and that'll work well for spells. Knowing you, I think you'll get great mana bonuses."

"Nine-one-one, what is your emergency? If you can't answer, please know that the police are on their way."

"Mana?" Brie spoke too-loudly, trying unsuccessfully to cover the sound of the phone. "Is this like in one of your video games?"

"Right. If one of you is a Body Player, and the other is a

Mind Player... it's—okay, it's like this. If we don't have food, we'll probably have water, so at least one of us will be able to fight. I was a Body Player before, an assassin, and I'm not going to change that. It's what I know, and I was the *best*."

Reuben tugged at his collar, his brow furrowed in puzzled concentration since Nacho hadn't made any moves to hurt them. "Let me guess: the better you do in the Evaluation, the better class you get?"

"Kinda. You earn points to spend." Nacho swallowed. His mouth was *so* dry. "Ah, I almost forgot! Evaluation! The water will disappear, as will the food. Mostly it's berries, like blackberries on bushes, and strawberries. Look at the ground *and* in the trees. There's also peanut bushes, or, uh, they look like peanuts. You'll see. Pick them and hoard them. Food is critical in this game. It was a..."

Nacho had run out of breath. He had to take a moment.

Reuben and Brie let him sit there in silence.

"I wrote this all down. Front pocket for both of you. If you have the time to read it when we get to the Starter World, please do, so I can answer questions instead of starting from the beginning. If worse comes to worst, the largest secret of that world..." Nacho inhaled shakily and powered through. "The Evaluation was a hint that none of us understood. I'm getting ahead of myself... you *will* die in the Evaluation. I didn't know that at first; no one did, so we were all *too* careful. You don't have to be. Take risks. It's the only way to get enough credits for an advanced class. Keep hydrated and eat. Collect water and hoard food."

"What else, what else..." He tapped at his head as he tried to think, moving to a ready position as Brie shifted slightly, only for her to slump down. "Okay, there's a shack to the south with weapons, baskets, and some supplies. On the rocky ledge above the central pool, you'll find some armor. There's also blackberry bushes there. Those ledges are a good base. There are a handful of weapon caches here and there. Use them to kill monsters to get Evaluation Points."

"Kill… monsters." Brie clearly didn't believe him. Nacho didn't mind. She would soon enough. "In five minutes, you're either going to leave forever, or we'll be in a new world."

"That's right. Kill monsters." Nacho echoed the only part he wanted to reinforce, even as a pang ran through his heart. "Don't eat any meat in the Evaluation world! It's all full of Putrid Mana. If you eat it, you'll get sick, and you won't be able to fight. You'll see the world slowly dying, so again, store food and water. Remember, choose Balanced, Instant. You won't be able to change it. You'll get what seems like a casual choice, but it's the most important decision you can make as you leave the mall. No one knows it until after the fact."

"Okay, we'll choose Balanced, Instant. Just curious, but what are all the options?" Reuben wasn't joking now, his eyes serious and locked onto Nacho's.

Nacho licked his lips and cracked a smile, now that it looked like his friend was starting to believe. "There are three build types in the game, but we're out of time."

Brie grasped her dress in two frustrated fists. "This is *not* the kind of wedding day I wanted. You know I'm not super girly in general, but I do like it when things I spend time planning work out."

"We do." Reuben squeezed her hand and quirked an eyebrow at his friend. "You do know if nothing happens at noon, you're out of the wedding, right?"

Nacho ignored the jab that felt like it was aimed right at his heart, grabbing a bag and revealing that the side of each held a long machete. "I have clothes, weapons, food, and water for us. We'll appear together, all at the same time no matter how long it takes you to finish everything else."

He glanced at the time on the microwave, then stood up fully and shouldered on his pack. Reuben helped Brie with hers, and then got himself taken care of as the sound of police sirens started drawing closer. The three stood facing each other in the apartment, and Nacho desperately wanted to say something in an effort to mend the bond he had just endangered. Luckily for him, years as an assassin had taught him how to keep his mouth shut.

As the seconds hand on the clock passed the large six, Brie let out a shrill, disturbing laugh. "Okay. One positive with either the end of the world, or dealing with the police that are coming to throw you into a little white room, is that I won't have to deal with my family."

Nacho smiled warmly at his two friends. "We'll be together again. We'll have gear. The Evaluation is going to freak you out, and you *will* die, but you won't stay dead. Then you'll be with me, and I've done this before. It'll be... better."

"I'm just glad I didn't want anything to eat or drink when I got here." Reuben rolled his eyes drolly and looked at his fiancée. "I'm looking for the grape Kool-Aid, but we're probably good."

Brie threw an elbow into his arm. "That's not even funny. It's noon, and time's up, Nacho. Get out of the-"

Her voice cut off, as did all physical sensations.

Armageddon had come right on schedule. It was time for the Evaluation to grill them.

CHAPTER THREE

"Yay, I'm not crazy!" Nacho was more relieved than he would ever let his friends know. That would've been awkward if the clock had hit twelve-oh-one and they'd just been standing in the apartment wearing their backpacks, not to mention a mountain of debt falling on him and the police ready to pack him away. "I guess the old saying is true: the best apocalypses are the ones you can set your clock by."

He had appeared in the Evaluation World wearing a tunic and sandals, which were basic clothes of antiquity. A belt cinched the tunic closed and had a little pouch tied to it. No underwear. "Ugh, forgot about this. People probably did so much conquering back in the day because of the chafing. Discomfort leads to irritability and the need to fight something. I get it now. They were all just looking for proper support."

A familiar scene that he had never expected to see again was spread out in his vision. He was staring into a forest glade, having landed in front of a pool of water surrounded by tall, rough-cut stones; basically Stonehenge around a crystal-clear pond.

That water would become vital, as would the wall of blackberry bushes growing along the rocky ledges behind him. Yep, this was the Evaluation World, all right.

Right on time, a message in a grand font flashed in his vision.

Welcome to the Juxtaposition! Your world has been chosen to participate in a game of adventure, luck, and skill. The first step is to evaluate you. Right now, you're in the Evaluation World. Relax, take a look around (wink wink wink), or kill monsters for bonus Evaluation Points! You will automatically gain EP based on the length of time you remain in this world, but some people strive to forge their destiny. Will that be you, or not? Either way, may your future be delicious!

Then, in a smaller font, there was standard legalese that made him roll his eyes, just as it had last time:

The Patrons are not responsible for your death or dismemberment. Some Patrons might give certain players boons, which may or may not be helpful. The Evaluation World is not the Starter World. 'May your future be delicious' is a trademarked term owned by the Dale Mountain System (DM System). All rights reserved.

Nacho remembered his first time in the Evaluation World. When that message had flashed in his vision, he'd thought he'd gone completely insane. Now, reading it again, all he could think of was how nasty the Patrons had to be to make something like this.

"Time to get some EP." He had hoped the location of various items would be the same, and so far, that was exactly the case. He hurried toward the blackberry bushes and began picking the berries off. He filled the pouch on his belt, making sure to pick the ones that were just on the verge of being ripe;

they needed to be firm, rather than squishy. Food was vital—that was the hidden meaning of 'May your future be delicious'.

He paused and focused on the deep purple berries, relaxing his mind and winking three times with his left eye to make the System View appear. In the next moment, he read the properties of the food.

Simple Black Berries
Tier 0
Note: Tasty on vanilla ice cream!

Once again, he was struck by how this experience was so different, now that he understood how to work the system. The average player wouldn't know that 'relax and look around' was required to access the System View and would likely think the system was generating innuendo with the winking. "Always so cheerful, aren't you, system? After seeing that for six months of torment, everyone is going to look at that and see taunting. I already do."

He ate a few of the berries, and they weren't bad—even though he could already taste the sharply rotten flavor of Putrid Mana. The only thing keeping him from hurling was the knowledge that plant-based food of the Evaluation World had low levels of the supernatural poison, so he could eat them without getting too sick if he rationed.

The meat was a different matter altogether.

After his quick snack, he clambered up onto a ledge and pulled down a helmet, battle kilt, and cuirass that were just floating there somehow. Touching them instantly equipped them, as he only had basic gear on, replacing his tunic with the chest armor and simple kilt that wouldn't do a thing to protect his legs. Though he tried to examine the items, he was locked out of the main System interface until after the evaluation, and the System View wasn't all that helpful.

. . .

Evaluation Armor Detected!

Note: Evaluation items are not transferable to the Starter World. Enjoy them while you can!

The sandals weren't helping even a little, but he'd not been able to find boots last time. "Maybe if I try going north?"

He had food, he had some armor, and now he needed weapons. Nacho also needed a container for water and suddenly remembered the shack in the swamp to the south. That had been vital to his survival, but it had taken a while for him to find. Heck, by the time he'd found the armor last time, he'd already taken damage from a variety of creatures. He'd been hungry, terrified, and thoroughly convinced he'd gone insane.

On the other side of the pond, right on time, the first monster shimmered to life. Only one appeared at first, but he knew that was going to change all too soon. Standing about two feet tall, the squirrel had a bushy tail and a cute face—except for the inch-long fangs bursting out of its mouth. It also brandished three-inch razor-claws on the ends of its weirdly muscular arms. "Why, hello there, Rocky Squirrel-boa; I see you've been skipping leg day again."

The Claw Squirrel chittered and charged at him like a gorilla, seeming to understand well enough to take great offense to the taunt. Nacho darted down the trail, running south for all he was worth. He found the first weapon, a club floating in mid-air over the dirt track. He didn't check it, but in the end, it didn't matter. He could use it to bash the Claw Squirrel into meat paste—not that he could eat it, as all meat coming from monsters or animals was *saturated* with Putrid Mana.

He grabbed the club and turned just in time to intercept the Claw Squirrel, drawing back and swinging as it got in range. A single blow was enough to bash in the monster's head, and he was struck by how much simpler the combat system was than on the Starter World. Right now, it was easy: hit target, don't get hit by target. He didn't need to factor in cooldowns on skills, nor manage his Hunger and Thirst matrix.

A message coincided with the kill:

Congratulations! You have murdered an adorable, fluffy little Claw Squirrel! Is it the monster, or are you?
Level 01 Standard Monster = 10 Evaluation Points
Awesome job! You get +1 EP for your first kill!

Nacho paused, knelt, and touched the squirrel, relaxing his mind to see the thing's properties.

Raw Tier 0 Meat
Note: Putrid but delicious!

Nacho rose, nodding in relief that the Evaluation World was exactly the same as it had been in his vision. That was useful. He hoped his information held true, and that everyone else was experiencing what he'd expected. If so, Reuben and Brie would at least get armor and whatever was in the swamp shack. They'd also know about food and water.

He never once paused, already partway to his next goal. The dirt path turned into a trail of flat stones, half-covered with dirt. They led south from Stonehenge Pond, which he knew was the exact center of this world. Howling rose somewhere in the distance, followed by the chittering of giant insects. "Yeah, the wolves and the beetles; I haven't forgotten losing an arm and an eye to you... let's see if I can return the favor."

Last time, even despite dying the second day, he'd done fairly well for himself compared to the other people he knew about. He'd been able to purchase a pretty good Body Player class from the Evaluation Mall; this time, he was *also* going to stock up on overpowered skills right from the start. Nacho ran down the path through the pine trees until the ground started to get muddy. More ferns appeared, and the pine trees were gradually replaced with cypress and oak trees covered with Spanish moss. As the ground sloped, the path's stones were soon nearly covered in black water.

A massive snake slithered out of the murk. Yellow, black, and copper-colored scales covered the thing all the way up to its shovel-shaped head. It started to turn toward him, but he was fast enough to close on the beast. His muscles didn't respond like they had when he'd been a Tier two assassin, but he was strong, fit, and had retained the years of memories in combat— if not the actual combat experience and musculature.

He anticipated the snake's movement and struck, whacking the club into the reptile's head. It immediately threw coils around Nacho, trying to hide its head, but he hit again and again until the whole thing relaxed, most of its big body lost in the black water of the swampy section of earth.

A flash of information cheered him on:

Congratulations! You have murdered a Copperopolis Anaconda that only wanted a hug!
  Level 02 Standard Monster = 20 Evaluation Points
  Awesome job!

Nacho bent and used the System View:

Raw Tier 0 Meat
  Warning: Putrid but ssso good!
  Note: A few potential recipes are anaconda dumplings, snake fricassée, and fried serpent with chili peppers. Yum!

. . .

Nacho left the snake, fully understanding that it was a trick and a test of willpower for anyone else that would have managed to take the thing down. Most people would have either died or spent *days* planning a way to kill something that big and would be on the verge of starvation. For him, the Putrid Mana warning was all he needed to know. The note was just an invitation for a night of nausea, diarrhea, and vomiting. "Not my idea of a good time, mmkay? Thanks."

He hurried across the stones, ducking under moss-heavy branches and keeping his eyes on the black water. It could be hiding big alligator monsters, or even a Tier one creature, that would kill him instantly. He'd feel better once he got the knives he needed. After proceeding with an overabundance of caution, Nacho reached the shack: a dilapidated structure covered in moss, ivy, and bugs.

The floor was broken, and half the room was submerged. The other half held some shelves and a table, along with the crumbling stones of an old fireplace. On the hearth, he found flint. He'd need it for a fire; soon the nights would be deathly cold. On one shelf sat several round clay jars, including the true prize of a full container of roasted peanuts.

Last time, he'd ignored the jars and only focused on the weapons—a rusty short sword, a long dagger in a sheath, and a bandolier of throwing knives hanging on a hook. This was where he'd discovered his love of knives, the reason he'd chosen to become an assassin. It had helped that he typically liked playing stealth characters and had a certain moral flexibility that others seemed to lack. Not surprising, since he'd grown up in a system that was oftentimes as cruel as this new world: foster care.

He'd been one of the luckier ones: Reuben and Brie had become his family. He prayed they'd do well in the Evaluation. He reminded himself that he had given them a better chance to survive than they'd had the first time around. He could only hope that it was enough.

Nacho threw the bandolier of throwing daggers over his shoulder and strapped on the short sword and long dagger. Thanks to the high humidity, he was sweating bullets and getting pretty hungry. The hunger brought back terrible memories, so he shook it off and kept working at his goal.

He left the club in the shack, as well as the pottery jars and some old half-rotten cloth he could turn into sacks. There was one thing he wanted to check on. The stone path kept going past the shack, and his old life of battle started invading his thoughts. Nacho found that he had missed the adrenaline dump. His senses came alive: the stink of the swamp filled his nose, the swish and burble of something swimming through the black water tickled his ears, and the cries of other monsters in the Evaluation World were felt on the skin from their sheer volume.

It took some time to reach the edge of the swamp, where it drained off into nothing but wispy clouds far below. "Look at that; the world is flat. How powerful do the Patrons have to be to be able to create a flat world hanging over clouds in some unimaginable place? I guess we just add it to the mystery that is the Juxtaposition."

The gray coloration of the leaves on the trees nearest the edge caught his attention, and he frowned. It seemed too fast, but the whole point of the Evaluation World was to kill him, so perhaps it was actually par for the course?

Having scouted the location and deciding that nothing was going to be coming for him from that direction, he made his way back to the shack.

Whizzz.

"No... I hate these things!" Nacho picked up the pace, but three goblin mosquitos had caught his scent. The carnivorous insects were bright green and the size of pigeons, though they lacked feathers. Mottled green flesh, whirring wings, and dagger-like proboscides were the only details visible when they were on the move. They didn't have eyes, at least none that he could see, and their six legs ended in sharp hooks.

Fighting two-handed—short sword in his right hand, dagger in his left—he chopped one out of the air. One of the insects went for his leg, but he stabbed his dagger into its pulpy body. The last one tried to hook a claw into Nacho's cuirass, scratching a groove, but the armor held. The monster mosquito flew over his head, and he hacked the thing out of the air before it could call for more of its kind.

That was the real concern with these things. When there was one, hundreds more might be right around the corner. Hurrying away from the freshly spilled blood, he glanced at a notification that granted him ten points for each of the monsters. "Nice… up to sixty-one EP already. Awesome. Time to get settled in and get ready to go full turtle."

He hurried to the shack and grabbed the earthenware jars, backtracking all the way to Stonehenge Pond. Once he reached the clear pool, he filled the empty clay jars with water and ate as many roasted peanuts as he could. These legumes weren't bad, and he didn't taste any of the Putrid Mana, which proved to be a nice surprise indeed. After gorging himself, Nacho filled the last jar by picking the blackberry bush empty.

"Some peanut bushes down the north path. I'll hafta check out the west and east portions of the world. Gotta watch for hostiles, but maybe I can grab some better armor. Need boots, for sure." He spoke aloud to himself—nothing wrong with talking to an expert, after all.

When he started gathering the nuts, two Claw Squirrels took umbrage to his presence in their territory. Now that he was equipped with his short sword and knives, they were easy to dispatch. With just a quick slash here and a stab there, he was up to eighty-one EP and was the territorial victor. "I am king of the peanuts! Fear me, squirrels!"

Of course, he made his jokes *very* quietly. It took a moment before he realized that he was smiling, and it occurred to him that being back with Reuben and Brie had really changed him for the better already. "Man, I hope they're okay."

Then again, even if they royally messed up the Evaluations, they could still buy classes or Skills in the Juxtaposition Store on Starter World. It would just be a lot more dangerous, expensive, and put all of them at risk. Yet, they'd still be together again, and Nacho had every advantage. He was going to use that to keep himself and his friends safe. What was a small issue like choosing the wrong starting Skill going to matter after ten years of practice? Fifty?

As for the rest of the world, the poor people who weren't prepared for the Evaluation would be going right past the frying pan and instead falling directly into the fire. "Sucks to be them, but everyone plays real life in hard mode."

CHAPTER FOUR

Nacho found a cave on the north side of the mound of rocks. Inside waited a trio of Rat Nasties, rodent monsters similar to the Claw Squirrels, but with exponentially less cuteness to them. The rats had filthy fur, diseased pink tails, and all four limbs were visibly muscled.

He reflected on the fact that he was doing *so* much better than his first go-through. Last time, he'd spent way too much time filling his non-existent underwear and running from monsters. Killing things in a video game was so much easier than killing things in real life.

The fact that the club was a terrible weapon also crossed his mind. When he had first found them, he'd only had the sword and daggers for about twenty minutes before the wandering reptile-bear-thing had pulled him into the black water and ripped him to shreds. Hence, a healthy respect for amphibious creatures had been born.

Nacho lured the Rat Nasties out of the cave, then flung knives at them. He killed two before he had to draw his sword to kill the third, which was almost on him by then. Having made short work of the pathetically weak creatures, he collected his knives and kicked their bodies into the tangle of bushes. He was up to a hundred and eleven Evaluation Points, and now had a well-protected base for his future operations. Carefully placing his jars in the back of the cave, he gathered dry wood and made a tiny fire on the flat slab of rock of his cave patio. The roasted peanuts were so much better than the raw ones that he just kept going, despite knowing he was probably eating too many. "I earned this. I need a treat after a day like today."

Whatever the glowing thing in the sky was, it was setting by the time he added a few more roasted peanuts to his stores. He piled wood in front of the shallow cave, knowing that it wouldn't keep anything from coming for him, but the noise of the clattering sticks would wake him up. As he lay down, he sneaked a peek at the night sky. There weren't any stars, just a fake-looking crescent moon that glowed like a papier-mâché sickle in the utterly black dome above. It was unnerving, like budget CGI. Filling the last crack, he spent the rest of the night in total darkness, worrying about his friends in their own Evaluation abysses—but he did sleep pretty well for laying on a bare stone floor.

In the morning, he drank deeply from his water supply, then re-filled it from the clear pond. Most people wouldn't have noticed that the water level was down a quarter of an inch, but Nacho did. He knew from horror stories of people that had done well in the Evaluation that, in the end, that pool would dry up.

"Two days and two hundred EP is my record. I gotta at *least* double that, if not triple it." After tidying up his cave, he took the north path in the hopes of topping off his clay jar with peanuts. The northern forests were full of the yips and yowls of monstrous wolves, probably level three at least. He'd eventually go hunting there, though he had to be careful. High-level Tier zero monsters were hard, but a Tier one monster would be impossible to even damage without skills or weapon masteries.

He remembered the wolves. They were smaller than the average timber wolf, completely hairless, and bright pink. Their eyes were dull black dots in their skulls, but frankly, their teeth were the largest part of them: big, spitty, and yellow.

Nacho had a plan to deal with them, but he wanted to make sure his stores were good enough for him to hole up if he got too injured to continue. To that end, a fence for his cave entrance would be a great idea. He didn't have the ability to make a door, but he had enough access to the materials around him, so he decided that he could create a screen of sticks.

After looking up, then down and to the left for the third time, he grunted in annoyance. There was no way to check his Satiation values here—how hungry and thirsty he actually was, not just how he felt at the time. In the Juxtaposition, Hunger and Thirst Points were tracked just like Health Points and Mana. "I can't... man, it's gonna be wild returning to that madness."

Part of him was excited to beat whatever twisted game the Patrons were playing. Another part of him didn't want to be thrust back into that chaos. Frankly, the 'nice' people from Earth didn't last. While he would do what he could to change that, the fact was that the vast majority of people that did survive too often turned out to be bloodthirsty and paranoid. Not always—Nacho had met a select few kind people, and there were natural leaders who knew that humans did better when they worked together than they did by going it alone.

"How about I watch the grass so I don't get eaten, instead of reminiscing?" he chastised himself. To the west of his cave home, he found a swath of tough grasses. He pulled a bundle out of the ground, filling one of the cloth sacks before returning. In about an hour, he had woven the grasses through his sticks and made a crude fence for his cave entrance. He looked over it with a critical eye, sighing at the wilting mess that he had put together. "Enough of this. Time to go wolf hunting."

The sky's glowing orb—as he couldn't really call it a sun, the world being flat and all—hung overhead as Nacho jogged up the northern trail without even breathing hard. That was a great sign, encouraging him that he was in very good shape.

When he was a kid, he'd thought that being in shape meant being muscular and cut, but now he couldn't care less how he looked. This was about his survival, and being lean with high endurance was the key to staying ahead of the curve.

Yip!

The cries of the naked pink wolves grew louder, all the way until a wolf came running from the undergrowth—easy to spot, given the fact that it was practically fluorescent. Nacho chose a tree with plenty of branches as his escape route. He waved his hands and called almost softly, "Hey, pinkie, wanna chew on some grade-A Evaluation butt?"

The wolf seemed to like the idea. Unfortunately, it didn't want to play along with his one-on-one plan. It lifted its head and gave out a howl, a signal for its buddies that it had found lunch.

"You filthy cheater!" Nacho hissed as he turned and sped to the tree, climbing up a few branches. He hung his helmet on a branch so that it wouldn't impact his aim, then whipped out a knife and sent it end-over-end into the throat of the naked wolf.

It was a perfect shot. The wolf choked and scratched at itself, but it eventually died drowning in its own juices.

Congratulations! You have murdered a Naked Wolf!
  Level 02 Standard Monster = 20 Evaluation Points
  Good job; those nudists have it coming!

The party was only just starting. Six other naked wolves came tumbling down the trail, drooling at the idea of prey and fully ignoring their fallen companion. Lathered into a frenzy, the naked wolves tried to scurry up the thick tree trunk, but all they tasted was his blade. Nacho slammed his short sword into an eye, an instant kill. One fifty-one EP. Another, he had to slash twice. One *seventy*-one EP.

Seemingly unconcerned about the prey in the tree, one of

the wolves turned and started eating an easier meal. The others had yet to give up, one of the final two leaping up and managing to get its paws over a lower branch.

The human was forced to switch to his long knife in the close quarters, hacking his blade into the monster's skull. At this point, normal canines might've run from the massacre, but these were monsters. Their job was to kill or be killed, and when they faced someone like him, he could prove empirically that it wasn't a good evolutionary route to success.

Nacho was soon out of knives, but the wolves didn't relent. Instead, even more started trickling out of the woods and joining in on the hunt. He didn't mind. If they were coming to him, that meant he didn't need to waste calories by hunting them down. Strike after strike, he killed them all.

By the time the final furless lupine lay bleeding out on the ground, he was sitting at two hundred and fifty-one Evaluation Points.

He'd gotten thirsty, but he knew that he had plenty of food and water back at the cave, so he pushed on, continuing down the north trail. This was new territory for him, and all he had to go on was second-hand accounts from people that were clearly exaggerating their time in this place. The last time he'd been in the Evaluation, he'd been forced to go running from the wolves, yet he still remembered the squawks of monsters farther into the forest. So far, he'd killed monstrous squirrels, snakes, and wolves. "Might as well take on some kind of bird. Task list is growin'. I need boots and leggings, and I wouldn't mind a projectile weapon. These throwing knives aren't ideal beyond like... ten feet."

He followed the path through the thick forest until he came to a river, which was a neat trick on a flat world. "Who needs physics anyway? See, this right here is why I skipped out on physics. Not because the world was ending. Totally not."

A half-destroyed stone bridge arched over the frothing water below. Farther north, the ramparts of a castle tower rose above the rainforest trees. Nacho checked the skies one last time, then started across the bridge. He was jumping from the cracked stones on one side to get to the crumbling bricks on the other side when the shriek of a furious monster split the air on his left.

Immediately following the first sound of alarm, the roar of a bear rose to the right. To be fair to his past self, it was actually a bear crossed with a lizard. That monster among beasts had killed him before, but that wasn't going to happen this time.

Nacho backed up onto the bridge, took three big steps, and jumped to the other side. Behind him flashed the black feathers and wicked yellow talons of the bird-creature. Nacho landed safely, then whirled, short sword and dagger ready. The bird was already flapping away in the distance. He got a good look at it: a misshapen crow, as if it had been dipped in candle wax and then left out in the sun. "*Tha~at's* upsetting. Ambush predator dropping from above? So unfair."

The lizard-bear roared again. It was close, and getting closer. Nacho was already at two hundred and fifty-one points. He'd broken his previous record, and as long as he was careful, he might hit his lower goal of five hundred. At that point, he wouldn't *need* to be an assassin; he'd have the points for a Paladin class, if he wanted to learn a whole new way of doing things. That wasn't the route he'd take, though; he'd stick with being an assassin. It just matched his personality too well. With this windfall, he'd buy any number of Skills and weapons from the Evaluation Mall and hit the game already overpowered, ready to kill anything and anyone who threatened him and his friends.

Satisfied, Nacho continued down the path. That bird thing was at least level five, as was the lizard-bear. If he killed both? He'd end the day at well over three, if not *four* hundred points. Blinking the sweat out of his eyes, he focused on his current survival. If he got taken down by some minor creature, his trip to the Evaluation Mall wouldn't be nearly as much fun. He wanted to go shopping while flush with EP.

Managing to reach the castle without further incident put him on high alert. It wasn't a huge keep; more like a stone outpost than anything grand. Near the back of the castle, the pine trees were gray, and he could see the trees near the front already losing needles. It would be happening across the world: the plants dying, the land turning to dust.

Peering around carefully as he passed through the half-destroyed gate and into the courtyard, he took in all the details of the area and plotted his escape route right away. Above him hung a loft area, as wrecked as the swamp shack. Half the floor was gone, and the wooden roof was open, granting him a full view of the melted crow that went soaring over him. The bird creature wheeled around with a distant caw, clearly waiting for him to come back into the open.

The first thing Nacho spotted was the boots, but after racing over to them and trying them on, he found that they were way too big, as were a pair of leather pants with rings on the side. The only things he found that he could use were a bow and a quiver hanging from a hook, along with a long halberd which gleamed silver. It was truly a mighty polearm, but far too heavy for his current musculature to use properly. Fortunately, there were also some leather satchels, all better than his current homemade cloth bag.

The melted crow finally came swooping down, landing on the front battlements across from the loft. It was a massive, ugly thing that regarded him with evil, beady eyes. It shook itself, and feathers a yard long fell to the courtyard floor as black fluid spattered the walls.

Cawing hoarsely, it launched itself off the wall and came hurtling into the open-topped building. Nacho was quick enough to grab the bow and quiver of arrows, scurrying up a ladder into the upper level as the crow smashed up the wall with its long black beak. Its talons shredded the floor, and the halberd went clattering to the cobblestones below.

Nacho was thrown against the wall as the crow bashed through the remnants of the roof, sending splinters flying through the air. The thing was big, clearly higher than level five. He could only hope that it was geared toward speed and ambush while perhaps having a glass jaw that he could shatter with standard weapons.

He nocked an arrow and let it fly, the too-high draw causing the string to slap back against his wrist and fingers. "*Ouch!* Stupid bird! Stupid bow!"

His practice paid off, even if it had cost him a bit of pain. The feathered shaft tore through the air to the neck of the beast… and bounced off.

"Uh oh." The strike was enough to drive the crow back and perhaps hurt it, but the corvid merely flapped its massive wings and blew an awful stink into Nacho's nose, then went soaring away. He wasn't worried about it leaving. It would be back; *that* was the concerning part. "What's going on here? That thing is way too strong for me… no… can't leave. I just *know* it's hiding something delicious."

Nacho glanced down the back castle wall, confirming that *yes*, this was the northern edge of the world. Below waited nothing but swirling mist. He wondered if he could walk on those clouds, maybe find a secret room, like in a video game? Would he find an easter egg from the Patrons themselves? It was an interesting idea, but he wasn't going to risk it. He could imagine himself smashing to pieces on rocks below the mist, or worse yet, falling forever and dying of thirst with the wind whistling in his ears.

It was rather unnerving to see the world end in nothing, bordered by a line of dead trees, dried roots, and dirt turning to ash as it dripped away into the ether.

The devil crow shrieked a challenge, declaring that it was coming back to dine on his very Nacho-y flesh. He remembered what he'd told Reuben and Brie—to take chances. This wasn't real. This was an *Evaluation*, and death would only send him to the Evaluation Mall. So… he decided to take a chance. He stood tall and waited for the devil crow to fly toward him, continuously dripping goo and losing feathers.

He didn't take the shot right away. He waited, waited… *waited*. Part of him wanted to shoot just to let go of the slightly shaking string. Another part, the war-weary part, told him to endure—that he would know when it was time to release the arrow.

Those claws reached for him. They were within ten feet of his face, and that was when he let the shaft fly with a grunt of relief. It sank into the chest of the devil bird just as another of the iron-hard feathers fell away, sending the corpse tumbling over him and into the wall to break through the stone and land on the other side.

Nacho spun, fingers stinging. That was nothing compared to the burn on his arm.

Congratulations! You have killed a Melting Crow!
  Level 05 Standard Monster = 50 Evaluation Points
  Nice work! Try a bite; it's practically ice cream!

"You're disgusting," Nacho called up at the system. He didn't need to check the meat; there was no way it *didn't* contain Putrid Mana. Getting off the castle wall was a little tricky, but he managed to find handholds and footholds in the stone. As he was still wearing the kilt, it wasn't a good look. "*So* glad I'm here alone right now."

Sitting amidst the ruins, he pulled on the pants. They were still too big, but the minute he used the wooden button to close the fly, they shrank to fit him, as did the thick leather boots once he stuffed his feet in.

Evaluation Armor Detected
  Note: Your new pants and boots are disco-leather-luscious. However, evaluation items are not transferable to the Starter World. Enjoy them while you can!

. . .

"Abyss, it really was only level five." While he had been hoping for a better payday, he was still pretty happy about the gear he had found. He hadn't been expecting leather to be as protective as the metal of his cuirass, but apparently, game logic was in charge once more. Nacho had been living a regular life for the last half-year, and he had gotten rusty. The fact of the matter was, reality had been reprogrammed to do whatever the Patrons demanded.

Fully armored up, he shouldered on the leather satchels, the bow, and the quiver. He didn't have any extra-dimensional Storage Slots yet, so carting around all the gear was getting cumbersome. He thought about leaving the halberd behind, but a devious idea of how to use it popped into his mind, so he lugged it along as well as he could.

Rapidly desiccating pine needles littered the ground as more trees died around him, some even falling as he passed by. He stopped and threw some pinecones, half-opened and dry, into the satchel, getting sticky sap on his hands. All he wanted to do was go take a nap, but that was the gamer college student in him, not the trained assassin. He had to get back to his camp, eat and drink, and then he could explore some more.

But first, he had a bear to kill and revenge to take. He was at three hundred and one Evaluation Points, but he wanted to end the day killing the monster that had once killed him. Fortunately —or unfortunately—the lizard-bear blocked his path on the other side of the bridge.

"Might as well get this over with." Nacho rolled his head around and dropped his gear, grabbing the bow and arrow from the pile. The beast stood on its rear reptilian legs, brandishing the massive claws adorning its paws. Fur mixed with scales; half the bear's face was mammalian and familiar, the other half lizard, ugly and scaly, with bulging eyes rotating in their sockets. Nacho was pretty sure the lizard-bear hatched eggs, if it procreated at all—not that it needed to. "Thanks, magic, for a treat like *this*."

Nacho retreated back down the path, then jammed the butt

of the halberd into the dirt that was already turning to dust as all moisture within it vanished at an unnatural rate. He lodged the spear tip against the lower limb of a dead tree, covering it with dead branches.

When he returned, the bear was pacing back and forth, roaring and huffing on the other side. The river was too fast and full of churning water to easily cross, and the creature was too smart to put itself in a disadvantaged position. It clearly wasn't confident in making the jump across, a perfect scenario for Nacho. It was like finding a glitch in a video game where the bad guys couldn't touch him.

He fired arrow after arrow into the bear, until the thing was so blinded by rage that it launched itself across the gap in the bridge. Bleeding and frothing at the mouth, it landed only seven feet from him and didn't pause. It sped forward, chasing after Nacho—who had started sprinting down the path as soon as he saw it leap.

The human dodged to the left just as the creature caught up, leading it straight into the halberd that was hidden by the dead tree limb. The bear rammed a shoulder into the spear point, driving it in deep, which served to anchor the creature to that position.

Seizing the moment of pained surprise, Nacho danced forward and drove his short sword into the monster's side, bypassing its ribs and puncturing both the heart and lungs. Then he ducked and swirled away to let the creature finish dying on its own.

Congratulations! You have killed a Gecko Bear!
Level 07 Standard Monster = 70 Evaluation Points
You did well!
Note: +5 Evaluation Points for killing it on your second day! Bam! You go, boy.

. . .

Nacho let out a sigh of relief, then returned to the bridge to gather everything he'd dropped. He couldn't keep a wide smile from spreading across his face: he was ending the day at three hundred and seventy-six Evaluation Points. That was almost twice as many as he'd had when he'd died the first time, to the creature he'd just finished off.

Jumping over the bridge, he hurried back to his cave home... and that was when he heard voices calling out in the distance. The words sounded human, if a little high-pitched and throaty. "This is new... are there *people* here?"

Everything he experienced from here on out would be new, but... he had never *once* heard about other people being found in the Evaluation, and some people had managed to survive for *four* days. He inched closer, but even up close, he couldn't understand their words. That was enough for him to decide to turn around and run for it.

Someone was talking. Nacho was sure of it. He wasn't alone.

CHAPTER FIVE

Not wanting to take a chance on a fire that night, Nacho cracked open the pinecones he'd collected and added pine nuts to his peanuts and berries, washing the meal down with a large gulp of water that had been cooled by the stone cave. For now, he could drink as much as he wanted, but the level of the pond had dropped another inch. "Trail mix and water. Hard to beat; harder to eat."

The strange voices had vanished into the west, but he knew that whoever—or *whatever*—those sounds had belonged to, they'd eventually be driven to the pool if they wanted to live.

The night passed uneventfully. Even so, Nacho had set up his grass screen and added plenty of sticks to give himself as much warning as possible if something tried to intrude. As the third day in the Evaluation World dawned, he left his cave to explore the plains to the east. The forest thinned out into a prairie, where steady wind drew patterns in the long grasses. A stone path led off through the undergrowth with a crumbling rock wall on either side. "Just like that, I beat my survival record."

A flash of red caught his eye, and his blade was half drawn

before he realized that he had found strawberry bushes growing next to the wall. Big, red, and ripe: the perfect sweets for Nacho.

He spotted a hill in the distance, as well as some kind of structure. Too bad it was already in the dead zone, where the grasses were gone and the dirt had turned to dust. Going out to that area, a space with no cover, was practically *begging* to be swarmed by monsters. "If the death zone keeps moving at this pace, I've got *maybe* another two days before it reaches Stonehenge Pond. If I ration the jars of water and the food, I could survive for at least another week past that before dehydration starts sending me into a death spiral."

He didn't find any exciting monsters that day, only managing to hunt and kill a few level two and three monsters on the plains. That included massive bark-covered grasshoppers that flung themselves into the air in hopes of landing on him and crushing his skull, as well as giant field mice covered with a thick shell like a turtle. The turtle-mice had hooked talons, and they were tough to damage, but they also weren't very cautious. Thanks to their apparent disregard for pain, Nacho was able to kill several with his bow, and a few with his throwing knives, finishing off the leftovers at close range with his sword and dagger combo. Overall, the time proved to be profitable, if not terribly exciting. "Exactly how I like it."

At one point, he did find a hill that housed a crypt-like room. It was clear of any enemies, and he didn't even need to worry about running into any undead, since the only zombies that existed in the Starter World were ones resurrected by Necromancers—one of the available Mind Player classes. There *was* a happy surprise: the crypt held long swords, battle axes, shirts of chainmail, metal boots, and most importantly: huge, empty water barrels! The alcove didn't have a door, which was unfortunate, but he was aware that he had found a true treasure trove.

Searching through the connected rooms, Nacho found another bow and quiver of arrows, as well as two crossbows with complicated loading mechanisms. There were only six bolts to be found, and it would take forever to reload one of them, but anything that would increase his odds of survival was worth collecting. In a small closet, he found a pick and a shovel, probably the things that excited him the most beyond the water barrels.

Outside, the wind blew the dust and dead grass around as the dead zone expanded... and Nacho was struck by a *very* good idea. Instead of using the cave right next to Stonehenge, he decided to fully relocate here, door or no door. Those barrels of water would last him a good long while if he filled them, and he still had a ton of blackberries, peanuts, and pine nuts.

So long as he moved at night and didn't draw any attention, he didn't think the monsters would seek him out on the dust plain. They'd all eventually be forced to congregate at the central Stonehenge Pond; it wasn't like turtle mice had the ability to collect water. Eventually, they would fight each other until only one select group had access to the water source.

As for the voices he'd heard? Nacho wasn't convinced they were human, but if they were alive, they would have to eat and drink. He didn't want to be forced to fight them directly for the last of the world's resources; instead, his preference was to snipe them at extreme range while they clustered around the pool. He'd been a very successful assassin for three years. He knew how to pick his moment.

Working until late into the night, rolling barrels full of water back to the hill crypt, Nacho started putting his plan into action. The crescent moon might have looked fake, but it created enough light for him to work in the otherwise absolute darkness of night. As he stood for a final moment outside his poolside cave, a new light source drew his eye.

There were *campfires* to the west, and at the same moment he saw the fire, he smelled cooking meat. His stomach grumbled, but then he detected the foul tang of the Putrid Mana. "I'm not gonna fall for that! I know how sick that makes people. I'll stick with my plant-based diet until I can buy a cheeseburger from the Store in the Starter World, thank you *very* much."

Then he remembered the quality of the Store's food and sighed. Perhaps he *should* have taken some time to go ahead and sample decent food in the months before the Juxtaposition instead of pursuing his single-minded training. But he was a disaster in the kitchen, and he hadn't wanted to waste the money he needed for more important things.

He continued rolling the last barrel home before setting up his screens to block the archway of the crypt. Utterly exhausted, he still had to take a moment to laugh at himself. If this had been him from four years ago, the stone slabs that could have skeletons under them might've freaked him out, making it impossible to sleep. But now? He laid directly on the stone resting space and prepared for his grand plan. Most likely, he'd be facing some high-level Tier zero monsters.

"Rig up some traps... but not today." He ended the day with five hundred and ninety-six points—basically triple the number of Evaluation Points he'd gotten in his last attempt—he had water for weeks, and food for a few more days. "I can live without food for a good long time. I hope I starve to death *weeks* after everything else here dies. What would that be worth?"

He woke to his fourth day with a howling stomach, but thankfully, he had the strawberries he'd collected from the rock wall near the forest. He'd also filled another pot with blackberries, and if he added that to the peanuts and pine nuts... Nacho probably had a week's worth of food, and so much water that he wouldn't be able to drink it all.

The next half-day was spent digging some shallow pits and covering them with grass. He unstacked stones from the wall and laid them out around the pits, then retrieved sticks from the woods and carved up punji spikes for the holes. He also hid weapons, including one of the crossbows, near the stacks of rocks and set up another halberd trap—it had worked on the gecko bear, and he hoped it would work again.

A sudden wind whipped up the dust, making him gag on the dry air and grains of sand that shot down his throat. He wished his helmet had a visor, or goggles, but instead, he took a bit of the cloth from the swamp shack and covered most of his face so that only his eyes were exposed.

Not forgetting that his main goal was the collection of EP, he spent the rest of the day hunting. Many of the weaker creatures had already gathered at Stonehenge Pond. From the look of things, the southern swamp must've been hit especially hard.

Long Copperopolis Anacondas and albino alligator insects slithered in and around the pool, chewing on Goblin Mosquitoes. The half-eaten remains of Claw Squirrels lay scattered about, mostly ignored by the swamp-dwelling creatures—indicating to his experienced eye that whatever had been eating them had been eaten in turn.

Nacho waited patiently to start killing until the dustification of the northern forests pushed the naked wolves south. As soon as the first of the diseased canines began arriving in the area, it wasn't long before they fought the alligators and snakes. That was when he knew the time for gathering EP had arrived. Bow in hand, Nacho began sending feathered shafts into the wounded, gathering the points for little to no effort. Even though the process was fun and easy, it brought back some memories of point poachers in the Starter World. "Whoever got the kill got the points. I can get ready for that in advance, at least. Then again... how do I prepare against myself? Heh."

He was doing well until a mysterious arrow flew through the air and killed a wrinkled pink wolf. "That wasn't mine, where...?"

That was when he noticed the Squirrel Lords. He'd killed Claw Squirrels on his first day in the Evaluation, and these things were similar... except they were six feet tall, with big bushy tails, and onyx demon horns poking out of their hairless heads. A closer inspection revealed no ears, black eyes, and wet noses leaking mucus; which had dried to a slime around their nostrils. Their arms were overly muscled: frankly, their only point of failure turned out to be skinny, crooked legs.

Hidden in his tree, Nacho counted six of the Squirrel Lords. They wore various pieces of armor and were equipped with a collection of swords, spears, and maces. One held a crossbow, and another hefted a heavy crank crossbow like the one he'd set up in his ambush traps around his crypt home.

They'd pulled along their camping gear as well; clearly, they were migrating to occupy the pool. The mucous-y Squirrel Lords attacked the wolves and alligators while Nacho stealthily watched. It dawned on him that the Squirrel Lords were the ones speaking the strange language he'd heard before, allowing them to coordinate their efforts. It was good to know that even though he was dealing with an intelligent enemy, he didn't need to fight people yet. Even so, their ability to think and plan together made them a hundred times more dangerous than even creatures like the Gecko Bear or the Melted Crow.

Nacho had already gathered another hundred points and was sitting at six hundred and ninety-six Evaluation Points. With a more powerful enemy on the field, it was time to retreat. He inched his way down from the tree and slipped away into the forest, allowing the sound of the fighting to grow fainter behind him. He didn't go directly back to his final home. Instead, he headed south through the dying trees.

Confirming that the southern swamp was gone—only brackish black puddles in dust remained—Nacho cut around to the southeast, making sure that his trail was wiped away, thanks to the wind, until he was back at his crypt in the blasted plain.

The next day, day five, Nacho took a little trip up north across the plain. The pine forest had decomposed into a mixture of dead trunks, rust-colored pine needles, and black dust. He killed five giant spiders—Argus Spiders, according to the System. The spider monsters had the expected eight legs and dripping fangs, with the main difference being the *gazillion* eyes on their black, furry bodies. He quickly gained an advantage against the creatures, finding that the shifting piles of pine needles made rapid movement difficult for the spiders. That detail allowed Nacho to stay back and use the bow and arrow to pick them off one by one.

They were all level six, which meant another three hundred

points for him. He was only four points away from a full thousand Evaluation Points, and he could hardly believe it. He gathered up some firewood, which was easy, since all the trees were as dry as barbeque in North Carolina, if less vinegary. That night, Nacho observed the glow of the Squirrel Lords around their fires, in their new location near Stonehenge Pond. "*So* glad I did the water barrels yesterday."

Nacho didn't exactly look forward to his next essential task. Though he had enough food and water to wait them out, he also wanted to maximize his points. The only issue was that facing all six of the demon rodents at once was a death sentence.

His knife was in his hand and a smile was on his face before he was even consciously aware of what he was doing. Nacho was an assassin.

It was time to use his training and even the odds.

CHAPTER SIX

The soon-to-be-official assassin started a tiny fire in the crypt, solely for a light to draw in prey, and prepared for his midnight run. Taking a burial shroud, he rubbed it in dust until it became a dark gray, then used it to cover his cuirass and anything else that might shine. He gathered his bow and his last five arrows, then noiselessly followed the low stone wall into the central forest.

Above him, the crescent moon wasn't doing him any favors, but there were thankfully still thick trees and undergrowth for cover near Stonehenge Pond. Nacho walked from dust to dirt, only coming to a halt when he laid eyes on the Squirrel Lords asleep around the pool. Only one was on watch, clearly not expecting trouble—since it was gazing down at a small fire with its black eyes, nearly asleep itself.

By now, even though there was still water in the pond, it was unfit for humans. He could tell even from that distance that it was full of swirling Putrid Mana. That was fine by him. Given how fast the swamp had dried up, that pond wouldn't last a day once the creeping death hit the center of the Evaluation World.

Soon his targets would be weak and dying, even without his intervention.

"Can't let all those EPs go to waste though, now can I?" Standing in the shadows of a tree, Nacho put an arrow to string. He found himself looking forward to the kill, pleased for the first time by how years of war and murder had changed him—twisted him, really. He'd become a player who was determined to win, no matter how grisly the game became.

It was a simple enough matter to pull the string back, take aim, and send a feathered shaft into the throat of the Squirrel Lord on watch. Since it was nearly asleep, the arrow strike caused it to try to inhale, only to get a lungful of blood and Putrid Mana. It went down without a sound; even the *thump* from hitting the ground was muted due to its thick fur. "Those lessons were totally worth it."

Congratulations! You have killed a Greater Flufftail Terror!

Level 08 Standard Monster = 80 Evaluation Points

Wowee! You're one special little warrior! These things are tough, mean, and unkind to their rodent parents.

Note: You have over 1000 Evaluation Points! You are killing *it! You're now a one percenter!*

A *cha-ching* sound followed, though it was only in his head and inaudible for the demon rodents sleeping around their fire. Nacho hung the bow and quiver on a branch, then crept forward with only his dagger, planning his route. He'd cut throats before; that was the gory truth. Pulling himself from his memories, he abruptly realized that he was sweating and breathing hard, so he paused to take a few deep breaths. "Huh. I'm still gonna call them Squirrel Lords in my head."

Under control once more, he continued edging silently forward. He nearly stepped on a sleeping figure on the outskirts of the campfire's flickering light but managed to pause and reposition. Nacho stared down at the target, knowing that although the task would be harder than it used to be—he didn't have any of his assassin stealth skills—he knew the basics. Grabbing the squirrel's demon horn gently, he tugged it back and exposed the monster's neck. A quick slash later, the thing was neatly dispatched.

Another eighty Evaluation Points went into his total, but he wasn't paying attention to that: the beast had managed to gurgle a warning with its last breath, jerking awake the other Squirrel Lords. Nacho dove behind a stone before the first of the blood started to pool, cursing his luck silently. He'd gotten two of the fluffy terrors, but he still wasn't going to fight the remaining four on their own turf that night. Eyes glittering as he marked his next prey, the man slithered south silently, retracing his path through dead trees and across ever-increasing dust... then running back to his hillside home.

Too amped to sleep, he watched the fake crescent moon cross the blank black sky. Nacho already knew exactly what he would do next: nothing.

That little glade of trees would vanish, the water would be gone, and all he would have to do was wait. Those beasts would get hungry, then thirsty, and when they saw his fire, they'd come to investigate.

Nacho let one day pass in total relaxation and luxury, by this world's standards. The following day was a nice, lazy one as well. Refusing to poke his head outside, he could only imagine what havoc a week in the Evaluation World had wreaked. The place was likely a parched, dead forest on a plain of dust. The temperatures, even in his shelter, began to swing from sizzling heat during the day to frigid death at night. Even so, Nacho didn't risk a fire. Not yet.

On the afternoon of the eighth day, he took his flint and steel and started a nice-sized fire in an area he had specifically prepared for receiving... guests. More important than the flames was the smoke, and to remove all concern that it might be a trap, he slid most of his water barrels—brimming with water—out next to the fire. It would only be a matter of time before the fluffy terrors came to investigate, driven by their desperation. He knew from experience that even a single day without water was a long day indeed.

Nacho dug himself a little hidey-hole in the dust and covered it with leftover dried grasses he'd woven together. He adjusted the blind so it blended into the gray, black, and yellow landscape. There he sat, with his crossbow, longbow, throwing daggers, and other weapons ready to go. A barrel of water that he drank from constantly was his only companion, as he needed to stay completely hydrated. Those oversized vermin might have meat to eat, but they had to be running out of water: he had checked to verify that there were no containers among their goods when he had scouted the camp.

Only an hour later, the Squirrel Lords came stumbling on weary legs with their tails appearing matted and sickly. Their hairless heads had grown pale, and they looked to be on the verge of collapse, though it was hard to tell with the horns and the inky black eyes. Frankly, they were just plain creepy. One carried a drawn bow, another a loaded crossbow. Both wore curved swords at their hips, though the other two had their melee weapons out and ready to deal with anything close-range.

Nacho braced the stock of his own crossbow against his shoulder and lined up his bolt with the lead bow squirrel. He was nervous, his hands sweating lightly. "This is all just practice; I have well over a thousand Evaluation Points."

He would enter that Evaluation Mall as *royalty*.

That thought was enough to let him pull the trigger with no fear. The bolt struck the bow squirrel in the chest, and it sank to its knees. A system message dinged to tell him he was eighty Evaluation Points richer. With no time to waste, Nacho immediately got to work cranking the wheel of the string and slipping another bolt in place. He carefully blinked sweat from his eyes as he settled back into position.

"One down, three to go." The squirrels hadn't seen where the shot came from, and they scrambled to take cover inside

Nacho's crypt. He felt violated. "Crypt, sweet crypt. Be it ever so humble, there's no place like crypt."

Nacho didn't have to wait long. The thirst drove them out. They sprang for the water barrels with cups, and the minute they dipped into one, the human nailed the crossbow squirrel in the back, right where his little evil squirrel heart should be.

It let out a cry, and Nacho heard the *cha-ching* that confirmed his kill. Sadly, the two remaining anthropomorphic vermin spotted his face. It was time for a few close-up kills, not that Nacho was going to play fair. No... it was time to put his traps to work.

He dropped his crossbow and launched himself out of his hidey-hole, screaming as he ran straight at the squirrels. He kicked away the dead beast's crossbow that lay in the dust as the others recoiled in confusion, triggering the action and sending a bolt shooting out across the dead ground. With the weapon rendered useless, he sprinted along the stone path through his pit traps.

The first sword squirrel followed him carefully, but the mace-wielding one stepped into a pit; his foot crashed through the grass and onto a spike. Macey-Demon let out a shriek of pain and rage. Hearing that the trap was effective, Nacho spun and knocked the sword squirrel against a pile of rocks—right where he had hidden the halberd away in the tangled grass. The demon squirrel found himself impaled but alive, but Nacho fixed that with a single thrust of his dagger.

The system allocated him eighty additional points as the last of the monsters limped toward him, the mace in its paw glowing a sickly green. Nacho sized up his opponent, realizing that this creature had some nice armor—if the assassin didn't let his eyes drop below the creature's knees. "Probably should've invested more in shoes than chainmail!"

Nacho used the moment the squirrel took to understand his words to dart forward, just before it could start swinging the mace. He drove his short sword into the squirrel's chest, but it merely rebounded off the armor. Macey-Demon whipped his fancy Morningstar around, crushing the human's left arm, but Nacho had already begun twisting, and managed to plunge his dagger into the exposed throat; driving the knife up to the hilt in the monster's arteries.

Those black eyes went lifeless.

Congratulations! You have killed a Greater Flufftail Terror!
  Level 09 Standard Monster = 90 Evaluation Points
  Stupendous work! +25 bonus points for killing the big cheese!
  Note: You are crafty. We like that.

Nacho checked, and he had one thousand, five hundred and eleven points in total. From what he'd seen of the area, there were no other monsters remaining on this little slice of paradise. He didn't get all of the points that were possible, thanks to the Flufftails killing the creatures who'd congregated around Stonehenge Pond, but his results were still more than acceptable. His left arm was numb from the mace strike, and he figured the bone was broken for sure. In the end, Nacho knew it wouldn't matter.

Using his healthy arm, he dragged the bodies of the Lords out into the dust. He doggedly returned to his crypt and laid down for a few minutes. Taking stock of the situation, Nacho breathed a sigh of relief. He might not have a door, but he had two barrels full of water, a clay pot half full of peanuts, one full of strawberries that were already going bad, a few pine nuts, and some blackberry pouch jelly.

"I did it. Everything here is dead except for me." He eased up and shuffled out to sit by his fire, and all was darkness except for the fake crescent moon in the inky sky. Then he had a thought that chilled him to the bone: he was going to starve to death unless he ate rotten monster meat. He had enough water to last him a good long while, but in conditions like this, the food would go bad. From there, it would be a slow decline into death by starvation.

"Well, that's a problem for *aged* Nacho cheese to deal with." He wrapped up in a burial shroud next to his fire and went to sleep, half-hoping some monster would just kill him as he slept so that he'd be done with this place.

No such luck.

He spent the next several days exploring every *inch* of the Evaluation World, which had been reduced to a dusty circle of dead plants. All the rivers were dry enough to start a fire on, the swamp had desiccated into cracked mud, and Stonehenge Pond lay empty. The western part of the realm might've been a nice place back before the withering had hit it—it lay thick with the parched remnants of trees, grassy knolls, and numerous sandy riverbanks.

He found a rambling cottage with eight rooms, more weapons, armor, and broken food storage containers. Nacho figured it had been the Squirrel Lords' home, since he found far too many empty walnut and peanut shells, as well as some rotting meat which might have been a chicken at one point. Why the Squirrel Lords had smashed up the clay storage jars, he had no idea. They could've used them to store water and avoid his homegrown ambush.

Nacho thought maybe his wounded left arm would kill him, but he didn't think it was going to be fast enough to avoid some thirsty days. His body was already healing, though he was getting hungrier. He'd run out of satchel jelly, he'd polished off the pine nuts and strawberries, and he only had a handful of peanuts left back in the crypt.

On the way home, he collected more firewood, deciding that even though he didn't need to return to the crypt, it was as good a place to slowly die as any other. He built himself a firepit inside the crypt and dug out a chimney, then rubbed sticks together in the sun, instantly creating flame—the wood burned like flash paper.

He wasn't sure if there was some kind of penalty for ending

the Evaluation himself, but given how terrible things were in the Evaluation World, Nacho figured some people just gave up all hope. He wouldn't.

In the end, he didn't need to.

A couple days later, weak from hunger, he woke up on the burial slab. It was his fourteenth day in the Evaluation World. Two weeks was a whole lot better than two days, and he had collected nearly eight times the points. Confused as to why he had woken up so suddenly, he realized that dust was shaking from the walls of his crypt. His fireplace crumbled, and it felt like the entire world was quaking.

Nacho slipped off his slab and stumbled out of the crypt, freezing in place as he watched a Godzilla-sized abomination rise out of the dust in the distance. On its head was a rocky crown he recognized even from this distance—those were the Stonehenge stones. The pond must've been part of the giant's skull.

"Gross," Nacho laughed dizzily. "I was drinking head water."

The giant had to have been at least four hundred feet tall, likely a Tier five monster, though there was no way for him to prove that. Whatever it was, all Nacho knew for sure was that it meant he didn't need to die from starvation anymore. It lumbered forward on massive feet, a veritable mountain of ambulatory stone crushing through the dust and causing a storm and landslide all in one.

Half the world seemed to have been drawn up into the monster already, and the ground seemed to be absorbing into its body like an earth elemental from legends. It grew larger every second, so Nacho grabbed his bow and started toward it. "Maybe a lucky shot'll score me another fifty points. C'mere... you. There's gotta be a prize for taking you down. What delicious secret are you hiding? I bet... I bet it's... *delicious*."

The rock monster came swaying over, not even noticing the frail human that was gearing up to take it on directly. Up top, there might've been a mouth and eyes, but at that distance, it was too high to really tell. Nacho started giggling as he fired arrow after arrow into the stone limbs, though they bounced off harmlessly.

It wasn't long before Nacho was gaping helplessly up at the giant stone heel of the final monster. The sun was blotted out. Air rushed past and around him.

Then it was Splatsville: population Nacho.

He didn't feel his death, which was a nice surprise. Being mauled by the Gecko Bear had been *awful*. This wasn't bad— just some air pressure, and then nothing.

Aww, we're sorry, Player, but you were killed by a Tier Five Stone Catastrophe!

Evaluation complete.

You died with 1511 Evaluation Points, but how many people would charge at something like that? You have been evaluated as Worthy. *Because you were cut off before going as long as you* could *have lasted, we're forced to round you up to an even 1600 Evaluation Points! Great job!*

Ready to mix up a delicious future?

Go get some retail therapy!

"Ha. Called it." Part of Nacho was disgusted that the Patrons had thrown such a wildly unfair monster as a Tier five at him. There hadn't even been a Tier *one* in the entire area; everything he'd fought was Tier zero! The other part of him realized that it didn't matter, except for allowing him to skip starving all by himself for weeks on end.

Mostly, Nacho was just glad to be alive. Again. He was back in his body, wearing a tuxedo, blinking at the bright lights of the weirdest mall imaginable. As he settled back into himself, he slowly smiled at the realization that he had a small hill of Evaluation Points burning a hole in his pocket.

Time to cash in.

CHAPTER SEVEN

Nacho scanned the mall surrounding a central abyss, and his inner safety-minded-self cheered over the fact that there were railings. He found that he was still without the backpack he'd strapped on before the Juxtaposition began, but he was confident he'd have it in the Starter World. His left arm was also completely healed, and he felt full and hydrated. "Everything exactly as expected."

All dressed up and formal, he strolled over to gaze down into the dark nothing below. Normally, there might be a first floor down there. Not in the Evaluation Mall. These stores were illuminated by bright neon lights, with even more light pouring from fluorescent bulbs covered by plastic amidst the ceiling tiles. What lay above? Nacho figured it was some kind of cosmic horror that would drive him completely insane if he were aware of its existence, but he might try to sneak a peek anyway.

The mall's store signs were written in Patronese, the universal language of the Starter World which everyone could understand. A common language made speaking with everyone possible, even if most conversations were usually punctuated with sharp objects instead of a witty turn of phrase. Nacho recognized each of the shops from last time: Terraseth's Body Pavilion, The Obliterator's Mind Wares, Gary's General Store, Big Al's Armory and Steelworks, Saavi Candoo's Skills Stall, and Wheezy's Weapons.

But what really caught his attention was the *new* store across the way. Had it been there the last time Nacho had been in the Mall? It was strangely hard to remember, but he knew that he would've checked it out if it had been available, so he could only assume it was new.

"Cinnabunny's Satiation Shoppe *wasn't* there before. I *know* it wasn't." Nacho would've remembered the plump pink unicorn bunny on the sign. He'd have to check the place out this time around.

A welcome message hit him like an annoying, unskippable UTube ad.

Hello, Player!
You survived your evaluation!
Just kidding, lol. We all know you were killed in the end, but great job returning to your updated body with little to no Patron intervention! While you were gone, we made some changes to your insides, so things will never go back to normal for you or everyone you love. How exciting!

Unlike everyone else, Nacho already knew that the changes to his body were critical. He wouldn't process food and water as he had before, as his levels of hunger would be tied to his Skills, but he would *need* to eat. Everyone else would be clueless about that, and he hated how the Patrons mentioned 'everyone he loved'. It was a threat, and he knew it, even if no one else did.

Another message followed.

. . .

Remember those Evaluation Points you earned? Well, this is where you get to spend them like a boss. This is the shopping spree of a lifetime! Buy your future character class, magic items, and other cool things.

To reach the Starter World, just go to the elevator near Gary's General Store. All unused points are forfeit. May your future be delicious!

Nacho shook his head at the seemingly inane messages that carried hidden context. He walked into Terraseth's Body Pavilion—the place was divided into seven sections like his local supercenter, except instead of Men's Sportswear, the departments were based upon the seven Body Player classes:

- *Warrior (100 EPs)*
- *Rogue (150 EPs)*
- *Assassin (200 EPs)*
- *Archer (300 EPs)*
- *Berserker (500 EPs)*
- *Ranger (750 EPs)*
- *Paladin (1000 EPs)*

The Paladin section—which had been impossible to see clearly the last time he was shopping—exhibited suits of gleaming armor positioned around a central basin which presumably held holy water. The Ranger's section sported studded leather armor, bows, arrows, and cool swords, all displayed among fake plastic vines and a plaster tree set into the wall. Rogue was all sleek black leather, while the Archer alcove offered wrist guards and finger guards. Lastly, the cheapest option, Warrior, presented a variety of chainmail armor with a cool central shield in the middle.

No one bought the actual clothing, weapons, or armor here. There were other stores for that. This was merely where a player purchased their class.

A welcome message from the shop appeared in his vision:

. . .

Greetings, Player!

Do you like chopping off the heads of your enemies? Do you enjoy close-quarter combat, or are you just an all-out hack-and-slash murderhobo in the making?

The Body Pavilion is a stop-and-shop heaven for those players wanting to armor up, grab a sword, and get busy sweating and questing. Any questions? Just ask Terraseth.

Note: Terraseth can't speak, but he can offer you silent moral support as you make your way through your options.

A Naga ran the place, though the snake-man was a true non-player character: not very helpful. Presumably, this was the aforementioned 'Terraseth'. The Naga slithered over, showcasing his midnight scales and dark flesh, though he incongruously wore a jaunty red vest and a fez on his bald human scalp.

"Howdy, S-s-seth," Nacho called to the shopkeeper, Drawing out all of his sibilant 's' sounds. "What deals-s do you have for Ass-sass-ssin classes-ss?"

A black tongue slithered out of the thin lips. Yellow snake eyes regarded Nacho with very little interest, then flicked to the assassin robes: everything from ninja black to cutthroat crimson.

A System information box appeared in his vision:

Assassin class! Includes two deadly—but exceedingly fun—killing Skills of your choosing!

To be an Assassin is to strike from the shadows and destroy your enemies, unseen and silent, leaving behind nothing but their death rattle.

Basic cost: 200 Evaluation Points

Browse for more info?

Yes / No.

Note: Additional Skills can be purchased at Saavi's Skills Stall, on the other side of the mall.

.   .   .

Nacho had figured he would just be an assassin again—he'd been *the* great assassin, and he planned on spending the rest of his life backstabbing beasts and people alike. There was no need to browse for more info; the Skills were pretty self-explanatory. It came with the classic Backstab, Lethal Anatomy Knowledge, Distance Death, Midnight Blend, Shadow Speed, and Ninja Hush.

Then again... being an assassin again did have its benefits, but... he had fourteen hundred extra points to spend. There was no need to dive into anything right away. Nacho *could* afford the Paladin, but he couldn't picture himself in plate mail with a long sword. Ranger might be an option, or Archer, since both prioritized bows, and he'd liked not being close to things trying to kill him.

He could buy those classes easily and then max out skills and gear; maybe he could even combine Archer with the Lethal Anatomy Knowledge. "That might be cool. Is multiclassing a thing?"

Terraseth sighed at him, slithering away to adjust the chain-mail in the Warrior's section. Nacho figured that Paladin would be what Brie would choose if she could afford it. Once again, he wondered how well she'd done during her Evaluation. She had the athleticism and physical endurance to do very well, but could she stomach the slaughter? Could Reuben? He was a sensitive, happy-go-lucky guy. Murder involved luck, yes, but not necessarily happiness... unless a person had been born that way.

He wondered what the System would assign his people as their native Skills. Nacho stood there, torn between upgrades, but the scent of pastries invaded his thoughts. He knew the truth: there would be no way to choose a class until he checked out the Cinnabunny's Satiation Shoppe.

Just the *name* made him hungry for a cinnamon bun. Sweet, sticky, hot out of the oven. Not that he was hungry—all his Evaluation World hunger was gone. Just one of the many benefits of his forever changed body. Leaving the Naga's store behind, he popped into the Obliterator's Mind Wares to procrastinate.

The Obliterator was a mysterious figure dressed in a black cloak and embellished robes. On her right arm were the words 'Happy, Happy' stitched into the black fabric. Her left sleeve stated 'Joy, Joy.' At least the Obliterator seemed like she enjoyed her work. "Nothing like Terraseth, amiright?"

Again, there were seven sections to the place for the seven Mind Player options.

- *Warlock (100 EPs)*
- *Illusionist (150 EPs)*
- *Elementalist (200 EPs)*
- *Necromancer (300 EPs)*
- *Healer (500 EPs)*
- *Druid (750 EPs)*
- *Wizard (1000 EPs)*

A second later, like before, another shop message hit him.

Greetings, Player!

Do you like standing back, casting spells, and causing collateral damage? Do you want to use your mind and spirit to delve into the darkest depths of forbidden knowledge? Or do you just like fire, lots and lots of fire? Either way, being a Mind Player might make you weak at first, but you'll become a living weapon at higher levels. Or, there's a lame Healer class for those softies who can't stand seeing their fellow players in pain.

The Obliterator Mind Wares is where you can find your magic and get your mojo working!

Any questions? Just ask the Obliterator!

Note: The Obliterator can't speak, but she can listen to you make your way through your incorrect options.

. . .

The Obliterator floated over with her sleeves clasped so her hands remained hidden.

"So, little O, can you tell me the difference between a wizard and warlock?" Nacho stood with his hands on his hips and addressed the character, wanting to see what the shop-keeper would do. She extended a slim hand with long scarlet nails... pointing to the section where the warlock robes hung near various statues of other robed men and women.

Actually, in the Mind Player store, it was all robes, all the time, though the healer's clothes seemed to have more of a sacred feel to them. In stark contrast, the Druid's section was unfortunate: mostly just loincloths. A lone mannequin stood there, sporting the band of leather hanging off plaster hips.

Nacho didn't bother to go over and check out the warlock class. He wasn't going to be a Mind Player. As for the difference between the classes, warlocks were jack-of-all-trade sorcerers fully reliant on being powered by a Patron. They could use a variety of spells, but they were significantly less formidable. For example, they could raise the dead, but their undead creatures would never be as deadly as those summoned by a true necro-mancer at the same level.

The now-undecided man meandered through the other stores to bother the shopkeepers, all of whom didn't say a word but merely stood there silently. If his friends' lives hadn't been depending on him, he would've punched Big Al just to see what would happen. Big Al was a huge man, garbed in a leather hood and greasy leather skirt, who sold all kinds of armor; from European mail, to Japanese lacquer armor, to African wicker shields. Of course, there were some interesting artifacts on display as well, though who would have the Evaluation Points to afford a powerful item like the Emerald Breastplate shining in a display case in one corner? The single piece of armor was five hundred points.

Nacho was shocked to realize that *he* could afford it. Maybe he *should* just buy back his assassin class? Then he could load up on artifacts... no. He was only dragging his feet because he didn't really want to go into the Cinnabunny's Satiation Shoppe, not with what he knew about the Juxtaposition. For the most part, Patrons only liked to complicate things. They liked making the players miserable, and he could easily imagine walking into that new shop and being eaten by cupcakes, or making some Faustian deal and trading his soul for blueberry muffins.

Fighting the inexorable pull of sticky-sweet cinnamon, he went out to the railing and stared down into the abyss. This place operated outside normal time and space, as the Evaluation World had, so he had time to think. Not that thinking was going to help him. No, he knew what he had to do. He just wasn't looking forward to it.

The truth was... he *had* heard rumors of Satiation Players, but that was all they'd been. Rumors. There was talk of a brewer up north who not only could filter Putrid Mana out of water, but could brew up potions usable by players on different Tiers. Then there was talk of a mountain man to the east who could take dead monsters and make them edible, much like the Gorged Guild's magical oven. It was *improbable*, but not impossible. Such player classes hadn't survived all that long. They had no combat skills, which meant they'd all died eventually.

Also, who would want to start out in a lethal world as a *farmer*? Why would a fighter, who had kicked butt during the Evaluation, ever decide to spend the Juxtaposition growing food? Short answer—they wouldn't. Even the gamers who enjoyed playing the support classes like a healer wouldn't willingly choose to be really good at making soup, bottling water, or grilling hamburgers.

But... if the rumors were true, a Satiation Player would've made all the difference in Nacho's life and the lives of everyone else in the Final Victory Guild. Nacho shut his eyes. He had a bad history with cooking. There was one time... it had been the best day of his life, and the worst. But he wasn't going to linger on those memories. It would be better to forget his past forever.

Nevertheless, it was going to be a brutal decision. Part of

him just wanted to go be an assassin and forget he'd ever seen the Satiation Shoppe. Also, why the pretentious extra 'pe' at the end? Those Patrons were as bloodthirsty as they were inane. Overdone naming conventions aside, Nacho knew that he couldn't leave without at least checking out the Satiation Shoppe. If he didn't confirm his suspicions, six months down the road, the regret just might kill him.

Nacho knew he was in a unique position. He knew it down to his bones, so he ambled over to the shoppe with the unicorn bunny sign. That had to be the Cinnabunny, and she smelled cinnamon-y and good. The fact that he wanted to lick her instantly put him on edge.

In the Juxtaposition, nothing was as it seemed. He was willing to bet that after the first taste, he would collapse into a hallucination or something. the first words out of his mouth were, "I don't trust you, rabbit."

Cinnabunny's expression didn't change, but he knew that she was probably devastated at the news.

CHAPTER EIGHT

Crossing the threshold of the Satiation Shoppe, Nacho received a variety of messages.

Greetings, Player!

Congratulations! You not only did well on your evaluation, but you scored in the top one percent! That's not easy to do. Your reward isn't all that great, sorry. You get the chance to become a Satiation Player!

Do you like chopping onions, dicing peppers, and standing over a stove for hours and hours? Or maybe you'd like to burn yourself on an oven rack in the same place, every time. Or perhaps you want to make your own hooch or concoct any number of intoxicating cocktails. Or maybe farming? Monster breeding is kinda fun, if you're into that sort of thing.

The Satiation Shoppe is the place to get your food on! Be the life of the party! Throw amazing wedding receptions! Steam cocktail weenies to impress your friends after they're done throwing lightning and calling down meteors!

Any questions, just ask the Cinnabunny herself!

Note: As it will become abundantly clear, the Cinnabunny isn't human. She's a bunnicorn. She can't talk, and she's actually an herbivore with a very limited diet. So you're on your own, Player. Good luck! May your future be delicious!

The proprietor of the shoppe stood behind a counter near the back, with all kinds of brightly colored candies arrayed in bins inside its glass display case. She was a big fluffy pink bunny with a single pearlescent horn sticking out of her forehead. A white apron covered her chest and belly. She might be an herbivore, but Nacho had a sneaking suspicion that she'd been snacking on her own sweet supply.

Like the other shopkeepers, she gazed at him with cool pink eyes, as though she could care less about his existence. She must've been the surliest bunnicorn in all of creation. Nacho glanced around and found that the place was part candy store, part diner, part post-apocalyptic stage play, and perhaps just a dash of backyard barbecue. In the far corner, things got fancy with shiny knives and cooking utensils that baffled Nacho. "Sometimes kitchen folk come up with the weirdest solutions to the simplest things."

Unlike the other shops, Nacho was going to review every class and get a good sense of the Skills, because if he was going to commit to such a lame character class, he was going to make *absolutely* sure there weren't any hidden 'gotchas'.

Over each class area hung a sign.

- Survivalist
- Scavenger
- Farmer
- Harvester
- Butcher
- Brewer
- Common Cook

Nacho immediately noticed that there were no price listings. Was this a case of 'if you have to ask, you can't afford it'? The

Cinnabunny half-hopped, half-slumped its way to stand next to Nacho, as if prompting him to hurry the abyss up.

He did *not* hurry up, instead languidly browsing, starting at the front corner of the shop. It resembled an army navy surplus store with lots of camouflage, netting, green canvas, and complicated-looking backpacks that appeared to be as much about the straps as they were about the pouches.

This display was way different than the other parts of the shop, to a crazy degree. Nacho was inundated with the informative message as he got close.

Survivalist Class! Including two isolating and slightly paranoid Skills of your choosing! Yes, they are out to get you, but you'll get them first!

To be a Survivalist is to live with a capital L-I-V-E! You'll be able to eat most everything you come across. While you won't have access to many combat skills, if you're careful, you just might end the day with a full belly and the knowledge that while other fools are dead, it won't be you, hearty survivalist. You'll outwit, outplay, and outlast your opponents!

Base cost: 1000 Evaluation Points

Browse for more info?

Yes / No.

Note: Additional Skills can be purchased at Saavi's Skills Stall. Blah, blah, blah, you won't see this note again.

Nacho was shocked at the cost of the class. No wonder the store hadn't been available before. His measly two hundred Evaluation Points wouldn't have bought him a sack of jelly beans. A quick browse through the Player information revealed that the Survivalist class could eat things with Putrid Mana and drink unpurified water with no ill effects.

That would've been a huge bonus if he were going to be alone again, and the list of Skills available included everything from camouflage to trap construction. At higher Tiers, the traps were *very* deadly. There was also a 'Good Doggy' Skill, which made it possible to tame a monster and keep it as a pet, and that was the extent of combat for the class.

If Nacho had been alone and had known what he knew about the way food worked in the Juxtaposition, he'd have been tempted. Instead, he moved on to the nearby display of the Scavenger, the station appearing as nothing more than a tableau of a highway—complete with cracked asphalt and the leftovers of a Styrofoam deer.

When Nacho drew near, the introductory information box appeared.

Scavenger class! Including two rank and smelly skills of your choosing! This is the 'are you going to eat that' class.

To be a Scavenger is to live on the hunt for leftovers! Like the Survivalist, you'll be able to eat above your Tier, but unlike that paranoid person, you'll have to carefully prepare your meals. Half line cook, half killer, the Scavenger is perfect for people who like to beat half-dead things to full-dead while not being too picky about their basic hygiene.

Ever wanted to be a laughing hyena? This is your chance!

Base cost: 1100 Evaluation Points.

Browse for more info?

Yes / No.

This one looked promising. Curious, Nacho pulled up more details about the class. Basically, the Scavenger could process the Putrid Mana out of monsters up to a full Tier above their level and Tier. Instead of being poisonous, the meat would be fine—or the vegetables, since there were monster plants as well. The Scavenger class also included some combat Skills, the ability to use blunt weapons, a recipe for bone broth, and instructions on how to make sausages out of intestines.

Nacho thought the class might be a good combination for him, though he'd spent the last six months practicing with small blades, and the combat of the Scavenger was limited to blunt weapons. If he was more of a club guy, he might've gone with Scavenger. So, he kept on shopping with the weird, silent, man-sized Cinnabunny following him creepily closely.

Farther into the store, the Farmer section consisted of several hay bales stacked next to a little end table with a lace doily placed on the polished wood. Of course there was a pitchfork, a kerosene lantern, and a little book on soybeans. Another glance revealed it to be a pamphlet on calming monster soybeans.

The Cinnabunny sulked next to him.

He decided to tease the thing. "Hey, Bunny, tell me about the Farmer class."

The big pink unicorn bunny wiggled its nose—that was cute. The hostile look in its pink eyes wasn't.

The information box did all the talking.

Farmer class! Including two skills of your choosing! Hope you like to get up early; a true Farmer gets up before dawn, milks the cows, feeds the chickens, slops the pigs, and squeezes the teats of their ogre cows. Warning: if you choose this class, you'll eventually know so much about corn that you won't be able to fit in at parties. You probably won't see much combat, and you'll have many lonely Saturday nights, but plowing the dirt is just as fun, right?
Base cost: 1200 Evaluation Points
Browse for more info?
Yes / No.

Nacho skimmed the Farmer class details and let out a low whistle. This was *powerful*, not for him personally, but for his friends. Basically, the Farmer could grow Tier zero crops and raise Tier zero animals. Both would be free of Putrid Mana. That would be useful for the first six months or so, maybe even good for a year, but once Players leveled to Tier one, everything changed. The Farmer could provide Tier one products, but they would still have to contend with Putrid Mana. It appeared that the Farmer class was meant to work with other Satiation Classes, like the Brewers or the Common Cooks.

One aspect was extra useful: the Farmer could also raise monster animals and monster plants to protect himself and his guild, and his monsters wouldn't attack him or his allies. That would be handy for someone building a base of operations.

The mainstay Skills of the Farmer weren't that exciting. It obviously came with the basic Oat Obsession, Monster Milking, Expert Egg Extraction, and other examples of Skills necessary for a fulfilling life on the farm. If he became a farmer, his people would have a ton of food... but it wouldn't help them long-term.

It *did* serve to make Nacho curious about the Common Cook and Brewer classes. Also, just from investigating the first three Satiation classes, he observed that the Patrons had specifically written the descriptions so as to discourage people from choosing a Satiation class. That was interesting, if not surprising —they had practically been pushing people into cannibalism back in the day.

If Nacho had been a normal Player, he would've spent perhaps five seconds in this store and left. However, he knew the value of food in the Juxtaposition better than anyone.

At the center of the shop stood a fake kitchen display for the Common Cook. If the order of class options was the same as in the other stores, this should be the most potent class available. Nacho approached it cautiously.

Common Cook class! Just like Mom used to make! Selecting this class will grant you two Skills, a grilled cheese sandwich, and some warm fuzzies.

To be a Common Cook is to slave away for hours in the kitchen, to keep yourself locked for days in the garden to find that perfect tomato, and to get up early because the bread won't cook itself. Tired? Too bad! Every night, you'll be staying up late because those dishes won't be washing themselves! The Common Cook is <u>uncommonly</u> boring, but hey, level up and at least you'll eat well. That's something, right?

Basic cost: 1599 Evaluation Points! Are we crazy? Yes, yes, we are, and so is this class. Crazy expensive!

Note: Yes, you can buy more Skills over at Saavi Candoo's Skills Stall; we've been over that. We just wanted to let you know that there's no such thing as too much garlic.

Browse for more info?

Yes / No.

Of course Nacho wanted to browse for more information. It was clear the Patrons were not fans of letting this class out into the wild.

Common Cook class—Enhanced Description. You weirdo. Stop looking into this class.

The Common Cook is able to cook anything, anytime, anywhere, and make anything edible. You know that one girlfriend you had who could walk into a half-empty kitchen and make a four-course meal in forty-five minutes out of the expired ketchup bottle in the fridge? The Common Cook is like that, but better—because your old flame, Hildegarde, couldn't add buffs to her cooking. That's right: not only do you get a gourmet meal, but your happily-fed friends will be able to go out and kill dragons right after! Common Cook will only receive System credits from their kitchen combat, so you'd better like garlic. You saw the note before: garlic-haters need not apply.

Browse Skills?

Yes / No.

Nacho was definitely going to be browsing the Skills in detail. He'd skimmed the others. Not this one. This one had him fully engaged, though he did have to wonder how many people had dated someone named Hildegarde in order for it to be added to the class description.

CHAPTER NINE

The human stood in the demo kitchen of the Satiation Shoppe and tried to ignore the annoyed sighs of the Cinnabunny. He was intrigued by this very expensive Common Cook class, and he was dying to know about the Skills, so he dove right in.

INGREDIENT PROCESSING (REQUIRED): The lucky cook with this Skill can process all kinds of monstrous fruits, vegetables, and beasts of higher Tiers based on their level. This isn't just killing, skinning, and dressing your average carrot; oh no. This gives the cook the ability to completely drain the Putrid Mana out of any kill. You can make the yucky into oh-so-yummy.

COOKING MAGIC: Enhance dishes with spices, love, and destruction. Cooks with this Skill will be able to make dishes that grant a single stat boost based on the level of the cook. When people say that your soup kills, they won't be kidding. Make hamburgers that dish out harm, or spaghetti that slays. Buff up your diners and then send them out to battle!

GOURMET LURES: Cook dishes that will be so crazy good that no one can resist them! Just the smell will pull in everyone from peasants, to princes, to dragon kings. Set traps with apple tarts or bait cages with cherry noodle kugel.

FEASTING FEATS: Have to cook for a battalion? Need to feed an army? This Skill will spread out the joy of cooking and feed the multitudes with a limited amount of food as long as your guests have some credits to spare. You've heard of the loaves and fish? This Skill is like that, except with demon bread and monster meat. Make a little go a long way for your paying patrons!

BLADE SHARPENING: Any cook cutting meat needs blades as sharp as their wits, and with this Skill, you'll be able to give your knives the ultimate edge. You'll be able to cut a tomato even after you saw through a tin can! But come on, ask yourself: why are you cutting up tin cans?

CYCLONE WHISK: Make mixing easy with this Skill! You can mix up your ingredients in a whirl of awesome, cutting down on cooking time and creating flavors as only a rogue tornado can! Make your kitchen a category-four hurricane of culinary love!

MOTHER'S LOVE: Create dishes that can heal the body, mind, and heart. Fix wounds at the same time you fix emotions. Time since you last called your mother: N/A. Oh, you're a monster. Ignore this Skill. Oh. Nope, our bad, sorry about that.

SUMMON STAFF: Any busy chef can tell you that sometimes they need help. With this, your next helper could be the potato peelings you just threw away. Summon kitchen help from everyday garbage and create trash golems that can divide the work!

MANY HANDS: Like the Summon Staff Skill, sometimes a chef in the kitchen doesn't have enough hands. With this Skill, you can grow an extra set of limbs! Then you can do it your way, baby. Whip the cream, beat the eggs, torture the goose to get the pâté, all at the same time! Number of extra arms will be based on level.

COMBAT CONVENIENCE STORE: You can't open the Juxtaposition Store if you are in Active Combat or Active Cooking. The Store is as closed as a liquor shop after 11 p.m. in Topeka. However, this ability allows _you_ to shop, though it is restricted to items you would find at your local convenience store. There will be canola oil, but it will be double the price. The Slurpee's will still be cheap, so you'll have that going for you.

· · ·

Nacho grew more excited with every line, and he knew right away that the most important Skills were the first two, the Ingredient Processing and Cooking Magic abilities. With those, not only would he beat the food problem, but he could actually help his comrades in battle.

He knew there would be strings attached, and he also knew the Patrons *really* didn't want Satiation Players to exist. But he was going to become one, and he pretty much knew right then that he was going to choose the Common Cook. He did notice the Active Cooking thing highlighted. What was Active Cooking? He'd have to research later; first, he wanted to finish inspecting the other Satiation sections.

At the back, at the grill display, was the Butcher class. It was basically like the cook, but only meat could be handled with any efficiency. The class *did* get twice the nourishment from meat, but only half from vegetables. Their Skills also included Blade Sharpening, but there were some Skills which helped with anatomy, the ability to make head cheese, and one called Basic Blood Sausage.

Being able to process monster meat efficiently would be nice, but the Butcher was thirteen hundred Evaluation Points, cheaper than the Common Cook. He knew there was a reason for that—being a Butcher limited a Player.

The Harvester was similar to the Butcher, only it was the vegetarian flavor of the class, hence being discounted slightly more at twelve hundred and fifty Evaluation Points. In keeping with that trend, a Harvester gained twice the nourishment from fruits and vegetables, and only half from meat. One of the Skills was Fool's Gold, which did grant the ability to make vegetables taste like meat. Another was Breakfast Grain Guru, which helped to make the most important meal of the day even more important by adding buffs to oatmeal.

Nacho easily discounted those two classes. As he moved to the back corner, he found a barrel of beer, some wine bottles, and a six pack of diet ginger ale. This was the Brewer, and it gave him pause.

. . .

Brewer class! Make mine a double, Larry. This will include two Skills, a few beers, and possibly a hangover.

To be a Brewer is to be the life of the party—if that party involves yeast and measuring. Sure, the Brewer is able to purify all water, but the fun doesn't end there! A Brewer can add high-Tier power to lower Tier food. They are the master of the soup and the stew, and they can take a Tier 0 deer and make it a meal for the Tier 1 hero! Even so, it'll take a herd of deer to feed a Tier 2 hero. Only choose a Brewer if you like soup. Because soup is good. Right? People can be passionate about soup. Probably.

Basic cost: 1450 Evaluation Points! This is wickedly expensive for what a lot of guys do as a hobby. You'd drink your friend's hobby beer, right?

Browse for more info?

Yes / No.

Nacho skimmed through the Skills quickly, though he paused on one called Stone Soup Master. Like the others, the description was amusing, but it hid how truly powerful this class would be later in the Juxtaposition.

STONE SOUP MASTER: Make a simple pot of water a satisfying meal with a little monster meat, a few devil potatoes, and a stock fashioned from dreams. With this Skill, you'll be able to keep your people alive and healthy as long as you have a water source and a few ingredients. Don't skip the celery! Like Feasting Feats, this stretches out your food supply—though you should probably find some crackers, because soup by itself needs a friendly carb to complete the meal.

Nacho immediately understood how this could be really powerful. Yet, he also saw the drawbacks. While Stone Soup seemed like magic, in actuality, it required a lot of ingredients.

Clearly, the Common Cook class was the best of the Satiation options, and he had the Evaluation Points to buy it. Nacho turned to the creepy pink unicorn bunny. "Okay, Cinn, I'm going with Common Cook. I want my Skills to be Ingredient Processing and Cooking Magic."

A flash of subtle interest lit up the bunny's eyes before the pink beast turned and hopped back around the counter. Nacho strode over, following in her cinnamon-scented wake. Inside the case sat bins of bubble gum, rows of licorice, a bin of beef jerky, some sausages that were a bit too bright pink—obviously raw—followed by trays of dried fruit snacks and sheets of cookies, including a single gingerbread man.

The bunny opened a sliding door in the back and reached to grab the gingerbread man, but the little guy leapt to his feet. Gumdrop buttons marked his coat, and his arms were bound by licorice whips. However his legs were free, and he tried to escape through the opening.

Even so, the bunny was faster. It slammed the door closed and cracked the adjacent panel. The gingerbread man scurried across the cookies and kicked a beef jerky against the glass while his frosting-marked eyes cast about for something to cut the licorice ropes off.

Pausing was his mistake. The bunny threw open the door and snatched him up, then slammed the squirming cookie form down on the counter. The unicorn rabbit seized another length of licorice and tied up the gingerbread man's legs in a flash of red high-fructose corn syrup. Nacho silently watched the confectionary conflict with both unease and enjoyment.

Before, when he'd purchased the Assassin class, he'd merely taken the robes to the counter and the Naga had rung him up. The robes had disappeared, since they'd only been a prop, and an elevator ride later, he'd appeared on the Starter World.

This time, though, the bunny waved a pink paw over the gingerbread man, who was glaring at Nacho like it hated him, knowing he was looking at his doom.

An info box popped up.

. . .

Are you sure you want to purchase the tedious Common Cook class as well as those two lame Skills?
Yes / No.

Nacho chose 'yes' without thought, but the gaming system wasn't going to make it easy on him. He couldn't believe he was choosing this class, and that he was paying so much for it. It was ironic in all the wrong ways, given his history both in and out of the Juxtaposition.

*Wait, wait, wait. If you choose the Common Cook class, you'll be spending your life in this exciting new world either in the kitchen or doing dishes. You could be an all-powerful mage or a dashing paladin. Are you **really** sure you want to purchase the boring Common Cook class and the two uninspiring Skills?*
Yes / No.

The Patrons clearly did not want their Players choosing Satiation classes. Nacho bought it anyway, losing the lion's share of his Evaluation Points. He only had a single EP remaining, and he knew where he wanted to spend it.

A final message gave him the last of his instructions.

Congratulations, Chef. You're now a Common Cook who can use Ingredient Processing and Cooking Magic. Good luck out there, back in the kitchen, missing out on all the fun. Eat Mr. Gingerbread on the elevator down.

The Cinnabunny stuffed the gingerbread man into a pink box and tossed the cardboard containment cell into a pink bag with sparkly silver handles. Nacho grabbed the sack and felt the cookie man wrestling around in the carton. Eating the thing wasn't going to be easy, physically or morally. He just hoped that biting the gingerbread man's head off would stop the rest of the wriggling.

Back out in the mall, he walked past Saavi Candoo's Skills Stall. He wasn't going to be purchasing additional Skills until he was on the Starter World, earning credits, and figuring out his new class. He was fairly certain that he'd get a knife Skill, since he'd been practicing so much, but he wouldn't know for sure until he took the elevator ride down to the planet.

Nacho popped into the Gary's General Store and used his last Evaluation Point to purchase a mundane combo set: a generic pot and a wide cast-iron fry pan. He figured that they would be good enough to fix up most easy meals.

On his first run, he'd joined the guild early on, but that didn't mean that he hadn't done some campfire cooking when he'd been Tier zero. Back then, he'd been far more focused on surviving monster attacks than on meal prep. Most of the time, he'd bought meals from the Store. They were cheap, but they weren't good.

Gary the shopkeeper was the most human thing that Nacho had seen in the mall, like someone from an Iowa farming supply store. He had thinning red hair, a ton of freckles, and overalls which worked overtime to keep his considerable gut in check. Gary wore sunglasses, and Nacho knew what that meant.

"Are you human, Gary?" Nacho scoffed as he shoved the pink confectionary bag into the thick cardboard apple box that held the cookware. Gary didn't respond, but Nacho was almost positive he knew what kind of eyes the shopkeeper hid behind those mirrored shades. The shopkeeper's grin was slow and evil as it split his pink, chapped lips.

Nacho laughed as he regarded the CrossHuman. "Even *you* are a clue to what's coming. Those Patrons are such sneaky sneaks."

Outside Gary's General Store, he spied a bench against a

wall, near enough that he might be able to push open the ceiling tiles. Could he climb up to where the Patrons sat? Or would he open the tiles to reveal some eldritch monster that would drive him insane?

Nacho wanted to look, but he ultimately decided against risking it. He wanted to eat the dratted gingerbread man and get to his friends. He couldn't shake a nagging feeling that if he went off-script, it wouldn't go well for him. He was changing the game right out of the gate by becoming a Satiation Player, and he wouldn't be surprised if the Patrons had already started gunning for him.

He hit the down button on the elevator, turning to take one last look at the Evaluation Mall. He'd never see it again. This time, there was no Kronos boon to give him another shot. This time, it was all for keeps, and he was a *cook*, of all things.

Somehow, even though he had planned to follow his previous path... he knew he was doing the right thing.

The elevator dinged, the doors slid open, and Nacho stepped inside. He bent, wrestled the gingerbread man out of the bag and box, and then bit the sugary, squealing head off. It was warm—unnerving—but very sweet. Once beheaded, the cookie went limp, and he quickly ate the doughy body. The frosting was sweet, the gumdrops chewy, and what he'd thought had been licorice just tasted like artificial cherries.

The System flashed.

Wow, a Satiation Player. You're a rare boy, aren't you? We have your selected skills listed as Ingredient Processing and Cooking Magic. Is this correct?

Yes / No.

Nacho chose the 'yes' option. A second later, he had another parameter to set:

. . .

Okay, last question before you get started, Cookie. What kind of build type do you want?

Self-Applied: 2 stats per level, can be placed anywhere.
    Balanced, Instant: 3 stats per level, applied to the stats evenly in a round-robin manner.
    Balanced, Delayed: 5 to each stat, applied only at each level that is a multiple of five.
    Choose now! All choices are final.

Nacho had been waiting for this. The first time, he'd chosen 'Self-Applied' like most people, and that had been... *fine.* No one, outside of Nacho, had even seen their stats yet. He already knew the last one was a trap, because while it allowed for sudden, massive power increases—granting the same number of stat points at level ten that a 'Balanced, Instant' had at level twenty—the Player would need to fully trust that the people around them would keep them safe and alive while they were weak. It was too easy to reach the verge of a fifth level, only to be killed while lower Tiers were still far more powerful.

Despite that, Nacho knew his friends would be there for him... if they had forgiven him by now. They had, he *knew* they had. He confidently chose 'Balanced, Delayed.'

The elevator sank down as if the bottom had dropped out of it, and he smelled the unmistakable greasy aroma of a grilled-cheese sandwich. "What is *happening?*"

A moment later, his new life began.

CHAPTER TEN

Nacho appeared in a forest south of a river. In a daze, the only thought he could process at first was that most of the trees had colorful leaves left on their branches. Underneath them lay a thick carpet of red, orange, and yellow. Around him rose the gasps, cries, and sighs of dozens of other people. Nacho recognized a few faces of his neighbors from the apartment complex. One man clutched his chest and dropped in the next second, and a few people cried out in alarm and moved to help him.

He ignored the man who had just died from the loss of his pacemaker and focused on Reuben and Brie, easily identifiable in their tuxedo and wedding dress, standing in bewilderment on the dirt of the Starter World. Nacho was also in his tuxedo, holding the box from Gary's General Store, but on top of it sat a paper plate holding a freshly grilled sandwich. He remembered that the description of the Common Cook class had promised him a treat, but he'd thought that had been flavor text.

Brie was *scowling*. She didn't look sad or scared, just furious, and a little odd with the big backpack buckled over her formal gown. Reuben hooked his thumbs into the straps of his own backpack. Face pale and sweat already dripping down his face, the big guy half-smiled. "Oh, hi, Nacho. Are you going to share your sandwich? Also, I can't speak for her, but in my mind you are fully forgiven for the whole, ya know, hostage thing."

"...Thanks." Nacho squatted and dropped the box on the ground, the first litter to grace this new world's soil. He touched the pot, pan, and sandwich, whisking them into one of his extra-dimensional storage slots. A breeze swept the paper plate off the box and into the grass. Standing took some effort, since his backpack made rising a little unwieldy.

All the people around them were having a variety of reactions: shouting, talking, whispering. The Oscreech attack would happen in a few minutes—cross an emu with a giant eagle, and the result was a nightmare bird experience. More than anything, he needed to get himself and his friends to safety.

The Juxtaposition had a little message for them first.

Nacho looked past the welcome message to see Reuben and Brie staring at their own screens, their eyes glowing blue to show they had their individual systems pulled up.

Hey there, intrepid Players, welcome to the Juxtaposition! You're on your Starter World, Tier 0. Everyone is at level 0, which means you have a long way to go if you want to rock 'n' roll. This is your System menu, where you can check your stats, your Skills, and your storage slots. Have fun and good luck! Kill monsters for System credits! May your future be delicious!

"Come on," Nacho ordered his people. "We *need* to move right now."

"But... that's Steve over there," Reuben protested as he halfheartedly pointed into the distance. "We should get him to come with us."

"No." Nacho glared at his dense friend. "I know what's about to happen, and we can't help them. We have to just make sure *we* survive. I didn't travel back through time and get you ready so that we could throw away this opportunity."

Reuben nodded, though he was already close to tears. Brie's eyes blazed with rage, and she clenched her jaw muscles. "What the *abyss*, Nacho? You knew the world was going to end and you didn't *tell* us? That little game on 'Death Island' sure was *fun*. When I say 'fun', I mean the exact *fecal matter* opposite, and what is wrong with my ability to swear!"

"Language filter, gotta keep the ratings up for the viewing Patrons." Nacho sighed and motioned around helplessly. "How well did telling you what was going to happen work out? How fast would you have started avoiding me, huh? I literally had to *force* you two to listen to me at the last minute. I did everything I could!"

Reuben only had eyes for Steve, another college student who was currently backing up with his eyes on the sky. Nacho knew Brie had a fairly utilitarian view of things, but his buddy was more soft-hearted. Nacho threw him a bone that he knew he'd never need to retrieve. "We'll come back for them, Reuben. Let's just go. I know a place we can hole up, and I can go over the game mechanics with you."

"This isn't a *game!*" Brie bellowed as her frustration boiled over. "This is real life. I should know. I spent a *week* in the Evaluation World slowly bleeding to death! I will *not* have you calling this a game."

"The System calls it a game," Reuben whispered to her, his soft voice a potent counterpoint to her maximum volume. "We're Players. But you're right, love. This is real."

Nacho pushed them both toward an outcropping of rock peeking out of the forest in the distance. "We can talk about all of this once we find higher ground. But not too high. Oscreeches will be coming through here any minute. Six feet tall, three toes, with talons as sharp as their beaks. Fun fact to keep your attention right here: emus have three toes, while ostriches only have two. Just bad luck to fight the level five monsters right off the bat. It's unfortunate."

"What?" Reuben twisted around and shouted, "Steve and… everyone else! Take cover! Demon birds are coming. Don't try to fight them, just run!"

Nacho wasn't sure if that would help anyone or not, but he no longer needed to physically *move* the big guy. Now that his team was on board, they ran as fast as they could manage in their formal shoes, with combat boots swinging off their backpacks. With their eyes to the skies, the trio headed off toward the river. A swift glance backward revealed that their apartment neighbors had congregated into groups of their own.

Nacho wished them luck. Perhaps being aware of an incoming threat might change things, hopefully for the better, but he couldn't say for certain. He single mindedly guided his friends to the rocky outcropping, a little hill that overlooked the forest. He remembered a narrow crack at the top where they could safely stop, talk, and change clothes. Those birds wouldn't see them, and any monsters on the ground would have to clamber over rocks to get to them. By that time, the assassin… no, the *cook*, would have his blades ready.

As soon as they were settled inside, he set his backpack on the ground, strung the bow, and got a few arrows ready before whipping off the tuxedo jacket and tie. "We need to change into better clothes. It's not cold now, but it will be soon. There's an easy dungeon about a day's walk from here, but we'll camp tonight and make our way there tomorrow. That'll give us time to get you caught up."

Reuben marched off to the corner of the crack. "But those people… come on, Nacho. I know you don't mind playing neutral to neutral-evil characters, but like Brie said… this is real life. You can *help* them."

Nacho wanted to yell at his friend to get with the new program, but that wouldn't ease the tension. He'd been patient and self-controlled up until now, and he couldn't allow himself to fall apart. "Let's just change and talk. Once we have a secure position, we can go see about helping everyone else."

It was a lie. The attack would be quick and brutal, and once

Reuben saw the result, he'd realize that holing up had been the right tactic. Brie was going to be a tougher nut to crack. "You *knew* this would happen. Nacho, that one morning… how could you go *months* and not say a thing about this?"

"Fifteen minutes before we were thrown into the Evaluation, how much did you believe me? When I *forced* you to listen, I seem to recall having the *police* called on me." Nacho met her glare with his cool gaze. Brie didn't say a word, but he knew the truth. Trying to prepare them would have only driven them off, and he would have been too far away to save them.

Again.

He powered through the silence. "If I would've insisted that the end of the world was coming, you would have cut me off. Reuben wouldn't, but *you* would've. *You* wouldn't have tolerated me seeming crazy. So I planned ahead instead, and did the best I could to keep you close and safe without damaging your trust before all of this started. Right now, I need you to change into better clothes. I need you to strap on your weapons, and I need for us to be *ready* if we're attacked. We have a real chance to not only survive, but to *thrive*. I was given the ultimate prize: I know how the game works, and I know what's going to happen… at least for the next few months. I plan to change things after that."

Their first challenge would be the Calamity class monster, but he didn't want to tell them about that particular nightmare just yet. Their faith in him was already hanging by a thread.

Brie glanced away and dropped her backpack. "Reuben, I need help with the dress."

Just like that, she'd shifted into competition mode. Reuben came back from the edge of the crack and unzipped her dress while Nacho moved to the other end of the area and changed into the fatigues he'd packed. He couldn't help but overhear his friends talking. Reuben was whispering, but the sound carried. "I'm sorry, Brie. Our wedding day… I wanted it to be perfect."

"I think we have bigger problems than that, Reuben. Don't

get me wrong, I'm *livid*, and someone is going to pay for doing this. There's an intelligence behind this; there has to be."

"Maybe. I just feel... the *people*." The big man's voice cracked as he tried to say what was on his mind.

"I know, Reuben. But Nacho knows what he's doing. He got us here, together, we have gear, and he really seems to be invested in keeping us alive. Let's just hear him out."

A shadow blocked out the noonday sun, and Nacho's eyes focused on the source. The Oscreeches were similar to eagles, but their plumage was tinted with varying shades of greens and blacks, while the talons were unnaturally oversized. Their necks and bodies were slimmer, almost serpentine, and they moved differently from the birds back on Earth—practically ignoring the physics of flight. That was the only explanation for the way they could drop into the trees, tuck in their wings, then run like ostriches... or emus.

Not a single Oscreech gave Nacho or his friends a second look. The monsters dove into the trees, followed by the antici- pated shrieks of pain and shouts of anger, and as he remem- bered, the attack was over in moments. The quiet afterwards was terrible, but Nacho filled it with information for his pale, shaking friends. "Long story short, we were scooped off Earth, evaluated, and now we're here on the Starter World. We even- tually started calling this area the AKC, or the Alternate Kansas City, since we all landed here together."

"Somebody *help* m-" The scream was cut off with a wet *squelch*, and Nacho started speaking louder to drown out any follow-up sounds.

"The point of the game is to kill monsters, gain credits, and upgrade our skills. The last time I was here, I was the *best* assassin in the entire world. That gave me access to information and people like you wouldn't believe. Believe me when I say: information is going to be the *hardest* thing for other people to get, but not for us. Now, the Store is like the Evaluation Mall, except virtual, and you don't physically go there. I mentioned this before, but in case you forgot, you can pull up your display just by winking left, right, then shrugging. Even *that* isn't discovered by other people for weeks. We have every advantage right now. Open it, look at the information, and then we can discuss."

Brie's and Reuben's eyes glowed, proof that they were inspecting their character sheets.

He pulled up his own Stat Sheet:

Eli 'Nacho' Naches
Kronos Boon—Probability Vision—1/1 used
Class: Common Cook
Level: 0
Experience Points: 100 to Level 1!
Current Credits: 0

Build Type: Balanced, Delayed
Body:

- *Fitness: 10*
- *Metabolic efficiency: 10*

Mind:

- *Mental energy: 10*
- *Circuit: 10*

Satiation:

- *Hunger: 100*
- *Thirst: 100*

Total Health Points: 30
Bonus Physical Damage: 5%
Health Regen: 10% Health Regen/minute
Total Mana Pool: 25
Bonus Spell Damage: 5%
Mana Pool Regen: 10% Mana Regen/minute

Skill Slots (3/4)

- *Small Blades (Passive) Level 0: 0% bonus damage on all knife attacks.*

  No Mana, Hydration, or Metabolic Cost

- *Ingredient Processing (Active) Level 0: Remove Putrid Mana from monsters up to Level 2.*

  Mana Cost = 5%
  Hydration Cost = 5%
  Metabolic Cost = 5%

- *Cooking Magic (Active) Level 0: Cook food that enhances a single stat by 0% of maximum.*

  Mana Cost = 5%
  Hydration Cost = 5%
  Metabolic Cost = 5%

- *Open slot*

Connected to his Stat Sheet were links to the Store, which offered everything a player could ever want—with some notable exceptions—for a price. Nacho was pleased to see that all of his practice with the knives had given him the Small Blades Skill. "Yes! I even have a small blade, so this is perfect. Thought I bought a pot, though? What's the difference between a pot and saucepan?"

He had so much to learn about cooking. Suddenly, he felt scattered: there was so much to cover, and he didn't know where to start. Thank goodness Reuben let out a laugh. "Okay, so the stats are pretty simple. Body for warriors, mind for mages, but what's up with those Satiation stats? It looks interesting. I can actually track my munchies? 'Look, dude, I have a level three craving for pepperoni pizza'."

Reuben's relaxed demeanor, even if it was forced, was very welcome at that moment. His joviality didn't touch Brie's focus; she ignored the joke and waited impatiently for more information. They all sat down on the rocky ground, and Nacho took a deep breath. "We'll get to the Satiation, but let's start with Body. Fitness is both strength and agility. I'm assuming you both have ten points there."

"Shouldn't I have less?" Brie interrupted him immediately. "I haven't been lifting weights, and I don't have as much testosterone as you two."

"If anything, you should have way *more* than us with how long you've been improving your physicality." Nacho leaned against the stone, trying his best to get comfortable but knowing full well that such creature comforts were probably going to be gone for a long time. "Game logic. A lot of this world defies biology."

Reuben's grin was infectious. "Look at me, sitting on my butt most of my life while you worked out every day, and now we have the same strength."

Brie rolled her eyes, then searched for a stick that she could hit him with. Nacho could only chuckle at the antics, loving being back with his friends. This was so much better than slogging through the Juxtaposition alone. "Your 'Total Health Points' is based on your Fitness level. Fitness affects your 'Total Physical Output', or in other words, gives you bonus damage. For now, we should all have a five percent bonus."

Reuben sat cross-legged and looked relatively calm, but the sweat dripping down his face belied that controlled exterior. "Gotcha. Health Points and combat bonuses. Good thing my crappy eating habits back on Earth didn't affect me too much. I have to say, the exercise you made me do *was* helpful in the Ew. Good call on the blackberries and peanuts."

"The 'Ew'?" Nacho itched his chin with the tip of the bow. "What?"

"You aren't going to keep saying 'Evaluation World' all the time, right?" Reuben shook his head in disbelief. "You did, all the time, didn't you? No wonder you're no fun. You weren't just the best assassin; you were a *joy* assassin."

The now-Cook wasn't sure what to say about that, so he simply moved on after a slight internal struggle. "Anyway... that brings us to food. The second part of your Body stat is your Metabolic Efficiency. That's how well you use food and how fast you heal. Basically, your Health Regen is your Metabolic Efficiency, times your Hunger, divided by a hundred. That gives you the percentage. You'll lose Hunger points when you use your Skills, but we'll get to that."

They hadn't talked about their experiences in the... Ew... and Nacho didn't know what classes his friends had chosen or what build types they had each decided on. They had so much to cover. Again, Nacho felt his mind racing, and he had to forcefully regulate his breathing.

Reuben nodded at the information, taking it in easily, while Brie sat frozen, listening intently. The groom spoke up as Nacho worked to bring his anxiety down. "I'm assuming Body Players have combat Skills that reduce their hunger, and Health Regen is really important for your fighter types. I went the Mind Player route. I work differently, amiright?"

"Yep." Nacho agreed with the assessment. "Let's talk about Mind Players for a minute."

"I wouldn't mind, probably because I'm a Mind Player!" Reuben laughed a bit too loudly. "I'm freaked out, people, but I'll make jokes until someone steals my voice box."

"Just keep talking, Nacho. You know he'll just keep going till you stop him." Brie practically deflated with the quip, amusing Nacho to no end. They really were perfect together. That made him wonder which class she'd chosen.

"For your mind stats, Mental Energy is like Fitness—it's your basic mental acuity. That affects your Mana Pool, in the same manner that Fitness is connected to your Health Points. Now, Circuit is how efficiently you use the energy to cast spells or use Skills. For me, I'm thinking that'll be what I draw on for my Cooking Magic, though I need to physically craft food, so I chose a build that should give me the best of both worlds."

Reuben made a face and raised a forestalling hand. "Hold that horse, mister. *Cooking?* I thought you said something about being an awesome assassin?"

Nacho held up a finger. "We'll *get* to that. Remember that the only way to eat an elephant is one bite at a time. Your Mana Regen is your Circuit, times Thirst, divided by a hundred. That means that while Body Players mostly use food, Mind Players mostly use thirst, and using your Skills reduces your Hunger and Thirst points."

"Actually, the only way to eat an elephant is in jail. Because it is illegal," Brie informed him seriously as she began rummaging through her backpack, eventually finding a hatchet in a sheath. She stood and threaded the sheath onto her belt. By now, her wedding dress and Reuben's tuxedo had vanished, meaning both were using a Storage Slot for their nice clothes. "I think I'm getting the hang of all this stuff. Beyond opening the screens and accessing it initially, it's fairly intuitive. Only the stats make no sense at all."

Nacho opened his mouth to clarify, but Reuben reached over and patted his shoulder. "Let me try, Nacho—Brie and I speak the same language. Darlin', Fitness and Metabolic Efficiency are your screams and grunts. The higher your Fitness, the more satisfied grunts of impact you hand out. That's how you get the damage bonuses our boy Nacho talked about."

"Screams and grunts." Brie looked at him incredulously. "That's what you call speaking the same language?"

"Did you understand it?"

"I mean…" Brie growled in frustration. "*Yes*, but *why?*"

Nacho looked between the pair. "Is this actually working?"

Reuben launched into the next part of his explanation. "Health is your scream canister. When your scream canister runs out of screams, you die. Health Regen is your scream re-filler. That seems to get faster based on your Metabolic Efficiency and your Hunger points. Eat more, and you'll be able to scream more. The Mind stuff works about the same. Only it's magical screams and grunting. Your Mana Pool is your magical screams. Your Circuit score, along with water, refills your magical screams faster. Get it?"

"Magical screams and magical grunts." Brie unclipped her sheath and lifted out the hatchet. "I want to stab you a little, but I think I get it. I also hate that you made sense."

Nacho had to laugh; his friends actually *did* speak their own language. However, Brie wasn't done asking questions. She started pacing while Nacho and Reuben tried to relax. "Food helps you fight and heal. Water helps you cast spells and refills your Mana Pool. The Skills drop our Hunger and Thirst points. Fine. What if you don't use any Skills? What if you just sit and don't move?"

Reuben tilted his head and slowly smiled. "Babe, you're a natural-born gamer."

"I like to win," the transported bride stated simply.

Nacho was impressed with the depths of world mechanics that her question dove into as well. "You'd be fine for one full day. If you go twenty-four hours without food, you get a Starvation Debuff, and you'll lose one hunger point each minute until you go negative. It's… nasty."

Reuben used his fingers to do the math. "When your Health Regen turns negative, do you start *losing* percentages of your health? Say you have a hundred Hunger points, but you lose one every minute. One hour, forty minutes, you go negative? A half an hour later, you'll be losing three percent of your health. Then four percent, then five, then dead."

Nacho was similarly impressed by how rapidly his friend had figured that out with so little information. "Yeah. Wow. That's right. Once your hunger tanks, it's a cascading effect. Thirst works similarly, but it's called a Dehydration Debuff."

Brie paced to the other end of the crack, turned and stomped back. "Lose all your Health, and you die. Just like Earth. Fine. Does emptying your Mana Pool kill you?"

Nacho grimaced up at her. "No, but if it hits zero, you go unconscious. You can't eat, and then you starve to death. Not eating gives you the Starvation Debuff whether you're conscious or not. Healing spells won't work, and I've never seen a spell to feed someone. But…"

He had to pause, because he'd never had access to the Satiation Player Skills before. He wondered if there *was* some kind of feeding tube Skill and made a note to check the Store.

"There's no tutorial, no information page. A lot of this makes sense, but why wasn't there some… I don't know, is there a logistics fairy to help us along?" A chill wind came down blowing through the crevasse, making the dried leaves crackle. Reuben's eyes flashed blue as he went back through his tabs. The big guy was smart enough to intuit how diabolical the System was in practically no time flat.

A coldness settled into Nacho's belly as he thought about the hundreds of lives that had been spent on buying information. "You can buy info packs from the Store, though they're expensive and—for the most part—useless. We'll get to the Store in a minute. Suffice it to say, whoever or whatever organized this game doesn't seem to care much about our general wellbeing."

Brie drilled him with a freezing stare. "But you know about all of this stuff. How?"

Nacho got to his feet and returned the stare. "A Patron, Kronos, gave me a boon called Probability Vision. Single use. I don't know much about the Patrons, but they grant boons to a few select players. Anyway, I had a vision of living through the Juxtaposition, a bunch of stuff happened, and I was killed. The minute I died in the game, three years from now, I was sent back to our apartment six months ago."

Following their lead, Reuben likewise got to his feet and shouldered on his pack. "Probability Vision. It sounds like your Patron ran a simulation of probable events, and you were at the heart of it. That's how you knew about this spot and the attack of the evil eagles and everything else. What's the next terrible thing that's going to happen? Can we play the lottery on this world? What's my stock portfolio going to be worth in three years?"

Nacho squeezed past Brie, crept to the end of the space, and readied his bow. Reuben held his own Gerber fixed-blade knife, and Brie had the hatchet as well as another knife.

"Let's keep moving." Nacho knew he hadn't answered Reuben's question, but he didn't really want to talk about certain things yet. "Once we get some credits, upgrade our skills, and get an artifact or two, we'll be in much better shape."

"Leveling up is always good," Reuben agreed slowly, trying to figure out what had just shifted in the conversation that made it end.

Brie eyed the weapon in her hand and shook her head. "I knew you two would drag me into playing one of your games at some point. At least a game that involves hiking is perfect for me."

She was making jokes—that was encouraging—but the look in her eyes indicated that she wasn't relaxing into her fate.

Good. Nacho needed her focused and fighting.

CHAPTER ELEVEN

Nacho didn't want his friends sleeping out in the open on their first night in the Juxtaposition. He had told them they were going to stop, but hearing all those people die had given him good leverage to make them press on willingly. Though he had definite plans, which he'd worked on in the six months leading up to the Juxtaposition, they still had a lot to discuss—but they could have their conversation on the move.

He and his friends left the rocky hill and made their way down through the forest, following a narrow dirt track; probably a game trail from the animals evolving into monsters. Nacho figured he'd recognize some of the wider paths, so he picked one that vanished in the same general direction he wanted to go.

Nacho, Brie, and Reuben had appeared on the Starter World with the sun directly overhead. The Cook kept them moving west, toward what would later become known as Armor Mountain. Even from a distance, the wall of limestone was visible as it rose above the trees, with more trees growing on top; one of the biggest landmarks around. Even more importantly,

Nacho remembered that a dungeon was located on the south-east side of the mountain.

It had originally taken a couple of months before the place had been discovered. People had clambered to get to the top of the mountain to defend themselves from the monsters, but little did they know that monsters would be the key. Nacho figured that at this point in the game, the dungeon would contain mostly low-level Tier zero monsters, not much harder than the initial Evaluation World creatures. It would take a bit for people to realize that monsters congregated in caves; if anyone wanted to level up fast, they went underground.

Nacho talked quietly while they traveled through the trees. He had his bow in hand, but his arrows wouldn't do anything against even Tier one monsters, since he didn't have an archery Skill to juice up his damage. Hopefully, they wouldn't run into anything too extreme.

He had worked hard and succeeded in gaining knives as his natively assigned Skill for a specific reason—namely, he was going to nab the MurderSong Blades. They'd clear the top floors of an easy dungeon first, grab enough credit to level their skills, then they'd journey over to win the Blades. He hadn't forgotten that Myron from the Gorged Guild had boasted the best knives around.

Guild Master Kala hadn't named her guild 'The Gorged' right away. Originally, it had been 'The Sunrise Brigade,' since they woke up early to kill the easier monsters before everyone else. That was the secret of their initial success. Nacho couldn't help but picture Kala and Myron somewhere, freaking out. While it was a nice mental image, he knew it wouldn't last long. They'd eventually come together and start their guild, but he had time to get his plans in place before then. To start a guild, a guild charter had to be purchased from the Store—and that price wasn't anywhere *approximating* cheap.

Reuben's curiosity pulled him out of his thoughts. "Tell us what you have cookin', Nacho. You *did* mention something about cooking, right?"

"I'd cook something right now, Reuben, but you'd probably eat it." The newly-minted cook shook his head at that thought. "In the 'you'd die' way of saying that. Not because I would *intentionally* make it poisonous, I was *really* bad at making food on Earth, and here… I need to start learning."

Brie let out a growl. "Why would you intentionally choose to do something you knew you were bad at? This isn't a game, it's real life! Why would you make this so hard?"

"Real life *is* played in hard mode," Nacho informed her grimly without meeting her eyes. The three of them had learned that early on: none of them had an easy go of it, not even Brie, who'd grown up in a wealthy family. Certainly not Reuben, who'd experienced more death than most. Definitely not Nacho, for his own reasons. "It looks like I was destined to cook for people, and not to kill them. Short version is that I spent two full weeks in the Evaluation World, and the Patrons pretty much killed the world to kill me. I could've lasted another week, easily. I had enough Evaluation Points to unlock the Satiation Classes, so I chose to be a Common Cook, the most expensive of those classes."

"Two weeks?" Reuben echoed in disbelief.

Nacho turned and grinned at his friend. "Two weeks. It was easy after I killed the Squirrel Lords."

"Those are the things that got me." Brie blew a strand of blonde hair out of her face. "What can you do?"

Nacho was surprised Brie had lasted long enough to face the Squirrel Lords. He answered her question openly. "I can process ingredients and add a little magic to my dishes, and I can chop like no one's business. Small Blades is my innate Skill—what we call a native Skill—that came over from Earth. It's a passive Skill, so it's always on. Ingredient Processing and Cooking Magic are active Skills. Each time I use them, there's a Mana, Hydration, or Metabolic cost. In other words, to process ingredients costs me five percent of my Mana, water, and food."

Exasperated, Brie closed her eyes for a moment. "I'm not going to get this until I can use my own Skills and see all of it in action. There are no help menus, and the system is all very cryptic."

"You're not wrong," Nacho agreed easily, even if he knew that agreeing was not going to help. "Let's talk about you guys. How did your Evaluations go? I'm dying to learn your classes and Skills."

"My evaluation was *terrible*." Reuben chuckled at the memory. "But it was better than most other people's, I'd imagine... all thanks to you. I got the armor and the club, and then went south to the shack to get the clay jars and weapons. In the end, I killed a bunch of insects and snakes. I got pretty good at luring them out and then smacking them from a tree. I made a spear, but I was taken down by a Gecko Bear."

Brie stopped walking and looked at him oddly. "I killed the Gecko Bear. Wait... Did we all have the exact same monsters? Did I do better than you?"

Reuben shrugged easily. "Knowing you, I'm betting yes. I ended the Evaluation at five hundred EPs. What about you?"

"Five hundred also." Brie's brow was furrowed. "I bought the best Body Player class I could. What did you grab?"

Nacho couldn't remember the price list, but he knew both of his friends had done exceptionally well. It almost made him self-conscious to think that he'd had a second shot at it. He had always known they would have done better than him, but this? Reuben grinned, but there was a troubled look in his eye. "With my history? I went full healer. But you both would've guessed that. My plan is to keep you two alive no matter what."

Brie's gaze was warm on her fiancé's face, and she scooted closer to give him a small peck on the cheek. Eyes devoted to searching the foliage, Nacho jolted to a harsh stop between two trees. The game trail they were following threaded its way through a tangle of brush, and he didn't want to get ambushed. When nothing jumped out at him, he kept walking, arrow to string, ready for anything. "What was your free innate Skill, Reuben?"

"I don't want to say." The big guy sounded completely

embarrassed, so Nacho didn't pry. "Didn't you show up with a grilled cheese sandwich? How did that even happen?"

Reuben always had been great at changing the subject. Nacho accessed his Storage Slots and drew forth the sandwich into his hands, happy that it was still warm. "You want some, Brie?"

She waved a hand carelessly. "Your pocket sandwich? Yeah, no thanks."

Nacho tore it in half. The entire meal was stringy, gooey deliciousness. Half was handed to Reuben. Both took a bite. Nacho figured it would be terrible, but no, the bread was buttery and crispy, the cheese was rich, and the whole experience was five-star. It was a huge surprise, since most of the time, Store food had problems. Reuben grunted in delight. "Now that's some *good* sammich right there, and a guy named Reuben *knows* his sandwiches, believe me."

Nacho motioned for Brie to continue. "Since Mister Sandwich is being all mysterious about his Skills, tell us about yours?"

She wiped sweat off her forehead, then reached back and began to braid her blonde hair. "I'm sure you both aren't surprised, but I got Athletic Endurance. According to your dumb gaming system, I get a reduction to hunger loss penalties when using my other Berserker Skills. It's a passive ability, so there's no cost."

Astonished, Nacho chewed and swallowed hurriedly. "Wait... did I hear you correctly? *Berserker?* You?"

"I liked the outfit in the shop." Brie stood with her hatchet tucked under one arm, both hands finishing up her braid. His eyes trailed over her gear with a frown; sure, she had that Valkyrie thing going on, but... the lifespan of a Berserker was measured in days, not years. "I chose Combat Dash and Defensive Whirl for my Skills. Both are active Skills. Both have a Metabolic cost, but no Hydration or Mana cost. That means it'll only affect my Hunger points, right?"

"That's right." Nacho finished off his sandwich, staring

longingly at the crumbs clinging to his fingertips. Celestials, he shouldn't have split it. "You'll see how all of this works once we fight monsters. Bottom line: you did really well in your Evaluation."

Brie cocked her head. "Of course. You told us where the armor and weapons were. I found a sword in a crypt and got to work. The barrels helped with water."

"You didn't go south?" That gave Nacho pause.

"I went east," she stated lightly. "Knowing I wouldn't die for real helped me take some chances I normally wouldn't have, just like you said. Killing the turtle-mice and those grasshopper things was a lot easier with a sword. I also loved having a bow again. I've always liked archery."

"When were you into archery?" Reuben questioned her around a mouthful of cheese.

Brie's smile was mysterious. "Wouldn't you like to know."

"Yes."

"Too bad. I also liked hitting things with a sword," Brie informed them after a while of hiking in silence. "The bow was fun, but there was something satisfying about chopping things up while getting up close and personal."

Reuben laughed. "That's my girl—a psychotic death machine."

"That's the plan." Brie's voice was only a little louder than a whisper.

Nacho adjusted his pack and looked at his friend dead-on. "Okay, Reuben. Out with it. What are your Skills?"

"First is… Marketing," the big guy grunted. "I know, I *know*. It's going to be super useful for us. I'm sure that running branding campaigns and optimizing online search results will be key to our success. You'll thank me someday."

Nacho winced but tried to hide it. "We might want to buy you out of that Skill. But we'll talk about the Store in a minute. What else have you got?"

Reuben laughed a little as he tramped through the leaves. "I could've gone with something called Soothing Touch, but nope,

Healing Hugs for the highest efficacy. A portion of your Health will be restored through me hugging you. It's an active Skill, so it costs me Mana and Hydration, but no Hunger points."

"I love your hugs, babe."

"Eh." Nacho didn't mind hugs, but that might be a little awkward during battle until they leveled up the Skill. "Healing Hugs it is, even if it sounds like a healing spell for kindergarten teachers. What else?"

Reuben responded immediately. "Positive Vibes, my brother. I can bless my team with extra combat effectiveness. They'll dish out extra physical damage based on my Skill level. Active Skill, costs Mana and Hydration. Who's the big cheese now, Nacho? I'm gonna be a hippie in armor. Healing Hugs, Positive Vibes, and eating a bunch of granola. Probably. I somehow imagine granola will be involved."

More good-natured laughter was cut off by the Berserker piling on more questions. "Okay, I get the basic mechanics of the world, but there are a few things you're not telling us about."

"There's a *lot* I'm not telling you. Some of it is... disturbing." Nacho wasn't looking forward to talking about the world's eventual food source.

Extolling the virtues of cannibalism was always so *awkward*.

CHAPTER TWELVE

Nacho led his friends down the game path, crunching through the fallen leaves. The sun was warm, though the chill breeze told them that it wouldn't be too long before the snow would begin. He could only hope they'd all be well on their way to being Tier one by then.

The Cook spoke to Brie and Reuben over his shoulder. "Now, about the Store. You can buy *anything*. Whatever you buy appears in your Storage Slots, which you get five of. Then it's just a matter of grabbing the items and placing them."

"Hold up." Brie stopped their march. Her face twisted in disbelief. "What do you mean by 'placing' them?"

Nacho pulled up the interface. "Wanna see my saucepan?"

Brie recoiled in disgust. "Is that some kind of euphemism?"

The cook rolled his eyes, went to his slots, and chose the stainless-steel saucepan. He then glanced at the ground, where he was shown a square box, a very game-like mechanic. With a thought, he placed it on the leaves, and there sat his saucepan. Reuben hooked his thumbs into the straps of his backpack. "Nice pot, man."

"Saucepan," Brie whispered softly as she eyed the metal

object that had just *appeared*. "I figured out how to put things in. I have my wedding dress in one of my Storage Slots."

Nacho put his saucepan back in his inventory and started walking. "Let's keep going. I want to reach the dungeon entrance before nightfall; it'll make for a good shelter. If I remember right, there's an antechamber we can stay in. We can gather firewood on the way and alternate watches."

Reuben belatedly nodded. "Watches, yeah, that's a good idea."

"Okay, this is real. We're in a new world that acts like a video game." Brie released a nervous breath. "We have Skills, storage slots, and whatever else. Tell us more about the Store. Is it like... Am-Prime?"

Nacho nodded and turned, kicking through a pile of leaves. "It's like Am-Prime if they sold basically anything in reality."

"You could have just said yes, then," Reuben quipped as his eyes flashed blue. The joking made Nacho feel better. As long as they kept their sense of humor, his friends probably wouldn't crack completely.

Even so, he needed them to be aware of a few things. "No guns. No bombs. No handheld video games. Modern weapons and electronic devices are forbidden. However, you *can* buy a castle, or a castle wall, or even a portcullis."

"Gesundheit," Brie shot at him, cracking a smile.

"Thank you," Nacho volleyed back. "We can buy a meal, anything from fried chicken to blowfish sushi. There's also a variety of beverages, including plain old water. The Tier zero food is dirt cheap, but that's a trap that lulls you into a false sense of security. We'll get to the, uh... food situation. Eventually."

The sun was heading westward, and the air was cooling. As they strolled along, Nacho went over a list of tasks they would need to complete. He had made sure each pack contained a non-electric Grill Bears Fire Starter; he'd thrown matches and lighters in as well, but the fire starter was waterproof and worked very well.

"They have donuts in the Store." Clearly growing comfortable with their new reality, Reuben was walking and checking out the Store at the same time. "It's clearly part of a delicious, balanced breakfast for only three credits. This feels very science fiction-esque. Credits and such... are you sure we can't buy a nuclear bomb?"

"Who needs bombs when you can literally buy a fire-breathing dragon?" Nacho paused to make sure he hadn't lost track of the ramparts of the Armor Mountain. "However, the Store can be tricky, like everything else in the Juxtaposition. You can buy the dragon, sure, but you might need a dragon-training Skill to keep it from killing you as soon as you place it. The Store won't tell you that. Near the end, most of us only used the Store for Experience and Skill Points."

"But dude, you can buy Excalibur, the ye olde magical sword of King Arthur." Reuben gasped at the find. "A meal is three credits, but Excalibur is just over eleven hundred? It *is* like Am-Prime, down to the categories and being overpriced! But you're right, the descriptions are short, cheery, and... kind of unhelpful."

"I hated the cheeriness the most," Brie announced behind Reuben. "In the Evaluation World, there I was, fighting for my life, and those abyssal messages were all, 'Great job! Be positive! You're super lucky to be playing such a wonderful game!' That made me so furious that I could barely keep it together."

Nacho suddenly felt *much* closer to his best lady friend as he waxed nostalgic about going through that same phase. "You'll learn to ignore the tone. But, Reuben, check out the Character Upgrades category. That's where you can buy Experience Points and Skill Points."

"Yeah, I see it." Reuben scoffed and read off what he found. "Two credits for one Experience Point? I see that you can buy points to upgrade Skills and level up, so obviously credits are the most important part of the game."

Nacho smoothly ducked under a branch. "It's *all* about the credits... once you have a full stomach."

"But food is so cheap!" Reuben burst out, tripping as he ran into the branch Nacho had ducked under.

"That's why you don't access the menus when you aren't in a safe place." Nacho felt a chill in his belly as he realized what Reuben had just said. "Food *is* cheap... at first. Now take a look at the price of the *Juxtaposition's Guide to Saucy Satiation*. It's an info pack, and it'll be near the bottom."

Reuben whistled at the price tag on it. "Five thousand credits."

"It's priced *not* to sell." Nacho walked slightly faster. "Specifically so that no one *would* buy it. By the time a player or a guild had enough money, they'd figured out the food situation, so that info pack became worthless."

His healer friend started breathing harder as they increased their speed on the incline, but Brie's Athletic Endurance had kicked in to keep her cool and poised, so she took over. "You keep saying it's called the Juxtaposition. I know you mentioned this months ago, but what are we juxtaposed with?"

"Crazy-ville... *gasp*... and cuckoo banana-pants!" Reuben panted out loud. "I stand by my assertion!"

"Ignore the healer. Some people think it's the juxtaposition of our former lives and our new lives; the real world and the gaming world; our old Earth and this new world." Nacho hoped Brie wouldn't ask for more details. The truth was complicated, and he was suddenly reminded of Gary from the general store in the Evaluation Mall. Gary wore sunglasses, which were astoundingly cheap—two for a single credit. There was a reason for that.

His answer seemed to satisfy her for the moment, but he didn't want to give her room to revisit the subject. Nacho hurried them along, anxious to get to the dungeon entrance as quickly as possible, but also to avoid more pointed questions. The shadows had lengthened behind them as they reached the base of Armor Mountain. He could smell the fires above— someone up there must've been a boy scout if they could start a fire without matches, a lighter, or flint.

They moved south along the limestone wall until Nacho found the dungeon. Its entrance was half-concealed behind the thick roots of some bizarre Starter World tree that was growing around a boulder. Its bark oozed a black substance, and pear-shaped, inky-black fruit hung from gnarled branches.

Nacho dropped his backpack into the leaves. "Time to get some hands-on experience. Keep in mind that monsters come in all shapes, sizes, and species. There are fields of monster corn and a wide-array of apple monsters that would just love to take a bite out of you."

"Hey! Let me try accessing the System View." Reuben winked his left eye three times, and they flashed blue. "This is an 'Oilbark Tree, Very Uncommon,' but nothing much else."

"You... you figured out the System View?" Nacho stared at his friend in shock, who had already started gathering firewood from beneath more normal trees.

"Ahh... yeah? What else would the triple wink thing have meant in the tutorial? That whole place was *oozing* with clues for gamers." Reuben's casual answer left Nacho flabbergasted, so he sputtered and continued explaining what was different about this tree. He noticed Brie was starting to wink at the tree, her face slightly flushed. It was comforting to see that he hadn't been the only one that hadn't realized it the first time it had come up.

"You'll find more Oilbarks around, but you *can't* eat the fruit. If you do, it gives you the Runny Tummy Debuff, and you lose both Hunger and Thirst points for a long period of time; long enough to kill us in our current creditless states."

"Good to know." Brie helped her groom collect wood and tried to act like she had known how to use the shortcut the whole time. "Why doesn't the System View give you more information?"

Nacho snapped a stick in half to show his anger. "The Patrons want you to buy an Inspect Skill from the Store. One of us might want to consider it at some point. You can also buy an additional Skill slot, so you have more room for Skills, though that's expensive."

Reuben lugged a big tree branch over. "You can buy upgrades to Skills? I saw that we could purchase new Skills, and from what I understand, you can also pay to get out of Skills? Like how you mentioned getting rid of my amazing Marketing Skill?"

"All it means is that we need to get as many credits as possible." Brie was getting into the concept, and her calculative mind was spinning at all of the new things she needed to learn. "Also, correct me if I'm wrong, but is that a watermelon?"

Nacho looked where she was pointing and found that there was indeed a sad little watermelon growing next to the Oilbark tree. The monstrous plant was taking all the nutrients out of the ground, and the watermelon appeared to be on the verge of death. "I think so, but… it *has* to be something else."

He inspected it, reeling back in surprise at the information that popped up.

Final Watermelon (Tier 0). This is the last watermelon on the planet. Be the one to make it go extinct for a special reward!

"Good enough for me. I needed to figure out Ingredient Processing anyway. Who wants a slice?" Nacho walked over to the vine and plucked it, returning to his friends a moment later. Pulling out his knife, he sliced the melon in half, then stared at the result in annoyance. The rind went all the way to just before the center of the melon, which offered a walnut-sized section of pink fruit and a single black watermelon seed. "Never mind."

His friends chuckled at the worst melon they had ever seen as Nacho tried to activate Ingredient Processing on the leftover melon. He had the feeling that something went wrong when mana flew out of him and into the melon, dyeing the seed golden for a moment before sputtering out. "Well, this was a waste of time."

Nacho scooped out the pink flesh and seed, throwing it away in disgust. Still irritated, he booted the leftover rind away and flinched instinctively as a huge *crack* resounded behind him. He whipped around, only to find that Reuben had slammed the Oilbark branch down hard enough to snap it. At first, Nacho thought his friend was upset about something, but upon closer inspection, it appeared that the Healer was just trying something out. "It's weird. All that walking, and I'm not hungry at all."

Brie used her hatchet to chop through a branch. "From what Nacho said, it's because we haven't used our Skills yet, and it hasn't been twenty-four hours."

"Woo, game logic." Nacho wiped sweat from his forehead, then waved his hands jazz-style. They piled the wood at the foot of the strange tree, then added some dried grasses and leaves, and soon had a small fire going. "We should eventually buy a lantern, but for now, we need torches."

He set some sticks from the Oilbark tree ablaze, and they each grabbed one. Anyone would have thought that something called 'Oilbark' would provide great material for torches, but just like an eighty-year-old chain-smoker, they sputtered, smoked, and barely worked.

Nacho had packed road flares, but he wanted to save them. Brie lifted her fitfully burning brand high in her left hand and gripped her hatchet in her right. "I'll go in first. I'm the warrior, after all."

"Berserker, babe." Reuben grinned at her. "Warriors were cheap. Berserkers are rare. You're one in a million."

"Yeah, I wasn't too surprised; she's always had a temper," Nacho agreed in a quiet voice, pitched *just* loud enough for his friends to hear him. One threatened him with her torch, while the other chuckled knowingly. "I'll have my bow ready, so I won't take a torch. Keep in mind, we're all level zero *everything*. Forget winning every battle we have the option of fighting; we just want to survive Active Combat. You'll see the System message, so just do the best you can."

Reuben took a fresh grip on his club. "Level zero everything. That sucks."

"You're not wrong, but we'll improve." Nacho and Reuben followed Brie down the stair-like roots, descending a dozen feet into a central square chamber.

A System message flashed in their vision.

Greetings, Player!

Welcome to the Deep Buggy Darkness! This looks like your first dungeon! How exciting!

There are a variety of treasures and artifacts that can be found in the Deep Buggy Darkness. You'll get bonuses for killing bosses, and others for wiping out every living creature! Be ruthless, Player, and fill these dark halls with the blood of your enemies!

Note: This place is deep. There is a high probability of bugs being present. There is definitely darkness. Have fun, and may your future be delicious!

"Still hating the cheery messages." Brie approached the archway, the official entrance, and peered down more root-stairs, which disappeared into the depths of the world.

"I kinda like them! Dark. Deep. No bugs yet, but a good shot that they will appear. They really do tell us the truth." Reuben glanced around at the big gray blocks that made up the walls and ceiling. "I'm feeling very Indiana Jones-y at this point. You know, if humans had controlled this place, I bet this would have been a guard room."

To the left sat a cold fireplace with the remnants of black-ened ashes inside. Nacho relaxed for the first time since appearing in the new world, setting down his bow and arrow and putting a hand inside the firebox. "I feel an air current, so this must have a chimney. We'll bed down here for the night, and then tomorrow, we'll start earning credits. This early in the game, we won't earn any bonuses for running dungeons, but that changes once we *need* credits. At that point, there'll be all *sorts* of incentives for bonuses."

"From other players?" Reuben asked as he unrolled their sleeping bags. "Or a System thing?"

"System thing. Stuff like running through a dungeon without armor, or completing a dungeon in a certain amount of time. I also knew a guy who got bonuses for beating a dungeon only using blunt weapons. There will be all kinds of exciting ways to die for a handful of bonuses if you want them." Nacho helped Brie pile wood near the root stairs leading out, as well as the stone stairs leading down. The heaps of tree limbs likely would not stop anything or anyone, but it would slow them down.

In a flash of insight while filling their packs, Nacho had included a few luxury MREs he'd picked up at the army surplus store. "I think we deserve to celebrate surviving our first day. Salisbury steak for everyone!"

The processed food wasn't terrible, but he could tell Reuben didn't exactly enjoy the meal. They had water from water bottles, and... that was their dinner. Without anything else to do, they started getting ready for sleep.

"I'll take the first watch." The big guy twisted the water bottle cap on and stored it away with a simple thought. "Neat. I don't think we've actually said it yet, so... thanks, Nacho. For making sure we were prepared."

Brie stretched and yawned, offering the Cook a tired smile. "Yeah, thanks. This is terrible, but it would be even more terrible if we'd had no idea what was going on. Tell me: if you've lived through all of this once, so did we, I would imagine. What happened to us?"

"You were at the church, getting ready for your wedding photos. I wasn't with you." Nacho had to force down the lump in his throat. He decided it was best to just be blunt. "By this point on the first day... you were both already dead. Killed by a

Dirt Devourer. Around now, I'd killed my first monster by beating it with a tree branch."

Reuben stumbled back, sliding down with his back against the wall facing the fireplace. He still had his knife, but he'd also found a cudgel, a good-sized stick with a thick knot on one end. "Oh. Well… well, we're *not* dead! Made it farther than last time, so that's good. Plus Brie won't have to deal with her family, and *that's*… oh babe, I'm so sorry, I didn't mean it like that."

"Never again," Brie agreed quietly. Using her backpack as a pillow, she turned away from them. "I won't have to deal with their nonsense ever again. Free, but… sad. Relieved, but hurt. On that note, good night, you two."

"*Nice*, Reuben," Nacho hissed toward his friend for the incredibly insensitive comment. Brie was tough—hard where Reuben was soft—but he thought he saw her shoulders shake with a light sob. He sighed under his breath as he followed suit and laid down on his side, warm in his sleeping bag, gazing at the fire as it crackled and popped. Silence stretched as the air became tense, and Nacho used the unexpected peace to surprise himself by falling asleep almost instantly.

He only woke once when Reuben threw another log on the fire, while Brie stood to take the next watch. It felt like he blinked only once more before she was shaking him awake for the final stretch. Nacho kept an eye on the archway until the rising sun became a glow at the top of the staircase. Hope filled him, a warm feeling that he had tamped down for over half a year. Keeping that feeling alive, he turned and gazed affectionately at his slumbering friends, his eyes slightly watery. He cleared his throat and gently nudged Brie, then kicked Reuben in the side. "Time to get up!"

They had a big day ahead of them.

CHAPTER THIRTEEN

The next morning, they didn't need breakfast—it hadn't yet been twenty-four hours since their dinner—and Nacho figured they'd be using their Skills a great deal that day. Before long, they would be eating, and eating, so much more regularly than they were used to. No reason to keep to a schedule yet. They were good on water, but that would be the next thing they needed, which meant another fire, since the water had to be boiled for a number of reasons.

Brie stood holding one of their homemade firebrands at the mouth of the archway, where ever-more root-strewn stone steps descended into darkness. She squinted as the shadows shifted. "These torches suck. We need a decent light source."

Nacho rummaged into his bag and pulled out six road flares. He handed a couple to Brie and Reuben. "We'll use these for now. I would've brought flashlights, but batteries don't work here. If I remember right, there are torches on sconces deeper down; it's just that the tree here destroyed the wall."

He pointed at a series of roots that had pushed through the rock. Reuben wiped sweat from his forehead. It wasn't hot; in fact, it was a cold morning, but it was clear the handsome

Healer was nervous. "Who built all this? I mean, this isn't a natural cave. Someone took the time to carve all this out of stone, so are these alien ruins?"

"Don't overthink this, Reuben." Nacho removed some extra clothes and supplies that wouldn't be too hard to replace, then put the pack back on. "I think it's safe to leave some of our gear up top. I'll bring food and water."

He struck a flare and tossed it down the steps, where the spitting red light painted the root-covered walls in a fiery scarlet glow. They had enough light to see that the top steps were clear as the odor of burning sulfur wafted up to them.

They chose a marching order, with Brie at the front and Reuben in the center, since they wanted to protect their Healer. Nacho had his knives strapped at his sides, but he'd start with the bow. Depending on what they came across, it might be a worthless weapon. He thought the Deep Buggy Darkness contained a mixture of Tier zero and Tier one monsters, but obviously the more powerful creatures should be much further down.

Within the first few steps, the System decided to get chatty with them.

Hey, Players!

It sounds like you're discussing party placement! You sure are getting chummy with these other players!

Would you like to create a party?

Yes / No.

"Let's all choose 'yes'," Nacho decided after a long moment. "The System checks to see how well we coordinate with each other, and that could eventually lead to bonus credits. Also, it makes trading easier if we can pool our resources."

"Is this like opening a bank account together?" Reuben chuckled as he pretended to haughtily glare at them. "I think I'll need to check both of your credit histories, especially the hot blonde. She looks shifty."

"I *am* shifty." Brie's joke came out tense, as she was too focused on the entrance to the dungeon, which very well might lead them to their deaths.

They all chose 'yes' on the prompt.

Yay! We love a good party that plans to live—and especially die—together! What would you like to name your party? Currently, it's Untitled1, and that's not very catchy.

Reuben actually laughed as the others grimaced at the incongruous jocularity. "Not very catchy at all, Patrons. How about we call ourselves the Cheesy Chasers. Mr. Colby, Ms. Brie, and Nacho."

"No 'Mr' on my name? Fine. What about 'The Dinner Party'?" Nacho suggested as he got into the spirit of having something that was *theirs*. A welcome smile flashed across Brie's face, and she snorted softly.

"The Dinner Party, it is!" Reuben affirmed for all of them. They didn't need to say more; the name was too perfect. The Healer hefted his backpack and tightened the straps. "So, uh, if we die now, we die for real, right? Maybe I should go first. I just don't like Brie risking her life for us."

Brie turned to menace him with her hand axe. "*I'm* the Berserker, Reuben. If I see anything, I'll go berserk and kill it. Don't worry about me. Besides, we both have the same strength. This is all dangerous."

"Just be ready to hug her if she gets hurt." Nacho chortled at the fact that he had just given an *absolutely* serious battle command.

Reuben lit one of his own road flares and held it aloft, just in time for motion from the wall roots to draw their attention. Not just the wall, but the ceiling!

"Brie, above you!" Nacho shouted as a three-foot-long grub, white with a marbled pink body, unraveled from above, where it had anchored itself into the root system. The back-end anchor was a bubble gum pink, while the bitey end was white with black eyes and obsidian mandibles.

The System chose that moment to inform them that their lives were in imminent danger:

Hey, Player, welcome to Active Combat! Active Combat is dangerous but fun! You cannot access the Store, and both your Health and Mana Regen have been paused for the duration. Good luck!

Gumdrop Grub
  Effective Tier/Level: ?
  HP: ?

The Patrons liked to keep monster stats hidden, for the most part, but Nacho wasn't fooled by the question mark next to the thing's Tier and level value. It had taken far too long for him to figure out what the punctuation meant. Even if the System View was garbage for the most part, it did have some uses.

The grub lashed out at Brie.

Nacho didn't have a shot, but the Berserker let out a shout and spun, raising an arm and trying to activate her Defensive Whirl. It didn't work. The grub drove its mandibles deep into the flesh of her arm, and she screamed in pain. As though she had rung the dinner bell, another grub crawled from the wall, its pale body pulsating. This one was a bright blue, but again, its segmented thorax shimmered with the glitter of sugar on a gumdrop candy.

Nacho *could* shoot that one and did. His arrow struck home, causing the thing to scream and fall to the floor, curling around itself. The familiar Active Combat message popped up.

. . .

Damage dealt: 5/5.

A second later, Nacho was given another message.

Congratulations! You have killed a Gumdrop Grub!
   Level 01 Creature = 0 Credits!
   Awesome!

It wasn't awesome—he'd gotten nothing for killing the monster. That wasn't how the system was supposed to work. *Everyone* got credits for killing a monster. Why wasn't... he?

"Nacho!" Reuben's call pulled his attention back to the fight, as three more of the grubs came curling out of the walls and ceiling—purple, light red, and green—though it was kind of hard to tell, since the flare's spitting light was on the redder side of the color spectrum.

Brie hacked at the pinkish one in the ceiling, driving her hatchet deep into the throbbing flesh. She pulled the monster down and kicked it away. It was finally dead, but she was bleeding.

Reuben waved his flare in the face of a third purple one. It shrieked as Brie spun and sank her hatchet into its pliant body. They'd killed three of the grubs so far. How many credits had they earned?

The red and green grubs had anchored their bodies to the wall on either side of the hallway. They lashed out at Brie's back, and Reuben stormed forward with his club in one hand and the flare in the other. Only, he wasn't holding his club for long. The red grub ripped into his arm, the pain causing him to drop the weapon. With an enraged cry, the healer pivoted and drove the flare into the beady black eye of the monster.

For a second, the staircase was dark, until the flames burned through the outer flesh of the creature, then lit it up like a big red sparkly balloon.

That left the green one. Nacho thought about using his bow, but at their current stage—being level zero everything—they *needed* credits. He had to assume that both Brie and Reuben were getting paid for their kills. Brie's body blurred with speed. Apparently she had figured out how to activate her Combat Dash. She swung her hatchet, hacking into the green grub until it stiffened in death.

Both Brie and Reuben were breathing hard, blood dripping from their wounded arms. The Berserker lit another flare and tossed it farther down the staircase. A rapid scan didn't reveal any more of the grubs.

Congratulations, Player! Active Combat is over! It looks like your friends were wounded, but they'll live! Have fun shopping, and enjoy the return of your Health and Mana Regen! May your future be delicious!

"Don't let that System message fool you." Nacho stood ready with his bow, though he was unwilling to use it if they didn't get paid. "We could get attacked right away, so don't let your guard down. Tell me you two got credits for killing the grubs."

Reuben bent and picked up his club. "I got five credits for my flare action."

Brie stood with her hatchet dripping the black ichor of the grub monsters. She clutched the sleeve of her shirt to stem the flow of the blood. "Fifteen credits for me. And I'm getting hungry, like I usually do after I've worked out for hours. That's the System, right?"

"You used your Skills." Nacho felt that was all he needed to say.

"Not that they *worked*," Brie complained bitterly as she inspected her bleeding arm. "My Defensive Whirl got me a bad gash, and my Combat Dash made me faster, but I didn't do any extra damage."

"Welcome to the drawbacks of having level zero skills." Nacho kept his eyes on the roots covering the walls and ceilings. The stone steps and root system descended... what? Another hundred feet? Five hundred? More roots waited down there, as did the shadows of something else; chittering bodies in a larger cavern at the bottom.

The steam from the flare in the eye socket of the red Gumdrop Grub had filled the hallway with the smell of cooked meat.

Brie went pale as she whispered, "Is it just me... or does that bug smell good?"

CHAPTER FOURTEEN

Standing in the middle of the stone staircase, surrounded by roots, Nacho wasn't sure how to respond to Brie's question. The cooked grub didn't smell too good to him, but he hadn't used his Skills, so he wasn't hungry. He also wasn't exactly sure *how* to use his Skills, in fact.

Reuben pulled Brie into a hug. He glowed, she glowed, there was much glowing in the stairwell. But when Brie pulled up the sleeve of her shirt, she still had the wound.

The big guy blinked. "*Nothing*? Not a single point healed? Then why am I thirsty?"

"Let's retreat for now," Nacho decided after allowing their confusion to increase. "You guys can eat, you can see your Health Regen in action, and then we can figure out where we go from here."

They marched back up the stairs but didn't stop there. All of them wanted to get into the sunlight after taking out the grubs—they had a mutual feeling that they were covered in creepy crawlies, and hanging out in the darkness would not help resolve that. Upon emerging into the sunlight, Reuben and Brie sat on a dead tree a few feet away from the Oilbark tree and the entrance to the Deep Buggy Darkness.

Nacho bent down to dig through his backpack. He hadn't bothered to bring medical supplies, because compression bandages and antibiotic ointment paled in comparison to the System's regenerative properties. Brie pulled up her sleeve and gingerly pressed at the flesh. "I was down ten Health Points, but now I'm all fixed up. Seven-point-five percent of my health is restored over every minute not fighting."

"Not ten percent?" Reuben raised an eyebrow at her in confusion.

Nacho checked his Health Regen, and just like Reuben, had ten percent of his max Health Points. Then he realized what had happened. "Brie's Hunger isn't at full. She must have seventy-five Hunger points."

Brie quickly confirmed his suspicions. "That's right. You had said that Health Regen is connected to hunger... makes sense."

Reuben tapped on a screen only he could see. "My Mana Regen is connected to Thirst, so I'm at nine percent regen."

Nacho took two Muscle Mania protein bars out of his backpack and tossed one to Reuben, the other to the Berserker. "Eat up, and we can talk more. We did well for our first Active Combat. Especially since it was an ambush."

"Not hungry, bro." Reuben waved the food away, tossing it back to the Cook. "But hit me with some water. I'm *weirdly* thirsty."

Brie tore into the bar, eyelids fluttering. "Oh, that's *good*. I used my ability twice and I was *already* getting hungry. My passive isn't helping me at all."

Nacho took a sip of water and tried to phrase his words delicately. "Let's talk about your skills more. We have twenty credits, so we'll have to figure out how to invest them. I shouldn't get anything, because I'm useless at earning credits in combat. I killed a grub and didn't get a single credit."

"Not normal?" Reuben questioned him.

"Not even close." Nacho sighed despondently, trying to figure out the reason for the lack of income. "I'll stay in reserve, only jumping in if you need help or are getting overwhelmed."

Brie was the one to come up with the most likely answer. "It bet it's because you're a Satiation Player. The rules must be different for those classes."

"Seems like it. Wait… I think that actually might have been in the class description." Nacho capped his water bottle as he tried to remember what exactly it had stated, but he eventually shrugged helplessly. "Let's get back to your skills, Brie. Tell me more."

Brie slid off the dead tree and began to pace. "My Athletic Endurance should give me a percentage reduction to hunger loss penalties. It's passive, so I don't have to pay, but it's not helping because of the level zero stuff. Combat Dash gives me bonus damage, as well as super speed. There's a ten percent Metabolic cost every time I use it. Defensive Whirl will eventually let me block attacks, and there's a fifteen percent Metabolic cost. I used both abilities, and I was down to seventy-five Hunger. Not sure why I got so hungry, since I was three-quarters full."

"You're not used to being hungry at all. The benefits of being in the American middle class." Nacho ran a quick System check on the Muscle Mania bars.

Generic Over-Priced Protein Bar
  One quarter portion

"Eating that should get you back to a hundred Hunger points." Nacho privately debated over which Skill they should boost with their twenty credits.

Brie stopped pacing as she confirmed his assessment. "Back to a hundred. You're right."

A System message appeared in Nacho's vision.

. . .

Special Bonus Sauce!
Congratulations! You have fed your party for the first time ever!
Bonus Credits = 5
Spectacular! May your future be delicious!

Nacho smiled slowly as he realized the answer. "Wait. Guys."

"Yeah, I saw your eyes flash. What happened?" Reuben's perceptiveness, while a great trait, still threw Nacho off slightly.

"I just got five credits for feeding Brie."

The woman grunted in displeasure. "Well *that* makes me feel like a zoo animal. I guess that's an apt description, since being in the Juxtaposition is like being in a zoo for Patrons, right?"

Nacho wasn't listening, unsure if he felt excited or baffled by his new Satiation class. "Okay, Reuben, what about your Skills?"

Reuben broke a stick off the dead tree and toyed with it. "Well, my Marketing ability costs five percent of my Mana, Hydration, and Metabolic points. Five percent across the board. Because of *course* it does. Ya know, getting people to buy your stuff is a hungry, thirsty, Mana-intense business."

"Probably not useful for now. What about your Healing Hugs and Positive Vibes Skills?"

Reuben didn't answer right away, needing to read off the details to refresh his memory. "Healing Hugs doesn't have a Metabolic cost, so that's why I wasn't hungry. It costs me in Mana and Hydration, though; ten percent of my Mana and five percent of my Hydration. I was down to ninety-five Thirst points, which wasn't that much, now that I think about it. It just felt right to drink."

"A lot of that is going to be due to habit." Satisfied that he had a better understanding of their function as a group, Nacho strapped up the backpack and stood.

"My Positive Vibes skill costs me five percent in Mana and

ten percent in Hydration. I'm assuming that's off the total, and not a declining percentage? I mean, ten percent of a hundred is different than ten percent of ninety."

"Right you are." Nacho sniffed the air. He could still smell smoke coming from the settlers on top of Armor Mountain. For a second, he felt sorry for them, but he couldn't soften his heart; not when his life and the lives of his two best friends were still in jeopardy. "So, we have twenty-five credits, and we should put them to use. A Skill Point costs two credits, and it takes ten Skill Points to upgrade a Skill to Level One. That means we can upgrade one of us, and then we can head back down into the Deep Buggy Darkness."

Reuben turned serious. "I hate seeing Brie get hurt. I want her to have her Defensive Whirl."

Brie stopped pacing once again, propping her fists on her hips as she stared down her fiancé. "Reuben, I can take care of myself. I'm going to be in combat a lot, so you'll *have* to get used to it."

The Healer cast his gaze down to the dry autumn leaves on the ground. "I know. It's just hard. I'd much rather *I* get hurt than you."

Nacho wanted to tell his friend that, as the Healer, they had to keep him back. During Active Combat, his hugs just might keep Brie alive. Nacho was the real problem. The fact that he didn't earn credits for killing monsters made his help in a fight an active hindrance to their growth. Brie grabbed Reuben's hand in both of hers, leaning in to give him a kiss.

"You're sweet, and I get that you want to protect me. But right now, I have to be the one to protect us. You have a point, though; leveling Defensive Whirl makes sense. It seems like it's a complete block instead of reduced damage. That'll keep me alive so I can inflict more damage." She turned to Nacho. "Is there a way to end Active Combat? Or is it just the System that makes that decision?"

It was a good question, and it had taken a lot of bloodshed for people to learn how it worked. Nacho was glad he already

DAKOTA KROUT

knew the answer. "You can retreat, and once you put a certain distance between you and the monster, Active Combat ends. We tried to map it out, but it changes every time. Normally, barring any sort of natural obstacle, it's a dozen feet away, but that also pre-supposes that the monster isn't chasing you. If the monster *is* chasing you, then it's harder—if not impossible—to end Active Combat until one of you is dead."

Reuben shook his head as he rose to his feet. "It both makes sense and is really ambiguous. So... that's terrible."

"It is, and it isn't." Brie shook her head in the negative. "It gives us some room to maneuver. If I can block attacks, and if we can retreat far enough, we can use our Health Regen to heal. It makes healing less important, and Positive Vibes becomes more important because that will actively help us dish out damage. This place really is about wholesale slaughter."

"You're not wrong." Nacho approached his friends. "I think Brie is right. Defensive Whirl is the right way to go. She'll take less damage and can continue to deal it. Are you ready to spend our money, Brie?"

"Always." She smirked as her eyes flashed. Nacho glanced at the top of his Stat Sheet to check their credits total.

Eli 'Nacho' Naches
> *Class: Common Cook*
> *Level: 0*
> *Experience Points: 100 to Level 1!*
> *Current Credits: 5 (25 total Dinner Party pool)*
> *Build Type: Balanced, Delayed*

Nacho had always thought it was weird that Experience Points weren't earned from straight combat and needed to be purchased like everything else. "Toilet paper or leveling up? It's so strange."

Brie's eyes lost their glow. "It's done. I was given the option

140

to pull from Reuben, so I nabbed his five, and not yours, Nacho."

"I'll be your sugar daddy." Reuben grinned at her, but she pointedly ignored him. Rested, healed, and with full Hunger and Thirst, the team went back down into the dungeon, pausing on the staircase. The flares they'd thrown were still spitting light, though most of their length was now gray ash.

Nacho appraised the dead grubs around them.

Raw Tier 0 Meat
 Note: Putrid Mana. Did someone say it's smoothie time?

He considered his Ingredient Processing ability. He could drain the Putrid Mana out of the insects, but could he *cook* them? Could he get credits for doing it? He thought so, but he wasn't sure. Nacho bent and turned one of the giant worms over. It wasn't getting gooey yet, but it would eventually liquify, thanks to the Putrid Mana. "Wait. I bet I could cook these things. Would you mind eating grubs?"

Reuben made a face while Brie shrugged. "Sure. Protein is protein. But how do we know they're not poisonous?"

"They are," Nacho replied darkly as he bounced the pound of jiggling meat up and down. "They contain Putrid Mana, but they're still Tier zero. We can eat them straight, though it makes everything taste terrible and would make us mildly sick. Not terrible, but not pleasant. Luckily, I can help with that. Should I try?"

Something chittered down below. Before the flare gave out a last sputter, they spotted movement in the corridor at the bottom of the steps.

"Cancel that." Nacho stood ramrod-straight. "This is the wrong place to do any kind of meal prep. I'm thinking the Gumdrop Grubs were just the warm-up act. What do you think grubs turn into?"

"Bigger grubs?" Reuben seemed hopeful.

"Bigger *bugs*." Brie pulled her knife out, arranging the hatchet in her right hand and the dagger in her left. "I'm only going to improve with practice. The more killing, the better."

"Spoken by my best little Berserker." Reuben kissed the back of her head.

"Oh, come on." Nacho gagged lightly, then got serious. "Remember, there wasn't a sign at the entrance that said, 'You must be this tall to run this dungeon'. It's totally possible that we could encounter something we can't hurt. If that happens? We need to run."

"I can run. Not well, mind you, but discretion is the better part of valor. I will discretion-fully flee." The look in Reuben's eyes told Nacho everything he needed to know. He'd sacrifice himself to save Brie and not think twice.

Nacho felt the tremor in his gut, wondering if he was starting to form an ulcer from all the stress. Yes, he had game knowledge that most likely no one else had, but he wasn't playing as an assassin, he wasn't alone, and he was responsible for a couple that loved each other beyond all good sense. He knew either one would jump to save the other. That might be a benefit; then again, it might be a recipe for disaster if they weren't careful.

He hardened his heart, trying to stay in the moment, focus on the dungeon, and get his party leveled and back out alive. Once they were safe, he could try cooking Gumdrop Grubs.

With a name like that, they wouldn't taste *too* terrible, would they?

CHAPTER FIFTEEN

Nacho tossed a fresh flare to the bottom of the long stairwell. Huge beetles, each about the size of a fully-grown Doberman, scuttled into the light. The insectoid monsters were strangely colored; each section of their carapace shone a different hue, the texture rough and pebbly. Their mandibles clacked, and their antennae waved wildly. Even so, Reuben chuckled softly. "Their shells look candy-coated. Did someone glue Nerds to their backs?"

"You're oddly cheerful about things trying to kill us." Brie squinted, attempting to make out the colors in the shifting light. "Don't really care what they look like. There seem to be a dozen of them, and I don't want to fight them all at the same time. Ideally, I could fight them one by one."

Nacho put a hand on the root wall, thinking rapidly. "If we could create an experience point farm, we could earn a ton of credits. We need to get closer to use the System View. If they are too strong, we'll just have to come back another time."

The candy-coated beetles ignored the stairwell but appeared to find the flare endlessly fascinating. Nacho sat on the steps and lit an emergency candle from his backpack so they weren't in complete darkness. "We know the beetles are drawn to the flare, but they could care less about a little romantic mood lighting. It would be nice to get a sense of the layout down there, but we'd have to fight through a good number of those bugs to get the info."

Brie stood, hatchet and knife firmly gripped in her fists. "My Combat Dash skill is more dash than combat at this point, so I could dash down and dash back. Maybe they wouldn't see me?"

"Or maybe they would." Reuben's worry was plain.

"The only way we'll know for sure is if I try. I can creep down and get close." Their Berserker shrugged dismissively.

"We can try it." Nacho broke their stalemate and Brie flashed a grin at him. "Gotta keep our eyes out for Gumdrop Grubs as we go. Once we get close, you can do your dashing."

"On the steps?" Reuben shook his head. "She could catch a root and go down."

"I'm very nimble," Brie asserted instantly, her frustration clearly mounting. "You call me a nimble little minx all the time."

"Quoting *Ghostbusters*?" The healer breathlessly whispered. "How *dare* you do so in public, where I can't properly thank you for it?"

"Yeah, let's move." Nacho left the candle on the steps and crept down. Brie was ready for more grubs to come springing from the ceiling, but none appeared, and the trio stopped six steps from the bottom. The corridor below was full of Nerds beetles, at least a dozen, scrambling over each other to get close to the flare. A candy cockroach convention.

Nacho chanced a quick System View, focusing in on one of the monsters.

Candylicious Weta Beetle
  Effective Tier/Level: ?
  HP: ?

. . .

The solitary question mark meant they were Tier zero monsters. What level, Nacho didn't know, but Brie *should* be able to hack them to pieces. He thought he might've heard of weta beetles before, back on Earth, but he wasn't sure. The Candylicious part was almost funny, except for the cruel mandibles of the creatures and their spiked legs.

One of the beetles smacked the flare down the corridor to the left, and the other insects followed the glow, tumbling over each other in a renewed rush to check out the spitting light. In seconds, the corridor was empty, which was very lucky.

It took a minute for Reuben's eyes to grow accustomed to the lack of light, but when he did, he called out in a hoarse whisper, "Something's glowing down there!"

Brie leaned over and hugged Reuben. Then she was running, moving like a shadow down to the bottom step, where she looked right, looked left, and then came running back, dancing over the roots until she was back with them.

She jabbed her finger upward twice, clearly indicating that it would be too dangerous to talk so close to the Candylicious insects. They might not be currently swarming at the landing, but they were far from gone. Each of the humans could hear the scuttle of all those big bodies.

Once they had retreated back to their little flickering candle, Brie spoke. "There's some sort of big chamber to the left with some stuff glowing in there. I'm thinking it's something with natural bioluminescence. It could be a plant, it could be an oversized Firefly; I have no idea. That's where most of the beetles are huddled up with their new favorite toy. To the right is a smaller chamber, full of roots. A couple of beetles are hanging out in there, but they seemed different."

Nacho had a fairly good grasp of the layout now. "Last thing: Are there roots on the ceiling and walls like in here like there in this tunnel?"

"It's the same as in here." She was sweating, but there was a definite look of excitement on her face: she wanted to fight.

"What if we hacked up the roots and tried to cause a cave-in?" Reuben offered a non-standard option for them to consider. It did not go unnoticed that his plan was one where none of them were fighting directly.

Nacho liked the idea, but the stone walls seemed strong. He had another suggestion. "What if we tossed another flare into the bioluminescent chamber? Then Brie could fight the two beetles in the root chamber to the right. If we make a barrier strong enough, we might be able to hold them off indefinitely. Then we'd be able to pick them off one by one."

Brie wiped sweat off her top lip. "We have enough wood up there around the dead tree. We could bring down logs and branches and wedge them into the root network on the walls and ceiling? Let's be real here: if we can't outwit beetles, we're never going to last in the game."

Reuben leaned close and gave his fiancée a regular hug. "She's amazing! Isn't she amazing?"

They retreated back up the stairs, but this time Nacho had them collect three of the dead Gumdrop Grubs. He wanted to cut them up and try to process their Putrid Mana... but he didn't get the chance. They were already liquifying. He didn't feel too bad; there was bound to be a learning curve in being a Satiation Player. This was completely new territory, for him and for everyone else in the AKC, as far as he knew.

They made it back to the antechamber where they'd spent the night without any opposition. It was going to be far harder to sleep there, now that they knew there were monstrous candy-colored bugs waiting below.

Outside, they gathered more logs while Nacho slowly built himself a saw. During those six months at home, he'd watched numerous UTube videos on backwoods survival, such as a Swedish backpacker making a saw using long sticks, a sawblade, screws, and some string.

Brie ate another bar to restore her Hunger—she was down to eighty points after her little stunt. Reuben pulled over logs, and when his saw was ready, Nacho cut them into lengths a bit longer than the corridor was wide.

It was late afternoon when they lugged the long logs and thick branches down the steps and piled them to the side. They could see the bluish glow from the bioluminescent chamber, but there was no sign of the beetles.

Nacho gave the emergency candle to Reuben. "This has to go quick. I'll light our flares and toss them to the left into the big chamber. That should draw the Nerds over. Once we see them scurrying, we might not need to fight the ones to the right. If we do, Reuben and I will build the blockade, and Brie will kill the beetles. If she needs help, Reuben, you'll have to go while I finish the barricade. How's that for a plan?"

Brie looked relatively calm. "You just be ready with the food. I imagine I'll be using my Defensive Whirl a lot. If I get hurt, my regen is going to be in the toilet."

"I have some raisins and peanuts," Nacho offered before creeping to the bottom of the descent. He plastered himself against the wall to the right, then hung his bow and his quiver of arrows on a root. Either Brie or Reuben would have to use it, since Nacho would only be wasting arrows if they didn't get a single credit from him during combat.

He could see into the grub room, where fat worms wiggled in glowing sacks of milky liquid, all contained by little alcoves enclosed by roots. These worms were smaller than the Gumdrop Grubs, but who knew if all these insects were the same species?

The Nerds beetles swarmed everywhere inside the big chamber. Nacho inched over to the other wall, just able to make out the colorful carapaces of the two beetles in the smaller room to the side. They must be acting as guards. That gave him an idea.

Nacho readied the last two flares, then motioned for Reuben and Brie to come closer before striking the starter on one flare, immediately spinning around the corner and hurling it into the glowing worm room. A dozen of the beetles knocked into each other in an attempt to get at it. At the same time, Nacho lit the second flare and tossed it into the smaller room on the right.

The two monsters in the small space squealed as if it had surprised them, before they too leapt on the spitting fire.

"Get them, Brie," Nacho hissed at the Berserker, who started forward, paused, then dashed into the root chamber to the right. Reuben set the candle down on the first step and sent a log scooting over to Nacho, who slammed it into the top corner of the corridor before wedging crossways into the floor to the left.

Brie let out a scream—a war cry—and slammed into the two beetles.

The System declared that Active Combat had begun, belatedly in Nacho's mind.

The cook watched Brie sink her hatchet into the face of the first distracted beetle, but it wasn't enough to kill the thing. It lunged, trying to hook her with one of its mandibles, and she reacted by using her Defensive Whirl and spinning away. The other monster rose up on its hind set of legs, bringing the spikes of its legs down on her. She sustained a bad gash but firmly drove her knife into the belly of the insect, causing it to shriek in pain.

That wasn't going to kill the bug either, but when it tried to catch her in its mandibles, she was able to Defensive Whirl away from its attack and find a chink in its exoskeleton to slam the hatchet into. The other monster attacked while she was thus engaged, ripping up her thigh.

Nacho could *barely* focus on her fight, since they had to get the barricade set up. Both he and Reuben were pulling the logs and branches over as fast as possible, slamming them into the roots. They placed the thickest logs diagonally to form a lattice, then shoved smaller branches to support them. The cook sank one support beam in place just as a Candylicious Beetle in the glow-sack room turned from the flare and lunged toward him, mandibles clacking.

The log jam squealed... but held!

"I need more wood!" Nacho yelled, the time for stealth long gone.

"That's what she said," Reuben breathlessly retorted. "Aw, *man*, I totally just self-burned."

Nacho heard Brie grunt in pain, followed by one of the other beetles piping out a dying shriek. He hoped that was good news.

Reuben drove a branch vertically to reinforce their barricade. The other beetles in the sack chamber had finally noticed them and were coming to bash down their wall. Mandibles tore at the branches as legs with spiky growths tried to pull the barrier apart. The structure creaked, the wood cracked, but Nacho and Reuben added another layer to their barricade, wood crisscrossing and holding.

His side of the barrier set in place, Nacho spun to check on Brie. Her clothes were bloody and gashed, but she'd hacked up both Candylicious Beetles. Their colorful carapaces were splattered with their black blood, and whole sections of their shells had been shattered.

Reuben set the last length of wood horizontally and anchored it in with his legs. The beetles were trying to shove their way through, but that wasn't going to work. If they were smart, they would've pulled away the barricade branch by branch, but... they were beetles.

Nacho joined his friend and pushed against the horizontal log, dodging an insect leg just before it could impale him. "Status report, Brie. Where are you at with Health? What's your hunger level?"

"Ravenous." Brie joined them and swung her hatchet, cleanly chopping off a leg. "I'm down to ten, I feel crappy, and I would literally eat one of those Gumdrop Grubs raw at this point."

Nacho turned and flipped his backpack upside down. "Hold the barricade, Reuben. I'll get Brie some food. We're still in Active Combat, so she won't heal on her own, but I can help with the Hunger. When this is over, she'll regenerate perfectly."

He retrieved the Muscle Mania bar Reuben hadn't eaten and also grabbed a big bag of peanuts and raisins. Altogether, it was a full portion, which would bring up her Hunger points to maximum.

"Wish I could hug you and make you feel better." Reuben let out a hiss of pain. "*Ouch*! Those spines are sharp!"

Nacho sprang back to the barrier, joining Reuben in holding it. On the other side of the barricade roiled a nightmare of beetle mandibles and insect legs. Their clacking and squeals were a storm of awful. "Reuben, grab the bow. Start shooting arrows while Brie eats."

The big guy ran for the bow and quiver where Nacho had left them in the stairwell. He came back holding the bow in his right hand, trying to get an arrow onto the string with his quaking left hand. Brie could clearly see that her boyfriend had no idea what he was doing, so she clamped the protein bar in her teeth and took the weapon from Reuben, and he grabbed the food out of her mouth as she chomped down.

She chewed and swiftly nocked an arrow, then sent a feathered shaft into the gullet of the nearest beetle—from its coloring, it was strawberry and grape flavored. The wounded bug went down under the whirring legs of the others. Reuben handed her a new arrow and lifted the bar so she could take another bite.

Nacho gritted his teeth and braced against the quaking log. "Tell me you're at least getting credits for these kills."

"I am," Brie mumbled around her mouthful. She fired the arrow into the face of another bug. Her fingers must've been throbbing from using the bow, and her sleeve was being shredded by the bowstring, but she didn't seem to feel anything.

Reuben sprang into action once the bar was gone. He scooped up Brie's hatchet and chopped off any leg that managed to poke through, also finding some eyes to stab while his far more fit fiancé emptied their quiver.

It wasn't long before the beetles had to crawl over their own dead to get to the wall, only making the barricade more effective. Once Brie was out of arrows, she reverted to her knife. She slammed the blade into the face-flesh of any of the Candylicious Weta Beetles that came close, and Reuben began to laugh maniacally. "We have our experience point farm! Only, we don't grow EPs here, we grow credits. Since these bugs are monsters, they aren't retreating. No survival instinct. Sucks to be on the wrong end of evolution, doesn't it?"

Brie continued to knife bugs as Reuben took a breather from swinging the hatchet repeatedly. She'd killed at least a dozen of the insects. "I *hate* bugs, and I'll never be able to eat Nerds again. Or… whatever. I'm still so hungry. Are you going to cook these, Nacho?"

The cook in question stepped back; the final horizontal beam had done the trick, holding their structure in place. The last of the bugs skittered forward, and Brie ended the thing, hissing out with relief as it slumped to the stone floor. "Now *that* was a workout. Gory. Disturbing. Probably not as bad as a typical Zumba class."

Reuben rubbed the small of her back. "You okay?"

She nodded, though her smile looked like it had been cut into her face from all the ichor that had splattered across it.

Nacho was amused by how easily she had shifted to accepting this as normal life: killing monsters for money. "How much are we getting per kill?"

Brie let out a shuddering breath. "Eleven credits per kill. Each had thirteen Health Points, so it took a few swings to put them down. I killed fifteen, for a total of one hundred and sixty-five credits. Did you get anything for bravely giving me the Muscle Mania bar, Nacho?"

Nacho cackled at that. "Not a credit. But that's okay; you did all the work."

"I helped," Reuben insisted indignantly. "I got three kills for another thirty-three."

"Hold on…" Nacho held up a finger. "Wait for it…"

Reuben cocked his head. "Wait for what?"

Right on time, the System messaged them.

· · ·

Congratulations, Player! Active Combat is over! Your little party certainly was clever, putting up that barricade. You get +1 credit for being so smart! Enjoy your Health and Mana Regen!

Nacho checked their credits. With the bonus five they had earned before, they were up to two hundred and five. This was excellent news. In a very real sense, such a windfall might've saved all their lives.

Brie staggered against the roots. With combat over, the scratches on her hands began to heal, as did the bad gash on her thigh. Her left arm had been ripped up by the bow, and her fingers were swollen, but not for long. She made a face. "It kind of… itches. The Health Regen doesn't help repair my clothes, so… good thing you bought us a spare set. Now I get why you asked me for my size last month. Hit me with more raisins and peanuts."

Nacho handed her the bag, and she dove into them. Meanwhile, he and Reuben dismantled a small portion of their very effective barricade. By the time they were done, Brie was all healed up. The three of them walked into the grub room, weapons ready. The chamber was fifty feet wide, fifty feet tall, and all roots—all the time. Only the glowing worms in their bioluminescent sacks provided some variety. The worms themselves were a kaleidoscope of colors all swirled together to create a rainbow pattern of larval wonder.

"Hey! What's that?" Reuben gestured to an alcove. The glowing bag of goo within didn't just have baby worms inside it —a skeleton also floated in the fluid. The three of them held their weapons ready, Reuben with his knife and club, Brie with her hatchet, Nacho with his bow. Of course, they'd retrieved all their arrows.

When they drew closer, they realized that *all* the glowing sacks enclosed skeletons, surrounded by the baby worms. Some of the worm bags also contained other items as well—armor, weapons, and gold pieces.

Brie wrinkled her nose. "Oh, gross. They were feeding their baby grubs with people."

Reuben let out a whoop. "Gross, yes, but do you know what this *means*? We have *treasure*, people! If we're lucky, one of those items might be magical!"

Nacho glanced at the hole leading out of the other side of the worm room with a worried look. They would need to keep an eye out for more monsters while they cut open the goo sacks and gathered the treasure. He knew from experience that in the Juxtaposition, a triumphant victory could turn into a wicked defeat in an instant, so he pointed to the suspicious exit. "Before we get too excited, we're going to move our barricade. We don't want any unexpected visitors."

"Abyssal right," Reuben agreed, finally managing to pull his eyes off the loot. "Monsters should call before showing up and trying to liquify our internal organs. *Tsk.* So rude!'

Brie sputtered a laugh, sounding unexpectedly joyful in the dark, strange depths.

CHAPTER SIXTEEN

Working together, The Dinner Party relocated their barricade to cover the exit hole in the roots. Down below, the passageway was more rockslide than stone staircase, most probably infested with monsters—whatever was living down there didn't smell appetizing.

Nacho couldn't remember what else they might run into in the Deep Buggy Darkness, but so far, they'd been lucky to only encounter Tier zero monsters. Everything about combat would change with Tier one creatures, and they weren't ready for that level of action. Especially because Brie was the only one of them who had a Skill that was remotely useful so far.

Once their barrier was secure, the blonde Berserker curiously regarded the sacks of goo, the skeletons inside, and the little worms floating among the bones. "If there were already people in this world—adventurers, I guess you'd call them—what kind of civilization did they have? How long have the beetles and larvae been here? What about the fossil record?"

"I didn't even consider that!" Reuben mimed his head exploding. "Mind. Blown. What do you say, big cheese?"

"I've found that it is best not to think too much about the

'how' of the Juxtaposition or the Starter World. The bottom line is that we fought Tier zero monsters, there's loot to be collected, and I better start learning how to cook. First of all, let's spend our windfall of credits sooner rather than later. We need to get you two upgraded as fast as possible."

Reuben rolled his eyes. "Come on, man. You must have *some* theory about all the fossil records."

"I do, but now's not the time. Short version: the Patrons, who created the world, have an interest in epic fantasy tropes and dungeon lore, so they whipped up a planet where they could observe us playing out various nerdy scenarios. All the while, they sit watching, maybe taking bets, or maybe just making themselves laugh over the deaths of innocent people. How's that?"

"You should have just stuck with 'I'd rather not say'." Reuben wrinkled his nose. "Bleak, man. That's super bleak."

"We need to find a way to fight back against those things," Brie declared with righteous anger. "The Patrons, that is."

"They are *giving* us our abilities, Brie." The cook sighed as he was forced to delve into one of the biggest debates that would spark rage through the entirety of the Apocalypse. "Let's be realistic. Someone who is granting you power isn't going to give you the tools you need to overthrow them. It's the same thing the government did back on our world; you can get a great education, but no one is going to *give* you the knowledge that you need in order to change their system."

"Just like that, we're back to super bleak," Reuben calmly joined in.

"Welcome to the Juxtaposition." Nacho held up a hand, stopping any further comments. "Treasure first, then we go shopping for Skill levels, and then we make our way to the next dungeon. We don't want to go too deep here; the deeper you go, the worse the monsters become. We don't have the tools we need to go much further than we already have."

"I'll make a note of it." Reuben regarded the foot-long worms suspended in the glowing goo bags. His eyes flashed blue as he used the System View. "What we have here are Gummy Grublings, and they're Tier zero animals, but I'd imagine they wouldn't be too tough to kill. Brie, would you do the honors?"

"I was going to say they kind of looked like gummy worms. Except, you know, with more teeth." Brie used her dagger to cut open a goo sack, draining the fluid. The Grublings, three in all, screamed at her with round, teeth-filled mouths, but that was the extent of their defensive capabilities. She made short work of them with her hatchet.

"Exactly one credit each." The Berserker shook the fluid off her blade. "Not bad. I don't suppose we could buy a meal with that? I still feel hungry."

Nacho thought about telling her to get used to the feeling, but he stopped and reminded himself that he did not have to be quite as cautious with food this time around... hopefully. The whole point of his class was that the people around him would no longer have to starve and only eat when absolutely necessary. Instead of explaining all of that out loud, he reached inside the drained sack to remove the skeleton and gingerly lay it on the floor.

He was given a list of items when he scanned the sack:

- *Simple chain shirt (non-magical and heavy)*
- *Rusted helm*
- *Leather belt*
- *Unremarkable boots that we shall not remark upon.*
- *Tier 0 Weapon: Splatter Mallet (Imbued with Mysterious Unknown Enchantments) x2*

It was basic stuff, all except the two 'Splatter Mallets', which looked like a pretty wicked weapon: a two-handed hammer with four dull knobs on each end of the chunky head. Brie picked up the weapon, undeterred by the grubling goop on its haft. Her eyes sparked with excitement as she took a practice swing. "Let me try this System View thing... it's a Tier zero weapon, so I guess that's good, right? Minor enchantment. Do I know what that is?"

"Once you use it, you should get the information on what it does pretty quickly." Nacho noticed she was holding the weapon as naturally as if she'd been born with it. "Otherwise you need to buy an info pack on this type of hammer, have the Patrons decide to tell you, or you purchase the Inspect Skill, which sometimes just doesn't work."

"Sounds like a good way to pick up a cursed weapon." Reuben stated aloud, as he rubbed his chin in thought.

Nacho nodded at that, but before he could say more, Brie gave the hammer a few practice swings and stated, "Pretty sweet. You know, it kind of feels like my old lacrosse stick. The handle does, at least, but the big hammer end, not so much. I'm surprised it doesn't feel... heavier?"

Reuben had his knife out and was standing next to the other sack. "I would think that's part of the enchantment. Do you want to give it a try on the next batch of worms? I'll cut open the sack, and we can let the worms spill out. Nacho-Cheese-meister, do we have to worry about anything undead?"

"Only if there are necromancers around. As far as I know, no zombies or anything like that naturally occur in the world." Nacho lifted the helmet and pondered where the closest river was, so they could clean off the items. "Mostly, we'll face monster animals, like Earth animals, only more grotesque."

"Monster cows?" Reuben idly wondered, making Nacho freeze in place. "You know cows kill more people than sharks per year?"

"Yeah... definitely monster cows." He shuddered as he considered telling them about the first Calamity, but he didn't want to ruin their mental state this early; not when things were starting to go well. It was too early.

Brie held the maul, perfectly poised to practice mauling some poor buggies. Reuben sliced open the bag, and five of the Gummy Grublings sank to the bottom. He yanked out the skeleton, moving quickly to avoid the round, squealing mouths of the foot-long worms as they came slopping out.

The Berserker slammed her mallet down, crushing two worms with one blow. The others writhed about in confusion, but she took care of them in rapid succession. "They only have three health each, and I'm doing *twenty-one* points of damage with each swing. What does that tell us?"

Nacho pondered the implications for a second. "You have ten in Fitness, which is giving you an additional five percent of damage. I would think that hammer would have a base damage of ten, but if you're doing twenty-one points, that means the hammer... doubles the damage? That is a *great* weapon, we need to figure out what restrictions it has."

"Not bad at all." Brie joined them in analyzing the skeleton's items after finishing off the final squirmer, smiling a slightly disturbing smile the entire time.

- *Simple chain shirt (non-magical but sparkly)*
- *Tier 0 Armor: Leather Helm of Helming*
- *Thin belt, big buckle*
- *Sandals that were fashionable at one point but now are embarrassing (do not wear with socks)*
- *Tier 0 Weapon: Splatter Mallet (Imbued with Mysterious Unknown Enchantments)*

"Hold on now, I *like* wearing socks with sandals." Reuben lifted the footwear. "I know I don't wear the look well, so... at this point, if these aren't magical, I'll stick with my boots. Gotta say though, I *love* that helmet. Helm of Helming? What does that even mean?"

"Maybe your fashion sense will kill your enemies for you. It'll certainly keep people from seeing us together." Brie shook her head at her groom, wincing as she thought of their lives together.

"You...!"

"After seeing how great it worked for Brie, I want this bad

boy," Nacho enthusiastically interrupted as he picked up the second hammer, the twin of the one in the Berserker's hands. Sadly, the instant he lifted it, the entire weapon glowed with a golden light and shrank, losing the pointed knobs as both ends became perfectly flat.

The System flashed a message in his eyes.

Item Update!
Tier 0 Weapon = Splatter Millet
Congratulations, Satiation Player!
You gain bonus damage against grains and wheat products!

"At least I know what it does, but…" Nacho clenched his eyes shut in confusion, taking a calming breath as his friends began to chortle. "The Splatter *Millet?*"

Then it hit him. Since he was a Satiation Player, items would update to match his class. He'd heard rumors of items changing to correspond to different Body or Mind classes, but this was the first time he had actually experienced it.

Reuben kept snickering as he watched their seemingly-all-knowing friend stare at the hammer in his hand with shock. "It's small now, perfect for your little baby hands!"

"Size doesn't matter. Just makes it look bigger when I'm holding it." Nacho tried to play off his hesitation as he hefted the item, which had been reduced to the size of a meat tender-izer. "Besides, I'll be facing demon millet someday, not animal versions of monsters, right? It's a cooking item now. It's strange, granted, but… small grains beware?"

Brie scooped grub goop off her arm and slung it at him. "Enough with the jokes! The Patrons try to kill our bodies with monsters and our spirits with puns. Don't help them."

"We can defeat them by *embracing* puns and letting them nourish our hearts!" Reuben argued on behalf of all the terrible jokes remaining in the world. Nacho ignored the playfully bickering lovers and moved to the third grub sack, the last bag that held a body. Naturally, they would go through the others and wipe out the remaining Gummy Grublings just to get the credits, but this was likely the most important.

To Reuben's delight, the base sagged from the weight of a pile of gold coins, and he abruptly broke off his debate with Brie as he happily scooted over to peer inside. "Treasure!"

"You'd think so, wouldn't you?" This time, Nacho was the one to cut open the sack and snatch out the skeleton. Four more Grublings were turned into paste on the floor, earning Brie four additional credits. They'd killed twelve of the overgrown gummy worms so far.

Reuben began enthusiastically scooping out the gold coins, despite their slimy state. Nacho was more interested in the skeleton, as he knew the truth about the 'treasure'.

- *Seventy-six gold coins*
- *Rusted scale mail (non-magical, unwearable, and awkwardly worthless)*
- *Gold circlet of skull squeezing (non-magical and uncomfortable)*
- *Belt that does nothing but hold your pants up*
- *Boots (Pretty good but probably not worth your time because they won't heel you)*
- *Gauntlets of Monster Destruction (Magical? Yes! Punch me, I'm dreaming!)*

Nacho noted all the exclamation points, then remembered that Reuben's most favorite thing in the world was the berserk powerup in the Goom video game—not to be confused with his new Berserker girlfriend. Reuben was too caught up in the gold to notice the gauntlets. "Nacho, let me guess. One gold coin equals one System credit. We're rich!"

"Ah, to be so naive." The cook picked up the gauntlets and patted his friend's shoulder. "We *all* thought gold was going to be super important. We were wrong. You can melt it down to make things pretty, and we *should* take it for trade. It'll act as a currency for a couple of months until the smarter people realize it's just a soft metal. Basically worthless."

Reuben sighed and tossed the coins into the air, catching them with a bright **clink**. "Let me guess. Only System credits make the world go 'round."

"You got it." Nacho slammed the big metal gloves into his friend's chest. "You wanna try these on? They might be right up your alley."

The big guy finally checked the loot drop. "I kinda like the boot puns. Also… how do we know these gauntlets aren't cursed? This is the kind of system that would have super cursed items. I don't trust these Patron guys."

"You're not wrong to be on the lookout for that stuff, which is why people are sure to specialize as appraisers after things settle down a little, but we won't find many cursed items initially." Nacho nodded his head, impressed by his friend's on-point paranoia. "That is a good thing to keep in mind. Things changed, the deeper we went. The Patrons started with providing relatively safe stuff. It took us a while to figure out that they were just lulling us into a false sense of security."

Brie rested the hammer on her shoulder. "Try them on—I liked the 'punch me, I'm dreaming' joke."

Things are looking up. I have to get close, but this should be fun." Reuben took the gauntlets and slipped on one, then the other, and made a fist. His eyes turned blue as he tried to access more info on his Gauntlets of Monster Destruction. "I'm not getting anything other than a comment about 'putting my dukes up'. Not helpful."

A creepy chittering echoed from the tunnel down below, making the hair on the back of Nacho's neck stand up. "That is our cue to get out of here. We can throw some of the better items into our Storage Slots until we can find a stream to wash them off, and then try them on."

Reuben decided to keep the leather helm and the chainmail that was non-magical and heavy. Brie selected the rusted helm and the *sparkly* chainmail, which was lighter and prettier. They stashed the gold in their Storage Slots, where it stacked into a single space. It desperately needed to be washed before they put it on.

Nacho kept an eye on the barricade while Brie and Reuben blew through the rest of the Gummy Grublings. There were an additional fourteen monster worms, which brought their total pool to two hundred and twenty-nine credits. As they walked through the dead Candylicious Weta Beetles, the cook sighed at the sight of the monsters turning into puddles. "Abyss it all."

"What's wrong, Nacho?" Brie stood with the Splatter Mallet propped on her hip, and Nacho remembered seeing her a hundred times in that same pose with a lacrosse stick.

"It's the Putrid Mana. I forgot how fast it corrupts the meat. I missed my chance to try out my Ingredient Processing ability. Again." He toed one of the beetle pools and huffed.

Brie grimaced and eyed the melting bugs with disgust. "You missed your chance to eat bugs? I think you'll live."

"We won't survive *long-term* if I don't figure out this Common Cook class," Nacho grumped at her, then took several calming inhalations and tried to stay positive. "We still have food, so I'm not *too* worried. At Tier zero, food is pretty easy to find. Even so, I don't think we should spend our credits on meals when we have another option. Especially when we could spend that income on increasing our Skills or levels. I can't *believe* I'm not getting credits from combat, but… I think the MurderSong Blades might change that."

Nacho remembered that Myron, his rival in the Gorged guild, had bragged that his knives could do all sorts of things. Maybe they could even allow a Satiation Player to get credits from combat? The trio returned to the antechamber and found their gear exactly where they'd left it. While not surprising, it was always good to know that someone hadn't arrived and rifled through their belongings.

The cook dropped his backpack and began to gather up the supplies he'd left there. "Let's pack up and start off for another dungeon. We'll hide the entrance to the Deep Buggy Darkness a little better so we can come back when we're more powerful. At this stage, just running the initial chambers is going to be our best bet on leveling without getting killed."

Reuben *clicked* his new gauntlets together, the sound muted thanks to all the slime it was coated in. "The anti-completionist strategy? Take what you can, until you can take it all. I like it."

Once they were packed, they left the antechamber and gathered more wood to toss over the roots of the Oilbark tree, causing the ground to look like just another deadfall. Brie inspected the work critically before smiling at the two men in her life. "You're getting pretty good at weaving logs."

Reuben sniffed the air. "Campfires up above. I can smell someone cooking something, but for some reason, it doesn't smell so good."

Nacho had also caught the distinct scent of cooked Putrid Mana, a hint of sulfur like raw eggs, along with a slightly chemical tinge. Those random people up there would learn the rules of the world quickly, with or without his intervention. "That would be the Putrid Mana."

"You keep saying those two words." Brie reminded him once more that he hadn't explained what was going on very clearly. "Is this some nerd culture thing? I need more than you're giving."

"We can talk while we walk." Nacho abruptly turned and led them away, south of Armor Mountain.

"I hate that we're not telling those people what's in store for them," Reuben grumbled as he gave his leader a sidelong glance. "What's our policy on dealing with other people? We're sure to run into someone eventually, right?"

Nacho didn't turn around, not wanting to reveal that he had been agonizing over that decision. "We keep to ourselves for right now. The initial Juxtaposition sucked for everyone, but it sucked more for some people than others. We have an opportunity to *eventually* help people, but we need to be smart about it.

Before I talk with *anyone*, there's a couple of artifacts I want to secure."

"Fine," Reuben reluctantly acquiesced. "We'll keep to ourselves for now, and I'm guessing these artifacts are knives?"

That surprised Nacho, which caused him to involuntarily stop and turn. "How did you know?"

Reuben stopped as well, visibly perplexed by the fact that *Nacho* was surprised that he had worked it out. "You've spent the past six months as 'Mister Knife Guy'. Kinda makes sense you would be searching for magic knives, but I thought we were going to do some shopping? We have a buttload of credits to spend. Also, correct me if I'm wrong, but didn't you tell us that the terrible watermelon you found was the last one on the planet?"

Nacho followed his chin thrust with his eyes, sighting a watermelon growing out of a thick mud hole. It looked a lot like the previous one, though this vine was far healthier and the melon looked less ripe. "You know, I threw the seed this way. Eh... it was all rind anyway. Maybe that's something else? Not worth going into the mud to check."

"What if we-"

Brie uncapped her water bottle and took a loud *slurp* to interrupt the jabbering. "Let's discuss our options on the road? We'll want to find a defensible position before nightfall."

"Great point." Nacho was relieved that she had jumped into the situation. Even with having her clothes shredded and being thrust into hand-to-hand combat, she seemed to be handling things well. "We can ask ourselves: 'to Brie, or not to Brie'."

"You're *sharp*, Brie." Reuben joined in on the compliments, the two men high-fiving as their Berserker rolled her eyes.

CHAPTER SEVENTEEN

The Dinner Party soon found a river winding its way through greenery, and stopped on the bank to wash their chainmail, helmets, and gore-coated weapons. Reuben took extra long washing his hands, as he had been wearing the gauntlets as soon as he found them.

Nacho set up a quick fire, perching his pot on two stones to start the process of boiling water. Brie pulled the sparkly chainmail over her torn shirt, and the armor shrank to fit her. Unlike in 'the Ew', even though her arms were bare, they'd still be protected by the shirt, thanks to this world's physics. She couldn't get the rust off the helmet, but once she put it on, it changed in hue to match her sparkly chainmail armor. Aside from her new pants and her combat boots, she looked downright heroic.

As for Reuben, the leather Helm of Helming had the absolute opposite effect. He gazed into the water, complaining loudly. "*Ma~a~n*, I look like Peasant Number Three in a historical drama—and not a good one. More like a season eight episode where they just cast homeless people and don't let them smile so they can hide their teeth."

"One good thing that came out of this: you're not watching anywhere *near* as much television as you used to watch," Brie muttered just loud enough to be heard.

"*Hey*, I still aced my classes!"

"Tell that to your 'C' in Economics!"

Ignoring the childishly bickering couple, Nacho fed another stick into his fire. Once the pot boiled, he poured the sterilized water into one of their metal bottles, then got another pot going immediately as Reuben tried to adjust his helmet.

Somehow, every position seemed to make him look worse. "The chainmail makes me look chunky."

"But will it keep you alive?" Brie questioned him drolly as she eased herself onto a flat rock on the other side of the fire. Her spirits were noticeably improved since she'd cleaned off her face and pulled her hair back. "Tell us about Putrid Mana. Is that why you're boiling the water? Or are we just dealing with normal bacteria?"

"Yeah, Nacho, can you *explain* why you are doing what you're doing?" Reuben joined them by the fire, his eyes glowing blue. "I'm checking the Store, and water seems to be *real* cheap. One credit for sixty-four ounces. That's a half a gallon to share between the three of us."

"Food and water aren't a problem for a while," Nacho agreed as he fed the fire with a stick. "But we don't want to use the Store unless we have no other choice. For now, Putrid Mana is everywhere: in the animals, in the plants, and in the water. Putrid Mana is what turns the flora and fauna into monsters— and yes, that includes bacteria. At Tier zero, the Putrid Mana just makes us queasy, but the higher the Tier, the more dangerous it becomes."

Reuben set his water bottle in the sand, looking pensive. "We smelled whatever meat those people at the top of Armor Mountain were cooking, and it smelled like sewage on a plate. That was the Putrid Mana?"

"Yep." Nacho nudged some coals under the... not a pot. The saucepan. Who knew there was a difference?

"Tier one animals would make us sick if we ate them?" Brie questioned as she glanced back in the direction they had come from. "So those people...?"

"If sick means *dead*, then yeah, eating Tier one things would make us 'sick'." Nacho carefully avoided looking into their faces. "But those people back there probably won't die from what they ate; yet they *are* forming bad habits. You don't want to have to experience what it is like to eat that, and *we* won't. Right now, a lot of people are desperate because they cannot figure out how to open the Store, but you had me around to explain it to you right away. The bad habit I am trying to keep you from acquiring is the ease of access that the Store provides. I can keep us fed on Tier zero monsters, and when we level, we'll be able to deal with the food situation."

"Tier this, Tier that; can you just explain yourself, *please?*" Brie snapped at him while gazing at the mountain, where she could have sworn she still saw smoke from a campfire rising.

"I'm sorry." Nacho couldn't help himself from keeping things from them; it was all just so... dark. "It's just so hard to remember that you don't know the most basic basics yet. This one is at least easy to explain. A 'Tier' is a qualitative change that occurs in both people and monsters every tenth level. That means level nine is still effectively Tier zero, which is why monsters under ten have been showing up as something like 'monster level: zero five', instead of just displaying a five. Upon reaching level ten, you're Tier one, level zero, and guess what? Tier zero food doesn't do anything for you anymore."

Brie frowned in consternation. "What do you *mean*, it doesn't do anything for you? Food is food."

"What I mean is that it does nothing to affect your Hunger points," Nacho explained somberly. "If you only had fifty Hunger points, and you ate an entire bull in a single swallow, you'd still be at half your Hunger points."

"Food just... stops working?" Brie shook her head, unable to understand how that was possible. "That's so messed up."

"Okay, so you just buy Tier one food." Reuben was back to

searching the Store. "Oh... I get it. At least, I *think* I get it, Nacho. Tier one food costs ten *times* what Tier zero food does. That's terrible. A Tier one donut is *thirty credits?*"

"You have no idea how bad it got." Nacho released a shuddering breath, trying to keep his hands from shaking. "*We* didn't know. All these superhero warriors that we collectively thought were going to be the leaders of humanity... they hit level ten and almost instantly began to starve to death. They were *all* forced to use their credits on food because they couldn't eat Tier one animals; the concentration of Putrid Mana was too high. A lot of people died trying before they found... alternatives."

He paused to let that information percolate, then forcefully attempted to lighten the mood. "For now, all we need to do is boil the Tier zero water, which kills the bacteria and removes the nastiness, and I'll start cooking. Let me check our credits."

He glanced at that part of his stat sheet:

Eli 'Nacho' Naches
    Class: Common Cook
    Level: 0
    Experience Points: 100 to Level 1!
    Current Credits: 6 (229 total Dinner Party pool)
    Build Type: Balanced, Delayed

Nacho chuckled dryly. "Not to brag, but an entire *six* credits of our party pool are from me."

"Please," Brie scoffed haughtily, joining in a beat late as she realized what Nacho was doing, "don't brag. You don't even *want* to know how many of the credits are from me."

"Peace and love, friends. We *are* in this together. *Aww.*" Reuben reached out and squeezed his fiancée's arm. "Two hundred and twenty-nine credits turns into a hundred and fourteen-point-five experience points. One of us can get to level one... so who should it be?"

"Skills first," Nacho denied his friend with a quick shake of his head. "I have my reasons."

Reuben scrunched up his face in disbelief. *"Really?* But we'll get more stat points!"

"Without a doubt, this is the right plan. Trust me: this cheese used to stand alone. I've learned everything the hard way." Nacho adjusted the fire as his saucepan of water reached the verge of boiling. "Leveling your class gives you improved stats, yes. However, it *also* comes with a hefty price tag. Everything becomes more expensive and more complicated, which means it's better to upgrade Skills first, as you're going to get more combustion for your credit."

"I think I get it; it is basic investment snowballing." Brie tapped on her hammer as she processed the concept out loud. "Upgrading Skills, especially my combat Skills, will help me dish out more damage right off the bat. More damage, more kills, more credits."

"Exactly," Nacho agreed with her, grinning with relief at being understood. "Upgraded Skills also let you take down more *powerful* creatures, meaning you will earn more credits.

Reuben snapped his fingers and pointed at Nacho. "Upgrade those Skills even more, and you'll eventually increase your level, which means you'll have to increase your Skills. It sounds like a vicious cycle, but if we start early, we will be able to afford the cost later on! Especially if we are not spending… *that's* why! I totally get why you want us to only eat the food you can make us!"

"Everyone plays life in hard mode. 'If you fail to plan, you plan to fail.'" Nacho stated softly, a counterpoint to his friend's enthusiasm. "Here's a more modern saying I came up with: 'if you aren't planning ahead, you end up trapped in an inescapable vortex of doom instead of snowballing toward greatness. Then you're dead'."

Reuben grimaced as he realized that he had fallen for the idea of convenience, just as his buddy was warning them would happen. "Hey, dude, you're the guy who had Probability Vision.

It's just... that's backward from any game I've ever played. Leveling your class was the point, and you did your skills kinda whenever."

"Some people figured it out." Nacho's voice was hollow as he replied. "But just like you're saying, most of us rushed to level our classes, and improving our stats really did help at first. The fact is, it's just better not to worry about your stats, and focus on your Skills instead. It's like Build Type. Those who chose Self-Applied were all excited to level their class and start cranking up certain stats, but it isn't the best strategy for long-term success."

Brie was listening intently, but her eyes glazed over at the mention of Build Type, so Nacho chuckled as she muttered, "Let's just focus on our Skills, yeah?"

Reuben rubbed his hands together in excitement. "Yeah! I want to be able to use my Skills and not stay a level zero experience leech."

Nacho checked the Store, then took a stick and scribbled some math in the wet sand of the riverbank. "It costs ten Skill Points, multiplied by the skill level, to level up an ability. Each Skill Point is worth two credits, so it basically goes twenty credits, then forty, then sixty, and so on. If we all wanted to level up all of our Skills to at least the first level right now, it would be forty credits for Brie, since she's already at level one with Defensive Whirl. We'd normally divide it into sixty credits for me and Reuben, *except* for the fact that Reuben's Marketing Skill just isn't a priority at this stage."

Reuben clutched at his chest as if he had been betrayed and stabbed in the heart. "You say that, Nacho, but what happens when we lose *market share?*"

"We'll burn that bridge when we get to it." Nacho briefly pondered the best way to move forward. "I'm honestly not sure if leveling up any of my Skills makes sense. Except for Small Blades. But even then, if I can't get credits through kills... it might be a waste."

Brie interjected just before he could announce that he

wouldn't be taking a share of the credits. "Being level zero with any Skill can't help us. Except, yes, maybe we ignore Reuben's overly expensive Marketing degree. That one costs you five percent Mana, Dehydration, and Metabolism across the board?"

Reuben shrugged and nodded. "Yeah."

Nacho drew the information out in the sand.

Brie:

- *Athletic Endurance = 20 credits*
- *Combat Dash = 20+40 credits*
- *Defensive Whirl = 40 credits*

Reuben:

- *Healing Hugs = 20 credits*
- *Positive Vibes = 20 credits*

Nacho:

- *Small Blades = 20 credits*
- *Ingredient Processing = 20 credits*
- *Cooking Magic = 20 credits*

"This look correct to everyone?" Nacho checked his work as they read. "That's a total of two hundred and twenty, but we'll bring all of our Skills to at least at level one—except Reuben and his highly suspect ability to market—and Brie will be at level two in her two most important Skills. We'll have nine credits left."

"Let's make it happen." Brie stood and her eyes turned blue as she accessed the Store, pointing her index finger like a grandma on a new-fangled smartphone. "I'm going to use a hundred and twenty credits to buy sixty Skill Points."

Nacho's water started boiling, but he ignored it in favor of savoring the momentous occasion. "You can just think of what you want to do, Brie. The System can understand your intentions."

"Right. Kinda like Am-Prime's one-click shopping." Brie sucked in a breath and began her spending spree. "I'm going to level up my Combat Dash first. Are we ready?"

"So ready!" Reuben grinned enthusiastically as he encouraged her to become more powerful.

"Using credits from The Dinner Party to upgrade my Skills. Go!" A second later, her glowing blue eyes turned golden, as did her skin. "Athletic Endurance is at level one. Combat Dash has been raised from level one to level two. Last but not least, Defensive Whirl is at level two as well. I'm feeling better, faster, stronger. This is amazing."

Reuben swept her up in a hug, swinging her around as they both celebrated their excitement... that brought on some intense kissing. Nacho grimaced, turning away and filling metal bottles with boiling water.

The Healer—who couldn't yet heal—dropped his bride to the ground and waved his arms in the air like a kindergartener as she yelped. "Me next. I'm ready to start striving toward ultimate power!"

Like Brie, the big guy gleamed with a golden light as he dumped credits into the Store to buy Skill Points, then poured those into his Skills. Once he'd brought both of his useful Skills to level one, he made a fist, and the harmless golden energy crackled around him before dissipating. "Sweet. You're up, Nacho."

The cook stood, a half-grin on his face as he got ready to boost his Skills. In his opinion, this was the best part of the new world. He accessed The Dinner Party's credits, relieved that he was able to move over sixty credits from their shrinking pool.

He brought up his Stat Sheet:

Eli 'Nacho' Naches
Class: Common Cook

Level: 0
Experience Points: 100 to Level 1!
Current Credits: 6 (69 total Dinner Party pool)

Build Type: Balanced, Delayed
Body:

- *Fitness: 10*
- *Metabolic efficiency: 10*

Mind:

- *Mental energy: 10*
- *Circuit: 10*

Satiation:

- *Hunger: 100*
- *Thirst: 100*

Total Health Points: 30
Bonus Physical Damage: 5%
Health Regen: 10% Health Regen/minute
Total Mana Pool: 25
Bonus Spell Damage: 5%
Mana Pool Regen: 10% Mana Regen/minute

Skill Slots (3/4)

- *Small Blades (Passive) Level 0: 0% bonus damage on all knife attacks!*

    No Mana, Hydration, or Metabolic Cost

- *Ingredient Processing (Active) Level 0: Remove Putrid Mana from monsters up to level 2!*

173

Mana Cost = 5%
Hydration Cost = 5%
Metabolic Cost = 5%

- *Cooking Magic (Active) Level 0: Cook food that enhances a single stat by 0% of maximum!*

Mana Cost = 5%
Hydration Cost = 5%
Metabolic Cost = 5%

- *Open slot*

He applied the Skill Points to Small Blades first, enjoying the tingles as they flowed through his body, starting in his hands. Nacho was rapidly filled with golden light, tied directly into the Juxtaposition's gaming system. There weren't any chatty messages waiting for him, and he was grateful for that.

There was only a simple:

Would you like to upgrade your Small Blades Skill?
Yes / No

He knew the answer to this question. "Yes."

- *Small Blades (Passive) Level 1: 2% bonus damage on all knife attacks.*

No Mana, Hydration, or Metabolic Cost

He made the same selection with his other Skills, and in the end, he had improved... but he didn't know if spending the credits had been worth it to get the minor improvements. Nacho wasn't an experienced Satiation Player, so he had no idea if he was choosing the best build, but all he could do was follow his gut.

- *Ingredient Processing (Active) Level 1: Remove Putrid Mana from monsters up to Level **3**!*

  Mana Cost = 5%
  Hydration Cost = 5%
  Metabolic Cost = 5%

- *Cooking Magic (Active) Level 1: Cook food that enhances a single stat by **5%** of maximum.*

  Mana Cost = 5%
  Hydration Cost = 5%
  Metabolic Cost = 5%

Nacho's whole body was vibrating with power after the upgrade. His eyes lazily drifted to his friends, and he told them the very iffy news. "I don't know if I did the right thing by becoming a Common Cook."

"We'll just have to try it out," Brie contradicted him, ending that line of conversation with, "Food and water are going to be extremely important in the game. You know that. Don't doubt yourself."

A subdued Nacho returned to his place by the fire, not having anything else to say. "Give me some good news. What are the amazing things you both can do?"

Brie, having just spoken, was poised to continue. "Thanks to my level one Athletic Endurance, I get a *two* percent reduction to hunger loss penalties when using a physical Skill, which in my case is all of them. I'll deal an additional four percent of damage on my Combat Dash, and my Defensive Whirl stays the same—but I can automatically fully block up to a single attack. I think I will be able to block two additional attacks at level three."

She tapped at her invisible status screen for a moment, stopping and blushing lightly when Nacho chuckled at her. His amusement couldn't dampen her excitement, though, and she powered through. "You know, it's interesting. Combat Dash and Defensive Whirl only cost me eight percent of my Hunger—or thirteen Hunger Points, respectively—because of my Athletic Endurance. If all of these increase, that can *really* come in handy as I level up. I think that's going to be my best bet for raising Skills: focusing on my Athletic Endurance."

"Not so fast." Nacho could totally see the possibilities, but he could also spot a few problems with that strategy. "Cost reduction is great, but we need you to be doing as much damage as possible, especially if we start facing higher-level monsters. Upgrading your Skills gets more and more expensive, so if we pour credits into Athletic Endurance, that's going to take away from our other options. While you might be able to Combat Dash on the cheap, if you're not doing more damage per strike... it wouldn't matter. We need to keep Brie's Athletic Endurance in mind, but that's *after* the other Skills are upgraded to a more useful point."

Reuben tossed a twig at his friend. "There goes Nacho, ruining our fun like always. Want to take a turn at killing my excitement about my super cool level one newbie abilities? Great. Every hug straight up gives you five Health Points. *Bam.* Every hug. Every time. Until I get too thirsty to hug."

"*Five* Health Points?" Nacho wondered aloud, causing Reuben to tense up... until the cook let out a low whistle. "That's a *lot* for the first level. Are you sure it's not five *percent?*"

Reuben shot an 'are you serious' look at him. "No? Why did you think I chose Healing Hug in the first place? We're not talking percentages here, we're talking a full five points, and you're right, that's just level one. I'll be doing full body heals by the time I'm fifth level. Yes, it takes a close-range hug to do it, but it won't be long before I'll be a full-service Healer."

"Color me impressed," Nacho relented with a relaxed sigh. "That'll be a ton of help."

Brie didn't see why it was such a big deal. "Such nerds. It's *five* points of health. I hit for, like, five times that amount of damage."

"But wait, there's more. It gets even better." Reuben was all smiles; clearly, he'd been goading her into speaking out. "When I rub my cheery disposition off on you, as in Positive Vibes, you'll get a deadly *two* percent more out of your physical attacks. Gonna juice up my baby and unleash her onto the world."

"Don't use 'baby' and 'juice' in the same sentence." Brie shuddered theatrically, but she was grinning the entire time.

"Can you juice yourself?" Nacho watched his saucepan as the last of the water got up to temperature.

"I think so. Not orange juice, though. I'll *apple* juice myself, because OJ kills people." Reuben laughed at his own joke, uncaring that he was the only one who did. "Lastly, and most important… I learned something interesting when I actually took the time to read about my Marketing Skill. Even at level zero, I can use it to lure creatures to a certain location—as long as they are level one. Let's never forget the power of a good marketing plan."

"That *is* interesting… we'll keep that in mind." Nacho put out his fire, contemplating how to try out Reuben's comical Skill at some point. If he really could lure in unsuspecting level one monsters, they might be able to create another credit farm and increase themselves faster. "We'll test it out, then decide if it's worth keeping."

"*Yes*! I worked way too hard on that degree to see it vanish. What about your amazing kitchen Skills?" Reuben still had a goofy grin on his face, the leather Helm of Helming not doing anything to help him look any less absurd. "When are we going to see you in action?"

"Let's see if we can't find something for me to cook up after Brie does some killing," was Nacho's calmly diverting reply.

"I get to kill things again right away?" Brie popped to her

feet with the Splatter Mallet on her shoulder. "Sounds good to me. Let's see how different combat is with level one Skills."

"Calm down, killer." Laughing at her eagerness, Nacho started packing the water bottles away. "We'll *never* run out of things that need to be dead. Pace yourself."

CHAPTER EIGHTEEN

It was already noon by the time they had finished spending credits, filling their water bottles, and taking stock of their meals. They each had enough food remaining for three portions a day, for three days. Teriyaki beef jerky, protein bars, bags of raisins and peanuts, some instant oatmeal, and a few Meals Ready to Eat—better known as MRE's. They also had nine credits left, so they could buy meals, and they *probably* would, but Nacho wasn't looking forward to it. Store food was just... wrong.

The Dinner Party left the stream and continued down the southern path. Every once in a while, Nacho would peek back to verify that Armor Mountain was still behind them, not trusting his sense of direction. Every time he checked, the mound of limestone had grown smaller and smaller.

Brie had stored her chainmail, since walking around in jingling metal didn't make much sense, especially *sparkly* jingling armor. She'd also threaded a strap on her backpack through her helmet to carry it more easily. Reuben had likewise put away his chainmail, but his leather helm wasn't overly heavy, so he kept it on.

Tragedy of tragedies—yet at the same time, unsurprisingly —the guy had fallen in love with the silly-looking thing.

Nacho wondered if the helm was cursed, until he remembered Reuben's unfortunate history with hats. He'd had a fedora in high school and wasn't even slightly shy about wearing it with shorts, a long-sleeve shirt, and crocs. That had been the year their friendship had survived its most difficult test.

The cook's mind drifted to their destination. If Myron had bragged accurately, he'd found the MurderSong Blades early on, hidden in a strange dungeon under a waterfall in the southwestern part of the AKC. Since the population of Kansas City had appeared in the same region of the Starter World, they'd basically transported the names from Kansas City to the new world. South of Armor Mountain lay Indian Creek, which stretched down to the Hallbrook Ponds before curving northward. The MurderSong Dungeon was actually behind Tomahawk Falls, down at Tomahawk Creek.

That was the exact location The Dinner Party was planning to use for their exclusive event.

Later in the afternoon, they found another rocky bluff with an overhang of granite to use as their campground for the evening. They opted to put their bedrolls in the back, and agreed to keep one person on watch as a lookout either at the entrance or up top.

Even better? They happened across a herd of Tier zero monsters: Wight-Tailed Deer. The creatures were standard deer, if you ignored their tails. The fluff was gone, and in its place, they had human arms—but white and chalky. Each corpse-arm appeared to be very useful. While they couldn't stretch to the mouths of the deer, the strange hands could shoo away flies, grab the limbs of opponents, or pull grass out by the roots, allowing the monster deer to then turn around and eat the bunch of leafy goodness.

Nacho crouched in the bushes underneath a tree covered in brightly-colored bark and used his System View to confirm his suspicions.

· · ·

Wight-Tailed Deer
  Effective Tier/Level: ?
  HP: ?

Brie recoiled in disgust. "*Yuck.* Is that an arm?"

"Wait a second… I think that one is writing a book with its dead hand." Reuben's eyes glowed blue for an instant. "Wight-Tailed Deer. That's a bad pun right there; I'm starting to like these Patrons. Love me a good, bad pun. Right, so, from what you told us, the single question mark means they're Tier zero, and it *looks* like they're still herbivores."

"That's correct. For now." Nacho spoke in a low tone, knowing whispering would be more attention-grabbing. "But there's Putrid Mana in the grass. As they eat more, they'll mutate up to Tier one. Then they won't be eating grass; they'll be trying to eat us. Some won't change, but every single one is going to get stronger, all because of the Putrid Mana. Let's kill and eat them first."

He sighed and handed Brie the bow. "You might as well practice—not like a kill on my end would earn us credits."

"I'm happy to take the shot." She took the bow and the subsequently offered arrow. "But never forget that *we* get the credits. We're here because of you. There's no way you're going to be allowed to remain weak as we get powerful."

"Thanks…" Nacho muttered with some unease. "I think I might actually be more nervous that I have to practice cooking."

Reuben patted him on the back as Brie tested the wind. 'Don't worry. It's only cooking. How hard could it be?"

Naho hoped his friend was right.

"Guys, quit talking and let me bring home dinner." Brie drew the bowstring back, waiting for one of the deer to turn perfectly. The most tasty-looking one was idly chewing on grass while its hand scratched at its thigh with jagged yellow fingernails. The Berserker lined up the perfect shot, yet she relaxed the bowstring, sweat dripping off her nose. "That arm coming out of its butt is freaking me out."

Reuben squinted as he tried to make out more details. "Technically, the arm is *above* its butt, not coming *out* of its butt. I can take over if you'd like? I'll get credits if I take it down, but you're the better shot."

"That's true," Brie agreed confidently.

"Another thing; why didn't I know you had this skill?" Reuben demanded with a slight chuckle. "Where on Earth did you learn archery, and why are you being so cagey about it?"

"Camp Sacagawea. Fifth grade. Archery unit." Brie's expression grew determined as she continued to watch the mutant ruminant. Releasing a controlled exhale, she drew back the string, took aim, and fired... the arrow struck home. The deer slumped to the ground while the other members of the herd fled. "I accidentally burned down about a hundred acres of forest trying to prank the boys."

Nacho started toward the distant meat while Reuben snickered at his fiancée's embarrassment. "They're still deer enough to run off? Good. In a year, they might charge us as a herd. Now, let's see what I can do with this Satiation ability."

Brie rubbed her reddened arm where the string had slapped her skin. "Well, we have eight more credits."

Reuben helped her down from her firing position. "That gives us seventeen credits total, but I don't get it. If a single arrow can kill a deer, it must only have five Health. Why is it worth eight credits?"

Nacho knew the answer to this one. Everyone did... no, everyone *had*. "Health Points aren't tied to credits; only levels and Tiers change what they're worth. That's good in the case of the deer, but bad when we start fighting nastier monsters. Kill something in a hit, earn just as much as spending all day fighting a tanky beastie."

Reuben helped him carry the big doe back to the rocks in

front of the overhang. Nacho had a vague idea of how to cook actual meat—apply heat and eat when it isn't bleeding anymore —and he'd watched a couple of UTube videos, but that was months ago. He checked the Store. There was an info pack called *Cleaning and Cooking your Favorite Ungulate*. It cost two hundred credits and was located under the 'Tier zero Class Item Gain' category. The info pack came with a recipe called 'Uncle Ron's Very Fine Venison'. That would be helpful... but only one recipe? That seemed like a rip-off.

Grumbling under his breath, he pulled up his Skill slots and went over the basic information on Ingredient Processing. It simply said:

Can remove Putrid Mana from monsters up to level 3.

He searched for more information, finally discovering an obscure note buried in the footnote of a page which clarified that all recipes were required to include at least three ingredients. "Three? One ingredient is the deer meat itself. What else could I add?"

Nacho knew that he needed to hurry before the Putrid Mana turned the animal into an inedible goo. Brie and Reuben stood watching him curiously, so he shooed them away self-consciously. "You're freaking me out. Uh, take watch, put together camp, or start boiling water?"

They left, but Nacho still felt the pressure to succeed. His imposter syndrome was hitting him like a sledgehammer. He *had* to get this right; he'd spent a fortune on becoming a Common Cook, and if this was just some Patron's ruse to make him lose everything, he'd never forgive himself. "I could be an Assassin with *amazing* Skills right now... what am I *doing*?"

With uncertain motions, he cut off the corpse-arm tail and threw it as far as he could into the forest, then found a basic price list for ingredients in the Store:

. . .

T0 ingredient=1
  T1 ingredient=10
  T2 ingredient=20
  T3 ingredient=40
  T4 ingredient=80

"Salt, pepper, garlic, even Herbs de Provence are all Tier zero ingredients? I know those words! Eh... most of them." Nacho wasn't going to take a chance on anything that sounded French just yet.

He broke down and used two credits to buy the salt and pepper, which came in nondescript plastic-feeling canisters, like most things from the Store. They appeared immediately in his two free Storage Slots, and he transferred them into his hand. Bright yellow packaging, blood red lettering—one marked with 'salt' and the other with 'pepper.' If cast aside, the plastic-ish material would last for a few days before melting away. If kept around, they would last indefinitely.

At least he got his money's worth—twenty-six ounces of salt and eighteen ounces of pepper. He set the canisters on a nearby rock and got a fire going: it was time to cook.

Nacho had to laugh at himself: he was *nervous*. Even when he'd chosen the Assassin route, when he'd backstabbed his first monstrous pig, he hadn't been this nervous. He had no idea why: after all, wasn't cooking just the chore you needed to do before eating?

CHAPTER NINETEEN

With a fire crackling merrily in front of their rocky overhang home, Nacho easily sliced off the back leg of the deer, thanks to his Small Blades ability. He peeled off the hide and set it aside —that seemed like the right thing to do. There was probably a tanning skill he could buy, or maybe an info pack on how to process deer leather? He'd get the cooking down first, then maybe tackle the leatherwork in a few years.

He glanced up at Brie, who stood above him on the rock to scan the horizon, bow in hand, while Reuben came back with more firewood.

"How's it going?" The big guy used his knee to snap a thick stick in half, a casual reminder that their bodies were no longer what they had once been.

Nacho cut off a slice of the meat, a pound at least, and dashed the salt and pepper on the chunk of flesh. It was pink and red and looked right—a steak in search of a backyard grill. "Not sure yet."

"How about a spit?" Reuben offered a stick he was holding. "We could do it old school."

"Let me just try to fry it on a rock." Nacho rubbed the spices on the meat. The sudden System message made him flinch, jerking his hand back.

Greetings, Satiation Player! Welcome to Active Cooking! It's like Active Combat, but this culinary chaos involves more butter... depending on how you fight, we suppose. During Ingredient Processing, or your more normal kitchen battles, you cannot access the Store. Both your Health and your Mana Regeneration have been paused. Good luck being delicious!

You have purchased two ingredients (salt and pepper) and acquired a third, which is full of Putrid Mana. Not so great for the bowels, am I right? Wanna start the process of eliminating the Putrid Mana from your newly harvested Wight-Tailed Deer meat?

Yes / No.

Nacho had no idea what was going on, but he remembered seeing something about this at the Evaluation Mall. He'd grown accustomed to Active Combat over the years, but Active *Cooking*? Were the Patrons serious? Regardless of his misgivings, he chose 'yes'.

The System message vanished, but not before the pound of deer meat glowed with a golden light and another cheery message popped up:

One whole pound of level 1 deer meat is being processed! You earn two credits!

Black goo oozed out of the meat, seemingly driven out by the golden light that Nacho had only just realized was a combination of Mana, Hunger, and Thirst points. He started to understand what was happening as the process continued, and found that he was able to push the power emitting from himself through the meat and into areas that were more densely packed with the filth. One pound of meat was not a large amount, but by the time the Putrid Mana had evaporated fully, he was sweating and shaking from the effort. He wiped his brow as the light vanished. "Abyss, I hope that gets easier with practice."

You have succeeded in draining the Putrid Mana from 1 pound of Wight-Tailed Deer meat! You earn two credits!

Side note, you might want to add ingredients after you force the Putrid Mana out of the meat. That salt and pepper... can't recommend eating it!

"That was... disgusting," Reuben commented from a few feet further away than he had been at the start of Nacho's Skill use. "How is there that much bacteria in that tiny chunk of food?"

"Not bacteria... it's mana." Nacho didn't want to argue the point; his hands were flying as he gathered the purified meat and shoved it into a Storage Slot. "It isn't exactly an organism, at least not fully. It's kinda like a virus that got mutated by a huge amount of dirty mana. I need to hurry; I have no idea how much longer I'll have to process the rest of this."

The deer meat was holding together nicely as he worked on the small amount, but he knew it wouldn't stay together indefinitely, certainly not with such a large amount of muscle tissue present. No one had spent much time figuring out the liquefaction mechanic, since it was pretty clear that eating monster meat wasn't a viable part of the game. All that meant was that at some point, Nacho would have to figure that out on his own; it would be totally new research that he could add to the world.

He knew enough about campfire cooking that the *coals* were what were used to cook; anything hotter would just burn the food. After studying the glowing pile for a moment, Nacho put a flat rock in the middle of the red coals, waited for it to radiate an even heat, and laid the deer steak on the surface, where it immediately started to sizzle. To his relief, it smelled good.

Mouthwateringly good.

The cook grinned and sprinkled fresh salt and pepper atop the steak. "Well, Reuben, I got a couple of credits for processing this little feast. I guess that's how I'm supposed to earn my share? It looks like it's cooking well."

"It smells like I'm standing outside of a medieval burger joint. You know, this one time, I-" Reuben stopped talking, sniffed, and pointed. "Uh, Nacho, this might sound strange, but your deer meat is… melting?"

The cook whipped his eyes back to the meal he was trying to create, feeling a spike of horror at the sight of the steak turning to fluid on the rock and dripping into the fire. The greasy runoff hissed in the fire and produced a huge amount of smoke, filling the entire area with the stink of burning meat.

"What just happened?" Nacho coughed, trying to wave the smoke away. Was it because he was only level one? Was the meat bad? Had he missed his window to make it work?

Worried that the black smoke would draw more monsters, Nacho grabbed his water bottle and upended it into the fire, the final ingredient needed to turn the mess of deer fluid and sizzling coals into a sludgy mud. At least the black smoke had shifted into huge white plumes.

Well, Cookie-Cook, your first round of Active Cooking was a disaster! Better luck next time! Active Cooking is over. You can access the Store once more, and your Health and Mana Regeneration will start immediately.

It took Nacho a minute to get to the message. He felt overwhelmed, shaken, and ready to admit to himself that this Satiation Player nonsense might have been the worst mistake he'd ever made. Then he calmed himself down, and drew on the core of steel that was his willpower. "No... someday I'll make enough meals to keep *everyone* full!"

The words made him recall that his skills required mana, and that Cooking Magic was *magic*. Not having Mana Regen while he cooked limited him in the number of ingredients he could process, and how much Cooking Magic he could add to his food.

The Patrons were clever. They were also evil.

Squinting through the last of the smoke with teary eyes, Brie called down to the two of them. "We're not being very inconspicuous, boys!"

Nacho wanted to grumble some rude words at her, but she was right. Reuben raised his voice but refrained from shouting. "Keep your eyes peeled; there must be other camps around here that are bigger, smellier, and noisier."

"Let's hope so," Nacho grunted as he reached for the butchered corpse once more. "I'm going to try this again on another fire. I'll be more careful this time. Maybe I can angle the rock away, so if the meat turns into liquid, it won't make so much of a mess?"

"Liquid meat! It's what's for dinner," Reuben fired one last dig at him before going to gather another set of firewood. Brie stayed on top of the overhang, keeping watch.

Whine.

The cook froze as the tiny sound reached his ears. It sounded like a... dog? There was no such thing here. His eyes scanned his surroundings, catching some motion at the edges of the firelight. Not wanting to make a scene, a knife twirled into his hand and he dashed across the distance like a streak of shadow. His blade plunged down, coming to a stop as his target flopped to its back in a show of submission and whined once more. "What is this?"

He was looking at a bright green... puppy. There was no other way to describe it. Nacho kept his knife against its neck as he peered around the surrounding meadow for more, but found nothing. A quick scan of the creature only revealed a series of question marks, as though the system was also confused by its existence. "Ah... shoo? Be gone. I don't want to stab a puppy, and I know you can't be tamed, since I'm not a monster tamer or farmer."

The puppy got to its feet and slowly ambled over to where Nacho had tried and failed to cook, then began lapping up the liquid meat failures. It shuddered and clearly found the taste disgusting, but took in as much as it could regardless. Licking the last droplets from its tiny green muzzle, it looked over at Nacho hopefully, letting out a little growl.

"I just *knew* you were going to get hostile." Hefting the knife once more instantly had the green puppy laying on its back, vine-like tail curled up to cover the stomach a little. Nacho stared at the monster, then lowered the knife and pointed. "*Get.*"

The monster puppy slowly left the area, looking back at him several times. "I know you're just trying to get me to lower my guard so that you can turn into something horrifying and scary, then eat me. Or I'll do something that sets you off and you reveal a hidden skill that kills me. Either way, I don't trust this situation. No. *Shoo.*"

There was a rustle of leaves as the puppy vanished. Finally alone, Nacho let out a sigh of relief and lit another fire near the first mess of a pit. He cut off another pound of meat and began the process of purifying the Putrid Mana. After a few minutes of mental struggle, he had a clean chunk of meat to salt, pepper, and place on a fresh rock angled away from the fire— gaining another two credits for his efforts. Just as he finished, the rest of the deer meat let out an evil **hiss** and deflated, turning into a foul sludge. "No third try, huh?"

Again, he got the System messages as he entered Active Cooking, but even though he felt that he had done everything correctly, the same thing happened. At least this time, the meat-goop ran into the dirt instead of onto the fire. "What am I doing *wrong*?"

Active Cooking ended with more gleeful sarcasm from the System. Nacho returned to the Store and found a section on

Common Cook-prepared meals, eventually discovering something interesting... if not helpful to his current situation. The grid displayed information such as recipe level, and how much he could charge per meal.

For level one recipes, he could charge six credits for any meal he made. As he had already found, all recipes required a minimum of three ingredients. A new chunk of information revealed that each dish prepared could feed *three* people.

Level *two* recipes were worth twelve credits, *three* were worth eighteen credits, and *fourth* level recipes were worth twenty-four credits. Nacho sat back and pondered his puddled steak. "I don't get it. Meat, salt, and pepper are three ingredients. I was able to process the ingredients; is it that I'm just a terrible chef? I mean, yes, but is there more to it?"

He went back to pondering the pricelist. In the end, when people bought his cooking, they'd be getting a good deal. A meal for three people for six credits? If they went to the Store, it was three credits for a single Tier one meal. For three, that would cost a total of nine credits, and it would be *Store* food— little better than cardboard with sauce on it.

There was only one problem: he couldn't cook anything.

Nacho took a stick and tipped the flat rock, sending the last of the deer smoothie to dribble onto the mud. At that precise moment, Reuben came ambling up with another armful of wood.

"Well, my friend, do you wanna eat our own food or shop at the Store tonight?" Nacho questioned defeatedly.

Reuben adjusted his obnoxious leather helmet. "It's our second night in the game. I say we celebrate!"

"Store food is *not* for celebrating." Nacho found himself hungry, thirsty, and grumpy about both of those things. A quick check of his Stat Sheet explained why.

Eli 'Nacho' Naches
Class: Common Cook
Level: 0

Experience Points: 100 to Level 1!
Current Credits: 9 (19 total Dinner Party pool)

Build Type: Balanced, Delayed
Body:

- *Fitness: 10*
- *Metabolic efficiency: 10*

Mind:

- *Mental energy: 10*
- *Circuit: 10*

Satiation:

- *Hunger: 90*
- *Thirst: 90*

Total Health Points: 30
Bonus Physical Damage: 5%
Health Regen: 9% Health Regen/minute
Total Mana Pool: 25
Bonus Spell Damage: 5%
Mana Pool Regen: 9% Mana Regen/minute

It took a minute to understand what was happening. He'd done two rounds of his Ingredient Processing ability, and at five percent each... that had used ten percent of his Mana, Hunger, *and* Thirst Points. He was still at ninety Hunger and Thirst Points, but his Mana was already back to full. Now that he was out of Active Cooking, he was getting nine percent of his Mana back per minute, a point under his maximum, because he'd used ten Thirst.

If his deer steaks *hadn't* turned to goo, he could've eaten some to keep his Hunger Points in check. He'd have to keep some Store water around to deal with the Thirst, but his Mana remained a limiting factor.

The next consideration: if a pound of deer steak was one ingredient, he wondered how much of the monster he could process before he ran out of Mana. How much meat *was* on a typical deer? Nacho sat silently, mind racing, not knowing what to do next, as the last lumps of the deer carcass turned into sludge.

"I should've cut it up and got as much as I could." Nacho growled at the waste, feeling like an absolute tool. "Why wasn't I thinking ahead? Why did I take one piece and only cut more off after it had already been wasted?"

"Next time, you'll plan better." Brie calmly attempted to offer affirmation. "You're new to this, just like we're new to the rest of it."

Nacho nodded sharply and walked away from the overhang, taking a minute to just breathe in the forest and let himself feel miserable. His first chance at cooking had been a disaster. He was disappointed in himself and furious once more that the Juxtaposition gave its players such little information, even if he had been able to piece together more than he should have by reading over the footnotes of information packs.

They weren't famished. No, he knew what starving felt like. Even so, his hunger was extreme enough to make him want to splurge that night. He returned to his friends, and all of them climbed to the top of the overhang to eat while they watched the sun set.

Sitting on the stone, Reuben pumped a fist. "I love eating out! Tier zero food for everyone!"

No one mentioned their lack of fresh venison steak as Nacho bought the chicken tikka masala plate from the Store. Brie went with fish tacos, while Reuben had Big Bubba's Burnt Ends BBQ Bonanza tray, which was a whole heaping helping of smoked brisket, whiskey beans, mac n cheese, and a lobster bisque. All three meals came on bright carnival-red trays with the word '*Enjoy*' scrawled in yellow across the front.

On the back, printed in tiny black font, were the words 'Tier zero'.

They weren't given silverware, but Nacho had packed an extra set in each of their bags for just such occasions. As they consumed the tasteless food, they watched the sky redden in companionable silence. In the distance rose the smoke from other cooking fires, marking the campsites of other groups of people gathered together.

Who was being attacked and killed? What were they eating? Tier zero food probably, meat and vegetables tainted with Putrid Mana. It wouldn't taste good, but it wouldn't kill them yet, and at least *their* meat probably hadn't liquified off their cooking surfaces.

Nacho picked at the chicken tikka masala that tasted horrifically... *fine*. Being bad would have been a step up for Store food. This was like eating someone else's frozen dinner, from the freezer at work, where it had remained for ten years, losing flavor the entire time. Store food wasn't *bad*. It was just *wrong*. But in the end, the taste didn't matter. They just needed food, so they could use their Skills to kill monsters, which would make them hungry again—thus continuing the endless circle.

Brie didn't complain about the soggy fish tacos, which she could've. Reuben didn't go on a rampage about how dry and tasteless the burnt ends were, despite the fact that messing up the deliciousness of barbecue took some real talent. Instead, he wondered aloud, "You think this food is an evil plot to break the morale of the players?"

"Yeah. That makes too much sense not to be the truth," Brie agreed easily, lightening the mood as they all got a chuckle from the observation. Nacho was able to mull over the situation without getting down, and he couldn't shake the idea that he was still missing something.

Muttering under his breath, Nacho pulled up the Tier zero Class Items list from the Store. For two hundred credits, he could buy the 'IMOP recipe—International Monster of Pancake recipes. Guaranteed delicious. Makes mornings worth waking up for again!' He also saw a Tier zero class item called the *De Re Coquinaria*, and decided to read its description.

It's no secret that the De Re Coquinaria is the most important single item a talented cook can possess, other than garlic and a heartbeat. This is the perfect gift for the preparer of food in your life, and it will bring you and them hours of pleasure and deliciousness.

Brie and Ruben were talking, maybe saying his name, and he thought one of them threw something at him. He was too focused to care. He had to figure out this cooking problem.

He turned his attention to the Tier one class items. Single recipes were available, for a *whopping* four hundred credits. He grimaced at the sight of one called 'Aunt Lilith's Blood Sausage'. Another winner was 'Carl's Fish Sticks and Tartar Sauce Surprise'. However, the Tier one class items also listed cookbooks. He skimmed some of the titles, but one stuck out— The Village Idiot's Breakfast Fun Cookbook.

If you are a Player in the Juxtaposition, you know that breakfast is the most important meal of the day! You can't kill monsters and loot dungeons without a well-balanced meal after a long night's terror. This cookbook has it all! The Juxtaposition's famous IMOP pancakes, Uncle Asmodeus's Spicy Sausage, Biscuits and Gravy, as well as omelets so fluffy and heavenly, you'll swear that the last monster killed you! Suffice to say, you can't go wrong with the Village Idiot's Breakfast Fun Cookbook. It makes early morning meals stupidly delicious!

"Stop that!" Brie demanded of him.

A piece of limp cabbage had hit Nacho in the face. He blinked and allowed the blue light that filled his sclera to fade. "Don't throw things at me!"

"You okay, buddy?" Reuben demanded an answer, hefting his 'food' threateningly. "Need me to smack ya awake?"

Nacho set his tray aside and unscrewed his water bottle. The boiled liquid was cold, and the metal gave it a flat taste. "I'm good. I just feel bad that I messed up the cooking, and maybe I know why. I think I need a recipe? I mean, I've been sorting through the Store, and I found all sorts of expensive class items and cookbooks."

"Ah. That makes sense." Brie's eyes shifted to blue while she accessed the Store. "I see what you're saying. Sorry for throwing cabbage at you. I think I might be losing my mind. Just a teenie lil bit."

"I know how you feel." He truly did, as he was living the Juxtaposition a second time. But he was not alone, and that reminder filled him with the determination he needed to do better at all of it.

As always, Reuben tried to lighten the mood. He grinned and banged his tray on the rock. "What happens to the trays? Can we collect them? Get a set? Use them as Frisbees? What?"

"They eventually melt, like the Wight-Tailed Deer did. You won't see them around. When we got really bored, we used to make bets on how long they would last. They *usually* last about an hour, just long enough for you to have a nice long meal and conversation. Probably made of Putrid Mana, given how they vanish."

"Hey, while you're already in a talkative mood, waxing eloquent on the composition of trays, we've had enough beating around the bush and waiting for you to be ready to talk on your own terms." Reuben reached out a hand to grab Nacho; showing his support in his own way. "You'll feel better if you just get it off your chest. How do you feel, Nacho?"

"I feel like... I'm missing something important." Nacho murmured as he fell back into thought. "That IMOP recipe. It's Tier zero if I were to purchase it alone, but that recipe is included in the Village Idiot cookbook. What does that *mean*?"

Brie leapt to her feet and shot-put her tray into the trees

from the top of their rocky home. "Fine. *You* won't talk about your stupid feelings so that Reuben can get all his warm and fuzzies out? Then *I'll* talk about my stupid feelings! You're not the only one freaking out here because they don't know what to do, Nacho!"

CHAPTER TWENTY

Brie paced back and forth across the top of the limestone overhang. It was dark, with a cold moon rising, giving them plenty of light but no heat. With the fire under the stone ledge which they sat atop, the chill of the evening was starting to seep into their bones. "I am not, nor have I ever been, a girly-girl. Even so, I wanted a *wedding*. I was going to be an *amazing* bride, and I wanted my family there to see me getting married to this man, so they'd know I'd never need *them* again! Abyss it, Nacho, I wanted to show them what *real* love looked like!"

"She means me." Reuben nudged Nacho with a warm smile on his face. "I'm the real love."

Brie didn't pause to acknowledge his interruption. "Fine, the world ended! I don't get a wedding, but on the plus side I don't get killed. I *was* killed in whatever weird vision Nacho had of this, right? Yeah, we've been over it, but still. This is *good*, right? I'm not dead. I even have to admit, I like this fighting stuff. It's like lacrosse, but with higher stakes and a lot more blood."

"It's all very bloody, yes," Reuben agreed soothingly, earning a sharp glare to keep him quiet.

Brie turned and jabbed a finger into Nacho's chest. "My

family probably didn't make it. If *I* would have died, *they're* dead for certain. I know that on some level, and I feel bad. I don't *want* to feel bad. My parents made it clear right from the get-go that if I didn't live by their rules—if I didn't go to their country clubs and act the way a proper young lady should—they'd disown me and not think twice about it. The wedding was going to be me cutting *them* off. I haven't had a family in a long time, so why do I feel so *crappy* that they're gone?"

She huffed angrily, braced her fists on her hips, and glared at the man that had saved them. "This is the part where you give me all your wisdom about death."

"Death." Surprisingly, Reuben was the one that spoke. "I know about death. Firsthand. Four times."

Nacho had shared in two of those deaths. It had hurt, but even before his three years in the Juxtaposition, he had been able to compartmentalize his feelings. Just as demonstrated when Reuben and Brie had unsuccessfully tried to get his attention while he was inspecting the recipes and cookbooks, Nacho had learned to shut out the world. It was a survival skill that the System hadn't given him credit for.

Brie made a face, the rising moon bright enough to reveal her features. Reuben's parents had died when he was in elementary school in a car accident. It had been their date night, and they'd left Reuben with his grandparents on his mother's side. Reuben never got to go back to his own home again. He'd been in fifth grade, old enough to know exactly what had happened.

Then his grandfather died when he was a senior in high school. It had been a blow for both of the young men, because by that time, Nacho was basically living with them as well. Reuben's grandparents' house had become the only sanctuary Nacho had ever known. Death had kicked in the door of the sanctuary and smashed all the windows. Grandpa Colby had succumbed to a heart attack, and only two years later, Grandma Colby had followed.

Nacho had given up on people until he'd met Reuben his sophomore year in high school, and the two had been best buds ever since. Reuben had started dating Brie behind her family's back during their freshman year, so the cook had always known them as a couple. They'd become family for each other.

Remembering that they had been together forever, and that they were tackling this as a team, was enough to shake Nacho out of his funk. "This is the last time I'll bring this up. Back then, I knew you were gone, right? But I'd hear someone that sounded like you, or hear someone laugh at one of my dumb jokes-"

Reuben cut him off, pretending to be affronted. "Hold up, cowboy. Dumb jokes are *my* thing. You can try, but stay outta my way."

Nacho shook his head at his friend. "I'll never have jokes as eye-rollingly awful as yours, Reuben. I am sorry that getting information out of me has been like pulling teeth; I'm just so used to doing this alone and needing to hoard knowledge. Trusting people... I kind of need to relearn how to do that."

"Yeah, but you love us." Brie exhaled, and the tension seemed to flow out of her. "Even if you got us ready for this in the absolute *worst* way possible, we love you too. That should make it all easier. We'll figure everything out."

The cook had to clear his throat to be able to speak again, and he smiled through his pain. "*Do* I love you guys, Brie? Pretty sure I just needed you to hit things for me, and Reuben for comic relief, so that I could learn how to make a proper barbecue during the Apocalypse."

"A true citizen of the great state of Kansas." Reuben slapped Nacho on the back. "That's all I needed to know. Off to bed, then."

Brie groaned at their antics. "Fine, Nacho. I understand you might need more time to tell us the worst parts of what is coming, so just make sure to tell us everything we need to know, and should know, in time for it to be useful. One thing for both of you to remember... I'm keeping that wedding dress in one of my Storage Slots until I'm forced to give it up. At some point, we *are* going to be married officially. We looked too good in those outfits to just throw them away."

"Present tense," Reuben admonished her, taking her hand and giving it a kiss. "You *look* good. Right now. I'd marry you right this moment."

"Ugh, you two..." Nacho abruptly stood up. "Who's taking the first watch?"

Brie was too full of shifting emotions to sleep, so she volunteered to go, on the condition that she would *not* be the first person to eat a meal that Nacho created in the future. Nacho grumbled about the stipulation as he lit yet another fire outside the overhang. He eventually took the second watch and left the little home after throwing a good-sized log into the fire. He stayed out of the light so that it would not impact his night vision, constantly scanning the surroundings while thinking about Reuben and Brie in their little almost-cave.

He did love them. They weren't just his friends. Even if he were not going to marry in, he would *always* consider them to be his family.

Nacho inhaled the cold air, smelling the strange scents of this foreign world. Taking a turn to scan the sky, he wondered again how similar the constellations were to his old world. Even the moon seemed the same. Most people in the Juxtaposition just assumed it was one more way the Patrons taunted the players—give the Earthlings a few things that were familiar: the sky, the stars, the moons, the seasons—but change literally every other facet of life. It would've been easier if there had been two moons, or three suns, or even a ring like Saturn.

Introspection aside, the nice thing about taking a watch was that Nacho had a ton of time to contemplate the food situation. He had to learn how to cook; that would let him change the entire landscape of the game, especially as people reached a higher Tier.

More importantly, he could keep his friends safe and powerful. The powerful part was even more important than safe—no matter how much Reuben would fight against it. The rest of

The Dinner Party had no idea how dangerous this world could get, and he hadn't even told them about the CrossHumans yet; just one more twist in an already pretzeled game.

He would learn how to use his class properly, despite the fact that it would cost them a hefty sum even when making something as seemingly ordinary as pancakes. If he needed, Nacho would perfect a single recipe and force-feed it to people for the next decade. If he had to reduce the entire game down to simple breakfast food to keep people alive, he'd do it and eat that meal a *countless* number of times.

"Maybe I should try to figure out a great omelet recipe? It doesn't get much easier than that, and I can always change what I put in them to add some variety. Good. I have my plan, survive, and win the Juxtaposition using breakfast food. I hereby dub this plan… Omelet Endgame."

CHAPTER TWENTY-ONE

Nacho awoke to a gray light filling the air. The fire had faded to white coals in the early morning cold, the rocks around them failing to retain heat. Although he was conscious, Brie slept on. That meant Reuben would be above them on watch.

He rolled over onto his side. It was nice sleeping in until the sun actually rose into the sky. The Juxtaposition wasn't pleasant; even on its best days, it was more 'death quest' than 'adventure fun', but the rhythms were far more natural than the rat race of finding a career had been on Earth. No one was forced to watch the clock; as long as they had the basics—water, food, and shelter—anyone could sleep as much as they wanted.

One small issue: quality sleep and life-threatening stressors didn't mix. Besides, Nacho knew getting out of his sleeping bag was going to suck. The air was chilly, and more than that... he had *just* gotten used to having good coffee again. He knew he shouldn't have, but having coffee just... *available* was a temptation that he couldn't resist, even with his years of training as a minimalist. Now, the only kind of coffee they had was instant, and they only had nine servings; three coffees for three days. "It's too soon...!"

He huddled deeper into his sleeping bag, shifting from side to side, because that's what people did when they slept on the ground. Nacho had considered grabbing sleeping mats, but that seemed like too much of a luxury—he figured that they'd eventually buy beds once they had a safe location all set up.

Finally, he gave in and pulled himself out of his sleeping bag. There was just no way that he could allow himself to waste time by lazing about. The fact of the matter was that they would all be happier about facing the horrors of the Juxtaposition if they had a little coffee to take the edge off.

Nacho didn't wake Brie as he quietly got the fire started again, putting his saucepan over the heat and filling it with water. He figured they could use their metal water bottles for the instant coffee. Upon observing his roused team member, Reuben swung down from the top of the overhang. "Quiet night. No screaming, bleeding, or random midnight encounters. Best night *ever*."

"So *loud*." Brie grumpily pulled herself upright, and Nacho forced himself to keep his mouth shut about the lion's mane of hair she was currently sporting. "A good night for *us*, at least."

That sobered Reuben. "Eventually, we *are* going to go help people... right? Last night when I was reading through the Store, trying to get ready to sleep, I found a 'create guild' option, and did some reading on the information it offered. We should start a guild, build a castle, get you a decent kitchen. I know, I know: first, we need to upgrade our Skills more, and you need to learn how to keep everyone fed."

"Leave it to you to start figuring out the game mechanics of the world. Speaking of food, especially now that it is breakfast time, I found a recipe for omelets." Nacho slid a stick into his crackling fire. "Do you guys know what a *De Re Coquinaria* is? Also, this might be a little strange... how much do you like omelets? Could you eat them daily?"

Brie held up a hand. "Wait. Guilds? Is that like a workers' union? More importantly, can *you* make omelets?"

Nacho smacked the little packets of instant coffee against a rock. "We could buy some eggs, and I could try an omelet, but I don't think it will work out very well. I'm pretty sure I figured out the issue; I'm missing the tools of my trade. I can't cook without a recipe, or a cookbook, or something. The problem is, we're talking about *hundreds* of credits for even the lowest recipes. I'm not sure it's worth it at this point."

"Fine, fine." Brie waved off his noncommittal explanation, rubbing the sleep out of her eyes with her other hand. "Which takes us back to guilds. What are they?"

"Coffee first?" Nacho offered weakly; he hadn't wanted to explain guilds yet. The discussion would only muddy their situation. "I have cream and sugar for you, Reuben."

"Nice try." Brie's exasperated retort dug into him, and he actually flinched. "What the abyss, man? Reuben? You want to let me in on what a guild is?"

"It's like a party—what we're in—only scaled up a *lot*. There seem to be definite bonuses for creating a guild, but there are also some drawbacks. Nacho might know more, since the System's free information is as cheerful as it is useless."

"Listen." Nacho poured the hot water from the pot into three of their six water bottles, adding the correct amount of sugar and creamer to Reuben's before handing them out. "You're right, and they are *really* important… but I'd rather not talk about guilds just yet. Before we get into the weeds, I want to level our Skills, get a bunch of credits, and be in a position of power. Starting a guild… well. Let's just say it's important, and leave it at that."

The last time he had joined a guild, he'd been forced by the binding compulsion of the contract to murder a ton of people, CrossHumans, and monsters. He added that to the list of things that he didn't want to talk about with his friends. The day he had run into other people and had found that they were members of a guild which he could join had started off great, and had turned into a nightmare not long after. Maybe that was

why Nacho had accepted life in the Juxtaposition so quickly—
he knew that life could change in seconds.

But they had changed *back*, thanks to the Probability Vision.
At some point, Nacho figured that Kronos the Patron would
come and talk to him, and he wasn't looking forward to it. He'd
known warlocks who'd had close contact with their Patrons;
there were always strings attached and terrible deals made just
to stay alive.

"It's unfortunate that every day that we don't help people
understand what's going on, more die, but that's not our fault,"
Brie stated lightly, sipping her coffee. That was her in a nutshell
—talking about people dying whilst enjoying a cup of joe.

"I'm *fine*, guys." Reuben, the marshmallow of the group,
realized that she was only saying that for his benefit. "I think in
this case, it's like in an airplane when the oxygen masks come
down, if you know what I mean? You have to put yours on
before you can help others?"

"Not that we'll have airplanes anymore." Brie's remark was
as bitter as her coffee. "I searched the Store, and there is *nothing*
modern, except for the materials some stuff is made out of. It's
all just swords, axes, crossbows and the like."

Nacho winced at the taste of his instant coffee, briefly
considering dumping sugar and cream in it, but ultimately
opting to save those for Reuben. "Look, this is all less than ideal.
I just want to get these knives first—then I think I'm going to
need this *De Re Coquinaria* book. *Abyss*, I just wish I knew what it
did. Buying stuff blindly from the Store is an iffy proposition,
but I don't think I have a choice."

Reuben pondered the implications. "This book sounds like a
beach town in California. Dude, tomorrow, let's head down to
De Re Coquinaria, and we can go surfing!"

"From here on out, I'm calling it the *Aria*, like it's a list of
songs or something. I'm dropping the rest of it." Nacho pulled
out their food, packets of instant oatmeal which he made in the
pot, and they passed the pot around and each took a few bites
with their own spoon. After breakfast, they broke camp. Reuben

turned back to wave at the rocks. "It was a good campsite. We should call it the Rocky Top. Good ol' Rocky Top, remember the good times we had our first day?"

"You can't force nostalgia, Reuben." Nacho was cut off before he could say any more.

"How do you know, if you don't *try?*" No one had an answer to that, so they lapsed into silence. They found the same game trail and continued to follow it south, ready to jump on any monsters they came across. A short while later, they surprised the same herd of Wight-Tailed Deer they had seen the day before, but the animals were too quick for them to ambush and sped away; the pale arms of their tails sticking straight up. If Nacho didn't know any better, he'd have sworn that those pale hands were waving goodbye.

They reached Tomahawk Creek by noon.

Being back in the world of the Juxtaposition was strange. Nacho knew he should be hungry, but he wasn't, since his Skills remained unused, and it hadn't been twenty-four hours since his last meal. It all felt strange, as well as perfectly familiar. They eventually found a section of the river with boulders rising from the water where they crossed, moving upstream until they spotted Tomahawk Falls. In the real Kansas City, there hadn't been such a place, but here, the stream fell from a cliff's edge, pouring about thirty feet down into a crystalline pool.

According to Myron, behind the pool lay a cave that led to the MurderSong Dungeon. After his announcement that this was where he got his amazing blades, it had been repeatedly ransacked. There were always new monsters worming their way into the caverns or climbing up from the deepest caves, where the high-Tier monsters lurked.

Nacho had run some dungeons to the north, but he'd mostly stayed above ground doing unwise things for the first six months. He had chosen to be an Assassin, and his prize for the ill-advised choice of joining a guild was to carry out assassinations, instead of delving to find excellent gear.

He and his friends kept winding their way through the trees, following the game trail, when they were stopped in their tracks by the shout of human voices. The Dinner Party dove into a thicket of dense bushes—a perfect place to hide.

"Aren't they just people?" Brie's voice was too loud, and Nacho almost slapped a hand over her mouth before thinking better of it. He didn't want to get punched.

"*Maybe*," Nacho cautioned her in a pointedly hushed tone. "Think of it like a zombie apocalypse. Not everyone is a friendly sheriff's deputy from rural Georgia; most people are just going to want to survive however they can."

Reuben grimaced at his friend. "Wow. A *Talking Dead* reference. That show-"

Nacho held up a hand, hearing a familiar voice that set his blood to boiling. "*Abyss*, Crave, why are we out here in the middle of nowhere? You dragged me away from that little settlement we were going to loot. The food would have been terrible, sure, but at least we wouldn't have to do any of the butchering—you know we get credits for the people we kill?"

That was Hogan, and the fact that he was talking to someone meant he'd be with Crave and Whitney. The three had hooked up early, and had never been able to escape the rumors that Hogan and Whitney had done terrible things when they first arrived in the Starter World. From the conversation the trio was currently overhearing, it seemed that was true.

As for Crave, he claimed he'd figured out the guild rules early and convinced people to join them because there was strength in numbers. It was only because of a good marketing campaign that Crave had gotten so rich so fast. If he and his goons were getting credits through all-out murder, Nacho didn't want to engage with them until it was clear that he and friends would win the fight.

Nacho lifted a finger to his lips to keep his friends quiet. They nodded with wide eyes, hearing the same things he was. Crave, Hogan, and Whitney walked right past them. All three carried sacks made from random clothes and rags they'd tied together. Crave was in a torn suit and expensive shoes that probably wouldn't last the week. He *did* have a pretty nice iron spear—not homemade—that he must've scavenged.

Hogan merely had a massive club that he'd augmented with nails. He must've bought those nails from the Store, then used a stone to pound them in. The huge man wore clothes that he had likely grabbed off someone else: the jeans didn't fit him, the shirt was far too tight, and the Crocs didn't exactly help the look.

Whitney wore overalls with a plaid shirt and a woodsman's axe to match the plaid. Funnily enough, Nacho had always known Whitney as a bigger guy, short but wide… however, right now, he was downright *slender*; meaning he had gained a huge amount of muscle and fat *after* the end of the world.

Crave stopped abruptly. "Wait, I'm feeling something from this boon thing. Something dangerous is near."

"You and the boon again," Hogan growled at the man that would someday be his boss. "Just tell us where to go."

"What is it?" Whitney swung his axe to limber up.

Nacho's killing intent sharpened as he thought about attacking them. He knew that he could put his years of effort to good use and kill them before they became an issue for him. When it came to Hogan and Whitney, he wouldn't care at all. But Crave…? Nacho and Crave had been close, and in the end, they would have been friends if the guy hadn't ordered his death.

Nacho knew Crave could be a hard man, hard enough to make decisions that killed people—Nacho, for instance. But right now, the three were killing people just to get a little bit of a head start. He wasn't afraid of a fight, but he also didn't want to let his friends see him murder a trio of people in cold blood.

Brie crouched lower, leaning against her hammer. Would she be able to use it against other humans? From the intense glint in her eyes due to their conversation topic, Nacho thought so. Reuben had equipped his gauntlets, and he'd fight if he had to, but it was clear the big guy didn't want to hurt other people.

Crave glanced around. "I had a definite sense there was

something important back there, by the waterfall. Can't put my finger on it. It *was* Dope, but this area is rapidly becoming more Nope than Dope. Something near us is considering killing us… and I think it will if we don't leave. My senses keep wavering as though it hasn't made up its mind."

"Just wow. Deciding what to do based on little emotions." Hogan's sardonic laughter clearly showed what he thought about Crave's 'feelings'. Whitney didn't say anything, merely standing with the axe resting across his left shoulder. "Can't believe we listen to this garbage."

"So far, my Dope or Nope Intuition has come in handy, *wouldn't* you say?" Crave snarled at the man. "Just like Fourtuna said it would. He also whispered about a cook that wasn't supposed to exist when I talked to him. If we had a cook, we wouldn't have to eat rank deer meat or those awful apples. We'd have *real* food."

"Store food is *fine*." Hogan spit into the weeds. "At least that pattern told you how to get at it. Tell you what, it's a lot better than the chow we had at Leavenworth."

"*Patron*," Crave rebuked his minion.

"That food tastes like socks," Whitney whined quietly. "Or old tennis balls."

Hogan snorted and rolled his eyes. "You said you thought there was a dungeon or somethin' back there. If we'd have found it, we could've got enough credits to buy food instead of needing to *axe* people to hand over their stuff."

"If we started a guild, we could collect credits on a *much* larger scale. Just like any gang large enough to become a legitimate government does: *taxes*." Crave frowned and turned to stare right where Nacho and his friends were crouched behind a thick tangle of bushes. Their camouflaged clothes blended in, just like Nacho had planned, so the man merely adjusted his ripped suit coat and looked away. "At some point, someone else is going to figure out that's how you get real power in this game. We need to leave. Let's follow the stream east. We can double back if we need to do so later."

The three men kept on marching down the path. If they'd had any ranger skills, they would've been able to see human footprints on the path, but Nacho was pretty sure that Hogan and Whitney were low-Tiered Body Players. Not Crave. Crave had done well enough in the Evaluation to become an assassin, just like he had. He'd kept that a secret from *almost* everyone for over a year, saying he hadn't done well enough to even buy a class. Crave had other secrets, like the fact that he'd always had close ties to a Patron—someone called Fourtuna; the same Patron who had bestowed him with his Dope or Nope Intuition.

Now it seemed that Fourtuna knew about Nacho being a Common Cook. If the Patron knew more about Nacho, that might change this iteration of the Juxtaposition dramatically. More than ever, Nacho wanted the MurderSong blades, and he wanted to level up his friends. If Crave came after him, Nacho wanted to have to *scrape* that team off the business end of Brie's Splatter Mallet.

Reuben laughed awkwardly. "Well, those three seemed nice. I mean, aside from the murdering, thieving, and what-have-you."

Nacho gave the Healer a reassuring pat on the back. "It seems like they're looking for a cook to make them dinner. Good thing I can't cook, eh? Let's go steal the dungeon he couldn't find. Listen... I know that guy. He's going to start a guild, and it's going to be big. But that's not for at least a few weeks, months if we can do enough to save the people that he would otherwise rob and kill. Abyss, maybe we can keep him from starting a guild entirely."

"You knew him?" Brie inquired with an arch look. "He seemed like a real charmer."

"I'm not telling you about three years of messed-up Juxta-position horrors, but I don't want to live like I did then. Long story short, that was the guy who kept me alive for a long, long time. We have a... complicated history."

He didn't mention that Crave was the same guy who had

rammed a knife into his heart. That was a little too gruesome to mention, especially when things were going so well.

CHAPTER TWENTY-TWO

"Well isn't *that* just great." Reuben was still shaking his head as they walked down the trail toward the waterfall, too perturbed to admire the crystalline blue pools beneath the falls. "Killing other people is directly *incentivized*? You get whatever credits they collected, as well as credits based on their level? That's just... why would that be allowed? This whole thing is just asking to turn into a drama about betrayal. All we need now is a proper love triangle."

"No love triangles." Nacho and Brie looked at each other, both shuddering at nearly the same time. Internally, Nacho found himself trying to defend the future Guild Master. Sure, the guy might have made some mistakes early in the game, like getting involved with thugs like Hogan and Whitney, but in the end... didn't Crave do a lot of good, for a lot of people? Nacho kept those thoughts to himself, knowing that his friends didn't have the moral flexibility they would need in order to accept that outlook.

He and his friends gripped the roots of the trees while they navigated the path until they could reach the waterfall, which completely hid the cavern. If Crave had done more gaming, and less Vice Presidenting—he had been the vice president of sales for some sporting goods company—he might've known there was *always* stuff hidden behind waterfalls.

The cook filled his pack with the last of the food, then hid the other two packs behind a mass of tangled tree roots. Grabbing a hanging root tendril, he swung into the open air, slamming through the cold water and onto a ledge. Diffused light glimmered off the sparkling walls, where an engraved archway spanned the stone hallway farther down.

Noting the lack of light further in, Nacho sighed. He didn't want to spend their credits, but he had no choice if they wanted to stay alive. Popping open the Store, he found a combo deal for a hooded lantern with four hours of fuel, costing only fifteen credits.

Brie swung through the waterfall and into the corridor, followed by Reuben. Both began shivering immediately. Reuben adjusted his leather Helm of Helming with hands covered by his Gauntlets of Monster Destruction. "Let me try out my new catchphrase. *I'm ready to hit things!* Is that a good one? What do you think? I could try to make something about love gloves."

"*No*. No battle cries, no branding yourself. I don't *care* if that's your entire degree, just no." Brie slammed her helmet onto her head, hammer at the ready. "We don't need catchphrases. Go kill things and collect credits."

"Ugh, now that's a *great* catchphrase, and you probably won't even use it!" Reuben lamented at his fiancée.

Nacho carried the bow with the quiver over his shoulder, planning on avoiding combat if he could; they needed every credit they could get. His current plan was to essentially be a squire for their resident Berserker: hold the light, swap out her weapons, and keep her fed while Reuben kept her healed. Lighting the hooded lantern, he called, "Good news? We can see. Bad news? We only have two credits left."

"Well, let's *fix* that problem!" Brie marched forward enthusiastically. That was the only holdover from their original battle order, as Nacho followed with the lantern raised, casting light on the dripping rock walls, and Reuben was their rear guard.

A squawk behind them made them all turn in confusion, just in time to watch bright blue birds with black beaks and eye-growths that looked like large black sunglasses come soaring around the waterfall, streaking toward The Dinner Party.

Blues Birds
  Effective Tier/Level: ?
  HP: ?

Nacho had noticed holes near the ceiling, and now understood that those black beaks were the cause. Then he registered what their actual name was: Blues Birds. He had vague memories of these monsters, mainly because of the sunglasses. If he remembered correctly, their song was considered one of the most beautiful to listen to at night. The problem was that they were some of the low-level monsters that morphed into bigger iterations. Some elites became Roc-Stars later on.

These Blues Birds came in all different sizes. The little ones were about the size of a chubby red-breasted robin, while some on the bigger end were the size of a small dog. A dozen of the things came flying in, but they weren't aiming for the holes—they dove toward Reuben, who was the first and largest target.

Even though he was a Healer, Reuben wasn't about to run from a fight. He pulled back his right fist and splattered the incoming bird with a giant metal glove. To everyone's surprise, the creature exploded into a fine mist of blood, bone, and feathers. The problem was that the Healer had thrown himself off-balance and there were eleven more of the birds. They began slamming into him, trying to drive their beaks into the chainmail.

· · ·

Hey, Player, welcome to Active Combat! You're fighting the Blues Birds, and they're looking for a good guitar peck. No Store or Regeneration during Active Combat. Good luck!

Nacho dropped the bow and set the lantern on the floor. He hurried forward with his knife drawn, hacking the blade into one of the birds and sending feathers exploding everywhere. These things simply weren't tough. Even though he had two percent bonus damage, along with his current Fitness bonus of five percent, that should have been nowhere near enough to create instant death on this scale.

Instant kill! Die, bird, die!
   Congratulations! You have killed a Blues Bird!
   Level 01 Creature = 0 Credits
   Incredible!

Reuben slammed himself into the wall, trying to squish or push off some of the monsters hooked onto him. Nacho dashed over, waving his arms and slashing at anything covered in feathers. For just a moment, Reuben was free of the birds. He flung out his hands. "Positive Vibes! Go, go, Dinner Party! You've got five minutes to slap some extra pain into these featherheads!"

Nacho felt the glow of Reuben's magic fueling him, making him a tiny bit faster and stronger, just in time to deal with the birds that abandoned Reuben to target him. He killed the first of them—eliciting a cut-off squawk— and once again gained zero credits.

As for the damage he was dishing out... frankly, two percent increased damage didn't help anyone much. At their levels, they just weren't dealing with the high damage output values that a percentage increase required. Meanwhile, Brie leapt into action with her Splatter Mallet, her Combat Dash ability turning her into a blur as she raced past Nacho. Her mallet slammed into a bird, mashing it into avian paste.

"Haha! Yes! Speed and pain!" She was using a larger weapon with a base damage value of ten, had her Fitness plus-five, her Combat Dash for four percent, and Reuben's two percent, meaning she was dishing out *twelve* points of damage with every hammer swing.

"Stop making awesome catch phrases if you won't let me use them!" Another bird came winging in as Reuben yelled, only to be reduced to gooey gore even without Brie's Combat Dash being active. Shouting ferociously, she rammed the shaft of her two-handed hammer into another monster bird, slapping it away from Reuben—who was actively bleeding from a number of small wounds.

The other birds swarmed back onto the Healer. Nacho had to help him, but losing credits on each kill frustrated him like nothing else. "Brie, pancake-batter up! Flatten those that make your beloved bleed!"

He plucked a bird off Reuben's unprotected thigh and sent it tumbling through the air like a feathery softball at the Berserker. She smacked it into the wall, where it impacted with a pulpy sound before sliding to the ground. "The Splatter Mallet is aptly named!"

"*Help* me, don't make jokes!" Reuben was frantically trying to save himself by using the gauntlets to squeeze the gizzards out of the creatures. Over the next half minute, between his gauntlets and Nacho playing bird baseball with Brie, they finally took out the first threat of the dungeon.

Congratulations, Player! Active Combat is over! Ouch! One of you is at single digits Health Points. Have fun shopping, and enjoy your Health and Mana Regen! May your future be delicious!

. . .

Reuben staggered over to lean against the wall. He was bleeding from a dozen bad wounds, so he wrapped his arms around himself and let out a sigh. "Wow. I can hug and heal myself. This is never going to get old."

His skin glowed gold once, twice, and the open wounds were taken care of. Brie hurried to her fiancé and rubbed his bloody arm. "Are you okay?"

"I will be. Give me a minute; that was... I almost died." He had his eyes closed as he used his healing ability again. He groaned and slid down to the ground. "Suddenly thirsty... I'll let my Health Regen do the rest."

"It's okay, everything is fine, Reuben." Brie tried to calm him as she stood watch with her hammer.

Nacho bent to look him over. "Let me get you something to eat. You'll be down on Hunger, too."

"More thirsty than hungry, but I could use a bite." Reuben leaned his head back against the wall. "I'm down to eighty Thirst points. It's really not that bad, I'm just not used to the *suddenness* of it, you know? Like the water was *drained* out of me. As if I'm a water balloon that someone didn't tie properly. My Mana Regen is at eight percent per minute...? Not bad. I can already feel my mojo coming back. But dude, Positive Vibes isn't doing much at this level. Only two percent... it's not worth it. Not for the cost."

"Probably not," Nacho agreed easily, handing Reuben a water bottle. The fluid was drained in an instant. Fighting back a grimace, Nacho accepted the empty container and packed up his bag. "I got nothing from my kills but blood I need to wash off my hands. How much were these things worth?"

"Seven credits each." Reuben slapped his gauntlets together to clear them of feathers and flesh, then started shaking his head back and forth. "Bleh, it got in my eye!"

Current Credits: 2 (72 total Dinner Party pool)

. . .

Most of the Blues Birds had been reduced to scraps—perfect for chicken nuggets—though a few of the bodies remained in pretty good shape. He could at least process them to get a few extra credits, even if he wasn't planning to actually cook them. Nacho nodded at the archway at the end of the cave. "We should make sure things are clear down there, and then you two should eat. I'm not even going to try to cook up these birds, but I *am* going to abuse the system as hard as I can for credits."

Reuben shrugged an arm that was almost completely healed. "I love that Health Regen is working overtime. Having a magical metabolism is the *best!*"

"Let's get inside so that nothing sneaks up on us while we're trying to recover." Brie's recommendation was met with grunts of approval, so the three of them walked down to the entrance, finding that steps had been cut into the cavern floor. With a silent glance of mutual agreement, they descended into darkness.

Carved above the entrance was the name of the dungeon, but it was pretty hard to read. After a moment of guessing, they decided that it was: The MurderSong of The Croaking.

Nacho squinted at the inscription, muttering softly as he tried to order his memories. "The croaking? Myron said it was only called the MurderSong, but to be fair… he wasn't the sharpest tool in the shed."

"Another *friend?*" Reuben questioned with a slight amount of concern in his voice.

"No… a competitor, a killer. He worked for a rival guild and ended up killing a lot of people. Long story… actually, no, that's the entire story." Nacho shook his head and glanced away from his queasy-looking friend. "Maybe frogs? Frog monsters. Croaking, that's a frog thing, right?"

"Does it matter?" Brie leaned on her hammer. "Whatever it is, we're going to kill it real good."

"It's a good thing to try to plan for the future." Reuben frowned at her blasé attitude, but he couldn't manage to figure out what he actually wanted to say to her. "Too bad we aren't getting incentives or bonuses for dungeons yet. It would be cool if we got credits for figuring out the names of a dungeon. You know, cash for puns? We'd clean up."

That put a smile back on Nacho's face. "If we could cash in on puns, you and I wouldn't need to fight anything ever again. We'd just retire in style."

Since nothing was charging up the steps, the cook led them back to the area where the defeated birds remained scattered around. He chose three of the most intact ones, each the size of a fat turkey, and gave one to each of his friends to pluck off blue feathers as fast as they could. Reuben rumbled with laughter. "You know, just thinking about these things cooking up is making me hungry."

"You just want to eat them as retaliation for them attacking you," Brie snorted as she ripped out a handful of feathers.

"Okay, maybe we know each other too well," Reuben admitted as Nacho looked at him for confirmation.

The cook, having the most experience with monsters and knives, got the feathers off thrice as fast as the others, then cut off the head and feet in two smooth motions. He wasn't about to lose credits to Putrid Mana, not this time. They'd already lost fourteen credits because he'd needed to kill two of these. He could only hope that the MurderSong Blades would allow him to harvest credits from kills. In the meantime, he was going to try to process the ingredients.

Once he gutted the bird and slopped the entrails onto the floor, he cut off the thigh and leg. He was ready for a System message to prompt him for cooking, but nothing happened. He frowned, had an 'aha' moment, and started purifying the meat.

Golden light washed out of him and into the flesh, and soon Putrid mana was dripping to the floor or evaporating into the air. Two credits hit his account. Now that the meat was ready, he was ready for a message to appear about cooking…

Still nothing.

By the time the small piece was clean, Reuben and Brie had finished plucking the feathers from their respective birds and

Nacho was sweating. The Blues Birds weren't liquifying yet, but they could at any minute. The rest of The Dinner Party gazed at Nacho in confusion, seeing his concern. Reuben eventually shook his head. "Wow. Here I am, at the entrance of a dungeon, but instead of doing cool stuff like slaying dragons… I'm plucking feathers off monster birds."

"I have the carcass of the bird prepped, so why can I not cook this? Why am I not being prompted for…? Ingredients!" Nacho didn't respond, too concentrated to join in on the joke. He whipped the yellow-and-red containers of salt and pepper out of his backpack and rubbed the spices across the carcass. "Yes!"

Greetings, Satiation Player! Trying to cook some more, Cookie? Well, welcome to Active Cooking. No Store access. No Mana or Health Regen. Are you gonna bake that Blues Bird? Or are you gonna pan-fry that bad boy? Either way, you have three ingredients. Wanna start cooking your meal?

Yes / No

"Now that I know for sure that this can be cooked…" Nacho wasn't going to let those messages mess with his concentration. So *what* if he didn't have Store access and Regen? At least nothing was currently trying to kill him. He lost five percent of his Mana, Hunger, and Thirst each time he worked to get the Putrid Mana out, but that was okay. He had plenty of food and water, even if they'd have to boil more water at some point.

"I got two credits," he tossed out to his friends, "but I'm going to keep on going. Don't touch the meat."

"That's what they kept telling me. I never listened. Made the whole flight awkward." Reuben patted his bird as he waited for Nacho to get to it. "These things are flesh and not goop, so keep going as long as you can."

Nacho felt his Small Blades Skill activating each time he

sliced and diced the Blues Birds, reducing them into eight piles of meat, each pile about a pound. Again and again, Nacho used the Ingredient Processing ability, switching over to Reuben's bird when his was gone. He kept going, powering through until another nine pounds of meat had been purified and was ready to cook.

He was starving, thirsty, and nearly out of Mana. Using his skill back-to-back, eighteen times in a row, had reduced his Thirst and Hunger all the way down to five points each, and he had a measly three points of Mana left. He'd gotten so caught up in getting the thirty-six credits that he'd forgotten to eat and drink: almost a deadly mistake.

Current Credits: 38 (100 total Dinner Party pool)

Seeing he had personally added thirty-six credits to their account made Nacho feel better. He peered around the cavern to see if there was anything else for him to work on, noting that by the time he had finished with the first two monsters, Brie's bird had turned into a puddle in front of her. It would be a race to process Putrid Mana before the animals melted. He had expected that, but it was good to know for certain.

Without the Putrid Mana, the piles of bird meat looked and smelled fine. They could try cooking them over a fire that night, even if Nacho didn't think it would work. It seemed he needed to have recipes to successfully cook anything; an *actual* recipe from this world, something purchased from the Store, since the scrap of information he'd found had hinted that he could sell meals based on the *recipe*, not on the food itself.

But… spending two hundred credits on a hunch could very well be a painful mistake. Nacho wanted to take the chance, and he had great reasons for being willing to spend the panic-inducing amount of credit. For one, he could imbue his cooking with buffs. Second, the food they'd brought would eventually run out, and Store food sucked.

With a grunt, he stopped working so he could start regenerating his mana. He gulped water and attacked the raisins and peanuts. Before he started drinking, his Thirst was all the way down to a mere ten points. "Went too far. Nearly fell unconscious."

"That's not good." Reuben considered that while munching for a bit, then sighed dramatically, gesturing at the food. "No M&Ms in the trail mix? I mean, it's just raisins and peanuts… you have a lot to learn about cooking, but even more about snacking."

"I know." Nacho grunted like a neanderthal between bites and gulps. "You'd think I would've worried more about taste when I was packing our food. I guess I got used to eating the bland Store food, and… other stuff."

"What other stuff?" Brie perked up at his hesitation, remembering that it was a topic that he did not want to discuss. "I mean, if you are going to bring it up…"

Nacho wasn't planning on exposing his brief two-year stint as a cannibal right then, so he merely shrugged. "I wasn't gonna be a Cook. I just wanted us together, I wanted you both to do well in the Evaluation, and then I figured we'd figure things out once we got here. But hey, I remembered your cream and sugar for your coffee, bud. Give me some credit."

"One credit." Reuben smiled as a credit jumped from his pool over to Nacho's. "You might be able to buy some spices for that crappy Store food."

"Maybe." Nacho tore open a protein bar. "The hungrier you get, the better even Store food tastes, and that's saying something."

"I don't know about that." Brie ate the last of her snack. "I don't think it was all that bad; it's like discount buffet food."

"Why do you think calling it discount buffet food makes it sound *better*?" Reuben struggled to come up with a way to make a better comparison. "Just gross, and that's terrible."

Nacho contemplatively chewed his Muscle Mania bar while packing up in the light of the lantern. "Tell me what you found out about your weapons. Did the Juxtaposition give you anything useful?"

"I'm almost *positive* that the hammer's enchantment doubles its base damage," Brie explained as she idly hefted it. "That means that instead of ten points like the hammer should be dealing, I'm doing twenty a pop. With my Combat Dash, I'm doing twenty-*three*. We use normal rules of rounding, I guess, since two percent of twenty-three is point four-six."

"You're hitting well above your level, then. Excellent. Also, yes, always round down if you're below point five, and up if you're at or above it." Nacho was practically vibrating with excitement at the quality weapon she had earned, though he did not let that impact his knowledge gathering. "How about you, Healer?"

"Ahh, what? Me? 'Kay, so, the gauntlets hit like a better weapon than they are. That's the 'Punch Me, I'm Dreaming' bonus; still haven't figured out the details. I also have something else, a 'Bad Case of the Clap' special move? That gives me two extra points of damage when it activates. Even so, I'm not doing *twenty plus* like Hammer Girl over there. What about you, Nacho?"

"No comment." Nacho shouldered the pack and collected the bow and quiver. "Let's just say I need to stick to cooking, when I figure that out. When I do, I'll earn my keep. I hope."

Brie gave him a friendly shove. "You've *already* earned your keep. We have thirty-six extra credits from you."

Reuben was there to shove him from the other side, though Nacho nimbly avoided the foot trying to trip him at the same time. "After a hard day's work in the dungeon, we'll have bird meat for days! We'll start a fire, cook some up, and it'll be like happy hour in the poacher's club."

"Maybe." Nacho didn't think there would be anything edible coming out of his cooking for a while. He still had a lot to learn about being a Common Cook. Even still, he could be helpful. The first step was to consider all their options. "You know, Reuben is only at level one with his Positive Vibes... we could upgrade him to level three, since we have a hundred credits."

Reuben brightened up at the idea of getting further empowered. "I think I'd give you guys an additional... six percent damage? That's still not great, but it would be at least an extra point if you were serious about rounding up."

"A point and then some for me, and five minutes per cast is great," Brie encouraged him. "Taking my Combat Dash to level three would give me an additional six percent, but you can help the entire team. Let's do it. Let's buy two upgrades for my love."

Reuben blushed and waved her off. "*Your* love. That's *me*. She's talking about me."

"I'll stab you if you keep doing that over and over. I know you'd survive it." Nacho warned jokingly. Once they spent the hundred credits, it was time to put those new magic powers to use. "Looks like the credits are all gone. Again. Let's fix that."

"*Abyss* yeah!" Brie led the way, with Nacho and Reuben following her into the first room of the MurderSong of the Croaking.

CHAPTER TWENTY-THREE

Nacho had vague recollections of people telling him stories about this place, though frankly a lot of tunnel-dungeons looked very similar. The stone steps didn't drop all that far; they were similar to the Deep Buggy Darkness, coming to a T-juncture. However, this corridor didn't end on the right, instead continuing to descend into darkness.

The floor was covered with white streaks, suspiciously similar to bird droppings. Somehow, he doubted the Blues Birds had come this far down—he'd handled them up close, and these smears looked far bigger than anything they could produce. The droppings gave the whole corridor a stink that was *just* below overwhelming.

"Left or right?" Brie whispered, the 'ta' sound from the word 'right' echoing off the walls as though a tiny person was hitting it with a hammer.

From behind Nacho, Reuben *clinked* his gauntlets off his chainmail, then spoke far too loudly for the trained Assassin among them to be happy. "Well, it kind of depends on why we're here. There's more guano to the left, so if we're here to kill monsters, that's the direction we want to take. The right smells fresher, so if we're here for fun, we should follow what makes our noses happy."

"There's no rush to go deeper." Nacho hoisted the lantern higher. "We're all about killing monsters and collecting credits."

Reuben started singing softly, "To the left, to the left, everything you kill in the tunnel to the left."

"Left sounds great." Brie strode ahead, hammer in hand as the tension in the air began to increase. She remained poised like a serpent ready to strike as the corridor's floor twisted down, then upward. The level of the hallway rose enough for them to smell the creek above and for occasional roots to grow out of cracks in the ceiling. Gradually, clattering and clicking became audible, joined by a few squawks, and then cawing— evidently, a murder of unhappy crows waited up ahead, and Nacho shivered at the memory of the Melted Crow that had nearly ended his Evaluation.

Brie stopped and looked back, sweat dripping down her face. "I always laughed at people who were afraid of birds. Now I think Hitchcock was on to something."

"We should focus on getting quiet now." Nacho squinted into the darkness, attempting to get his System View to lock onto the moving figures ahead... and failing. They were big, though not man-sized—still, they were larger than the Blues Birds from the cave entrance.

"Hit me with some Positive Vibes." Brie took a fresh grip on her maul. "I don't mind the fighting so much; it's the anticipation of the fight that drives me crazy."

"Crazy awesome, like the Berserker you are." Reuben moved forward and wiggled his hands at his girl's back. "Positive Vibes for everyone! Let's hit these things with an extra one-point-two-six points of damage! Whoo, six percent of twenty-one!"

"Twenty-three, with Combat Dash. Math shouldn't be this fun." Brie cheered under her breath. A shimmer of golden light flashed up their bodies from feet to helm, or in Nacho's case, his dark hair.

The cook gently pushed Reuben forward, which pushed Brie forward, and gave them their first glimpse of their next adversaries. The creatures were definitely crow-shaped up top, though instead of wings, they flapped stumpy arms that ended in bone hooks. Their beady eyes were as black as their beaks, and their feathers appeared to have been dipped in oil. Nacho got a definite vulture vibe from them, until he noticed that instead of a bird's clawed feet, they had the paws of a panther, complete with bright white claws.

He finally managed to get a lock on one of the things:

Caw Paws
 Effective Tier/Level: ?
 HP: ?

"Caw Paws?" Reuben wasn't impressed. "More like ka-*pows*! Get 'em, baby!"

Brie shouted an inarticulate battle cry and raced forward with a Combat Dash, tearing through the corridor and into the middle of the bird monsters. She used her Defensive Whirl to parry a striking hook, returning the favor by splattering the skull of the offending Caw Paw. As she pulled her weapon through a backswing, she shifted her grip and hammered into the chest of another, but a third one climbed up her legs, digging its claws into her thighs and attempting to disembowel her. Happily, the chainmail held, though she was facing two of the things alone for a long moment thanks to getting so far ahead of the others.

Then Reuben arrived like a Kansas thunderstorm, bellowing in fury at the sight of his future bride in danger. He ripped the crow off her, mashing it into the wall and punching the thing repeatedly. "I. Want. To. Do. More than. Twelve damage. At a time!"

While Reuben beat the Caw Paw into oblivion, Brie brought the hammer around on the last of the mutated animals. It let out a loud **croak**... as she drove her Splatter Mallet *through* it and into the floor.

The Active Combat session came to a sudden end, and the gash in Brie's leg immediately began to close.

"Was the dungeon named after the croaking of the... things? I kinda feel that it's more, ya know, squawking." Reuben wheezed from the exertion, something Nacho knew the man didn't actually need to do, thanks to his modified body. The cook merely shrugged and lifted the lantern higher. The tunnel contained a mixture of dirt, roots, rock, and guano—and was laced with small passages that opened to the outside. Unfortunately, those small tunnels were not empty. Dozens of Caw Paws came racing in, cawing and croaking in fury as the scent of fresh blood reached them; then even more loudly as they spotted their dead comrades. In a flash, a flurry of feline feet frantically flew forward.

"Fall back to the stairs! Regroup!" Nacho shouted to his friends as he turned and ran. They retreated, Brie limping slightly as her Health Regen repaired her legs—technically, they had not yet engaged in active combat. The party made it to the steps and turned just in time to open the fight against the river of monsters on their own terms.

The Caw Paws came tumbling over each other in a flurry of hoarse cries, feathers, and hooks. Brie gasped at her teammates as her hammer flew back and forth, "Guys, I can't fight all of those things at the same time!"

A rhythmic **thumping** drumbeat filled the air from down below, echoing from the corridor to the right. The tidal wave of hooked crow-panther hybrids all came to a screeching halt, then reversed course, the ones in the front clawing over the ones in the back in their frenzy to retreat. In seconds, the corridor was empty as the bird-cats flew out of the tunnel and escaped into open air.

"Don't," Nacho warned his friend, but he was too late. The Healer's mouth was already open.

"Drums," Reuben quoted solemnly. "Drums in the deep."

Brie didn't comment. She was done bleeding, but she appeared to be close to hyperventilating. "That was *way* too close. A few Caw Paws turned into thirty so *fast*…"

Fortunately, Nacho had quickly devised a plan in the event that they had to defend themselves again. He was pretty sure that the left corridor ended close to the surface, so all they had to do was find out where those holes emerged, and then they could pick off the Caw Paws a few at a time. If they played their cards right, they had just found a credit generator. He quietly drew his friends back and explained his thoughts. "Let's go back to the entrance cave."

The drums continued to throb with the beat of an impressive musician, the tone reminding Nacho of… *something*, but he just couldn't put his finger on it. Back up in the cave, they passed the slowly liquifying Blues Birds. The stench was nauseating, so the cook led them out past the waterfall. Though the water was cold, it washed the top layer of sweat and blood from their bodies, and allowed them a minor moment of relief.

"Where are you going?" Reuben finally questioned as Nacho climbed up the roots to the top of the cliff.

"The front door is a bad idea, so I'm trying to use my mental picture of the underground hallways to get us a better starting point." Nacho and his friends would have to cross the river; not a problem, since it was autumn and the river wasn't as swollen as it would be in the spring. While crossing over exposed rocks, they began locating exit holes on the other side. They noted Caw Paws emerging, so the trio only needed to follow the feathery creatures until they began surrounding a carcass, which turned out to be a dead Wight-Tailed Deer.

Scurrying with as much stealth as they could manage, Nacho, Reuben, and Brie squatted in the undergrowth between the stream and the monsters. Brie quickly washed her leg off, revealing that under the scabbed layer lay healthy, pink skin. She'd used both Combat Dash and Defensive Whirl— even in the brief combat, she'd lost approximately twenty-five percent of her Hunger points. Her Athletic Endurance was kicking in, but unfortunately, that only saved her a half a point at its level.

"Don't judge me, but the raw Wight-Tailed Deer looks... tasty?" Brie was obviously feeling her hunger, but she interrupted Nacho before he could stop her line of thinking. "Hold on, I want to say this. Humans can't eat Putrid Mana. At their same Tier, it only *tastes* gross and gives a few symptoms, but higher-Tiered meat can kill. Now, what I'm wondering is... do humans contain Putrid Mana? They don't... do they?"

"You're right." Nacho's heart fell as he spoke heavily; he knew what was coming, so he kept his eyes on the Caw Paws dining on the deer corpse.

"Wait. Humans are plentiful, slow, and easy to trick." Reuben had begun to put things together. "If humans aren't tainted by Putrid Mana... *no*..."

Before the big guy could finish the thought out loud, Nacho pointed at a good climbing tree above the well-traveled brush of the clearing. "If we get Brie up into that tree with the bow, she can pick off the Caw Paws. Reuben and I can lure them out, get them into position, and we take them out a few at a time."

"We *will* be talking about this later. If nothing else, you have to let us know what we need to watch out for." Brie turned and gave Nacho a long look. "Why do I need to be in the tree? What if I want to bash their little crow heads in?"

Both Nacho and Reuben were speechless at the sudden turn in conversation, so much so that Brie laughed and gestured toward the tree. "I'm *so* kidding. If we can kill from a distance, let's do that. As long as we get the same number of credits."

"How much are these things worth?" Nacho questioned their resident credit-earner.

"Thirteen a pop. We'll have another thirty-nine credits to add to the kitty." It was a relief to see Brie relaxing enough for a pun. But when they didn't laugh right away, she had to point out her joke. "Get it? Add to the *Kitty*? Since... they have cat feet. Anyone?"

"We love each other because we have *complementary*

strengths," Reuben offered soothingly, getting a glare for his efforts. "You have so many strengths, that maybe we leave the puns to me?"

"Just gimme the bow." Brie scowled and practically ripped the bow out of Nacho's hands before stalking toward the tree.

CHAPTER TWENTY-FOUR

The arrows did a base damage of five, requiring a couple shots to take each of the monsters down, but Reuben also jumped in to help as the monsters swarmed. Darting out of the undergrowth, he'd punch the head of a distracted monster and take it to the ground. Nacho stayed ready with his knife, but he never ended up needing to use it.

The Caw Paws didn't get wise to the ploy until a good number of them had already fallen, at which point the rest went underground. Once the last of the crow-panther-things had retreated, Brie stationed herself over the entrance to the lair, waiting for one of the creatures to return and stick its head out. Each time one tried, she dropped the hammer and crushed its head to paste.

Meanwhile, Nacho kept an eye out for Crave and his two goons, but they didn't reappear. He was hopeful that they had been warned off by Crave's intuition, but he couldn't fully trust that his luck would be so good.

Once the majority of the remaining Caw Paws were dead, the cook got busy. He bought more salt and pepper and quickly plucked one of the crows. Its little hook arms didn't have much meat, but the thighs were plump and muscled; unfortunately, they were covered in a thick fur that proved to be more difficult to remove. As soon as the meat was finally ready to be processed, the System happily let him know that he had wasted his time.

Greetings, Satiation Player!

It looks like you're trying to process a meaty ingredient! That Caw Paw thigh looks <u>delicious</u>! Anyway, wanna process your meal?

Yes / No.

"Yes-"

HA! Just kidding; great job wasting resources, though! This is a level 5 bird of predator. You can only process up to level 3. Try again once you've seen the inside of a kitchen or two—also, we suggest Colonel White Beard's poultry seasoning. Enough of the salt and pepper. Boo, boring!

Nacho felt Mana, Thirst, and Hunger points leave him. He narrowed his eyes and checked the party funds. To process the Caw Paws, he'd have to spend enough credits to upgrade his Skill... but it *should* be a wash. If he hurried, he'd be able to process a hundred credits' worth of meat. With that in mind, he upgraded his Ingredient Processing Skill to level two, then three, and savored the feeling of the golden tingleys filling him.

Reuben and Brie didn't notice, and he felt pretty bad that he hadn't clued them in on his expenditure ahead of time. Trying to make sure it had been worth it, Nacho started working as fast as he could to slice the meat off bone.

He soon had piled up ninety credits' worth of meat and was covered in blood, yuck, and feathers. Ignoring his grimy state, he attacked his food and water supply to bring his expendable points back to tenable levels.

Within a few minutes of Nacho completing his project, Reuben and Brie returned from the tunnels, heaving for breath. Reuben flicked a glance at his gore-coated friend as he choked down a gulp of water. "Well, that was some good exercise, and it looks like our boy Nacho has been working hard. You might want to try letting *some* of the blood drop to the floor instead of covering your clothes."

Back-to-back Skill usage had left each of them feeling weak, thirsty, and hungry. A bad hunger. Nacho couldn't manage to rebut his friend, instead tearing open a protein bar and swallowing it in three bites. Altogether, the bar and peanuts were only worth a half-portion, but after swigging down a bunch of water, he forced himself to talk. "Let's go get our stuff and move back to the waterfall cave. From there, we can figure out our credit situation. With all of these monsters out of the way, it should be fairly safe to camp in the tunnels; certainly more than being out in the open."

As they hiked back to the waterfall, Nacho couldn't help but feel frustrated. They were doing well with credits, and they were progressing, but he *still* wasn't convinced they should spend their money on his Satiation class, despite bumping up his Ingredient Processing Skill to grind for credits. It was already day two, he hadn't been able to cook anything, and combat Skill increases *was* an immediate need.

"We should continue to spend credits on Brie's combat Skills. Food is still cheap from the Store, and it's not like my supposed ability to cook food right now would help us any." Nacho was muttering under his breath and trying to be convincing, but there was a part of him that wondered what a full-power Satiation Player looked like. This was *completely* new territory for him. Yes, there had been rumors of other special classes during his three years in the Juxtaposition, but he'd learned long ago that truth and rumor were distant cousins, twice removed, and most of the time related by marriage only.

They rappelled down the roots to the trail and retrieved their hidden backpacks, then trekked back up and swung through the waterfall. Nacho was pleased by their current location: the dungeon entrance was a pretty good camp. They couldn't smell the Caw Paws, and though the waterfall kept things a bit chilly, it made for a nice view. The roar also drowned out the now-constant drums from deep underground.

They cautiously waited for a short amount of time, but no new birds came flying in. It appeared they had been successful in killing the entire roost. After purchasing more lantern fuel, they stood around the light source and tallied their credits. They'd killed thirty-three of the Caw Paws, earning thirteen credits each. Reuben looked at his friends with a happy smile. "Four hundred and seven credits. This is *awesome*."

Brie nodded at Nacho, "Are we buying your cooking stuff? I'm getting hungry every few minutes."

He winced and shook his head. "I just can't justify spending even *more* credits on my class stuff before we get you guys more combat-effective. My previous expenditure hasn't paid off yet, even if it was close. I'm thinking-"

Reuben opened his mouth to agree, likely about to reference his own Skills, but Brie dug her heels in. "Can't you imbue your cooking with magic to increase one of our Skills?"

"At level one, I could *theoretically* cook something that will boost one of your stats by five percent. But this early in the world, that is only a *fraction* of your damage." Nacho gestured despondently at her, as if to ward off money being spent on him.

Brie pondered the numbers, eventually shaking her head. "So... instead of a five percent damage bonus, I get a *seven-point-five* percent bonus. Fine, I see your point, but we need you to be able to keep up eventually. I guess the Store food isn't *that* bad."

"We can buy M&Ms for our trail mix!" Reuben called as he gave Nacho a friendly punch on the arm.

Their willingness to *not* eat his cooking didn't make Nacho

feel any better. Then again, after seeing steak turn into goo...
he couldn't blame them. He lit a small fire for light and warmth,
even managing to position it in the path of a flow of wind that
swept the smoke out through the side of the waterfall. The
constant moisture made the cave damp, but at least the corpses
of the bird monsters had fully melted away into nothingness.

He skewered some of his Blues Bird meat and tried to cook
it, but gave up as soon as it turned into goo. "No, I can't just *not*
be able to cook food. There *has* to be more to it."

It was Store food for dinner once again, at the low cost of
nine credits. Reuben ordered a meat-lover's pizza, Brie went
with shrimp enchiladas, while Nacho got the Dr. Salisbury's
Salisbury Steak. Nacho remembered it as the best possible meal
from the Store. In his mind, all Salisbury steak tasted exactly the
same. Was it good or bad? There was no way to tell.

During his six months back in his old life, he'd looked up the
name of the meat, having always wondered where it came
from. The answer somehow didn't surprise him even a little bit.
Dr. Salisbury had invented the meal during the American Civil
War: it was soldier food and tasted like it.

Nacho had warned Reuben to stay away from the pizza:
mediocre pizza was a heartbreaker. Reuben hadn't listened and
was now doing a lot of sighing. Finally, the Healer erupted.
"I'm telling you, I've had cold, week-old Domino's pizza that
was left in the box on my counter that tasted better than this!"

"You should have never put that moldy filth in your mouth,"
Brie informed her fiancé sternly. "The fact that you can legiti-
mately make this comparison bothers me."

"Also, I *did* warn ya," Nacho chuckled as his friend tried to
backpedal. "Same watches as last night? Actually, since the two
of you are doing most of the fighting-"

"Hold it. Not tonight, Nacho." Brie stopped him from
volunteering to do two shifts. "You need to *sleep*. We need some
clarity on this stuff, and interrupting your night messes with
your ability to think. At some point, we're going to need to
invest in your cooking abilities. There *has* to be a reason why

Satiation Players weren't a thing, and why you suffered so much because of it."

A thousand responses leapt to Nacho's mind, but he couldn't voice any of them. She was right, blast it.

"Hold on..." Reuben furrowed his brow, and his eyes flicked back and forth between the other two. "I thought *I* was the leader."

Brie leaned over to him and kissed his cheek. "You're the leader of my heart, but you'll never be able to order me around. Now get to sleep. You're taking second watch. Nacho will go first. I'll take last."

"You can't just..." Nacho literally had no idea how he had been planning to end that sentence, so instead, he threw another stick into the fire. "Fine, but first we upgrade you, Brie. We pour *everything* into your Skills."

"In the morning," she insisted sternly.

"No, wait." Reuben shook his head, his gamer intuition starting to spin. "Nacho's right. There's a chance that whatever is down there drumming might come up here to party. They might be tough, and we don't want to die with unused credits. It's like those guys who die of thirst in the desert with full canteens because they hoard water, thinking that they will use it when they need it. Or me, when I used to play video games, and I hoarded ninety-nine of every potion since they were supposed to be used 'rarely'."

Brie tossed her hands into the air. "*Fine*! I'm fine with being the best and the strongest, but what happens when I'm busy and you all need to fend for yourselves? Pumping everything into me just sounds... it's just a bad idea!"

"We trust you to do your job, and we can both fend for ourselves long enough for you to come save our butts." The Healer stretched out, then snuggled into his sleeping bag.

Brie's eyes glowed as she accessed the Store. "At this point, hunger hasn't been an issue because we have food, so I'm not going to increase my Athletic Endurance just yet. *Only* Combat Dash and Defensive Whirl."

"Oh, hey!" Nacho abruptly remembered a function of the system that had almost never been used by people in his first attempt. "Since we're a party, you can share some of the Stat Sheet. Do you mind sharing your Skills? I'm not a hundred percent on what your levels are."

It took a second, but soon both Nacho and Reuben were poring over Brie's Skills.

Brie McCurdy
Skill Slots (3/4)

- *Athletic Endurance (Passive) Level 1: 2% reduction to hunger loss penalties when using physical Skills*
- *Combat Dash (Active) Level 2: 4% Damage on Dash Attacks, 10 meter dash*

Mana Cost = 0%
Hydration Cost = 0%
Metabolic Cost = 10%

- *Defensive Whirl (Active) Level 2: Spin toward your enemy, auto-blocking up to 1 strike*

Mana Cost = 0%
Hydration Cost = 0%
Metabolic Cost = 15%

- *Open slot*

Nacho pulled up the Store, noticing that to get both her combat Skills to level three, it would take one hundred and twenty credits—sixty each. Fourth level would be one hundred and *sixty* credits each. They had enough to get her to fourth level for both with some extra left over. He leaned back on the stone wall, using his hands to cushion his head. "Brie, keep up with your Athletic Endurance. We have the extra points, and the less hungry you get, the better. It'll make a difference, I promise."

"So will your cooking," Brie insisted as she waffled between a spending spree and what they *should* be doing with the money.

Nacho wasn't sure about that. They eventually convinced her to take her Athletic Endurance up to level two for another forty, and he pondered what else they should make happen before settling in for the night. "You know, I think the best thing to do next would be to upgrade Reuben's healing ability. We haven't needed it so much yet, which is great, but there is no world where having a Healer that can give you more health right when you need it is a bad thing. That's only another forty."

Brie's eyes gleamed as her Skills increased. Keeping her Stat Sheet open, Nacho watched it happen in real time:

Level 2 Athletic Endurance!
  Level 4 Combat Dash!
  Level 4 Defensive Whirl!

Reuben upped his level while completely hidden within his sleeping bag. "Just like that, I'm a level two hugger. Fear me. Thanks for cheesing us up, Nacho."

"No problem, buddy. Just like that, we are down to thirty-seven credits." Nacho didn't comment on the inside joke. As his friends drifted to sleep and the minutes of his solitary shift turned into hours, the cook reflected on how different things were this time around.

Misty-eyed, he watched his friends as they slept, whispering so softly that only he could hear, "Can I just say... doing this with you is so much better than fighting through it alone?"

CHAPTER TWENTY-FIVE

Near the end of his watch, the drumming had started again, and Nacho realized why the rhythm had sounded familiar: it was reminiscent of an electronic music festival. "I guess we'll get to find out what kind of messed-up rave is going on down there."

Morning came all too quickly, and despite the thirty-seven credits The Dinner Party still had between them, they went with the cheaper option for breakfast. Anything purchased from the Store would be just as disappointing, so they pulled open the backpacks Nacho had prepared. Soon instant oatmeal oozed down all three of their unhappy throats as quickly as they could force the goop inward.

They still had two days' worth of food supplies remaining, but they were quickly realizing that Earth food was even more precious than they had originally thought. Nacho felt better after getting nearly a full night of unbroken sleep. Reuben was already rubbing at bleary eyes, and the cook felt for him. Middle watch was brutal. Patting his large friend on the shoulder to show solidarity, Nacho ate his breakfast without speaking—in fact unable to speak around the sludge.

Brie had been correct about sleep and the need for his abilities, and Nacho had to laugh that it was the maple and brown sugar flavored oatmeal that finally convinced him that they *needed* to invest in his Satiation class. As he well knew, even though Store meals were cheap, they weren't free. They needed every credit possible to advance their Skills, and if he waited until they *needed* good food, they wouldn't be able to spend the credits on advancing him.

Eventually, he would even be able to sell his food—six credits would purchase a meal for three people? That was a full one-third cheaper than the Store, and likely three times more delicious… maybe. Once he got some practice.

After tidying up their campsite and banking the fire, they left Reuben's and Brie's packs leaning against the entrance wall. Both of them armored up with whatever gear they had available, while Nacho filled his backpack with some of the food from their packs.

"Everyone ready to risk it all today so we can start the day with eggs tomorrow? No? Too early to talk?" They groggily descended the steps to the T-junction, and Nacho found himself bouncing with nervous excitement. "Remember that communication is key! We have our Berserker leveled up, so now she just needs something to berserk at."

"Did you guess what the drummer pun is going to be?" Reuben finally broke the monologue that Nacho was starting up. "Going by the bird theme, I feel like I already know what the monsters are called. It's brilliant."

"Even if I can see the humor in them, unlike Brie, I try *not* to think in puns or memes." Nacho lifted the lantern, sending light scattering along the tunnel.

"Excuse *you*." Brie glared at him, her bloodshot eyes reminding Nacho that their front-liner hadn't had coffee in a full day. "I will be up at the front. Move it."

He hurriedly changed both his position and the subject. "Before we go seek out the drummers, let's check out the Caw

Paw lair? We can wipe out any we missed, and maybe we'll find some treasure?"

"I'm up for that." Reuben inhaled sharply and tapped his gauntleted fingertips together with a grin. "I *love* the smell of treasure in the morning!"

They followed the trail of guano down a corridor to the cavern where the Caw Paws had clustered, which ended in a mess of feathers and droppings. They spotted some gold coins encrusted to the floor, but nothing of any value. It was ironic to the cook that gold coins weren't worth the effort of bending over to gather. They already had seventy-six coins of dubious value, and weighing themselves down wasn't a great plan.

Having determined that there was nothing to loot, they inched back down the hallway in the same marching order. They turned to the left as the hall ended, finding a new set of steps leading downward, spiraling around, and likely leading deep under the ground. "I want to explain to you both that the deeper we go, the more Putrid Mana saturates *everything*, meaning the monsters become more powerful. Abyss, even the walls become harder to chip. Also, these creatures of the deep don't need to eat to level up; the poison leaks into their bodies automatically. At least, that's the leading theory."

"The longer we go without killing them, the more likely something *way* too powerful comes out?" Reuben's query reminded Nacho of the not-distant-enough Calamity, but he merely nodded in agreement as they continued onward. The helical stone staircase ended at a vast abyss, where a narrow ledge cut into the side of the bedrock allowed them to ease along the edge of the pit. A handful of lights were visible deep below, flickering as they were occasionally blocked by figures moving and glowing strangely. The drumming sounded louder here, seeming to come from the bottom of the crevice.

Brie looked a little pale, though Nacho couldn't be too sure: the lantern wasn't helping anyone's complexion. "I can't stop thinking about how glad I am that I leveled my combat abilities.

I have no idea how you're so calm about going into this as a Basic Chef."

"He's a *Common Cook*. Specific words matter." Reuben grinned at the double eye roll he earned. "Look, I'm only here to give you some Positive Vibes, maybe a hug or two."

"Sounds good right now," Brie admitted as she gripped her maul tightly, "but me and Milley are gonna focus on making the monsters hug the wall with their blood."

"Eh... I'd give that one a four out of ten." The Healer grinned at the fact that his bride didn't look back at him. "I *knew* it! You *are* trying to figure out a catchphrase."

An increase in the drumming below hushed them. The syncopated beat went *boom, boom, boom*, the same deep bassline of every EDM song Nacho had ever heard.

The ledge offered them a choice: keep going straight—over a narrow bridge—or descend a ladder. Something about that bridge felt like a trap, but why would a nice, convenient ladder be here? Nacho wracked his brain to remember what Myron might've said about the MurderSong Dungeon way back when. Likely nothing that would be useful to any of them, seeing as he'd forgotten to include anything about croaking. More probable, the Assassin had intentionally misled people with his stories.

"Down the ladder?" Brie motioned to the iron rungs hammered into the rock. It looked fairly new, not a spot of rust, but... something about this situation...?

"Down the ladder," Nacho *very* reluctantly agreed.

Brie's Splatter Mallet—now apparently named 'Milley'—vanished into her Storage Slot, and she started down with Reuben right above her. The Healer wasn't about to let his fiancée descend without being there to hold her together if something got in a lucky attack. One major benefit of his gauntlets was that he could climb with his weapons ready.

Nacho slung the bow and quiver over his shoulder, along with his backpack. He climbed down with the lantern clenched in his teeth, wishing momentarily that they had headlamps like the miners from movies. He pushed the thought away; there *was* an option for an oil-based light that attached to your head, but he'd once seen a guy get hit and wind up with his face on fire. As he started down, he whispered under his breath, "*No~o* thank you."

They ever-so-slowly descended a good five hundred feet from the ledge, all the way down to a smaller crevice in the rock face, where a tunnel led off into the darkness. They could take it… or they could continue to make their way down to what appeared to be the lowest floor of this missile silo of a hole. Then they'd know who—or what—was drumming. Something told Nacho that the MurderSong Blades wouldn't be found that deep. Myron had gotten them early on, when he'd been weak and clueless. Even then, he must've gotten lucky; something powerful would guard such valuable artifacts. Currently, his team was so deep that there was a good chance they'd face at least one Tier one monster, and they'd need to run.

With that concern in mind, Nacho nearly called off the operation. They wouldn't be able to even *damage* a Tier one. Fighting across level gaps was already hard; fighting across Tier gaps was *impossible* without the skills and gear to even things out. as they were.

At the bottom of the ladder, where the crack continued descending to the floor, Nacho gathered his friends around him while the air thrummed with the drumbeat. "Listen… this is getting too risky. I didn't realize how far down this was. As long as we're facing Tier zero monsters, we *should* be fine as a team. *But.* If we encounter something that's Tier one, you physically will not be *able* to pierce its skin. I think we should leave before that becomes an issue."

Brie waved his concern away with a harsh, "Wait, we won't be able to do *anything* to them? You probably should've told me this back in the first cave before I started running ahead. It's fine, I get that you aren't perfect, but I need to know… do I *need* to pierce its skin to kill it? I have a hammer. Brie *smash* monster with hammer."

"You've never been more beautiful to me than you are at

this moment," Reuben whispered without allowing his eyes to leave her face.

"Technically… no, you don't need to cut it." Nacho went through the logistics of inter-Tier combat quickly. "At Tier one, Putrid Mana reinforces the skin of the monsters with their mana, giving them supernatural armor. The only way around that armor is to inflict just *crazy* numbers in damage with a single strike. As far as research shows, you generally have to do at *least* a tenth of the thing's total Health Points, or the attack just bounces off. We've been able to kill beasts pretty quickly, but they were all pretty low level, not to mention within our own Tier. I'd imagine that whatever is guarding the Murder-Song Blades is going to be quite a bit tougher: they are *amazing* knives. Most artifacts lose their potency once you hit Tier one, but not these. I know for a fact that you can buy upgrades for them at the Store."

"Do you mean that Brie-Hulk is going to have to give up her Splatter Mallet?" Reuben questioned with a concerned glance at his clearly hammer-obsessed bride-to-be. "Brie-Hulk… Bulk? Can I call her 'Bulk' and get away with it?"

"Give up Milley? Say it ain't so," Brie breathed with misty eyes, which hardened as she realized what Reuben had said *out loud*. "You can get away with calling me 'Bulk' *once*. That's right now, and never again."

"You'll probably have to get a new one." Nacho tried to rip the bandage off as gently as possible, patting the hammer as Brie clutched it close. "If it's any consolation, it's fairly likely that we can find you another maul that does *horrific* things to monsters. Back to the *point* of all this: I'm pausing our little strike team to tell you, if you can't hurt a monster, we run. We beat feet as fast as we can out of this place, and hope that whatever we're facing can't fly."

"Oh. Oh no." Reuben looked a bit taken aback as realization dawned that they might be in over their heads. "Ladders and fighting don't really go together, Nacho."

"No, they do not." Nacho enunciated each word grudgingly.

He *hated* that he was so driven to get the knives. They could've stayed up top, killed random wildlife, and leveled up safely. His major issue was that once he fixated on a plan, it was incredibly difficult for him to deviate from it. It was a failing he had never found the time to address, but he knew the root cause: growing up in chaos, he clung to order as soon as he felt that he had found it.

With the lantern's light mostly blocked, Nacho noticed a myriad of strange, multicolored light issuing from the floor itself. He also noticed polished footholds in the rock that would allow them to reach the floor below without much trouble. They picked their way down the stone wall until they could clearly see the floor and the bizarre creatures.

Once again, the monsters on their battle menu were crow-themed, but these things were man-shaped and wearing leather armor, cat-pelt stoles, and feathery cloaks fashioned from the Caw Paws, or that's what their garb looked like. No wonder the Caw Paws had retreated when they heard the drumming; they didn't want to become some other monster's accessory.

The man-shaped bird-men had the heads of giant crows, with those same unblinking stygian eyes. The same sharp, curved beaks. They likewise brandished weapons of obsidian, the sharpened wedges of rock strapped to wooden handles with leather thongs. Constantly in motion, the crow-men clutched the axes and spears with thin fingers at the end of their feathery arms.

There were five of the man-shaped creatures that they could see: four were dancing, and one kept rhythmically slamming a drumstick on a single huge drum sitting on the floor. That drum was like a timpani on steroids. Every time the drummer struck the skin, the impact echoed off the walls, sounding exactly like an electric drum. It was almost… mesmerizing. Nacho could easily see himself enjoying this music, falling into a flow state as he worked. But unfortunately, these beasts needed to die so that he could get a few extra credits, and that was all that mattered.

Five crow-men. One drumming, four dancing, but then things became strange. The crow-men wore glowing anklets, bracelets, and necklaces shining with a mixture of pink and green. The big timpani drum was also painted with the neon-colors, but blue and yellow had been added to the pink and green.

"Do you get the pun yet?" Reuben whispered directly into Nacho's ear, his eyes sparkling.

"Sadly... yes." Nacho closed his eyes and answered with a defeated sigh. "They're 'Rave-ings', aren't they?"

Reuben had to wheeze to hold in his laughter. "I *knew* it. I *called* it. I should've told you up top, but you never would've believed I hadn't snuck down here to get the answer ahead of time."

Nacho eyed his friend suspiciously, but the Healer merely continued to look innocent and a touch naive. Stifling a disbelieving snort, the cook used the System View to zoom in on one of the crow-men.

Rave-ings
  Effective Tier/Level: ?
  HP: ?

That single question mark next to the Effective Tier/Level put him at ease for about three seconds, until he recalled the name of the dungeon. He said the last word out loud as he applied the puns he had been intentionally ignoring suddenly bloomed into realization. "That sign didn't say The MurderSong of the *Croaking*. It was the *Crow King*. These things have a leader, and I'll bet you anything he'll be right at the edge of Tier one... if he's not there already."

The five Rave-ins were getting their groove on when another five came running up. These were clearly not part of the same group, as the intruders' jewelry glowed yellow and blue. The Dinner Party watched in stunned silence as the inter-lopers used the blunt ends of their weapons to bash the original crow-men to the floor. Once the last of the pink and green Rave-ings crumpled to the ground, the yellow and blue ones stole the drum and rolled it off into the darkness waiting at the bottom of the pit.

The pink-greenies got to their feet, stood motionless for a moment as if stunned, then chased after the yellow and blue interlopers, squawking harshly. Reuben watched the bird-men as they ran, nodding sagely as he observed the skirmish from their hidden position. "That explains why the drumming starts and stops. They have rival DJs. DJ competition can be fierce. There might be a dance fight, and we need to go see it."

"No, we need to *strategize*. There were at least ten of the Rave-ings, and probably a leader. Like with the Caw Paws, we need to divide and conquer. Wait here, and be ready," Nacho whispered, scurrying out long before Brie or Reuben could stop him. He didn't want to get mired down in a long discussion when they needed the lay of the land. There were a few things that didn't rely on Assassin skills, and he'd been training himself to move swiftly and silently for months, in addition to his previous years of experience.

The walls were full of cracks and alcoves, and he immedi-ately found a fissure to dash into. His eyes glittered in the dark-ness as he tracked the colorful glowing drum into the resulting hiding place. It had been rolled to the north end of the floor— at least, Nacho thought it was north—and had been positioned directly next to a throne, as well as a collection of sticks and sparkly things.

On that throne sat what had to be the Crow King.

He was a giant beast, seven feet tall at least, and his Caw Paw pelts were far more ornate than the others. They gleamed with gold, jewels, bits and bobs, as well as random shiny objects that a humanoid crow might collect and weave into cloth he'd made out of other crow creatures. The Crow King unabashedly sported neon warpaint in the colors of both sets of Rave-ings, as he was their king. In the end, he was a savage specimen of monster crow madness.

A yellow and blue drummer thrummed on the giant drum with his timpani mallet and the other four yellow and blue crow-men danced, while the pink-and-greenies stood on the outskirts, cawing, croaking, and brandishing their weapons. Every time one of the five pink-and-greens tried to steal the drum back, the others let out raucous shrieks and swiped at them with blades that had been hidden only moments prior. In the face of such a zealous defense, the pink-and-greenies were forced back.

When the Crow King saw their plight, he croaked out twisted laughter.

The System View didn't work at long range, so Nacho couldn't get a read on the Crow King, but he would've bet anything that the monster on the throne was a too high level for them to fight. Even so, the cook had an idea, and he swiftly slipped through the shadows and back up the footholds to where Brie and Reuben were waiting.

"Not. *Cool.* Nacho." Brie's lips were pressed together so tightly that she could barely get the words out.

"Sorry. I'm used to doing this alone, and I wasn't thinking. I'll try not to let it happen again. Listen… I ran some recon." He quickly detailed what he had seen… and then outlined his plan.

"I like it a lot." Reuben grinned in the lantern's dim glow. "An old-school ambush, just like Grandma used to make."

CHAPTER TWENTY-SIX

It wasn't long before the pink-and-greenies caught their opponents off guard and beat them to the ground, stole the big drum back, and came rolling south with it, screaming with what The Dinner Party could only assume was laughter the entire time.

They passed obliviously by the crevice where Nacho and his friends sat, and once the coast was clear, the cook led them into the darkness between the Crow King's throne and the clearing where the pink-and-greenies had already resumed dancing. Brie quietly asked how the bird men could continue dancing and drumming for days on end, and Nacho interceded before Reuben could make a joke.

"It's the Putrid Mana. The same thing that made them monsters gives them almost unlimited stamina," Nacho explained in a low tone, "I'll admit, the steal-the-drum game between the Rave-ings is… inexplicable. Maybe it's an inside joke from the Patrons? I've never seen something like this before, so I just don't know."

He found an alcove big enough for Brie and Reuben in the cave wall on the left side, then crossed to the right and located a crack for himself. The plan was fairly simple: they'd attack on Brie's signal after Reuben gave them both some Positive Vibes. When the Berserker attacked, she'd keep it quiet, because they didn't want to face all ten Rave-ings at the same time. They'd take care of the yellow-and-blues first, then deal with the pink-and-greenies. If all went well, they'd wrap up by sneaking to the north and taking down the Crow King.

For a long moment, while Nacho waited in the darkness, he wished he was alone. He *knew* that he could easily get to the end of the chasm and kill every single one of these things—except perhaps the King—all by himself, even as weak as he was currently. More than that, he wouldn't have had to worry about his friends dying. He shook off the misplaced anger and tried to just focus on the plan.

Motion pulled him back to the present.

Five neon-jeweled figures carrying stone weapons came creeping across the cavern floor, awash in yellow and blue. They were clearly planning their own ambush, making the ambush on the ambush an extra-effective ambush.

Brie was just another mote of darkness until she blurred into motion and sheathed her hammer in the skull of one of the crow-men, clearly landing a critical hit combined with sneak attack damage. The other crows shrieked with shock and rage as Reuben grappled another, beating on it with his gauntlets.

The Juxtaposition's routine notification of a session of Active Combat materialized just as the punching started. Enraged, the crow-men cawed above the muted din of the battle. The party had chosen this space for attack because it was unlikely that battle would be loud enough to draw either the Crow King or the pink-and-greenies. At least, that was the hope. Either way, they had to put the yellow-and-blues down fast.

Brie whirled through the vibrant crow-men, effortlessly drawing their attacks. Because her Defensive Whirl had been raised to level four, she managed to perfectly block two axes before they could slash within a foot of her chainmail. Reuben shouted a warning as he threw the crow he had grabbed toward his fiancée, and she used her hammer to sweep its legs, then adjusted her grip, swung, and took off a chunk of its head.

With a grunt, Reuben crushed his hands together with a Rave-ing's head between them. It didn't kill the crow, but the odd blow did stun it. Brie cracked the skull of another of the monsters, then spun and killed the crow whose cheeks Reuben had clapped.

The Healer sputtered as bone fragments and gore geysered into his face.

Nacho took advantage of the chaos, approaching from the back and driving his knife into the kidneys of a crow-man before it could attack the distracted party members with its spear.

One, two, three thrusts, finished with a twist to ensure no healing could ever manage to meld the pieces back together. Nacho gripped it by its feather cloak with his left hand while he stabbed with his right, then gently set the corpse on the ground as it stopped struggling, though he continued to press the blade to the base of its neck as a precaution. "Reuben!"

The Healer whirled, spotted the crow on the ground, and sent a fist into the back of its skull, driving the beak into the stone and cracking the beast's neck.

The System message ticked down the damage from his attack, happily not giving Nacho credit for the kill.

Damage Dealt: 20, 12, 11! You're moving too fast for individual updates!
The first hit was a critical sneak attack for double damage!

Noticing the combo backstab and haymaker, the last Rave-ing still on its feet turned toward Nacho, and the cook found himself about to get a stone axe in the face. The Berserker spotted the advancing crow-man just in time to Defensive Whirl her way out of two attacks, dropping her hammer where beak met face. The wet *crunch* as it landed caused enough pain that the drummer crow attempted to flee.

The mutated creature turned and ran back toward the king's throne, and Brie allowed it a few steps before Combat Dashing her way up to it and releasing her full kinetic load on it. The feathered biped went down with a weak croak, then lay unmoving.

Active Combat ended with a cheery message from the Juxtaposition.

Whoa! You put the 'murder' in 'attempted murder'! Tasty! Combat is over!

Nacho was shaking from the adrenaline, a wide smile on his lips as he felt the thrill of combat once more. His blade came up toward his mouth, practically of its own accord, and he needed to use all his willpower not to lick the Putrid Mana-filled blood off of it. Instead, he flicked the weapon, sending the blood spatter onto the wall and floor. Luckily, Brie and Reuben hadn't observed his near-lapse; they were both breathing hard and sweating, faces bathed in the neon glow of the dead creatures' jewelry.

The cook gathered himself into the most non-insane posture he could hold at the moment, then made a shushing motion in the hopes that his friends would realize they needed to keep quiet. They complied and sank into the shadows, listening carefully for the expected warning of another attack. Nothing converged on them, neither the Crow King nor the pink-and-greenies.

Instead, the drumming continued echoing through the area uninterrupted, a funky beat that had completely covered the sounds of their ambush. Nacho glanced north toward the Crow King's throne, then at his friends. "How much were they worth?"

Brie's eyes flashed blue as she wiped some blood off her chin. "Looks like they were twenty credits each."

"I *missed* this." Nacho was glad he hadn't killed the one he'd tried to backstab, feeling nearly as glad that he had managed to keep his bad habits hidden away where they belonged. Twenty credits was a *lot* per monster, right at the top of what any Tier zero monster could pay out. Better yet, they'd survived the fight and taken down five of the mid-level Tier zero Rave-ings in one shot. This was *very* good news. Now, if they could get lucky with the pink-and-greenies, they could wipe out the Crow King's minions without him suspecting a thing.

Nacho perked up with another great idea. "Okay, for the others, Reuben will juice you up with Positive Vibes, Brie. You'll go in hot, whirl, and start smashing things. Reuben, you grab the drummer. I'll pick up the drum stick and try to keep those beats going. Recap: you guys fight. I drum. We'll stop for a quick snack, then go for the king. Brie, how much did you use up?"

"I'm only down thirty-eight Hunger points, so I'm good for another battle like that. It's uncomfortable, but I'm getting used to it." She winced as her wound started to heal and pulled together her torn flesh. "It might take a minute for my Health Regen to fix me up, though. That axe got me good."

"Eat food, and it'll go faster. Actually, no, that'll take too long. Just hang out for a few-" Nacho corrected himself, clumsily moving on to contingency planning, only to be interrupted by the Healer.

"We are *not* waiting for that axe wound to stop bleeding on its own," Reuben growled as he stepped forward and hugged Brie, and two seconds later, she was at full health. He reached for a water bottle to replenish his Thirst points as Nacho sighed and rubbed at his head.

Brie gestured to him as she reached for a bite of food, only to get her hand slapped away by the cook. "You know, if we had some delicious Nacho snacks, it'd be no big deal to just eat something right now and be fine. Instead, we need to use precious resources-"

"I *get* it, I get it," Nacho cut her off with a growl. "Just understand that eating takes longer than drinking, and we need to hurry and kill the rest of the dancers to get to the king. Still, it looks like you're dishing out enough damage even *without* Combat Dodge to put these things down. Use Defensive Whirl sparingly, and we've got this. After we finish off the dancers, we can break for a proper meal. Okay… a snack. Small one. Raisins and peanuts, at most."

"How generous and gracious of you!" Reuben commented drolly, then snapped his fingers. "Abyss. I forgot to buy candy from the Store to help your… snack."

"You'll learn to love any food you can shove in. Savoring only makes it harder to get up to maximum Hunger Points," Nacho informed The Dinner Party grimly as they crept south, abandoning the glowing crow bodies littering the cavern floor. Before long, they approached the leaping and strutting pink-and-greenies. Reuben boosted them all with some Positive Vibes, as he'd figured out how to dole out his power without a revealing light show.

Brie trotted toward the Rave-ings, hammer in hand. The pink-and-greenies were expecting another good-natured attack from their rival gang at some point, and so didn't react as quickly as they should have. Instead of friendly feathered faces, they were set upon by a Berserker in chainmail and a helmet, running forward in combat boots and swinging her oversized hammer.

Active Combat had begun.

Brie activated her Defensive Whirl as she hit the Rave-ins, but the Skill could only automatically block two attacks at its current level. The third blow came from a crow-man slamming a hatchet into her chainmail. Nacho winced sympathetically as she let out a pained *wheeze*. That was going to leave some serious damage. Reuben would have to hug her as soon as possible to bring her back into proper fighting form; unfortunately, the fight had just gotten tricky.

As for the big guy himself, he rammed his fist into the crow holding the timpani hammer, and the stick clattered to the stone floor. The Rave-ing reached for a pair of obsidian daggers sheathed around his midsection.

Reuben grabbed the crow-man and flung him into the back of one of his buddies, sending both creatures sprawling. "You're Rave-ing mad, but you're not very good at fighting!"

"No trash talk until they're dead, please!" Nacho sprinted over and grabbed the timpani stick, trying to match the drumbeat and hoping he had at least as much rhythm as a monster crow. The beat once more boomed through the chamber, and the fighting shifted slightly as the tempo subconsciously began to impact the combatants.

Reuben punched the crow three times, matching the rapid staccato beat that Nacho was drumming out. Brie whipped her hammer around as hard as possible, the blows landing on each of the drum's fourth beats. One such strike shattered one of the Rave-ing's beaks, and the Berserker immediately spun and tactically retreated from the three surviving crows; she needed to try to staunch her wounds.

The monsters didn't mind, instead turning on Reuben as he raised his blood-coated fists and taunted them. "Come on, you prime candidates for bird flu! Wanna be my patient zero? Your beats are the opposite of sick; they're practically *healthy*. You're metronome dancers!"

"What did I say about trash talk?" Nacho shouted over the beat of his own drum. With their enemies thoroughly distracted, Brie came charging back in and flattened one of the birds as it tried to turn on her. Another whirled a pike and slashed Reuben's thigh, sending blood streaming over the camo pattern. The pants didn't offer any protection, but to his credit, he didn't let the wound stop him: instead he promptly punched the Rave-ing's lights out.

Once he'd cleared himself some breathing room, the Healer

started doing his actual job, forcing Brie into a hug and giving her a full ten health, even though he was also injured. The effort cost him, and he cried out as he took a heavy chop from the final crow, who was expertly wielding an obsidian axe. The razor-sharp stone blade sliced through the meaty part of Reuben's thigh, striking bone and sending the Healer to the ground with blood fountaining from the wound.

Brie flashed forward in a blind rage, using Combat Dash to save her fiancé as the monster reared back for a killing blow. Her hammer landed against the Rave-ing's left peeper, the weapon getting a true bird's eye view as the strike followed through and crushed its face. The beast spun around, already dead on its feet, but another hammer stroke slammed the carcass into the stone.

As soon as the Juxtaposition ended Active Combat, Brie was instantly on her knees next to Reuben, frantically wrapping his arms around his own body for him as he shook from shock and blood loss. "Hug yourself! Activate the Skill, Reuben!"

"Mmkay." Reuben glowed lightly, and his eyes began to focus once more. He reached up with trembling hands and wiped blood from his eyes, leaving a long streak across his face. "Remind me not to party in caves anymore. That DJ is giving me a headache."

"Doing the best I can over here." Nacho had kept the beat going steady, but now he started to throw in some fancy, quick beats, just in case the Crow King got suspicious. They needed time to heal and eat. "Too close guys, I'm so sorry. Get some food and water, and focus on healing. Should we get out of here?"

He must've been doing decently on the drum, because the System gave him a cheery message.

Hidden quest completed: It's Only Manslaughter if There is Probable Caws!

258

Good job drumming; you've kept the big bird entertained and compla-cent for five full minutes while you killed its subjects. Fifty credit bonus!

Nacho's teeth flashed in an excited grin. "Guys, I just got a bonus! Abyss, the rarest stuff just keeps throwing itself at us. I didn't get my first hidden quest for nearly a year the last... in the simulation."

"I didn't think those birds would be so ferocious. They're rave dancers! But I gotta give it to them..." Reuben hugged himself once more, a line of light covering the gash on his leg and closing the wound from the inside out. "...they had real chops."

"Patrons above, Reuben. Don't nearly die just to make a joke!" Brie threatened her groom with a water bottle, then stuck it in his mouth to cover the water leaking from her own eyes. He started chugging the water, because as Brie had correctly noticed, he was rapidly burning through Thirst points. The Berserker breathed a sigh of relief as Reuben's passive Health Regen finally kicked in, even though most of his bleeding had already been taken care of with his healing self-hugs.

Confident that her man was going to be fine, Brie went and pulled Nacho's backpack off, took a mouthful of water, and ravaged the teriyaki beef jerky. Normally, she was a stickler for manners, but she'd used her abilities to kill most of the ten Rave-ings and was utterly voracious. "I'm beginning to under-stand how critical eating is going to be in this game. The main problem is that I cannot get enough nutrients in my stomach fast enough. Does having higher-quality food let you eat less and still fill up your points?"

"Exactly that," Nacho called over. "At least in theory. I've literally only ever had the food from the Store, and one full meal is only ever one portion. Are you both ready? Or should we leave?"

The Crow King was next, and they all knew it.

Nacho continued to bang the drum as his friends hesitated.

He knew what the issue was: this was the first time they had killed anything even *approximating* a human, and it was already beginning to mess with them, now that their adrenaline was fading. "If we stay, here's the plan for the king: we'll roll the drum up the cavern after we go back and grab the blue and yellow jewelry from the first Rave-ings. He'll think it's just the other team stealing back the drum. I *would* suggest we hit him with the bow and arrow, but none of us has an archery Skill. We *need* to smack him with a bunch of damage all at once. Again, it's going to be all Brie, all the time."

"Brie *smash*." Reuben was ignored by his bride, but apparently he hadn't expected anything different. Being the gamer that he was, the Healer went over the bodies to see if they had any treasure—magic or otherwise. Sadly, all his efforts produced were the Caw Paw clothes, their stone weapons, and the neon jewelry that he tossed aside. "I'd take it, but pink and green just aren't my colors. I'm *far* more blue and yellow."

"Pink is nice. I think you'd look good in a crisp salmon shirt and white shorts." Brie casually attempted to sneak fashion sense into the man, but as per usual, she rolled a critical failure. "I want another minute, Nacho... but then I want to end this. We aren't going to be able to thrive without big windfalls, and that means taking risks."

The cook could only nod silently. Once everyone was ready, Nacho dropped the stick and started rolling the drum north toward the Crow King's throne. He only stopped once, just long enough for all of them to throw on the blue and yellow neon jewelry: anklets, bracelets, and necklaces. Thus outfitted, they progressed toward the floor boss, who continued croaking with laughter in the darkness.

While Nacho rolled the drum, Reuben jogged with Brie. Nacho was so glad they'd forced the huge man to work out ahead of the event. He was winded, in no way as conditioned as the lacrosse player or the ex-assassin, but he wasn't bent over and sucking wind like he would have been in the original time-line, had he lived.

When they got close enough to sight the throne of sticks, bones, and glittering trinkets—which was somehow outshone by the flash of the Crow King's multi-colored warpaint—Reuben gave them all a shot of Positive Vibes while draining a water bottle. In preparation to support the Berserker, he'd brought his Thirst back up to one hundred percent, and he had full Mana. Brie had polished off enough jerky to top off her Satiation stats as well, and Nacho was… hopeful.

Juiced up, Brie shot forward as they got in range, easily outpacing Nacho and Reuben. She ran directly up to the throne, adding spice to her initial blow with a healthy dose of Combat Dash. Fortunately, the Crow King realized he'd been ambushed a *beat* too late. He leapt to his feet, only to take Brie's hammer right in his side, though he managed to avoid a face-shot.

The neon-glowing bird-thing released a squawk full of fury. Nacho let the drum fall as the System message hit everyone involved.

Hey, Player, it's Active Combat time! You're facing your first boss monster, and it's the one, the only, Bob Bass, the Crow King! The Promoter Prince, the Duke of Dance! Better get your groove on, or else you might find yourself doing the worm dance six feet under. Remember: no Health or Mana Regen, and no Store fun!

Brie stood in front of the throne and cheered, "Twenty-five points of damage done! I can hurt him, and it's a *him*, all right."

"Where are you *looking*, Brie?" Reuben called with mock fury as he got into position.

Brie played it off easily. "You saw what the System said; he's Bob Bass!"

The Crow King acted as though he could understand them —either that, or he didn't take kindly to being attacked. He leapt into the air, a dagger in each slim-fingered hand aimed at

Brie. She whirled away in the nick of time, and Bob's attack was deflected to merely slice the side of her neck. Squawking angrily, the Crow King launched himself off the floor as she stumbled. He couldn't fly, but he still managed to glide right toward Nacho.

Reuben flung himself protectively in front of the cook. The Crow King's daggers pierced his back, though the chainmail protected the Healer from taking too much damage. Before his pained cry had even escaped his lips, Brie was there, her feet blurring with speed and her hammer swinging down like the pendulum of death. The head struck Bob Bass with the force of a freight train, crushing a wing and sending one of the daggers falling to the ground with a *tink*.

The Berserker leapt backward, gasping in a breath. "Damage done is fifty Health Points out of one hundred and sixty-five!"

They were unsure if this monster was Tier one, but they needed to act like it was. That meant that if she was going to kill the thing, she needed to continue to hit with a minimum of twenty-five points—which meant she needed to use her Combat Dash. Each strike took ten percent of her Hunger, so they *should've* been okay, but she'd used her Skills three times in this fight and was already down to sixty-five points. If every subsequent blow landed and she got a perfect hit, she should leave the fight with a quarter of her Hunger points left. The complicating issue was that she kept needing to use her Defensive Whirl, which cost her fifteen percent of her Hunger each time.

Reuben was already hurt—how bad, Nacho didn't know, but two knives to the back certainly couldn't feel good. The cook was going to have to deal some damage if they were going to make it out of this.

He got the drum moving and rolled it into the crow, who still couldn't fly. Bob *could* hop; in fact, he leapt effortlessly and nigh-instantly over the drum and onto Nacho. The human was trapped under the weight of the seven-foot-tall Crow King, and the monster drove his beak into the top of Nacho's chest like a spear.

The System flashed an ugly scarlet message:

Health remaining: 20/30!

"Oh, you're gonna pay for *that*." Nacho's voice was rough, nearly a snarl as he slashed his weapon into the beast ineffectually. The fact was, the cook knew the damage messages only too well. He'd managed to avoid being hurt up until now because he was neither a Body Player nor a Mind Player; but he had known it couldn't last forever.

Even worse, since Nacho didn't have any armor, he was being bashed up without any protection. The Crow King took advantage of the lack of resistance and slammed his remaining dagger into Nacho's arm.

Health remaining: 15/30!

Nacho felt the pain, but he also couldn't help but wonder why the damage wasn't worse. These *were* the MurderSong Blades, right?

"Get off him!" Brie punctuated her demand by smashing the Crow King's already damaged wing with her mallet. "Seventy-five points out of one-sixty-five!"

They had a long way to go, but Brie's Splatter Mallet had knocked Bob off balance. Reuben must've heal-hugged himself, because he came in slugging without any blood dripping off his back. His punches sent shockwaves through the feathers, sending Bob back-pedaling.

While the feathered beast was still reeling, Brie's hammer

came speeding back in and bashed the Prince of Promoters in the spine. "A hundred points even!"

Three more strikes. Three more rounds of Combat Dashing.

Nacho tried to get up, but he was dizzy from blood loss, and the pain was making it hard to concentrate. "Down to half Health and combat just started."

Reuben couldn't heal him, because he was currently trading blows with the Duke of Dance. The Healer managed to duck the dagger, but the Crow King's beak caught his silly leather helmet, and it was torn loose. He earned a gash on his scalp at the same time, yet it was nothing in comparison to his ridiculous headgear. "My helmet! Abyss, Bob, why are you and your crow DJs going after my helmet?"

"They know better than to let someone wear a hat like that in public!" Brie sprinted in, and her hammer strike sent the Crow King staggering. "Take the hint!"

Nacho finally forced himself to his feet and dropped his backpack. Wincing, he pulled out the bow, fitting an arrow to the string just as Bob charged forward. The Crow King acted like he wanted to finish off Nacho out of sheer spite. He wasn't even going after Brie, but to be fair, she was zooming around like a pain-inducing breeze.

The cook got an arrow off, merely hoping to distract Bob. The shaft bounced off the Crow King's face and left a small mark, causing the king to fling up his arms to protect his face in response.

Brie took the opening to rush by and crushed the disoriented king's leg. "One fifty! Only fifteen points left!"

As she sprinted around for another pass, Reuben tackled the beast, his gauntlets gripping Bob's wings. He might've been able to rip a normal Rave-ing's wings off with those metal gloves, but with the Crow King, he just barely managed to hold the thing still.

Frenzied to the point of panic, Bob spun and threw Reuben

to the ground and stabbed his beak into the big guy's exposed skull. A harsh, if glancing, blow.

The bow clattered to the ground as Nacho tackled the monster, mounted his feathery shoulders, and started twisting back and forth. "I'll choke you to death, if that's what it takes! You think you can attack *me*? My *friends*? I'm going to rip you apart and turn you into breakfast. I bet you're hiding something delicious under all those feathers! You're nothing more than a rotisserie chicken!"

He yanked hard, and the Crow King tripped and fell, landing heavily on his side as the cook struggled to keep him down. Out of the corner of his eye, Nacho could see that Reuben was still conscious, which was enough to help the cook hold it together while Brie sped forward and swung her hammer.

Hammer met crow skull.

Crow skull lost.

Congratulations, Player! Active Combat is over! Succulent success!

"That was… literally insane." Huffing in exhausted breaths as she hit her knees, Brie's hammer clanked off the stone floor. She brightened visibly as she went over the notifications, "Ooh. Twenty five credits with a fifty credit bonus for clearing a dungeon floor? We're up to three hundred and sixty-two credits! We can buy Nacho his cooking stuff, and I'm not going to lie… I'm so flippin' hungry right now. I only have fifteen Hunger points left."

Nacho found himself being gathered into Reuben's arms, and the cook could see that the Healer had already tended to himself. "I gotcha, buddy. Have some health. Now *that* could be my catchphrase. Have a heal. Hug a heal? Build a Bear?"

"I really liked 'Wanna be my patient zero'. It was ominous *and* confusing." The weary cook sagged in his friend's embrace as he felt the Health Points fill him. Once a full ten points sank in, he was back up to a comfortable twenty-five. "My Health Regen can take care of the rest; save your mana."

Brie was already face-first in the beef jerky, eating with gusto. Reuben chuckled at her... *ravenous*... consumption as he started shaking water bottles. He'd emptied a good number of them, so he breathed a sigh of relief when he found one that was still full, then sucked it dry.

Nacho reverently stepped over to one of the fallen daggers. He picked it up and used the System View... only to find that it was just a normal dagger. Concern filling him, he hurried over and lifted the other knife. Same thing. "These weren't the MurderSong Blades? Did we just kill a monster on the verge of Tier one for nothing? How did Myron do it?"

Nacho's lips pulled into an unconscious snarl. Those blades were *going* to be his.

CHAPTER TWENTY-SEVEN

"Not what you were expecting?" Reuben saw Nacho's thunderous face and reached out a reassuring hand. "Dude. It's okay. I know it sucks. Bob was this big feathered killing machine, and he was only worth twenty-five credits. We got twenty apiece for the Rave-ings, and they were a *fifth* as strong."

Again, Brie spoke with her mouth full, her voice garbled slightly. "We got the bonus, though."

"Cold comfort, I tell you!" Reuben shrugged as he drank more water to refill his mana pool. Utterly despondent over his failure to earn his prize, Nacho couldn't respond, despite the increasingly concerned glances the other two shared. While there were other passages into the MurderSong of Croaking dungeon, he couldn't imagine Myron would've wandered around too much.

No, the MurderSong Blades *had* to be a part of the Crow King's loot.

That only left exploring the room. His eyes turned to the throne.

He peered more closely at the messy nest. The big pile of sticks and partially visible fragments of scavenged items had been woven together haphazardly with copious amounts of feathers. His curiosity spiking, Nacho re-lit the lantern and slid all the neon jewelry off his limbs. They definitely wouldn't be taking the ridiculous pieces with them.

Squinting, the cook lifted the lantern hood so that the full flame was exposed.

The flickering light reflected off a few rusted trumpets, a splintered guitar, and some album covers—which was odd, given the fact that they weren't on Earth anymore. Nacho gingerly removed the guitar, hoping he wouldn't have to dig through the entire throne... and there they were. There, nestled among the sticks, were two daggers—one thick with an almost cleaver-like blade, the other a full-on battle dagger with a grand cross-guard to prevent the wielder's hand from sliding along the blade when they hit bone.

These were unquestionably the MurderSong Blades. "I *found* them."

Nacho didn't bother with the System View. He reverently lifted the pair of blades with unshed tears glistening at the corners of his eyes... until they simultaneously shifted right before his eyes. "*No!*"

Suddenly, he was holding a full-on cooking cleaver and what had to be a chef's knife. Neither would be found in a medieval weapons museum, true, but they could be purchased at any local high-end grocery store. Before his panic could override his brain, the System cheerily granted Nacho astounding information.

These were the MurderSong Blades (Tier 0 Weapons, Upgradeable), but you're not a simple murderer! You're so much more, and these lil beauties gotta match that!

Item Update!

Weapons: MurderSong Blades become... HungerCry Knives!

Congratulations, Satiation Player! You'll earn bonuses on chopping, dicing, and other kitchen-related activities.

Would you like more info on these amazing blades of deliciousness?
Yes / No

Nacho realized a couple things in that moment, and his shock must have shown clearly on his face. Reuben, still holding his water bottle, came close. "You okay, my cheesy chip?"

Brie stood back, ripping into a hunk of jerky with her teeth. "I think the knives are either better than he thought, or way worse. Don't tell me they're worse. I don't want to know if killing the big bird thing gave us butter knives."

"Don't know yet." The reply came out as a raspy whisper. Nacho's mouth had become so dry he could hardly talk. He'd come for powerful Assassin daggers, but the Juxtaposition had other ideas. As far as he could tell, just like the Splatter Millet, the daggers had changed because he wasn't a Body Player. He was a Satiation Player, and he had finally realized what that meant for his ability to do... anything.

Brie's chewing slowed as she grasped how serious the situation was. "Nacho, what's going on?"

He lifted the cleaver, then the chef's knife. "This is Hunger, and this is Cry. Say hello."

"Knives don't talk, Nacho. How could they say hello?" Reuben chuckled at himself and motioned with his water bottle. "Why are you getting all weepy over knives?"

"It's just... everything has changed. I figured if I got the MurderSong Blades, I might be able to use them to hack apart monsters and still get paid." Nacho let his arms fall to his sides as he huffed out a long sigh and stared at the ground. "You know, I thought I'd be useful in fights—get us more credits—but I don't think that's going to be the case. I'm going to spend the apocalypse in the kitchen. Cooking."

Reuben immediately grasped his dilemma and nodded along at the assessment. "Oh, man. Before, you were Mad Max, and now you're Martha Stewart. But, you know, look on the bright side? Anything you cook *has* to be better than the Store food."

Brie quirked a skeptical eyebrow. "So far everything Nacho tries to cook turns into goo, and he refuses to try to improve."

"I'm hoping with a recipe, I'll do better." Nacho inhaled and tried to let go of the massive disappointment filling his chest. "Okay. I'm not going to be helpful in battle, so I shouldn't fight unless it's absolutely necessary. We need all the credits we can get, and I can help both by using my Ingredient Processing skill, as well as selling the food I cook."

Reuben smiled brightly. "That means people—customers— which makes my marketing skill useful again! Just you wait. I'll have people lined up outside of our shop. Cart? Kiosk? Cart Kiosk? Yes, the combination is different from the individual version. Oh! Food truck!"

"No internal combustion engines," Brie pointed out kindly as she stretched.

Reuben shrugged and kept rambling. "Market stall. Get your Nachos here! Fresh, hot nachos!"

"If I wanted someone to eat me, I would just find an over-sized monster." Despite his doleful reply, Nacho was already feeling better; his best friend had always had that effect on him. He had to admit that he was still curious about the benefits his cooking could bring, so he took a look through the Store once more. The three of them had a collective three hundred and sixty-two credits, but he needed more—two hundred for a recipe and two hundred for whatever this *Coquinaria* was. He didn't want to risk going deeper into the dungeon—an actual Tier one monster would annihilate them. That meant going back to the surface and hunting up there.

In preparation, he and Reuben finished ransacking the stick throne, mostly freeing bits of broken glass, some buckles, and a few jewels and gold pieces. They added a couple of diamonds and a fist-sized sapphire to their inventory along with the seventy-six gold pieces.

They were about to give up when Reuben unearthed a pair

of metal boots—shining steel, gold trim, and golden buckles securing sturdy leather straps. The System View proclaimed they were Tier zero Armor called the 'Saucy Sabatons of Lower Half Protection'.

"Sabatons? They *rock!*" Reuben grabbed at the boots and mimicked an air guitar. "Do I look good? I feel like I look good."

Brie was unamused. "No man has *ever* looked good playing the air guitar. A real guitar? Yes. Oh my, yes. But the time, place, and hair all play into the equation. As does a helmet that an ogre should be wearing instead of a human."

Chuckling at their good-natured banter, Nacho idly bent and tore a handful of sticks off the base of the throne. Something small glittered from within a deep mess of feathers. "A ring? Listen, I don't have an opinion on the cute factor of guitar players, but I do agree that sabatons rock—also, Brie should get the boots."

"Hey! Traitor!" Rueben yelped as Brie snatched the boots and sat down to pull them on. "Just because she's cute doesn't mean she gets all the shoes she wants!"

Nacho ignored the spluttering Healer and extracted the innocuous-looking gold ring, earning another message.

Congratulations, Player! You've found the Ring of Cheese (Tier 0 Magic Item)! Magic rings don't get any cheddar than this! Don't swiss out! It's not bad, it's gouda!

Nacho held up the ring for the others to see, his brow furrowed in confusion. "Well, I found a magic item in all the mess. Not sure what it does, but it seems... cheese related?"

"Summon fondue?" Reuben's eyes widened hopefully. "Do you know that cheese is as addictive as most *drugs* back on earth? I've been thinking about it all day, but I didn't want to say anything."

"Not sure what it does yet, but is it okay if I keep it?" Nacho requested with a wince. "I don't mean to be greedy, and I already got-"

Reuben nodded and waved to quiet him down. "Sure, sure. It might go with the knives? Maybe you'll get bonuses for chopping up a cheese plate? Brie... help me out here... does one *chop* cheese?"

Nacho tucked the ring away, not willing to put it on yet, just in case it might be cursed. "You cut cheese-"

"Can do!" Reuben let out a massive stench and fell to the ground laughing as the others scrambled away from him in disgust.

Scowling at her fiancé's antics, Brie finished securing the metal boots, which matched her chainmail and helm fairly well. She took a few experimental steps and examined them carefully. "Even though there's a slight gap between the chainmail and the boots, my legs are now fully armored. These sabatons appear to be magical."

"As is my love for you," Reuben crooned as he reached out for a hug, waving his arms to spread the filthy air around him at the same time. Brie shoved him away, laughing and shrieking her adamant refusal to let him get closer at the top of her lungs.

Nacho grimaced as he found that backing up wouldn't let him escape anymore. "Gross. Let's get out of here."

They hurriedly climbed back up the ladder and raced up the corridor. As they approached the T-junction, they were greeted by caws, calls, and croaks rising in a cacophonous din from Caw Paw alley. Luckily for them, five more crow-panthers were milling about, which Brie and Reuben took care of quickly.

Another thirty-nine credits joined their pool, and they were that much closer to having a useful chef.

Outside, Nacho found a good place to camp downstream from the dungeon, well protected on one side by a solid chunk of limestone. The cold breeze smelled good as it rustled through the autumn trees, and the stream gurgled away, providing a relaxing serenity to their bivouac. After closing his eyes briefly and savoring the atmosphere, Nacho started a fire on the bank, which only added to the perfume. It truly was a pretty campsite, and he hoped to add a delicious meal to make it even better.

They had four hundred and *one* credits. He couldn't believe they'd earned so many so quickly, and it was even harder to swallow that he was about to burn nearly all of those credits on *cooking*. The sun was dropping below the horizon when he finally accessed the Store. He was going to buy this *Aria* first, since it really did seem like the requisite basic item for a Satiation Player.

He winced as he forced himself to press the button to spend the money. A book appeared in one of his Storage Slots the next moment, and he transferred it to his hand with a thought. It was an unexpectedly big tome with an embossed cover, reminiscent of a medieval grimoire. He opened the book to the first page, and suddenly things started to make sense.

Welcome to your own, personal, private cookbook! The dining options will be endless! You'll craft dishes that will make even the angriest chef delirious with happiness. This is your personal De Re Coquinaria, or in the original Latin: "On the Subject of Cooking"; in the updated Latin: "Cooking is the Thing to Make You a King!" This might have been one of the first cookbooks. Don't ask us, ask Caelius Apicius!

Have fun cooking up victory, Satiation Player!

Nacho's excitement was short-lived. The volume held nothing but blank pages, which was a formidable letdown after the triumphant introduction. However, if this was his cookbook, he'd eventually be able to fill it with recipes. "I *will*, right?"

"Now that is one big, juicy book." Reuben tossed a stick onto the fire. "Level with me, Nacho... do we eat the book?"

"I think I'm supposed to fill it with recipes. The problem is... recipes are obnoxiously expensive. Right now, I'm only considering a pancake recipe. For one, the required ingredients are cheap if we have to get them from the Store. For another, we can make them ahead and eat them cold. It's either this, or the 'Very Fine Venison' recipe in *Cleaning and Cooking your Favorite Ungulate.*"

"There seem to be quite a few Wight-Tails around, so the venison recipe might be the way to go." Reuben rubbed his chin. "On the other hand, I do love me a good pancake."

Nacho's mind spun as he considered other options. He was beginning to feel scattered by all the choices. "We've been fighting a lot of bird monsters. Maybe I should find a poultry recipe?"

"I like chicken, but will a chicken recipe work on cooking something bigger, like a Caw Paw?" Brie was using the Splatter Mallet to mash logs—she didn't so much cut the wood, as pulverized it into submission. She also employed her hatchet from time to time, which worked excellently on smaller sticks.

Nacho frowned indecisively and grimaced at the near-empty account. "I just don't know."

Reuben, noting his friend's rising anxiety, sat down on a log and held his stomach. "No worries. This is like any game. At the beginning, we have to make some hard choices, invest in late-game skills, the usual."

Brie smashed her hammer into another log, which cracked enough for her to pull it apart. "Keep it simple, boys. I think we start with pancakes. They're easy to cook, and if they aren't terrible, we can sell them to other people and start generating credits. Once Nacho gets better with the simple things, he can graduate to something harder than 'flat bread'."

"Pancakes it is." Nacho shook his head in horror as he opened the Store once more. "I can't believe I'm doing this."

In seconds, he had the recipe for the International Monster of Pancakes in his Storage Slots. When he brought it forward, the paper didn't appear in his hands; the recipe went right into his *Aria*—and suddenly, he had a table of contents under a new category: *Breakfasts for Champions, As Well As for Losers.*

. . .

Congratulations! For buying your first class Grimoire and spell, you earn three bonus spells! Now you can make pancakes, oatmeal, grits, and turkey sausage!

"That's neat... how did it...?" Reuben leaned forward to read from the book. "*Please. For one, pancakes aren't just for break-fast. For another? I resemble those remarks.*"

Snorting a laugh, Brie dumped an armful of wood onto the ground, then eyed the cook. "How much food do we have left? I polished off the jerky before we left the caves."

Nacho thought for a minute as he mentally tallied their reserves. "We have some trail mix left, some oatmeal, one protein bar, and a few MREs. Our coffee runs out tomorrow."

"That's a problem," Brie informed the two men sternly while trying to maintain eye contact. In turn, they tried their hardest to avoid her warning glare.

Nacho broke first and was drawn back to the Store in search of decent coffee. That was when he realized his mistake: they were down to a single credit. He had been so focused on purchasing the book and recipe that they couldn't afford to buy the ingredients: flour, baking powder, sugar, milk, eggs, and melted butter—not to mention it called for a lightly oiled griddle or frying pan. He had the pan. He'd also need to buy some cooking oil. Or could he fry them up in butter?

Maybe if he didn't buy all of the ingredients, he could still cook the recipe. He only needed three, so in theory, he could make the pancakes without the melted butter or the sugar. But did he really *want* to take chances on his first meal?

Reuben looked up from digging through his bag and heaved an exaggerated sigh. "He said we have trail mix, but we *don't*. We have raisins and peanuts. No M&Ms, Brie. Nacho brings us to this blasted world, and he doesn't bring M&Ms."

The woman sat down with them on a log. "*Nacho* didn't

bring us here. The Patrons did. Nacho kept us alive, and *we are grateful.* We don't *need* M&Ms."

"Tomorrow, we'll need roughly five credits, but I think I can cook us some breakfast." Nacho closed his cooking grimoire, then remembered the Splatter Millet. "Wait, I have my little hammer! If we find wheat, I might be able to make flour myself."

"Do you have any idea what wheat looks like?" Reuben snorted at the thought. "Because I don't, unless we're talking about video games."

"You have a point." Deflating, Nacho reluctantly tucked the tiny hammer away in his pack.

They didn't have enough credits to buy even a single meal from the Store, and while they had some food, they needed to save it for when they really needed it. Fortunately, Nacho hadn't used his Skills, so he could push on for a few more hours. He had a vague notion that he was hungry, but it was easy to ignore.

Reuben was in the same position, though they did boil more water to fill their water bottles. He didn't *need* food until he hit the twenty-four-hour mark, and Brie had eaten all the jerky after their fight to get her Hunger levels back up to a hundred percent.

Instead of a happy little meal around their fire, they sat in silence on their logs while keeping an eye out for monsters. Nacho almost wanted something to come racing out of the woods so they could kill it, earning enough credits to make food, or maybe just to pass the time. Instead, he settled for pulling up more info on the HungerCry Knives.

The Juxtaposition message was unexpectedly helpful this time.

The HungerCry Knives (Tier 0 Weapon, Upgradeable) are an amazing addition to any Satiation Player's inventory of cooking utensils. High-quality tools mean high-quality output!

- *All slicing and dicing will give the chef 50% more ingredients. Cut off a chicken leg, and get a leg and a half of meat!*
- *Cut things 100% faster! Double your cutting time with 0% chance of hacking off a finger! This is important. Cooks need their fingers.*
- *Carve up high-Tier meat like a pro! Using the HungerCry Knives, you can pierce the skin of monsters one Tier higher than you, leaving damage even if you don't meet the damage threshold!*

Upon learning what the knives could do, he was regretting his pancake decision. In the end, making pancakes had to be easier than gutting and processing a Wight-Tailed Deer. It was ironic that the HungerCry Knives didn't do double damage like Brie's hammer. In fact, from what he could tell they would just function like normal daggers in combat.

With his curiosity piqued, Nacho tried to look into the Ring of Cheese, but there was no information available. Just a lot of bad cheese puns. An Inspect Skill would be handy, but that was *thousands* of credits. He lifted the ring up between his index finger and thumb, studying the glittering accessory in the fading light. "I'm going to put the ring on, guys. If I can't take it off, you'll have to wrestle me down and cut off my finger. Are you good with that?"

"You wanna tell us why?" Brie wondered while giving him a concerned glance. "Are you okay?"

"Classic cursed ring." Reuben gave him a comprehending nod. "We'll horribly dismember you if we have to do so, Nacho. You can count on us, but maybe not your fingers in a few seconds. At least not to ten."

Nacho laughed nervously as he put on the ring… and nothing happened. He carefully slid it off. Still nothing.

"Did you feel anything? Reuben inquired of his friend. "Probably not, just like your last girlfriend; hence third-wheeling it with us."

"I did feel something just now." Nacho narrowed his eyes. "The overwhelming urge to stab you in the mouth."

"So nothing out of the ordinary?" Reuben chuckled, even evoking a laugh from Brie.

"Nothing." Nacho stood and brushed off his rear. "Okay, let's go through the routine."

With Reuben coaching and Brie watching, Nacho began to test what the ring could do. He tried to fly by jumping up and down, as well as just thinking really hard of flying. "Nope. Appears not to be a ring of flight."

He put his hand close to the fire, but instead of being fireproof, he got a little burn. "Not fireproof, but Health Regen will take care of that. I suppose I could jump into the river to see if I could breathe, but I just don't care that much. Finally… nope, can't make cheese out of nothing. I might buy some later to see if I can control it."

Brie made no effort to hide the little grin on her face. "Well, that was entertaining."

"Thanks." Nacho tossed the ring into the air and caught it, using some minor sleight of hand to make it vanish into his inventory. "We'll just have to hope we figure it out eventually."

After killing Bob Bass the Crow King, they had a lot to celebrate, but sipping water around the fire didn't feel much like a celebration. Instead, they decided to turn in early; Reuben once again took the middle watch and woke Nacho up for the last watch.

The cook kept the fire going through the frigid cold of the early morning. When the light streamed over the horizon, he gazed dreamily across the stream and spotted an old friend: a Puckered Granny apple tree.

An idea struck him, and the simplicity of it made him smile.

He was going to make this Satiation Player thing work for him.

CHAPTER TWENTY-EIGHT

In the dazzling light of the new day, Nacho took in the camp's surroundings. There was no sign of monsters, and the fire was going well, so he summoned his pot and crossed the stream to a Puckered Granny apple tree.

The firm apples were bright green with stark black stripes, which would deepen and start to rot as they absorbed the Putrid Mana of the Starter World. As they grew in power, the rot would sprout an eye or two, then a mouth, then teeth, ending with insectile legs, which resulted in them snapping free of their stems and scurrying through the forest as packs of carnivorous fruit.

These fruits were definitely Tier zero, probably level one, since the Starter World was still in the early stage. These weren't the only monster apples that Nacho had seen during his three years in the Juxtaposition; he'd heard rumors of the Kai-juicy Fruit, a hideous building-sized apple tearing across the world and creating havoc. Just another example of a Calamity-class monster that had started out as something minor.

Nacho filled the pot with apples and carried it back to their camp. After selecting an apple, he held it up and concentrated.

He was attempting to use his Ingredient Processing skill to drain the Putrid Mana out of the apple as he started chopping, and it worked perfectly. That was a good start.

He took a quick look at the bonus recipe for a sweet apple oatmeal in his newly purchased cookbook. He needed sugar, an apple, and some oatmeal. He had two out of the three, but when he tried to access the Store, the System barked at him.

Nice try, monster-turd! You are in Active Cooking. You cannot shop during Active Cooking.

"Well, now, that was rude. Is it the chopping?" Nacho got up and backed away from the fruit. "Or did that happen because I was processing the apple?"

He even put away his knives. He whistled as though he wasn't trying to do anything but stand there and whistle, even as his nerves started to fray. Every second he waited, there was a chance those monster apples would turn into disgusting jelly.

Finally, the System grudgingly let him out of Active Cooking.

Nacho immediately bought some sugar from the Store, which materialized in a bright yellow round container with red letters on the front. Apparently, this was 'Juxtaposition Sugar'. He'd used their last credit, and he truly hoped it was worth it. He got a pot of hot water boiling, prepared his oatmeal and sugar, and then found a nearby log to use as a cutting board.

The System detected what he was doing, and he was back in Active Cooking once more. He held his breath as he sank the Cry knife into the apple and cut the next apple, feeling a strange moment of disorientation as the blade reached the bottom of the fruit. Instead of two halves, he somehow got four halves as its special ability activated. Nacho blindly reached for another apple, placed it on the log, and had nearly pressed his knife to it when it wiggled slightly. He blinked and stared down at his impromptu cutting board, finding a pair of sad green eyes looking up at him. "*Dog*! Plant dog, thing! What in the… are you following me?"

There was no answer, other than the fact that the strange green dog lifted slightly toward the knife, evidently trying to get itself sliced like the apples had been. Nacho pulled his blade back and pushed the strange animal-plant hybrid off his impromptu cutting board. "Stop that! I didn't intend to cut you up, I was trying to grab an apple."

There was a tiny tail wag now that he was paying attention to it, and he inspected the creature more thoroughly. It had grown larger, now easily the size of a proper banana, though it still looked like a tiny puppy. His desire for it to leave wavered and he opened his mouth to name it, when the dog leaned forward and bit into one of the apples. Instantly, the entire fruit turned black and rotten, and the animal slurped it down greedily. It looked back up at Nacho, panting like any dog would and sending the stench of Putrid Mana rolling across the human's face. "Gah! Get out of here!"

The verdant canine froze in place, then dropped its head and slowly slunk away, only looking back one single, sad time. Nacho was going to throw something at the stray to make it *run*, but if his previous experiences with it were any indication… the creature would take the hit and try to get itself eaten or something. "It's *gotta* be a trap. As soon as I let it in, it'll attack, but if I try to kill or eat it, I just *know* something bad will happen."

Shaking his head and forcing the pup from his mind, he got back to his apples. Having had a little practice, he processed the Putrid Mana out of the apple at the cost of a percentage of his consumable bars at the same time as slicing the fruit. The black rot disappeared with a much smaller struggle than fresh meat had required, and he earned two credits for his efforts.

Two credits from processing a *single* apple. A wide smile appeared on his face, and Nacho sliced into one of the halves, hoping for additional halves… but of course it didn't work that way. Otherwise, he'd be able to cut an infinite amount of slices out of the apple. Instead, he got two quarters like a normal chef would.

A sudden spike of hunger hit him, and he felt his mouth water. He paused to question whether he'd ever actually eaten Puckered Granny apples before. He'd killed one, ah... a bushel of them, but had he tried the fruit? No. They'd all learned early on to only eat from the Store. Tentatively, Nacho lifted an apple slice and took a bite. The sourness hit him at once. It wasn't sour-sweet, it was sour-*salty*. His first instinct was to spit out the fruit, but no tang of the Putrid Mana assaulted his taste buds—still it was far worse than eating a Sour Patch Kids gummy rolled in salt.

He swallowed, and cautiously waited for any nausea to hit him. When he continued to feel fine, he actually began looking forward to the next bite. It wasn't *pleasant*, by any stretch of the imagination, but it was at least... interesting. He liked the disconnect of the salty when his head was telling him it was going to be sweet.

Better yet? He checked The Dinner Party's credit pool, and they were already starting to make a return. He ate a full apple, and each bite was better than the last, now that he knew what to expect. The Hunger points he'd used to process the fruit were replenished, and a quick sip from a water bottle refilled his Thirst points. He was still down on Mana, and he couldn't get out of Active Cooking to trigger his Mana Regen, so he just had to make the best of it.

"This is pretty easy." Nacho repeated the process, eating apple slices and drinking water as he went, until he had a pile of perfectly clean bright green Puckered Granny apple halves laying on the stump in front of him. "Practice makes better."

He'd processed a dozen of the fruit, for a total earning of twelve credits, which meant... he had enough to buy all the ingredients for breakfast! So long as he wasn't going to buy syrup, of course. First, he needed to see how cheaply he could make the meal. Waste not, want not. He thought about adding the Puckered Granny apples to the pancakes, but he wasn't sure if they would mess up the recipe or not.

While Brie and Reuben slept on, Nacho set a flat rock in the coals of the fire. Active Cooking had ended, so he was able to buy the remaining ingredients from the Store, including the melted butter, which came in a little yellow and red bowl. As always, all the ingredients came in Store containers: flour, baking powder, milk, and eggs.

He figured he'd mix everything up in his saucepan, so he poured the water he'd boiled into an empty water bottle to use for coffee once his friends woke up. Nacho didn't have a whisk or anything similar, but he found a suitable stick. "Now that this is proven to be viable, I'll have to splurge on better equipment. Is this why it seems like the Common Cook class is considered so powerful, and is so expensive? Sheesh... if I could raise plants and animals with a farmer, I could *literally* make my own credits."

His current line of thought didn't even include *selling* his cooking. Right now, his mind was filled with a life of peace, in which cooking would generate a ton of credits without ever risking his friend's lives. He could just process ingredients all day, and the credits would flow in. "*Cha-ching.*"

There was one major issue that needed to be solved: his Storage Slots were full. He was going to need a cart or some kind of fancy backpack that could hold even more than the one he had brought along. Another issue was the sheer number of *tools* he needed. To start with, he didn't have any kind of measuring cup, so he had to eyeball the ingredients. He *thought* he knew how much a cup of flour was, but how big was a teaspoon?

Was a normal spoon a teaspoon, or was that a tablespoon? He shrugged at the errant thought: it likely didn't matter *that* much. He kept his grimoire cookbook open on another rock in his makeshift kitchen, dumped the ingredients into a bowl, and found that the System was there to aid him along. When he had originally gotten started as an Assassin, the System had offered a few helpful tips amid all the cheery nonsense, and he'd met wizards that talked about how the System got chatty with them while they created spells. Finally, it seemed like this function was coming into play for him.

Hey, Satiation Player, you're still in Active Cooking, but we wanted to have a little chat. It looks like you're trying to make the International Monster of Pancakes recipe. Is that true?
Yes / No

Nacho chose 'yes', and the page flashed. The font for the ingredients turned red, and his heart leapt into his throat in excitement. "If this is what I think it is...!"

He threw in one and a half cups of flour... or as close to it as he could guesstimate, and the line for flour turned black! Every time he added enough of any one ingredient, the red font reverted to black. He was practically vibrating with excitement as he used his stick to mix the ingredients until his batter was thick and milky.

"Is it the right consistency? No idea, but this should be fun." Setting his cast iron skillet on the flat rock surrounded by hot coals, he slowly poured canola oil in the pan, and it was soon bubbling and smoking. "That should be hot enough."

As a last step, Nacho activated his other Skill, Cooking Magic, which should imbue the pancakes with the ability to increase one of their stats by five percent of the maximum value. That would only be half a point at this stage, but all signs pointed to the Juxtaposition rounding that up to a full point, so Brie would have an effective *eleven* Fitness instead of a ten.

Nacho accessed the Skill for the first time ever, and the System sent him a message:

. . .

Hey, Cook Boy! You're not just cooking, you're cooking with <u>love</u>. Give your favorite murder-machine mate motivation to be murdering. I'm sure you'll be proud when your dear friends go on a killing rampage with a belly full of your Cooking Magic.

Nacho rolled his eyes but was surprised to find that his mixture had developed a certain glow. Every time he swept his stick around the saucepan, that glow grew fainter and fainter. He squinted closer and realized that a piece of his stick might've broken off. He'd have to keep an eye out for it.

Curious, he checked his Stat Sheet.

Body:

- *Fitness: 10*
- *Metabolic efficiency: 10*

Mind:

- *Mental energy: 10*
- *Circuit: 10*

Satiation:

- *Hunger: 90*
- *Thirst: 90*

Total Health Points: 30
Bonus Physical Damage: 5%
Health Regen: 9% Health Regen/minute
Total Mana Pool: 22.5/25
Bonus Spell Damage: 5%
Mana Pool Regen: 9% Mana Regen/minute

Again, he felt a distant hunger, but at ninety points out of one hundred, it was easy to ignore. He'd used ten percent of his Mana on his Cooking Magic, but he couldn't regenerate that until he was out of Active Cooking. Funnily enough, in combat, he'd frequently checked his Health Points and Mana. During Cooking, he'd have to keep his eye squarely on his Satiation stats. "The kitchen has literally become my battlefield. So strange."

He poured enough batter to make a single pancake on his pan. The oil spat and hissed, but the whole thing didn't immediately turn to goo, which Nacho took as a good sign. As the batter bubbled cheerily in the pan, Reuben rolled over and sat up, blinking owlishly and sniffing with interest. "Hey, that smells good. Are you cooking breakfast?"

"I am." Nacho furrowed his brow as he considered the resulting sad disk of hardening batter. There was a new issue: how was he going to turn the pancake? It had to cook on both sides... right?

Brie rolled onto her side with her back facing the fire. "Food is fine, but who do I have to kill to get a cup of coffee?"

Reuben chuckled darkly. "In this world, that is a *very* valid question. More like *what* do you have to kill, and how many?"

"I can help with your coffee situation, Brie." While Nacho's pancake continued to cook on the same side, he poured a sachet of instant coffee into an empty bottle and added the hot water he'd reboiled. He set it next to Brie, who accepted the container to sip while still in her sleeping bag.

Reuben rubbed a hand over his head to calm his wild hair, failing spectacularly. "Wait a minute. We only had one credit left last night. Hey, Nacho, did you already kill something this morning?"

"No, for once, I'm seeing the benefits of this class. I found some Puckered Granny apples and processed them. Once I got that dog to leave my food alone, I went through twelve apples, earning two credits each." Nacho grabbed another stick and worked on turning his flapjack by strategically poking it. It was cooking, *really* cooking, and not just turning into goop. He *did* need a recipe! This changed everything! He wrestled around with the pancake to turn it, but instead only managed to smear it across his pan. A distinct smell of something burning rose into the air, which was never a good sign.

"You saw a dog?" Reuben awkwardly worked himself out of his sleeping bag, grinning with excitement. "Really? Also, a Puckered Granny? Gross. Toss me one."

"It's a puppy that was following us. I took care of it." Nacho flung him a piece of fruit, still watching his burning pan helplessly. The thought of warning Reuben about the taste crossed his mind, but it was too late.

His friend yelped and started spitting out the sour, salty fruit. "Ugh. Is that what Putrid Mana tastes like?"

"Nope. What's the matter? Don't like some salt with your monster fruit tart?" Nacho managed to awkwardly scoop out the crumbled, half-burned pieces of pancake to the side of the pan. "First one is ready. Who wants some?"

"With coffee? Sure." Brie crawled over and scooped up some of his nightmare breakfast food with her fingers. She blew on a piece, then took a bite without even hesitating. "You didn't —*mmph*—kill the dog, did you?"

"Of course not." Nacho grumbled at the direct stares both sent his way. "Fine, maybe the 'of course' isn't super believable coming from me, but I really didn't."

"Good. That's 'how to tell if someone is the real villain' one-oh-one. As for you, Brie, it's your daring side that really makes me like you so much. There's actually a *lot* I admire about you, now that I think about it." Reuben blinked rapidly at his wife-to-be, getting a snort and a grin for his efforts.

"I'm in total agreement. You're pretty great, as a person and as a friend." Nacho smiled warmly at his friend and gestured at his first-ever food creation. "Well?"

Brie's eyes flashed blue, and she read off the menu. "Five percent of max bonus to any one skill. Let's go with Fitness. Hey, I get an additional two Health Points for just one point of Fitness, and an extra point-five percent on my damage bonus. It's not Earth-shattering, but it's not bad since it rounds up."

"But the taste?" Nacho prodded her expectantly.

"Let's not talk about the taste."

"I see." Nacho made another pancake, having the same problem with the turning and the burning. "Well, Reuben is up next, then."

"You know, I think I can get behind this salty apple taste." Reuben chased the burned food with a Puckered Granny. "It helps with the... charred... flavor."

Brie munched another bite and screeched, pulling a rogue piece of stir stick out of her mouth. She held it up and glared at the cook. "What is this doing in here, Nacho?"

"Uh. I didn't exactly have the right utensils. There was an accident, and a small stick may have been harmed in the making of this breakfast." Bracing himself, he tried his own cooking. To say the pancake was bland was an insult to Store food. It was so bad that he started looking forward to the burned parts just so it would actually have some flavor. It didn't just need syrup; it needed a complete culinary overhaul. In short, the tasteless Store pancakes were *better*. "That was a depressing thought."

"Thinking about Store food?" Reuben nodded along knowingly. "I can tell. So was I."

Brie ate two apples just to fill her gut—certainly not munching for pleasure. Nacho continued with the rest of the pancakes, and they forced themselves to eat a full meal of the tasteless charcoal-seasoned discs. He saved some, though he didn't have much packaging to work with. Now they had battle food.

Also, their food situation was... better. They might get tired of his bad pancakes and the apples sponsored by Morton Salt, but as of right now, there was no more fear that they would starve to death. However unpleasant the food was, Nacho was feeling exceedingly cheerful as he put away pancakes for the road. Active Cooking finally ended when he ran out of batter and the last of his pathetic pancakes was completed. He ended up dumping the remaining flour into his saucepan and using the emptied container for the pancakes.

As they broke camp, Brie spoiled Nacho's good mood. The blonde Berserker finished strapping her sleeping bag to her backpack, then stood up and fixed Nacho with a stare. "Nacho, I've been keeping my mouth shut, but I need to know... if people don't have Putrid Mana in them... you can eat them, right?"

He managed to wrench his mouth closed after an instant, but he knew that she had seen his shock and revulsion. Wincing, Nacho finally nodded and took a deep breath. He knew that he needed to tell them the truth of this world, but it wasn't something he had been looking forward to explaining. He'd put it off for as long as possible, for good reason.

Cannibalism always made for very *distasteful* conversation.

CHAPTER TWENTY-NINE

"I wish we didn't need to have this talk, but I promise we'll speak about that… later." Choking down bile and paranoia over how they would judge him, Nacho stuffed his backpack full of food containers and refused to meet her eyes. "Let's get going. I want to get to the overhang before nightfall."

Nacho guided them back to the game trail that bordered Tomahawk Creek, then did his best to avoid the subject. "Other than the burned parts and the pieces of wood in my pancakes, I think the real problem is the measurements. Too much baking powder and not enough sugar. I should probably upgrade my Cooking Magic Skill."

Reuben marched behind him, while Brie took the front. Brie had her helm and boots on, but just as before, they were traveling with their chainmail stored in their extra-dimensional Storage Slots. The Healer appeared uncomfortable with the tense mood and started to babble. "You have to practice cooking, which means we need credits for ingredients, and we need customers. Are we going back to Armor Mountain?"

"Eventually," Nacho replied, clinging gratefully to the safe conversation topic. "I want to hunt more, so keep an eye out for

Wight-Tails. We also might want to go deeper into the Deep Buggy Darkness, now that we have more Skill levels and some new magical items. I'm hoping the Ring of Cheese does something awesome. Once we've leveled a bit more, we'll eventually check in on the people on top of Armor Mountain."

"Question about that." Brie abruptly turned and appraised Nacho, then asked him the question he had been worried about. "Are we going up there to sell pancakes to the people… or to eat them? Was that the plan all along?"

"We're going to eat the *pancakes*, not sell them," he replied lightly, only getting a solemn headshake in reply as they stopped in a clearing. A few Blues Birds drifted from tree to tree, but never got close enough to become a concern.

From the way she was digging in her heels, Nacho knew he couldn't get around the topic any longer. "We need to do this now, huh? Fine then. You've seen how expensive food gets. A Tier zero meal is three credits, Tier one is thirty, while Tier two is *sixty*. That's right; sixty credits for something that tastes like week-old buffet leftovers. But remember, once you hit level ten, Tier zero food doesn't do anything for you—despite the fact that the creatures we were fighting were powerful, as you've seen—that doesn't translate into more credits. Kill a big demon thing for one meal? *Maybe*? It wasn't worth it, especially since the entire world was growing more powerful, more intense, and the amount of Putrid Mana was always increasing."

Brie remained silent, and Nacho felt awful admitting the depths they'd had to sink into. Reuben, as always, could feel the tension in the air. Like the good friend he was, he offered Nacho a way out. "Look, man, it's not like all the things that you experienced actually happened, right? It was just in your Probability Vision thing."

"I used to eat people." Nacho exhaled, his heart twinging with guilt as they edged away from him slightly. There. He'd said it. "At the end, we all did. It was just more… *economical*, however awful that was. Tier two players could eat Tier zero people and it would count as a meal."

"*Abyss*, dude. Did they… taste like chicken?" Reuben weakly joked, though he was beginning to look a little on the pale side.

"Pork," Nacho replied honestly, meeting their eyes directly. He had already gone through the mental gymnastics necessary for him to be okay with surviving. Now he just had to get through their reactions.

"I'm *not* judging." Brie put a hand on Nacho's arm, then waved the other hand side to side. "Okay, I'm judging a *little*. Kinda hard not to."

"It can change this time. It doesn't need to be like that." Nacho looked into Brie's eyes, desperate for redemption he knew that she couldn't give him. "*We* can change things. But it's going to be a stretch for me. I was alone before, but not only that. It's true that I was an Assassin, but the reality was that I was magically forced to obey orders. My job was to kill people for the Final Victory Guild."

"Run by the Crave guy?" Reuben questioned him with concern. "Was that how you knew him?"

"Exactly that." Nacho swallowed as the memories flooded back. "Being a Cook is practically the opposite of being an Assassin. I'm going to be keeping people alive."

"With *your* cooking?" Reuben's bark of laughter fully broke the tension. "No, you're still an Assassin. I've tasted your pancakes."

"Wouldn't a *Healer* be the opposite of an Assassin?" Brie pointed out with annoying accuracy. "You know what? It doesn't matter. We have a way of earning credits that no one else has. That's going to help us in the end, so let's just keep walking. Thank you for finally telling us."

They continued on in uncomfortable silence through the forest. Nacho figured his big confession was done, but he was so very wrong.

"Tell us about your time alone," Brie casually requested over her shoulder after a while, like it was no big deal. Nacho had figured he could avoid all this talking with more hunting, but naturally, there was no sign of the deer. Where were all the animals? He figured other deer hunters had felt the same way over the centuries.

With nothing else to distract them, he reluctantly continued his confession. "Very long, very sad story short, I didn't trust anyone—I was mourning the loss of you two, and I became a not very nice guy. Basically, I'd stalk behind parties of people, lie in wait while they'd dish out damage on some monster, and then I'd come racing out of the shadows to deliver that last hit. Whoever gets the last hit gets the credits. I was known as the Shadow Killer, and I was kind of a legend."

"You sound like a total scumbag," Reuben snorted as he pictured Nacho running up to an orc and stabbing it in the butt, then running away as fast as he could. "Going in and grabbing the credits while other people did all the work? You're the worst."

"Your sense of right and wrong always astounds me. Why is it that *this* part of what you are hearing is the thing that makes you mad at him?" Brie groaned at her groom. "Two minutes ago he told us he ate people."

"I didn't want to explain any of this," Nacho protested with false bravado. "None of this shows me in a good light. But you saw me abandon the survivors on Armor Mountain. You already know I can be kinda soulless. Fact is, I'll do anything to make sure *we* survive this mess. Even if that means letting people die, or doing the deed myself."

The couple winced as their eyes were drawn to the long knife strapped to his belt. Brie looked away and squared her shoulders firmly, as if to ward off undesirable thoughts. "You have a good point. I can't judge you too much for doing what you had to do."

"You're *sharp* cheddar these days, Nacho. So edgy." Reuben tromped down the path behind Nacho. "Let's all just... think of it like this: you're feeling guilty for a dream you had, right? It was *kind* of you, but not really. Like you said, we can change things. You didn't do that, not really. You just watched a super realistic movie."

"It's an interesting idea," Brie agreed right away. "Use the experience from the dream, but don't repeat the actions in real life. Also, if it's only the last person who hits the monster that gets the credits, we could have Nacho fight, as long as he doesn't kill whatever he hits. We need to put him to work."

"Yeah, in the kitchen and in our restaurant: The Three Cheeses." Reuben gripped at his chest as though he were missing a dear friend. "People will come from across the land to buy our gourmet pancakes and succulent venison. It's so very yummy."

"The Three Cheeses..." Nacho closed his eyes and tried to accept that they were willing to move past this. "I can get behind that."

Around noon, they finally encountered a herd of Wight-Tailed Deer. It was a slaughter-fest that resulted in thirteen kills. They also picked off three Blues Birds that came in to eat the carrion, earning one hundred and twenty-five credits in addition to the credits that Nacho had earned processing apples that morning, minus the money he'd spent on ingredients for his pancakes. All told, they had brought in one hundred and forty-two credits with the annihilation, but Nacho wasn't going to let all that free meat lying in the field go to waste.

He processed as much of the flesh as he could before the remaining carcasses were liquified. It was a race to the end, eating pancakes as he went, chugging water, and only stopping for mana to regen until the work was done. Using the HungerCry Knives, he was able to skin the deer and cut steaks far faster than with any other blade he'd tried before. The Juxtaposition chided him on his salt and pepper recipe, but reluctantly allowed him to continue using it repeatedly.

They'd managed to bring down two level two deer. Working as fast as he could and taking regeneration breaks as needed, Nacho was able to complete *twenty* rounds of Ingredient Processing. He received four credits for each pound of flesh he cut from the deer, for a total of eighty credits to add to their stores. That brought them up to two hundred and twenty-two credits. "Already made back half of what we had to invest in me!"

The rest of the day was spent hurrying back to Rocky Top by climbing up the trail through the boulders, until they once again found their overhang and the charcoal remnants of their previous fire. From what they could tell, no one else had slept there.

Reuben and Brie kept watch while Nacho spent a few credits on basic cooking supplies, which were surprisingly cheap. He had expected the System to charge him up the wazoo for a set of measuring spoons, a half-cup measuring cup, a whisk, and a spatula. Then again, the Juxtaposition didn't have many Satiation Players to begin with.

Nacho also splurged on a blue Outdoors Enamelware coffee pot. That was for Brie, who insisted she could live without a lot —Netflix, hot showers, a toothbrush—but she would *not* live without her morning coffee.

By the time he was done, they were back down to one hundred and seventy-two credits.

The food he'd brought was almost gone, but they still had three Chicken a la King MRE's left. Reuben said those had been voted the military's worst MREs of all time. The Meatballs in Marinara sauce meal was better, and Nacho ate that one. For the first time, he was the one who needed to eat more because of all his Skills usage.

The next morning, the cooking went *so* much better. With actual measuring utensils, Nacho's pancakes were better... but the coffee from the Store was like yesterday's gas station sludge warmed up in a rusty pot. Nacho was fairly certain that Brie would massacre entire ecosystems for her coffee, so she didn't complain, but she wasn't happy. They'd have to look into upgrading the coffee using the rarity chart, a part of the Store that Nacho hadn't explained to them just yet. Survival came before comfort.

Nacho's pancakes turned out *exponentially* better, though they were still so dry that it took an extra few cups of coffee and some more water to get them down. He wasn't sure what he'd done wrong, but that was what practicing was meant for.

They even bought some Store maple syrup, but that didn't help much.

Reuben sighed over the meal—he was a guy who liked to eat—but Nacho reminded him that they were suffering through an apocalypse. Sacrifices had to be made. The Healer still shook his head sorrowfully as he choked down the breakfast. "I think it was Aeschylus who said that in war, truth is the first casualty. The second? Breakfast. Oh, the humanity."

"Let's really hunt today." Nacho scraped burned remnants into the fire. "Maybe we'll get lucky and find some more apples. Or maybe a Boarconator. It's like a Baconator, only more boar than bacon."

"We should level your skill," Reuben suggested instantly. "If there is bacon involved, I will happily stand aside so you can get boosted."

"Not unless we need to." Nacho shut him down instantly, already knowing this conversation was going to happen. "I want to buy that venison info pack along with the recipe. I need to get good at it. Then, when we show up with actual steaks and *good* non-Store pancakes, people will actually want to buy what I'm cooking."

They finished off breakfast, secured their camp, and only took their most important supplies. The rest they hid under the overhang. It wasn't long before Nacho found a grove of Red Pernicious apples, though he had Reuben and Brie pluck them. These apples had already grown teeth, but unlike Puckered Granny apples, they never developed eyes and legs of their own. They could only drop onto unsuspecting prey, eat into their head, and take over their bodies. Truly pernicious predators, the fruits were. A few of the red apples had already mutated into level three monsters, about the size of bowling balls, and were ready to drop off.

Brie found that she could Combat Dash under the limbs, slam her hammer into the tree to send a bunch of Red Pernicious fruit falling to the ground, then dash out from under the tree without being hurt.

Due to his comparative lack of speed, Reuben tried the bow and arrow. He wasn't bad, but he wasn't anywhere near good—there was a lot of wincing involved. Brie taunted him by muttering that he could've spent some time at Camp Sacajawea to improve his archery. He retorted that he didn't like to be in forest fires. Luckily, the monster apples were easy to kill. The ones with teeth were worth five credits, though the regular fruit weren't worth anything; at least, not until Nacho started processing them.

He followed in his team's wake, collecting the pierced fruit and extracting the teeth. Once they were processed, he was left with a huge pile of sliced apples, though the big ones unfortunately tasted like sawdust. The smaller ones were pleasantly crisp, though they had to be eaten with caution, because sometimes additional teeth were growing inside. Reuben discovered a few molars at one point and nearly hurled. Nacho merely grinned and said, "Looks like a monster apple a day keeps the Healer away."

Feeling far more confident in his abilities, Nacho splurged on more ingredients and spices, and it was cinnamon-apple pancakes for lunch—not that they needed regular meals anymore, as long as they didn't use their Skills and ate once every twenty-four hours. However, the habit of eating at intervals still ran deep.

Between killing the fanged apples and processing out the Putrid Mana, the team ended the day with another couple hundred credits. Nacho had been worried that changing the recipe would turn his cinnamon-apple pancakes into goo, but the Juxtaposition seemed to take a liberal view with additions, subtractions, and substitutions—as long as he had the minimum three ingredients.

If he could take a neutral recipe and augment it, he wouldn't have to fork over their precious credits on recipe variations. He knew there would be limits, of course, because the

Juxtaposition wasn't going to make it easy on him, but it was a thrilling discovery nevertheless.

Reuben added a fair amount of cinnamon and sugar to his pancake, but it had still turned out dry. Nacho wasn't sure what was wrong. Did he need to use canola oil instead of the melted butter? Bacon grease? Avocado oil?

The Dinner Party was sitting at a comfortable three hundred and seventy-two credits, but Nacho couldn't believe he was going to waste their precious credits on yet another recipe. Perhaps the Juxtaposition made it easy for Satiation Players to gain credits, but they also made the recipes so *expensive*. Then came the real question: was he really ready to cook deer meat when he couldn't even get simple pancakes right?

Regardless, he spent the credits on *Cleaning and Cooking your Favorite Ungulate*. That night around the fire, Nacho started reading. He'd gotten one thing right—he was definitely supposed to cut off the Wight arm and toss it. It was *banefully* poisonous.

After that, a cook was expected to do unspeakable things to the deer, starting with the back end. However, if done right, the entrails could be removed without too much fuss, and then it was a relatively simple matter to strip off the hide. The ironic thing? Very Fine Venison was basically a roasted deer haunch with only a little salt and pepper, though it additionally suggested vegetable oil and a little bit of lemon juice.

He also had to get the temperature of the fire just right, which wasn't going to be easy. All in all, the information pack and recipe was clearly worth the money. Again, he felt himself getting nervous about cooking, which further devolved into cycling his anxiety into anger about *being* nervous. He'd spent three years in the Juxtaposition killing all manner of man and beast, so how was *this* what threw him?

"Anything good?" Reuben's face glowed in the firelight.

"I think so." Nacho closed the book. "Tomorrow, we need to try my skills out on some Wight-Tailed Deer. We can't get distracted by more monster apples."

Brie poured water into the blue pot to get it ready for

tomorrow's coffee. "I found this rarity chart while I was looking for better coffee; what does it mean? I don't want a repeat of this morning's terrible caffeine sludge."

"Ah… you found that." Nacho grinned sheepishly and started drawing out a simple matrix for them.

Common: Price as stated
  Uncommon: +50%
  Very Uncommon: +60%
  Fairly Rare: +70%
  Rare: +80%
  Very Rare: +90%
  Epic: +100%

Brie's brow furrowed. "At one credit, a hundred percent increase is only two credits. I'm going to buy us epic coffee, and everyone else is going to be perfectly fine with that. It has to be better, right?"

Nacho thought so, but he wasn't sure. The Juxtaposition's rules weren't exactly… fair. No one had bought single ingredients back in the day. They'd all basically just grown accustomed to the Store coffee that came with breakfast meals.

Sitting around the fire with his friends, Nacho still felt weird that Reuben and Brie knew about what he'd done his first time in the Juxtaposition, and he felt the need to talk about it. "Hey, so with all the things I told you about my Probability Vision… all of what happened… are we still good?"

Reuben made a face. "We know you, Nacho. We know you have this side to you… because of—how do I put this as nicely as possible…? We had *always* voted on you as the most likely to eat another person. Be happy our old yearbooks got left in the old world."

"You did what you had to do, and we're grateful." Brie set the pot down into the dirt, the top loaded with epic-grade coffee. "We've always known that if you didn't have us to keep you stable, you might become too self-interested."

"When you're not distracted, scattered, and perfectionistic, that is." Reuben picked up a little pebble and tossed at him to show he was half-kidding. But only half. Nacho knew that he could be driven and self-absorbed, though he wouldn't go as far as labeling himself narcissistic. Then again, he might be fooling himself that his selfishness didn't run deep. It was funny. During his first time in the game—once he had lost Reuben and Brie— he hadn't cared much about stealing credits from other people and hadn't even cared too much that his guild had frequently used him to remove key targets. Nothing had seemed to matter except the mission.

Now? His mission was food, pure and simple, and everyone —not just The Dinner Party—was going to benefit.

There were still a couple of secrets he was holding back. For one, he didn't know how to tell them about the impending Calamity… or the CrossHumans. The entire AKC had some time before they were in danger of delving into that particular mystery. Even so, his mind kept drifting back to the incoming horror.

How could he explain the Bove to someone that hadn't witnessed it?

CHAPTER THIRTY

Three days later, they were celebrating their first full week of surviving in the Juxtaposition.

The Epic coffee turned out to be just that: *epic*. It was well worth doubling the credit cost, and the comforting beverage came out dark and rich. While Reuben complained that he had to use more sugar and cream than usual, Brie's shift to a rapturous demeanor reduced even that complaint to mere mutters.

It took a couple of days, but they eventually found another herd of Wight-Tailed Deer. Nacho and his friends played it smart and didn't try to pick them off one by one. They enacted their plan by building a makeshift corral, weaving together a fence of different lengths of wood and grasses.

Then it was only a matter of chasing the deer into the corral. The main issue was that one of the deer had leveled faster than the others. His back tail-arm was well-muscled and sported long yellow talons, and some of its teeth had become fangs. Other arms had started growing out of the thing's hide, but fortunately, they were rather short and skinny, with half-formed fingers. Reuben shook his head in disgust as he stared at the beast. "That thing looks like a potato that was left in a cupboard for too long."

That horror didn't run away like the other ungulates, but instead charged them. As expected, Active Combat began with the normal System message.

The creature effortlessly knocked Reuben aside—since the man wasn't wearing his chainmail at the moment—and rammed into Nacho. Its pale hand's filthy claws raked down his unprotected face. The cook's first impulse was to use his knives and kill the deer, but he didn't want to lose credits for his team. Also... Nacho didn't feel any pain. "What's going on?"

A Juxtaposition message flashed in Nacho's eyes.

Damage taken: 0. 5 Health Points Cheesed!

The mutated deer monster pivoted and rammed Nacho with its antlers once again. He staggered back, hands clutching his tattered shirt, but no blood oozed between his fingers.

Damage taken: 0. 10 Health Points Cheesed!

While Nacho was staring at his unharmed torso in shock, Brie took care of the nightmare deer with her hammer. She sped up, whirled to block the thing's antlers, then Combat Dashed its brains out.

Active Combat ended, and Nacho stood there shaking, pondering the strange messages. A sharp tang of limburger hung in the air, or as the French would say, the stench of angels feet.

"Why do I smell like... cheese?" He'd received fifteen points of damage from the mutated Wight-Tail's attack, and yet his Health Points hadn't gone down. Nacho eyed the Ring of

Cheese. "Cheese the champion… this ring absorbs damage done to the person wearing it. I don't know how much it'll take, but this changes a lot about how we'll be able to approach combat. I shouldn't wear it. Reuben, put this on."

Brie dragged Nacho away from the deer corpse before he could remove the item from his finger. "One thing at a time, Nacho. We need to keep the deer herd penned. We need the credits!"

Reuben was already waving his gauntlet wildly, scaring the wide-eyed ungulates back into the corral. Some were trying to climb over the hastily-made fences, but between the logs, the undergrowth, and the other trees, they were forced to stay inside.

Brie's fifth grade camp experience paid off once again. She brought down thirteen of the deer singlehandedly before the remainder managed to break out of the corral and race off through the forest in a scamper of hooves.

Well, they now had plenty of meat for Nacho to practice on. He flipped the Ring of Cheese to Reuben. "Here. Put this on. I'm not sure how much damage you can absorb, but it's at least twenty Health Points. That makes it a powerful magic item, though we'll never know how powerful it actually is until we're able to test it properly."

Nacho started on the deer pile by selecting the big monster deer and its various arms. He hacked the budding limbs off with Hunger, his cleaver. Using the ungulate info pack and his Cry knife, he successfully cleaned out the entrails and stripped the hide. Having the info pack open in his vision while he worked on the deer was like having two computer screens to watch as he prepped the carcass. It was very convenient, if sometimes distracting. He started to slice off a few steaks and tried to process one.

Hail, mighty deer hunter! Wanna process your newly acquired Wight-Tailed Deer meat?

Yes / No

Nacho chose 'yes' and earned a harsh buzz along with a bright red flash in his vision.

Sorry, Satiation Player, but you've bitten off more jerky than you could chew. This is a level 6 hunk of meat, and you max out at level 5! Either increase your skill or watch the meat go rancid! Don't let life leave a bad taste in your mouth!

Nacho tossed the meat to the side and addressed his friends. "Looks like we got a more advanced deer. You okay if I spend credits to level up a skill?"

"Yes, and do it fast! We don't want to lose all this meat." Brie waved her hand in a 'hurry up' motion. "I figured you might have trouble with this one. He was worth fourteen credits."

That brought their hunting adventure up to two hundred and thirty-two credits. Nacho used eighty credits to upgrade his Ingredient Processing skill to level four. He quickly closed his system view and processed the level six deer, making the steak glow a golden color as the Putrid Mana was strained out of the meat.

The System congratulated him.

One portion of level six deer meat processed! Twelve credits! That's some mouthwatering money!

"I got *twelve* credits from one steak!" Nacho had hit the jackpot. The big deer would take him a while to get through; there was just so *much* meat. Also, it had taken time to gather the bodies, and they'd spent some time figuring out the Ring of Cheese, so he had no time to waste. He didn't want his payday to liquify on him.

He had to prep and cook the meat right there in the forest. On the plus side, It was a good day to grill out: the skies were cloudy, it was a chilly day, and it could start raining at any minute. Working as quickly as possible, Nacho was able to go through nine more rounds of Ingredient Processing, bringing the group credit pool up to a total of three hundred and fifty-two credits.

The cook figured they could use that to upgrade Reuben's and Brie's skills. More than anything, he wanted to try cooking the meat. He was nearly starving, and Brie would be hungry— she'd used her Combat Dash and Defensive Whirl to bring down the big buck.

He had his friends find some firewood and at least one flat rock.

His cooking grimoire, his *Aria,* laid open, flipped to a whole new section, *Entrees for the Carnivorous Adventurer.* With an eye on the recipe, he triggered the magic and soon was throwing in salt, pepper, a generous portion of canola oil, and lemon juice he'd bought from the Store.

Just as they had with the pancake recipe, the ingredients started out red on his paper, but turned black as he adjusted them. Nacho was too hungry to add any additional Cooking Magic to the deer meat. He wanted to get those steaks sizzling.

His fire had reduced to bright red coals, and he could've laid the steaks directly on the rocks, but he preferred his cast-iron skillet. He arranged three steaks in the pan, even if they didn't fit perfectly. Soon the air was filled with the delicious smell of the venison sizzling and spitting. He had his spatula and his knife, but still ended up somehow dumping one of the steaks into the fire. He gingerly fished it out and mentally debated buying a fork… or tongs?

All the while, the meat continued cooking, and he kept having to move the slices around, including the one coated in ashes from the fire. He glanced at his friends guiltily, and he could tell that they were having a silent argument about who would be getting the ash-coated meat. "That'll add to the flavor, right? No? I'll eat the ashy one."

"You're a cooking saint." Reuben put his hand on Nacho's hand to let him know that he appreciated the sacrifice.

The cook stacked the three steaks on top of one another and finally got into the rhythm of moving them around. First one, then another, up and down they went, until they started to blacken. The coals of his fire seemed too hot, but how did one adjust the temperature of a fire's coals?

Nacho was sweating, stressed, and praying that he hadn't screwed up the meal too much. Reuben and Brie squatted down around the fire, staring at the meat like wolves. It was the big guy that pointed out the obvious. "They're done, Nacho. At least the outsides are. I like my meat pink, but there are limits."

Brie disagreed just as Nacho moved to take the meat out. "Do you mind cooking mine longer?"

Nacho wasn't sure if that was a good idea, but he managed to scoop out his ash-coated meal out onto one of the Store trays they'd saved from one of their mediocre meals. Brie's meat continued to cook, though Nacho knew that the blackened part wasn't going to get any *less* burned with more heat. While he waited for her to allow him to remove it, he pulled out a leftover pancake to wrap around his venison to make a primitive sandwich.

Reuben finally slung on his gauntlets and pulled Brie's steak off the pan. He held the hunk of meat in his metal gloves and blew on it. "Hey, look, even better than tongs! These things are great. They fit around my new cheesy ring—aw man, I can't wait to get hit and see how much damage I can absorb! Or how smelly I can get. Do you think it will cycle through the smell of different cheeses? Or just the one set scent?"

"No kisses for you, stinky boy." Brie took out a knife and fork and cut into her steak. The outside was black, but the inside had remained pink. "Ugh. So close."

Probably *too* pink, but the Putrid Mana was gone, and it was comparable to rare beef from a fancy restaurant. Nacho waited for her to take a bite, as did Reuben. Brie rolled her eyes at them. "It's going to be *fine*. It's Nacho's first attempt, and it can only get better."

"See?" She took a bite, chewed, and swallowed. "It's *fine*."

Reuben bit off a chunk of his portion of blackened meat. He chewed, chewed, chewed... and chewed some more. He reached for his water bottle and managed to force the deer meat down. "Exactly what I would expect from monster meat; it's not that bad."

Concerned, Nacho tried his, and once he got past the taste of the ash, he got to experience burnt meat. Eventually, he chewed his way through the charred exterior only to encounter the half-raw center, which tasted disgustingly gamey. He detected a hint of the salt and pepper and lemon juice, but it was akin to smelling something on the side of the road on a freeway while going eighty on a hot summer day. He unexpectedly recalled a cooking term and searched his memory. "What's a marinade?"

Brie didn't answer, continuing to chew with a determined look on her face. Reuben, looking for any excuse not to be ingesting the meat at that moment, was happy to answer. "It's letting meat sit in a sauce to make it more flavorful and tender. Grab some water, man. It helps."

Nacho survived his first deer meat like he'd survived his first attempt at pancakes: using a lot of grit and determination. If the kitchen was his new battlefield, he was getting his butt kicked. "All this means is that I need to practice. If anything is true, it's that practice makes better."

After banking their fire, Nacho and his friends returned to the overhang, the cook hauling ten pounds of the uncooked meat. His plan was to spend the evening practicing cooking. Once settled, they started another fire before the sun set on the cold day. The flickering flames gave them some much needed heat and light, in addition to preparing a cooking arena for

Nacho. To top it off, if the ominously gray clouds started spitting rain, they were in a good position to retreat under the overhang.

They still had to discuss their plan for the three hundred and forty-two credits they'd accrued. It was a windfall, and Nacho wanted to buy some barbecue tongs to avoid the dropped meat mistake he'd already made. Cooking was so much easier when you had the right tools... as was everything else in life.

He'd just bought the tongs when they heard a man's voice call up to them. "Hey! We saw your fire! Can we come up?" From the sound of the chattering, the man wasn't alone.

People had found them at last. Nacho's knives twirled in his hands—he didn't remember drawing them—and his friends watched him nervously. "What do you guys think?"

CHAPTER THIRTY-ONE

The evening was gray and cold, so the strangers *might* just want to enjoy their fire. Or they might have murder on their minds. When his friends didn't answer right away, Nacho made an executive decision. "Stay down there!"

Brie shot to her feet. Accessing her chainmail from a Storage Slot, she was dressed for battle in a flash. She gripped her hammer firmly and angled it over her shoulder in anticipation of an ambush. Reuben clearly didn't believe they were in much danger. "Guys, it's just *people* down there. They're probably scared, hungry, and totally clueless. Why are we freaking out again?"

"Think of *any* zombie movie." Nacho stood and grabbed his knives. He might not get credits for murdering other people, but making sure he was the one to kill the bandits meant his friends would suffer less.

Reuben grimaced and tried to wave his friends down. "This isn't a horror film, this is just life. Okay, so maybe there is *some* overlap-"

"Don't come up. We're armed. Give us a minute to talk." Nacho cut his friend off as he yelled to the people below. Then he looked back to his friends, his expression firm. "We have over three hundred credits. We bring Reuben up to three with Healing Hugs and level four with Positive Vibes—we bring Brie up to level five in both her Combat Dash and Defensive Whirl. Reuben can be the damage sponge while Brie brings the hammer down."

"Let me upgrade my Marketing Skill instead," Reuben added quickly. "Trust me, it's cheap. Just twenty credits, and I talk these people into giving us credits for your iffy cooking."

Nacho feigned being hurt. "Ouch, Reuben. Cooks have feelings too. No, we can't splurge on your Marketing skill just yet. Upgrading you both will leave us only twelve credits."

"You're going to regret that." Reuben adjusted his misshapen leather helmet. "It's all about branding."

"Says the guy in the abomination of a hat." Nacho twirled his knives again and again, idly evaluating their maneuverability. If only he'd been able to add to his Small Blades Skill.

"Are you all still up there?" The fact that the guy was shouting was a good sign. Shouting was better than screaming bandits rushing up with clubs and sticks. Or with swords, crossbows, and magical armor.

Nacho hopped up onto the rocky ledge facing east but quickly slid onto his belly and crawled to the edge. If the group had somehow managed to find bows, he didn't want to give them a target, especially since he didn't even have a shield to protect himself. Brie and Reuben joined him a moment later.

In the gray light, they could see most of the people, though some were partially obscured by the shadows of the forest. A portly man in a ragged suit, smeared with mud, waited at the bottom of the tumble of rocks. He had a pretty decent double-bladed battle axe—he looked like the mayor of a small town who had raided the props closet at a local theater, and he was the guy doing the talking.

Next to him stood a gawky teenage boy with dark skin and thick freckles, wearing a leather cuirass and holding an arrow nocked to a great bow. A few of the other people gripped rusty short swords and shields, but most only carried long sticks and knotted clubs. At least a couple dozen people had clustered at the foot of the cliff.

Reuben squinted and counted everyone. "They look like normal people. I'm going to stand up and talk with them. Don't worry; even though I'm a level zero marketer, I know the ABCs of selling: always be closing."

"Wait." Nacho didn't like any portion of this situation. He'd wanted to march up to the top of Armor Mountain, with his meat already cooked and with Brie standing tall and proud.

Reuben patted Nacho's back. "It's okay, man. I have my cheesy ring. If the kid takes a shot at me, I'll just absorb the damage."

"Then I'll smash his bones into almond butter," Brie hissed, a promise that made Reuben shudder.

"T-that's so sweet!" He stuttered as he got to his feet. The Healer was wearing his chainmail, which was good, but also the leather helmet—which was bad. The big guy smiled and waved at the motley group below. "Hey! Sorry it took us a bit. We had to level up our fighting skills, in case, you know, you were unfriendlies. But you all don't look like bandits to me."

Nacho liked that Reuben had started off by emphasizing that they had fighting skills.

To further drive the point home, Brie stood up with her fiancé. She looked tough with that big two-handed hammer over her shoulder, let alone her sabatons, mail shirt, and gleaming silver helmet. She could've played an extra Valkyrie in a movie and sold the bit by not saying a word, just standing there and glaring down at the people.

"Hey, we're not bandits, I assure you!" the portly man with the battle axe claimed. "I'm Dan Chronour. I was the mayor of Bonner Springs before, you know, the Juxtaposition."

"You look like a mayor," Reuben agreed with the man, putting him on the off foot. "Well, better Bonner Springs than Liberty Missouri, right?"

"Ha! I get that all the time." The battle-axe mayor paused.

"You know, we smelled meat cooking earlier this afternoon, and it didn't have that terrible stink to it that all our food does. That wouldn't have been you two... would it?"

"It was our group, yes." Nacho got to his feet reluctantly.

Reuben stroked his chin with a big gauntlet. "You know, Dan, we have a special player with us. Our buddy can cook food that doesn't make you sick, not like the Putrid Mana-filled meat around here does at least. I'm sure you've tried to eat the animals around here, and it probably tastes like warmed-over green dog feces."

"There isn't any better option," another voice called out sadly.

Reuben stood with hands on his hips. "Hey, Dan, how about you and... let's say five of your people come up, and we can talk. Maybe have something to eat? We were going to open a little restaurant and sell our food. It's delicious, and a lot cheaper than the Store. Maybe you can tell us your story, and we can tell you ours."

Whispers erupted from below, the main one being, "There's a *store*? Where?"

Nacho didn't like the situation: two dozen people, even with stick spears and tree-branch clubs, would be hard to deal with. Even six against three wasn't too good, depending on their levels.

Even so, Nacho could safely assume Dan and his ragtag group of underdressed and ill-armed people weren't a threat. He didn't want to teach them the command to open the Store yet; they'd probably use whatever meager credits they could get their hands on to buy food or to level up their classes and not their Skills. It was a rookie mistake that his party now had the option of teaching them to bypass.

In the end, Mayor Dan came up with only two other people: Taye, who was the freckled guy in the leather cuirass, along with a Mind Player named Kristie. She was a big girl with sparkly pink hair and a happy grin. Just the fact that Kristie was there—an obvious magic-user, and so very *nice*—was a clear attempt to put Nacho at ease. But he wasn't taken in. She could just be a lure.

Nacho put on three fresh steaks to fry in his pan. This time, he knew to flip them as they cooked, and he knelt to prepare dinner while Reuben and Brie chatted with their guests.

Taye eyed the piles of deer steaks with obvious hunger in his eyes, while Kristie was growing as pink with nervousness as the fading dye in her hair, which left Mayor Dan to do all the talking. "Listen, you three seem to know what's going on. I mean, you have very nice armor, and you have the ability to cook without making us sick? This smells better than anything we've tried, at least. I'm with some people about a day's walk from here. We've been searching for dungeons. We found a little one, just a bare room, but we were able to get some things from it."

"So my question is…" He slapped his battle axe onto the ground. "Can you offer us any advice?"

"How about we eat first?" Reuben suggested easily, trying to bring the conversation to where *he* wanted to take it. "There's three of you, and the going rate for a Nacho's Famous Venison and Hotcakes Tray is six credits. How about he cooks you something special? Not only is the food better than the Store, it is far cheaper too."

"You keep saying 'store' like it means something to us." Taye laid his huge bow on the ground. "No offense, Reuben, is it? How do we know this isn't a trick? Or if it's poison or not? Or if it's good? It might not be good."

"Is Nacho your real name?" Kristie stared at Nacho with her big doe eyes, which backfired spectacularly, making the cook hunk over the venison and glare. She didn't relent.

"Eli Naches." Nacho ground out the admission begrudgingly. "Nacho for short. Taye. You're smart to be suspicious of people. Have you had trouble?"

"Some. Initially." Taye shrugged with a dismissive air, as if the 'trouble' had been something minor. For all The Dinner Party knew, it had merely been a few tussles.

Nacho didn't care about losing a sale at this stage in the

Juxtaposition, but he knew these people needed to be set at ease. "Once these are done, we can give you a free sample. We'll eat some, you'll eat some, and we'll come to an understanding."

He closed his eyes and added some Cooking Magic to the thickest of the deer steaks. It was close to being finished, so Nacho sliced off a few pieces with a series of slashes that made the other people nod appreciatively at his clear skill with the knives. Then he lifted a hunk on Cry and took a bite. The meat had the initial squish of juiciness, which was a good sign, but it turned dry after a few chews. He had a long way to go, but still not bad.

The System gave him a flash of a message:

Hey, Player, the Common Cook who prepared this Wight-Tailed Deer cooked it with love and slaughter in mind. Would you like to increase one of your stats by 5% of max?
Yes / No.

Nacho chose the 'yes' option and increased his Mental Energy stat. A second later, he checked his Stat Sheet and found that his maximum Mana had increased to twenty-six-point-five, though he was down ten Mana from using his Cooking Magic. He stood and offered up pieces of the meat to the guests.

When Taye took his bite, his eyes flashed. "Hey, I get a stat bonus? Cool; there's no terrible aftertaste either. We've been cooking deer ourselves, but I think we got zombie deer or something. It was like... their bodies were okay, but their heads were kinda decayed. The meat had this rank smell, even the unde-cayed meat. It also wound up tasting rotten by the end of the first bite. Super gross."

"Ghoul deer." Nacho's lip curled in disgust. "I'm surprised you tried to eat them. They *start* as necrotic flesh."

Mayor Dan took a piece of steak, looking embarrassed as he

tried to explain. "We were desperate. To be honest, we're still desperate. Can I have some more? We'll pay."

Kristie looked embarrassed. "I think someone mentioned something about hotcakes? I'm assuming that's a pancake? I miss pancakes."

"I have some cold ones," Nacho told her, his tone as dry as the meat. "They're leftovers and probably not the best. Definitely not my finest work."

Kristie didn't hesitate. "It'll be fine, I'm sure."

"Why is this meat so much better than what you made us eat for dinner?" Reuben joked lightheartedly.

"Practice makes better. I'm a fast learner." Nacho knew the System would weigh in on the business transaction.

Hey, Cookie, looks like people are noticing your culinary expertise! Do you want to sell a three-person meal of your deer and pancake jamboree? Fun fact: people can't just steal your food without running into unspecified issues! You can just give it away, but we don't recommend telling people that. It's all too easy to chain a chef to a stove!

Yes / No.

Nacho chose the 'yes' option, and Mayor Dan scowled. "This apocalypse is bad enough, but those 'happy' System messages are a pain in my keister."

"Hey, now, Mayor, let's not start using such foul language," Reuben chuckled as the group collectively rolled their eyes.

Nacho heard a *cha-ching*, and suddenly he had six more credits to his name, bringing them up to eighteen credits. If they could sell meals to all of Mayor Dan's people, they could really clean up. "Let me put the hotcakes on the pan to at least warm them up. They might have a little more flavor after being fried in the deer grease."

Brie picked up on something. "You said you were about a

day's travel from here. You wouldn't happen to be from Armor Mountain, would you?"

"Armor what now?" Mayor Dan furrowed his brow as he considered all the landmarks he was familiar with.

Taye figured it out. "The big limestone mountain that appeared about where Armor Hills might have been? I mean, in the old Kansas City, not in this new place. Yeah, a bunch of us ran from the monsters—animal *and* human—and we took cover up there."

"We passed by a few days ago." Brie was slowly starting to open up. "We smelled you cooking."

"*Trying* to cook," Taye sighed dramatically. Nacho was glad Brie had left out the part that they had found a dungeon under the mountain. The meal was finally ready, and Nacho passed out deer steaks and pancakes to the three newcomers, who had gathered around the fire.

"How many people are up there on Armor Mountain?" Reuben inquired of the small group. Mayor Dan didn't respond right away, as he was too busy chewing. It finally started dawning on Reuben that even Nacho's terrible cooking was better than *any* alternative on the Starter World, and at that moment the Healer looked at his friend in a new light.

When Mayor Dan finally swallowed, he clearly still didn't want to answer the question. "Is it just you three? I mean, I want to trust you, but if you're part of a bigger group, I wouldn't want to give away our numbers."

It was Reuben that broke the tension. "Mayor Dan, it's just us three, and yes, we're amazing. We've figured out a lot of things about this world, but we have the same question. How can *we* trust *you*?"

Kristie, holding a piece of pancake, rolled her eyes. "Please. Look at us, then look at you. We're barely making it, and you're up here, eating like kings and wearing fancy armor and all outfitted in survival gear. It's not like we have the option *not* to trust you."

Taye was the one that pointed out the reality of their situation. "If we wanted to try to take your hilltop and your food, we would've had another group circle around and attack your rear. I took a chance on eating your steak, which very well could still be poisonous, or it might be some kind of food spell that you could activate whenever you wanted. At this point, we've been honest, and it seems you've been honest with us. Let's cut the malarkey."

"Malarkey?" Reuben recoiled and wrinkled his nose. "Were you homeschooled, by chance? I like it. Let's open this up to the rest of your people. We can all sit down, eat, and hash things out."

"We'll pay," the Mayor firmly promised. "This doesn't need to be a charity. We have some credits we've earned from various kills. But whatever information you can give us would be far more valuable than the food. How do we get this 'Store food'-"

Taye and Kristie raised their hands to show they wanted to know as well.

"-and how do we eat cooked food without getting sick? That stuff isn't fun, but it does keep us alive. I'd love to get rid of the 'getting sick' part, and you seemed to have figured that out." In the end, the Dinner Party allowed them to call up the rest of their people, and everyone took seats on the rocks while Nacho got to work.

He bought another cast iron skillet, then widened his fire so he could cook pancakes on one pan and deer on the other. The cook finally broke down and bought a mixing bowl as well. He only had ten pounds of clean deer meat, but luckily, the HungerCry knives turned that into twenty portions.

Nacho was pleased to see that he was getting quite the kitchen going, but he wasn't sure how he would be able to carry everything without purchasing some additional massive back-pack. He'd have to see if there was some kind of funky storage for Satiation Players.

Soon the cliffside was filled with laughter and more sounds from the System as Reuben collected the money. Twenty-one people buying meals turned into seven meals for six credits each, and just like that, Nacho had been able to boost his team back up to forty-two credits. If there were hundreds of people encamped on Armor Mountain, they could start collecting credits by the fistfuls.

The people ate and chatted, mostly with Reuben, who loved people. The Healer took some time to teach people how to open the Store, and soon gasps of excitement and shock resounded through the stony outcropping.

Brie was polite, but she wasn't relaxing; her hand was always on the shaft of her hammer. However nice Mayor Dan's people seemed, it would take a bit for her to trust them.

Nacho fully appreciated that.

It was Taye, who was obviously the gamer of the group, who asked a critical question as he searched through the Store. "I see menus to start a party of adventurers, but I also see building orders for a guild. Do you know anything about that?"

Reuben opened his mouth to answer, then closed it. "Maybe Nacho can expand on that option. He's the real gamer here."

Nacho bit back a grin as he flipped a pancake with an actual spatula. It was so much easier than trying to use sticks on half-solid batter. "Let me finish cooking first. Then we can talk more about how *terrible* of an idea that would be right now."

He had seen the benefits of guilding up, but he also knew about the drawbacks. The cook knew that he would have to proceed very carefully, or else they might wind up with a nightmare situation that would be nearly impossible to escape.

CHAPTER THIRTY-TWO

At first, it was strange having so many people around Nacho and his friends. Of course, Reuben loved it—he genuinely enjoyed people. Brie was friendly, if a little cold, while Nacho worked on keeping everyone fed.

Reuben invited Mayor Dan and his extended party to camp out at Rocky Top, the halfway point between Armor Mountain and the MurderSong Dungeon. Nacho and his friends would get the prime spot under the overhang, and the others would find other places. As long as it didn't rain, no one would need tents. Lightning flashed above, and at times, the wind swept through at a gale force before subsiding, but as Reuben had optimistically continued to point out: there had been no rain so far.

There were a few concerns that the breeze would take the scent of their fire and cooking east, and might draw monsters. But between the humans, things seemed to be fine. Once it was clear that there wasn't going to be any kind of fight, epic betrayal, or even an argument, Nacho felt himself relaxing. After all, if he was getting into the restaurant game, he was going to have to learn to be polite.

Reuben must've been using his Marketing Skill near-constantly; even at level zero, something was clearly going on to smooth tensions. People came back for more of Nacho's cooking, even when they didn't need to eat. He rapidly sold out of deer meat, but he could make as many pancakes as they wanted. In less than an hour, The Dinner Party had eighteen more credits to add to their forty-two. Nacho marveled at how well the whole system could work once he got better at cooking, expanded his recipe library, and added more cooking Magic to his dishes.

However, Taye's question about guilds still hung in the air. Seeing as it was going to be a major topic of conversation, the cook convinced everyone to have that talk in the morning so that he could explain things as clearly as possible. With full stomachs and sleepy eyes, most everyone was happy to acquiesce to that decision.

As it grew later, different people from Mayor Dan's party offered to take watches, which meant that Nacho, Reuben, and Brie could all sleep through the night... though Nacho wasn't sure he trusted these folks that much yet. How could he? He knew how people could be. He'd *been* one of those untrustworthy people.

Nacho finally found himself sitting around his cook fire with Reuben, the mayor, and Taye, who were an odd pair. Some gamer kid and a middle-aged mayor, at least fifty, with a paunch and a battle axe, would never have made sense as a team prior to the Juxtaposition. Brie and Kristie were talking at a nearby fire of their own, along with some other of the ladies from the larger party.

"Tell us more of your story, Mayor." Reuben had splurged and bought a root beer from the Store in celebration. The tepid beverage was flat, watered-down, and not very good. It definitely wasn't worth the single credit he had paid for it.

Nacho stuck with water, though he did wonder if he could play around with drink recipes. He didn't think that would be the case. There was a whole separate Satiation class, known as the Brewer, that cornered the market on drinks, though finding one would be a real trick.

Mayor Dan had bought a beer from the Store, and it came in a yellow plastic can with the word 'beer' printed on the front in red. Every sip made him grimace. "Well, I got lucky, I have to say. My wife and I came down from Bonner Springs to have lunch with my daughter. She's a sophomore at UMKC. We were in a restaurant at noon when the trouble happened… this Juxtaposition business."

The Mayor's eyes got misty. "The Evaluation was difficult, to say the least. I wanted to protect my wife and daughter, but I couldn't—the rules of the game weren't as clear as they could've been. I didn't last long. Actually, my wife did the best. Her momma bear came out in a big way. She chose to be a Mind Player, as did my daughter. The kid's an Illusionist, while my wife is an Elementalist. I only had enough Evaluation Points to buy the Warrior class."

The fire popped and cracked sparks up into the darkness. The mayor shook his head wistfully. "I didn't know what to expect. I was just glad to see my wife and daughter again. It was Taye that actually saved our bacon, though."

"Well…" Taye looked sheepish. "I've been kinda waiting for this my whole life—to live in a video game? The System is exactly what I expected, and I did okay in the Evaluation. Archer. What class are you, Nacho?"

"Common cook." He had to grin. "I'm a Satiation Player, which is… rare. In the end, I think we're yet to find out how powerful meal prep can be."

"Already you're earning credits by just cooking," Taye pointed out, making Nacho grimace at the use of the word 'just' in reference to his efforts. "With your party, you can dump those credits into leveling your friends. What level are Reuben and Brie by now? Three? Four?"

"Zero," Nacho replied curtly. "Leveling your Skills is far more important than leveling your class. Yes, you get more Mana and Health at higher levels, but I read that hitting Tier one, also known as level ten, comes with a whole world of sugar honey iced tea."

"I like these fine young people!" The mayor spouted happily. "They've already learned a workaround for cursing!"

Nacho had been observing how open Mayor Dan was, how friendly the rest of the people were. He shouldn't be so suspicious, and yet...! Reuben caught the cook's conflicted expression, taking the chance to quickly jump in at that moment. "Actually, Mayor, we're graduates of UMKC. Well, Brie and I are. Nacho left his senior year. He was already preparing for... for life. *Ahem.* What about you, Taye?"

The young guy shrugged. "I'm in high school, you know, just a gamer. I liked math and science, and the chess club, which probably doesn't mean much. I don't know. My parents... my sister... they didn't make it. We were across town when the Juxtaposition hit. They were killed by this cow thing, or at least I think it might've been a cow. It was the size of a semi?"

At that moment, Taye had Nacho's full attention.

"I was able to buy a bow from the Evaluation Mall, and I had arrows, but nothing I did could hurt it. It mowed through a whole crowd of us. It was almost funny, we'd been sitting in traffic at noon. We all appeared where we'd been in the car on the Starter World, and the c-cow blew through us like we were nothing." A tear dribbled down Taye's cheek. "We were close. The irony is stupid. Here I am, living a video game, but I have to do it after my family died for the second time. I mean, we all died the first time in the Evaluation, right?"

"That's right," Nacho gently agreed, getting a strange look from Reuben.

Taye scrubbed the tears off his face with balled fists. "After losing my family, I ran for a long time, and I guess I should feel bad about that. I found the Mayor and his group after a couple of days. Mayor Dan organized a bunch of people into a party; all the people from the restaurant and everyone else he could find. There's a couple hundred of us on Armor Mountain. The mayor saved a lot of people."

"After you saved *us*." Mayor Dan tipped his plastic can at Taye. "Then we found a little dungeon, started finding gear and getting credits. I'm a level one Warrior. I put my two stat points into my Fitness, though you wouldn't know it with my gut."

Taye exhaled heavily and itched the side of his head with his bow. "We all lost people. I just worry about my grandpa. He's in a nursing home across town, and I'm wondering what happened to him. Or to all the little kids. Babies, or whatever. I haven't seen a single one since we were brought here."

"I… found an info pack on this. They age up or down into the game." Nacho suddenly found himself talking, spilling a bunch of information he hadn't meant to share. "Fifteen to fifty-five all are brought in. But if you're older, you age down. If you're younger, you age up. A year from now, someone who's fifty-six will age down to fifty-five, get thrown into the Evaluation, and then they'll appear here. I guess they're held in a buffer of some kind. The Juxtaposition is pretty messed up, but the sick or disabled, they're given new bodies after they die in the Evaluation. I guess that's something, right?"

"You guys must have gotten really lucky to figure this all out." Taye shook his head in wonder. "I don't know. My grandpa is like… seventy or whatever. Are we really going to survive another fifteen years? If that cow thing finds our group on Armor Mountain, we won't last five seconds against it."

"That would be the… *the Bove*." Nacho flipped a log in the fire as he tried to contain the roiling emotions in his gut. "At this point, it's a high Tier one monster, almost Tier two, and it'll only keep getting stronger. It's some kind of mutant herbivore-turned-carnivore. It doesn't ever seem to sleep, and its hunger is endless. Right now, it's gaining Putrid Mana by the metric ton and increasing in power from every person it kills. The vast majority of people in the area won't survive the year if we don't take care of it, which brings me to a very important question. Do you know where it is?"

"I don't." Taye gave Nacho a long look. "It took off east, but I imagine something like that is hunting for large groups of people. There would be more ways to get… what did you call it? Putrid Mana? How do you know so much, anyway, Nacho? I can see the Store now, too. Those information packs are way too expensive to just *have* them all."

Nacho glanced at Reuben, and his friend nodded in encouragement. "Just tell them. We're trying to build something here, and we're going to be stronger together than we will be alone. We still haven't talked about this guild thing."

The cook shook his head at his too-trusting friend and decided to go with an amended version. He closed his eyes, took in a deep breath, and released it slowly. "I was given a boon by a Patron. I'm assuming you know about the Patrons. If you have gathered a couple hundred people together, you're bound to have at least one Warlock."

"Kristie is a warlock," Taye announced that secret as though it didn't matter. "She says her Patron is 'Caelius Apicius', but he's been pretty quiet so far. Kristie can throw magic bolt things."

Nacho perked up. He'd heard of Caelius before—it was the Patron who had inspired the name for his cookbook grimoire. It was in that moment that he realized that Reuben was right: they needed to work together. Forming a guild *would* be the best way forward, though he would have to be careful how he organized things.

He felt strange telling even *this* much about his boon, but he brought the mayor and Taye up to speed on some general information. He still didn't mention the CrossHumans, deciding to keep that information in reserve. He also didn't bring up the whole cannibalism thing. As quick as Taye was, he would probably put it all together before long. Taye had already learned that killing humans gave them credits—the people on top of Armor Mountain had already needed to repulse raiders. Nacho wondered which group or guild had attacked them. Had it been Crave? Or was it Kala and Myron?

The mayor had trouble grasping the fact that the nature of food would change once they hit level ten, which the cook had to explain was better known as Tier one, level zero. Nacho couldn't blame him. It had all taken them by surprise.

Taye's Skills were the next topic of interest, which turned out to be superior hand-eye coordination, from his many years of being obsessed with his PlayStation, and Eagle Aim; basically a sniper ability. He also had bought Fast Quiver, which allowed him extra shots when using his bow. The kid had obviously done well in the Evaluation.

As for the mayor, he had a definite oratory Skill, but that was it. He hadn't had enough money to spend on any sort of class Skill. Mayor Dan had totally biffed the Evaluation. Once he had earned some credits, they planned to evaluate the best way for him to move forward.

His wife, Becky Chronour, had a counseling Skill since she'd worked as a counselor at a middle school before the Juxtaposition, along with being a teacher. She also had a special affinity for ice magic with her defensive spell Skills, Ice Shield and Ice Wall. The group talked late into the night, until even Nacho was having trouble keeping his eyes open.

Reuben settled into his sleeping bag, which was quite the luxury item compared to the others' makeshift bedding. The mayor's people had all bought cheap Store blankets and used their new Store backpacks as pillows. For Nacho, the sight brought up a million memories of his first time in the game. The blankets were scratchy, the backpacks were lumpy. Part of him was afraid the people would get jealous and come after them. But... Taye had looked hopeful when Nacho had told him about his 'information pack' and what it could do for his allies.

Taye was smart enough to want to be one of Nacho's allies.

The cook could help these people. But would they agree to join a guild? It was a big commitment, and he knew some would walk away. Abyss, it had taken a lot for Nacho to join the Final Victory. It was only because he'd come to know Crave as a guy he could trust... right until the end. Pensive, he drifted over to Brie and sat down next to her little fire.

Brie pointed at the two people who had taken watch, identifying them under her breath. "That's Jimmy. She's Abby. They seem okay. But are we really going to trust these people?"

"How was your conversation with Kristie?" Nacho quizzed instead of answering her directly. "Did she seem all right?"

Brie winced and growled. "She did. She just seemed *normal*. I mean, she didn't do very well in the Evaluation, and she gets her powers from a Patron, but yeah. She seemed okay."

"Maybe we're being paranoid." Nacho sighed deeply and gazed around at the quiet campground. "Perhaps people haven't gone rotten in the single week that they've been here. Perhaps they're still hoping to go back."

Brie stared into the fire. "Just because we're paranoid doesn't mean there aren't people around us who would cut our throats to take what we have."

"Don't I know it," Nacho agreed with a groan. "You go to sleep. I'll stay up."

Brie crossed her arms, frowning. "You cooked for all those people. You must be exhausted."

Nacho shook his head and somehow managed to suppress a jaw-cracking yawn. "I'm good for a while. I'll wake up Reuben for the next shift. He just went to bed as though we've been with these people since the beginning... which started a week ago. Hard to believe."

"Hard to believe," Brie agreed, drifting into silence. In the end, Nacho got her to go curl up in her sleeping bag next to Reuben in the overhang. Nacho kept the fire burning for a while, but there were other people keeping watch, and he ultimately felt like he was being silly. After a while, he let himself drift off next to his little fire.

He fell into a dream, or he thought it was a dream, until he stretched out his hand to feel the fire. No, he was awake.

Standing before him was a tall man with unruly sideburns and a wide smile. He wore a white toga and golden sandals. On his frizzy hair sat a New York Yankees baseball cap. The strange man tipped his hat, which didn't match the outfit in the slightest, and it was that gesture that fully solidified for Nacho that he wasn't dreaming. The man in front of him wasn't exactly there. It was more like he was appearing through the gaming system, glowing a soft blue.

Mr. Toga's grin widened. "Sorry, buddy, about what's going to happen. But remember, you got a vision of what *could* be, not what *must* be—it was called Probability Vision; not Time Travel."

He was about to add another thought when the roar shattered the early morning air. It was a mixture of a cow's moo, a demonic scream, and an angry Tyrannosaurus Rex off its meds. Mr. Toga immediately vanished from the cook's gaming sight.

Hooves the size of doors clattered on the stones, and along with the noise came the smell—as though someone had dropped a septic tank into a factory farm.

Nacho blinked and stood subconsciously. The Bove could move impossibly fast, strike from the darkness, and be on them in seconds. Yes, they'd taken watches, but the Bove was already too wily to be seen until the very last minute.

The gargantuan Bove loomed above the encampment like a house of awful—the huge bovine body, filth-encrusted hooves, massive horns, and the black and white Holstein markings. It was a cow, all right, but instead of flat herbivore teeth, fangs gleamed cruelly from a bizarrely offset mouth, as if a lizard's maw had been crammed into that of a cow. The thing had a serpentine tail which also ended in a mouth, this one more snake than lizard. Throw on some leathery wings, and that was the Bove. It couldn't fly, but it could leap and glide… because the Calamity-class monster didn't care about physics or aerodynamics.

It only liked killing and eating people. The more people, the better.

Those oversized wings had allowed it to come swooping in from the darkness and approach without anyone spotting it. Nacho thought he was dead for a moment, but at the last second, the Bove lurched to the side and grabbed one of the Armor Mountain people, someone Nacho didn't recognize.

He was glad for that small mercy.

That guy was dead in an instant, half of him already in the Bove's gut. Other half-awake people launched themselves to their feet, including Reuben and Brie, who had both streaked past Nacho. If anyone were able to take out that monster, it would be the two of them. The Bove threw a horn that should've skewered Reuben, but instead, the big guy was smacked back, surrounded by the rank smell of parmesan cheese.

Brie attacked the Bove with her hammer, but Nacho couldn't be sure she'd done enough damage to hurt it. The fact that the Bove ignored the blow was indication enough that the attack was ineffectual.

Chaos had come to Rocky Top.

The entire hillside was rapidly illuminated by fire—both fireballs and flaming arrows. Jimmy, one of the Armor Mountain people, took an arrow in the chest. The cook watched it happen, and there was only one thought on his mind.

Nacho didn't think that was accidental friendly fire.

Another person on watch, Abby, dove for cover from both the blazing arrows and the Bove. "It's not just the cow monster that's attacking us! There are others! They killed Jimmy!"

Figures in black swept up the stone, engaging people in combat as the Bove tore through their ranks. It wasn't until the shadowy figures realized that the cow monster didn't care who it ate—nice, peaceful people or black-clad bandits—that they paused their assault.

Nacho stood frozen for an instant, but then he thought he might as well do some backstabbing to even the odds. He couldn't kill the Bove, but he could take care of a few of the raiders that had taken advantage of that unfortunate moment to attack.

Out of nowhere, a familiar face appeared in the darkness—he'd been using the Midnight Blend ability, an elite Assassin if there ever was one. This particular Assassin, Nacho knew, would later start the Final Victory.

Crave brushed a feather across Nacho's face.

Nacho knew that feather. He also knew he had about three seconds before falling asleep. In that time, he performed one very important task while everything else went up in flames.

He dropped the HungerCry blades into his Storage Slots.

CHAPTER THIRTY-THREE

Nacho suddenly knew he was awake, but he didn't open his eyes right away. Crave had taken him, he remembered that, but he couldn't let the Assassin know that his prisoner was armed and extremely dangerous just yet. Later in the Juxtaposition, forcing a prisoner to empty their Storage Slots became routine. But early on? People forgot about them, if they had even discovered them yet. Crave had made a mistake, and it was only a matter of time until Nacho capitalized on it.

Unable to sense anyone nearby, he cautiously opened his eyes and took stock. He was tied to a tree, unsurprisingly located in the middle of his enemy's camp. He was fortunate to have been tied close enough to a campfire that he hadn't frozen his fingers. That would've been a problem. He was still in the forests of the AKC—he recognized a Sickamore tree with black goo leaching into the branches and turning the yellow leaves the color of ink.

The cold sun had risen, and Nacho couldn't help squinting against the glare. The air was chill and felt damp, though it hadn't rained so far. A woman with short, dark hair, outfitted in ornate black leather armor, eased into view and called out, "Crave, he's awake."

Nacho had heard stories of Suzy Blacke, also known as Red Suzy Blacke. An Elementalist with a bow, she crafted her own fire arrows; a powerful combination she'd paid a massive number of Evaluation Points for... or so the story went. She was even better known for being a vindictive killer that Crave had needed to personally put down. That act had been seen as heroism, and solidified his 'good guy' persona.

Crave was sitting with Hogan and Whitney, but they'd picked up a dozen other people and added them to the party. This realization jogged Nacho's memory; they were the original thirteen, the very earliest members of Final Victory.

Nacho squeezed his eyes shut, trying to clear his head and remember what had happened the night prior. Who was the guy in the toga and baseball cap? Had he mentioned something about time travel?

The memories of the night before were hazy, but Nacho felt a sharp spike of fear. Had Brie and Reuben survived the fight? He checked the System settings and saw that he was still a part of The Dinner Party, which still had three members. That made him feel *worlds* better. If either had died, they would've been removed from the party.

However, they weren't close enough to transfer credits, which meant that Crave had managed to whisk him pretty far away. The Assassin strolled languidly into Nacho's line of sight and squatted down. He had classic good looks, brown hair, and a solid jawline. At some point, he'd lost the bad suit and picked up an Assassin's black leather armor with some magical chainmail thrown in. It was good stuff. He also had found a scimitar for slashing and a long dagger for backstabbing—and the feather, in a special little holster on his hip.

Crave smiled at him with a pensive look in his eyes. "I don't know who you are, exactly, but I do know you're either important now, or you're *going* to be important. I'm Crave."

"Richard Crave." Nacho grinned at the shocked expression

that crossed the Assassin's face. "Yeah, I know who you are, Rich. I also know you're going to regret most of what you've had to do so far."

The man grew pale and had a knife out and pressed against Nacho's throat in a flash. "You know my first name? Who in the abyss are you?"

"Eli Naches, but you can call me Nacho. As to why *I'm* important? I can cook." Nacho played one of his cards right away. "You have passive intuition, right? I've heard stories about you."

Crave snapped his fingers and waved someone over. "Hogan, cut him loose. We should get going. His friends are sure to come after him, but I think we can *explain* to them that things are different now. Nacho is with us, and they won't be much of a threat so long as we're holding his reins."

Hogan slammed a massive sword into the back of the tree, cutting Nacho free by destroying the rope. Nacho considered making his escape attempt right then and there, but he'd only wind up with a flaming arrow in his back. Red Suzy Blacke was already looking at him with a gleam in her eye, clearly hoping he would try.

As for *fighting* his way out of their camp? Hardly. Hogan already had good armor and plate mail, including heavy silver sabatons. With no small amount of satisfaction, Nacho felt confident that Brie's were better.

Whitney was in his own armor and he carried a round shield. The guy had a shield Skill that kept him safe, and an oversized sword of his own. Nacho wondered how much of their weapons and armor had been looted from their raids. Probably most of them.

A rat-faced man Nacho *didn't* recognize skittered forward, nervous and twitching. He had sickly pink eyes and thinning dark hair. "Hey, Boss, the dungeon is about four hours to the south. We should get going."

That statement stirred Nacho's memory. This was another guy that died early: the Dungeon Rat, Paul Rizzo. Again,

Nacho had only heard stories. Rizzo had gained a boon as well, a potent one: the ability to find dungeons. He'd been a rogue, but like Suzy, he wouldn't live to see the summer. At least he hadn't in Nacho's three-year vision. Hogan tied Nacho's arms behind him, and they started moving.

Crave walked next to him. "Okay, Nacho, I have a vague idea about you. Well, enough for my benefactor to make sure I nabbed you. How do *you* know so much about *me*?"

"I have a Patron myself, and a boon." Nacho wasn't going to tell Crave everything, but he had a couple questions his former boss could answer. Nacho also had a plan forming between his ears. Crave and his cronies had a lot of resources at hand, and a man with money was likely to spend it. "Hey, Dick, you haven't happened to see your Patron visit you in the gaming system, have you?"

"No, just a message." Crave frowned at him. "Also, addressing me as *Crave* is what will be happening. Not Richard —not Rich—and definitely not… that last one."

They walked on, Hogan not letting Nacho drag his feet. The bruiser kept him moving at a fast clip while Crave marched with his left hand on the pommel of his scimitar, eyeing Nacho curiously from time to time. "You don't seem very upset about being kidnapped."

"You didn't kidnap me to kill me." Nacho kept his eyes on the ground to avoid tripping on anything. With his wrists bound behind his back, a fall might snap his shoulder. "I'm thinking you watched me cook my deer meat out in the open, then saw those other people walk up, and then waited. The Bove attack was the perfect excuse for you to rush in. Shouldn't have killed Jimmy, though. People liked Jimmy."

"I don't *like* killing," Crave spat defensively.

"Probably shouldn't have chosen the Assassin class, then." Nacho laughed mirthlessly as Richard flinched. His class was supposed to be a secret.

"Killing has been *necessary* to get where we are today. Hard

times call for hard decisions." Same old Crave, casually justi-
fying things that most people couldn't.

Nacho kept up with Crave as they walked, as he didn't like
being shoved by Hogan. "Listen, Crave, your party is more
well-equipped than the people I was with before. I have to say,
though, they were happy to invest generously in my amazing
ability. I hope you're willing to do the same."

"What can you do?"

Nacho smiled widely. "I can cook actual food."

Whitney giggled like the wormy jerk he was. "But we can
buy food from the Store, *genius*. We don't need to cook, and the
trays make great Frisbees!"

Hogan huffed at his friend to quiet the man down. "Store
food tastes like my grandmother's week-old leftovers."

Nacho turned slightly to appraise the two dirtbags. "Grandmother's leftovers don't include buffs. I can make *magic* food, or
I will, once I get a few more recipes and level up my skills."

Rizzo laughed like a hyena having a conniption. "Well,
that's good; me and this other crew found a kitchen in the top
level of this dungeon we're going to. Looks like we can have
Cool Ranch here whip us up something special."

Nacho winked at the rogue. "Cool Ranch, instead of Nacho
Cheese. Funny. Paul Rizzo, you're a laugh-riot."

"How do you know my name?" The ratty little man scowled
darkly, all traces of humor evaporating as he lunged at the cook.
"How? Start talking! I'll *cut* you!"

"Magic, Rizzo. Magic." Nacho waggled his eyebrows as the
rogue was held back by the others. "If you see a Wight-Tail or a
ghoul deer, bring it down. Venison is my specialty. Pancakes too,
but you'll have to splurge for your own syrup."

Crave studied Nacho closely. "Out of all the things you
could've chosen, you chose to be a cook? Not a Warrior, not a
Wizard, but a chef? What is *wrong* with you?"

"Patron. Boon. What can I say? When a god-like entity
suggests something, you generally do what they tell you to do."
Nacho casually waved off the questioning.

Crave obviously wasn't so willing to drop the subject. "Do you think the Patrons are gods?"

"They created the Juxtaposition. They can give boons. They power Warlocks. If they aren't gods, they at least have power to a godlike degree." Knowing he would get farther by talking as little as possible, Nacho let silence finish that thought.

Crave sighed after a moment's hesitation and opened up to his captive. "I keep thinking about Fourtuna, my Patron. I think the Patrons are gambling on us, that they are picking favorites, and weighing the odds. Some people get boons, while others get killed, and I bet there are betting pools right now over what is happening to us."

"Well, boss, we're going to win," Hogan growled and hefted his sword. "The Patrons should put all their money on our party, because we're ruthless, and we're going to do anything it takes to own this thing."

"*Not* anything," Crave ordered firmly. "Nacho is right. We didn't need to kill… was it Jimmy?"

"I got thirty credits for Jimmy—for him, and for the credits he had," Red Suzy Blacke called out. "Not many monsters are worth that."

Crave's face wrinkled deeply. "We have to come up with some kind of code of conduct, or we'll turn on each other. People are more powerful together than any *one* is alone. At this point, we have some good armor and weapons, and we're going to hit the Chaos Coop hard. We'll do some deep diving, and we'll get a ton of credits for the kills. According to Rizzo, the dungeon contains a whole flock of these chicken-bats we can kill."

It was a little odd for Nacho to be traveling with the Final Victory Guild at their beginnings. Crave had left out the part about murdering and stealing from other people when he, Hogan, and Whitney had first created their Victory Party. However, Crave had said in the past that the Chicken Coop of Chaos was what had earned them credits faster than anything. The thirteen raiders used to divide up into three groups and go on killing sprees, leveling themselves up, finding magic items, and generally making a bundle.

Crave would eventually stumble onto a guild charter that he didn't even need to pay for, and others would see his power. People would join the Final Victory Guild by the hundreds, then the thousands.

Nacho wasn't surprised to see that the meadow where the old wooden shack sat was the same meadow where the Final Victory's Guildhall would one day stand. Nacho experienced a moment where his head spun a bit, and then he spotted a ghoul deer grazing on the dying green grasses.

Crave's people made short work of the monster, a massive thing the size of a horse, with a rotted head and super sharp antlers of an unsettling polished black. The single beast would be enough to feed Crave's dozen raiders, but Nacho wasn't going to use his HungerCry Knives; or eat the nasty meat it provided. He was going to keep those secrets until he really needed them.

Under the watchful eye of the others, Nacho used his old knife to butcher the ghoul deer once the party had taken it down, removing the rotting head and casting it aside with the legs, which were also a little decayed. The thighs, haunches, and ribs were thankfully all intact. He was provided some water, and they were once more moving.

Rizzo talked nonstop, explaining how he had risked the Chicken Coop of Chaos with other dungeoneers in the past week, before they had joined up with Crave, and had good information on it. The top floor had been completely cleared of the chicken-bats, and they entered it as soon as they arrived.

The Guild Master promised to have Hogan and Whitney carry deer meat down for Nacho later as he escorted the cook to the kitchen himself. The galley was connected to a barracks, where the Tier zero chicken-bats had been roosting. Nacho wasn't sure what a chicken-bat looked like, since all of the previous kills had long ago melted away. He recalled running across some hamburger-bats later on, which mimicked the shape of a Whopper, but with wings.

Once they had advanced through the first empty floor of the dungeon, Crave led Nacho into the kitchen proper. Entering the doorway with Crave, Nacho thought he might faint for a second. He was standing in the very room where Crave had killed him for political gain. First, the magical feather, then the knife to the heart... then the Probability Vision had ended.

In the three years they'd had together, the guild had made certain upgrades to the kitchen—knocked out the wall into the old barracks, completely removed the useless stoves and ovens, and built a long rectangular table. Currently, the kitchen was a rudimentary space of rock and metal, mainly housing a little cooktop above a fire bin with an oven next to it.

Dusty firewood was stacked next to the stove, and a long row of shelves held a mixture of pots, pans, dull knives and other implements that belonged in a kitchen. That didn't include the cast-off armor, a broken shield, and a few swords scattered here and there. The Patrons had evidently added a couple of cobwebby skeletons just for fun. A square table with four chairs sat in the middle, but one wall was dominated by a long counter filled with cutting boards.

A water pump sat in the nearest corner, so Nacho walked over and gave the handle a few pumps. At first, coppery water that smelled like swamp gushed out, but it was soon followed by crystal clear water that swirled down a drain in the basin. Nacho would still have to boil it to process out the bacteria brimming with Putrid Mana, but that would be easy with a big pot.

It was ironic to him that this room had become his first actual kitchen.

Crave watched Nacho's face closely. As always, his old Guild Master was quick. "I'm thinking this is better than the campfires you were cooking on."

Nacho forced himself into an outwardly pleasant mood as he turned and nodded to the Assassin. "It is. I'll get started on ghoul deer steaks and pancakes, and I'll load everything up with my cooking Magic. But like I said, I'm going to need credits, a *lot* of credits, to upgrade my abilities and to keep up with cooking. Thirteen people is a lot. I'm only used to cooking for three."

Suspicion clouded the leader's eyes. "But you were camped with a couple dozen back up at that hilltop. That was substantially more than three."

Nacho met his gaze steadily. "That was my first night with those people. I didn't know them at all. In fact, when I woke up tied to that tree, I thought they had betrayed us at first. No, I was just traveling with a couple of strangers for a long time, but no one I really cared about."

The story came easily, because when the truth could destroy his life, lies were all he had left.

Nacho was playing a dangerous game. He wanted to use Crave and his credits to upgrade himself, and he wanted to do it quickly, but he had to escape before Reuben and Brie came to save him. Hogan and Whitney were tough, and with Suzy and her flaming archery skills to back them up? The fight could easily turn against Nacho and his people in a blink.

For a second, Nacho actually considered joining Crave, until Crave snapped his fingers and Hogan came forward with ankle-cuffs and chains they had bought from the Store. The big bruiser *clicked* one of the metal loops around Nacho's leg and attached it to an iron ring set into the floor. Once he was satisfied the chain was secure, he stood there with his arms crossed, glaring at Nacho.

"We'll see if you cook well enough for us to invest in you," Crave informed him indifferently. "If you do, I'm sure you'll find a home with us. We have big plans, Nacho. I hope you see that, because for now, I'm pretty sure you're not telling us very much of the truth. Besides, there's something... *familiar* about you. I can't put my finger on it."

The leader idly drew his dagger to toy with as he spoke. "There's also another problem."

"What's that?" Nacho grumped as he tried to get comfortable.

"As you know, I have this boon. I can sense if things are dangerous or... useful. With you? Well, son... you're both. A whole lot of both. Not sure what that means, but you best be cooking. I want to send my people down into the Coop with whatever magic you can whip up. When we use our skills, we starve, so we're going to need lots of food."

Whitney, dripping wet, barged in and dumped an additional deer quarter onto the counter for Nacho to butcher. It seemed that the rain had finally hit. The sodden man marched over and grabbed Nacho's chin in a bloody, beefy hand. "If you poison us, if your food is bad, if you try anything funny... I will *end* you. I worked at a prison before the Juxtaposition. I know how to handle criminals and anyone else who crosses us."

That was a laugh. Hogan had been *in* prison before the Juxtaposition. He was a liar, but he was Crave's dog to unleash on anyone he wanted. Crave could be a good guy...when it suited him. But deep down? Crave was all about surviving, and he'd literally eat someone else to make sure he thrived.

Nacho was going to use the user, and then get the abyss out of there. But first?

It was time to break their fast.

CHAPTER THIRTY-FOUR

Crave's party rotated in shifts to grab venison steaks and pancakes before going out to kill for credits. Everyone who ate both dishes was given the option to upgrade their stats, and most chose Fitness for ultimate kill potential. They all commented on the food, saying it wasn't *bad*, but it wasn't good either. Having topped off their stats and selecting their meal-generated buffs, they went into the caves, taking their rudeness with them.

Nacho stayed in the kitchen without complaint and started on the next batch. He had to eat and drink periodically while he cooked to keep his Hunger and Thirst Points up. By the end of his first day, he was *exhausted*. He found a nice place by the wood-fire stove, a little dry niche, where his chain would stretch, and settled on an old wooden chair.

He leaned back in the seat, eyes closed, and it felt good to get off his feet for a second. He couldn't forget about the chains, nor about the fact that his friends were coming, but he managed to get somewhat comfortable in his little home away from home regardless. Crave had given him fifty credits for cooking supplies, which was substantially more than Nacho needed, but he was going to milk this opportunity for all it was worth.

The cook could charge Crave's people directly for the meals, since it was built into the gaming component. He *didn't* tell them he could've given them their food for free. Nope. Six credits, at a minimum, for a sit-down meal for three. From the work of processing the food, then selling it, as well as Crave's gift of fifty credits, Nacho already had a hundred and four credits to play with—though he wasn't going to be using that little nest egg without dire need. Instead, he'd claim poverty and milk these mother lovers for more.

Checking his Stat Sheet, he still wasn't in range to send a credit transfer to his friends. They remained alive, but not close. Good. Nacho needed to get out of his chains before they arrived. There were three keys, one each held by Crave, Hogan, and Whitney. The trick was going to be snagging one without getting caught.

Speaking of Crave, the eventual Guild Master sauntered into the kitchen, grabbed a chair from the central table, and pulled it up to where Nacho was snoozing. "Nice trick with the buffs, and your cooking isn't bad. What else do you need?"

Nacho didn't open his eyes. He was too tired, and he wanted to let Crave know he wasn't concerned about what the guy thought of him. Nacho was just a Common cook doing a job. "I'll need a recipe for the chicken-bats, otherwise I can't cook them. There's an info pack in the Store on chicken related monsters, and it comes with a recipe. But there's also a Tier one recipe that would give me more variety. I'm thinking your people are going to get sick of my deer-pancake combo pretty quick."

"Let me look at the Store." Crave's eyes flashed. "*Patrons!* The Tier one recipe book is pricey. Four *hundred* credits…? I don't understand the differences between the Tiers. Are they like levels? How big of a deal are they, really? My intuition makes me think there's a catch there."

"I have no idea," Nacho only partially lied, not needing to

feign exhaustion. "I'm still figuring this stuff out, just like you. But I do know that food is important, which is why I went the Satiation Player route."

"*How* did you know that?"

Nacho had to be careful, so he opened his eyes to ensure he saw the entire situation. "My boon gave me certain pieces of information, but at the end of the day, people have to eat, you know? If I can become important for cooking, my chances of survival go up. I mean, that's why you *abducted* me instead of killing me, right?"

"Your deer meat smelled a lot better than ours." Crave smiled and sat forward, steepling his fingers. "I'm serious about moving beyond the crime thing. At this point, if the Chaos Coop works out, and if we can keep getting credits fast, I won't be forced to keep doing the things I've had to do up to this point. I found something in the Store about guilds. I'm still doing research, but I think that's the route I want to take. It's best for people to work together because they want to, not because they are forced to."

At that point, Nacho recognized the reasonable man he'd joined up with in his previous game. It had always seemed strange that Crave had started out as a murderer. Then again, everyone had their own unique way of reacting to Armageddon.

"Coworkers are better than slaves, I agree. Listen, Rich-" Crave frowned in anger, so Nacho hastily backtracked. "Listen, Crave, if you can keep me in credits and working, and if I can continue to eat and cook, this will work out fine."

He jiggled the length of chain. "But I would like my freedom. I won't run."

Ah, the lies came so easily after spending three years as an Assassin. Crave shook his head. "Listen, Eli-"

"*Nacho*. Isn't getting corrected fun?"

The soon-to-be master of the Final Victory Guild nodded in wry acknowledgement. "Nacho. I'm going to drop a thousand credits into you, because if I can keep my troops happy with a cook, and if you can add buffs to the food, this will go a long way to convincing people to join my guild. I don't quite have all the details, and the contract can be a little beefy, but I think there are definite benefits for us all to join together."

Nacho didn't let his disappointment show. He'd hoped to get away before Crave created his guild. He'd have to adjust his timetable somehow. However, a thousand free credits? Yes, *please*. He was ready to take advantage of that. "A thousand credits? You have a *thousand* credits to burn on me."

Crave raised a finger. "Not burn. An *investment*, and I want to watch you spend them. I want to be the first person to taste your new recipe. I'll have a chicken-bat brought to you, but first, let's buy the cookbook that costs four hundred credits."

A second later, the System was cheerfully asking him if he wanted to accept a transfer.

Hello, Satiation Player! Looks like someone wants to give you a whole bunch of credits. Will you accept four hundred credits from this assassin in black?

"That would be a whole lotta yeah." Nacho promptly opened the Store and bought *Colonel White Beard's All Things Chicken and Breakfast Happiness*. The book appeared in a Storage Slot, and he instantly pulled it out and waved it for Crave to see. "There you have it. Everyone loves Colonel White Beard."

"I hope so," Crave rumbled dangerously, "for your sake."

Nacho took a minute to peruse the book. There was a quick introduction to the livestock ideal of a chicken and how to pluck them, clean them, and chop them into the kind of chicken parts people wanted to put inside themselves.

Crave watched him carefully. "I need to know I didn't just throw away four hundred credits. Show me something."

"Give me a second." Nacho found a way to merge *Colonel White Beard's All Things Chicken and Breakfast Happiness* into his

Aria. Then he turned to the breakfast section—which was filled with Chicken and Biscuits, Chicken and Waffles, and at least one spicy southwest chicken omelet. Better yet, there was an Intro to Omelets section.

In the Soups and Stews section was a chicken noodle soup recipe that looked tasty, and under Entrees he discovered a fried chicken recipe, fajitas, and a chicken tikka masala, as well as a sesame chicken that looked very much like something found at any Chinese food restaurant.

Nacho let out a low whistle. "This is an example of the System being a pain in the butt. Last time, I bought a single recipe for two hundred credits, but I could've gotten a lot more by buying the Tier one cookbook, which actually only contains one Tier one recipe, *Poulette a l'Orange.* However, I can start with this. I should be able to do some things with eggs and with chicken, and what's this? A scone recipe?"

Crave made a face. "I hate scones. They reek of all things British. But this is good. I'm hoping if you can do scones, you can do biscuits. Better make sure we have lots of honey for that, though."

An excited grin lit up his handsome face, and for a second, it felt like old times, with just the two of them figuring stuff out. Happily, this scenario would end in a delicious meal, and not with Nacho murdering someone in another guild or backstabbing a monster in some deep dungeon somewhere.

"Honey, yeah." Nacho tapped his chin. "Now, let's talk about my skills. If I'm going to be processing chicken, I'll need to upgrade my cutting abilities. Right now, I'm limited to low-level ingredients. If you bring me something tasty, I won't be able to process out the Putrid Mana, which is what makes people sick. Lastly, I'm only second level when it comes to my cooking Magic. That's what gives me the ability to add buffs to stats. We definitely want to improve that."

Crave's frown deepened with every word. He'd claimed he was willing to spend a thousand credits, and he had thirteen players risking their butts to collect that cash, but thinking about spending money and actually seeing the money go out the door were two very different things.

A sudden burst of clashing rose from below, and it sounded like trouble. Crave sprang to his feet and whirled away. "Just make a list of what you would like to upgrade. Meanwhile, I'll start sending chicken-bats for you to process. I'm *not* kidding about the biscuits."

Crave left Nacho's kitchen—gone in an instant. Was that Shadow Speed at work? The man had done *very* well in the Evaluation; better than Nacho's first attempt, at least. Nacho used one of his own credits to buy a pad and pencil combo, then sketched a matrix of which skills he wanted to upgrade.

The prospective Guild Master had promised him six hundred more credits, and for a second, Nacho felt kinda bad. Then he remembered Jimmy taking one of Suzy's arrows in the chest. All of his credits had transferred over to Crave's party, as well as those for the kill itself.

No, Crave was being foolish to trust Nacho. Then again, Crave *did* have him chained in the kitchen, so how much was he *really* trusting him?

Eli 'Nacho' Naches
Class: Common cook
Level: 0
Experience Points: 100 to Level 1!
Current Credits: 103 (103 total Dinner Party pool) No Transfers Possible Due to Distance Parameter!

Build Type: Balanced, Delayed
Body:

- *Fitness: 10*
- *Metabolic efficiency: 10*

Mind:

- *Mental energy: 10*
- *Circuit: 10*

Satiation:

- *Hunger: 100*
- *Thirst: 100*

Total Health Points: 30
Bonus Physical Damage: 5%
Bonus Spell Damage: 5%

Skill Slots (3/4)

- *Small Blades (Passive) Level 1: 2% bonus damage on all knife attacks*

  No Mana, Hydration, or Metabolic Cost

- *Ingredient Processing (Active) Level 4: Remove Putrid Mana from monsters up to Level 6*

  Mana Cost = 5%
  Hydration Cost = 5%
  Metabolic Cost = 5%

- *Cooking Magic (Active) Level 1: cook food that enhances a single stat by 5% of maximum*

  Mana Cost = 5%
  Hydration Cost = 5%
  Metabolic Cost = 5%

- *Open slot*

Nacho spent a little time on math. To boost his Small Blades and his cooking Magic up to fourth level, it would take a total of three hundred and sixty credits: eighty to get to second, one hundred and twenty to get to third, and one hundred and sixty to get to fourth.

Spending other people's credits was a *lot* more fun than spending his own.

To get a single Skill to fifth level would cost one hundred credits. Really, he could get two of his other Skills up to fifth level and max out at five hundred and sixty credits. Forty extra credits for this and that? It would be reasonable.

Nacho didn't *want* to be reasonable. He wanted to take Crave for every credit he could. Jimmy would've wanted it that way. With that in mind, he'd have to needle Crave for an additional sixty credits to get all three of his Skills to fifth level.

When Crave eventually returned, he was flanked by Hogan and Whitney, both grinning at the cook. Nacho didn't like the grins. He *did* like Crave easily agreeing to the extra sixty credits.

Crave authorized another transfer, and Nacho promptly leveled up all of his Skills. Just as a System message flashed before his eyes.

Current Credits: 103 (103 total Dinner Party pool) Transfers Possible! Party members in range!

Nacho's heart leapt into his throat. Reuben and Brie were still alive; that was good. The bad news was that they were probably close enough to spy on the entrance to the Chaos Coop and were likely planning a rescue.

That would be fine, if they weren't killed by Crave's dirtbag friends. Nacho kept all emotion off his face, but Whitney stared at Nacho and giggled while Hogan did the talking. "You're going to be with us for a while now, guy. Your old friends have been poking around up top, looking for you. Me, Whitney, and Suzy are just biding our time. First, we're going to take out the chick with the hammer, then the moron in the leather helmet."

Crave looked disgusted and left the room. He wasn't actively stopping his evil underlings from being evil, which made the Assassin just as culpable. Nacho shrugged as nonchalantly as he possibly could. "Only the two out there?"

Hogan slapped him on the back. "Wouldn't *you* like to know."

With a malicious grin, he and Whitney left a stunned Nacho alone in his kitchen, chained up tight. The cook's heart felt like a dirty charcoal grill in his chest.

His friends were in danger, and he was literally locked in the kitchen.

CHAPTER THIRTY-FIVE

Nacho was kicking himself. He'd had the perfect opportunity when Hogan and Whitney had been alone with him, since Crave and his knockout feather hadn't been present. However, taking on both bruisers at the same time wouldn't be easy—especially with the chains on his ankle.

He'd have to play the long game.

Until then, he had the chicken-bats to prepare. The creatures were a mishmash of poultry and flying mammal, with fur instead of feathers, and fighting talons a rooster would have been proud of. Their faces were a nightmare of huge dark eyes and golden beaks edged with razor-sharp metal, accented by a red wattle underneath; that was their actual weak point, though he wasn't going to tell anyone for now. Each was about the size of a medium dog, which meant they produced a whole lotta meat.

These things attacked in swarms of all ages and levels, so Nacho had a large variety of carcasses to work with. A few were even level three creatures, granting him six credits for each portion. He worked tirelessly to drain away the Putrid Mana, collect his credits—a fact he'd never tell Crave about—and then start on prep. In a flash of inspiration, he decided to save the fat because he had plans to make a deep-fat fryer if the worst came to pass and he ended up with the guild permanently.

Then again... that wouldn't happen under any circumstances. If Hogan, Whitney, and Red Suzy Blacke ended up killing his friends, Nacho would kill them right back. He kept checking his Stat Sheet obsessively to make sure The Dinner Party hadn't lost any members. "Within range, and not dead. Good start. Keep at it."

At first, it was easy to get caught up in the cooking. He was making biscuits for the first time, and he would've thought that the quick breads would've been fairly easy. Nope; there was a definite art to them that he didn't understand in the slightest. He ended up making several rounds of tasteless hockey pucks, which he chowed down on to keep his Hunger levels up.

Then he remembered that a lot of people had used cans of premade buttery biscuits, the paper-roll kind that had to be smacked on a counter and produced the satisfying *pop* as they opened. He contemplated buying some from the Store and trying to pass them off as his own work, but they would've been terrible. It was all too easy to know when something was from the abyssal Store.

Once he had hacked up the chicken-bats with a dull knife, he pan-fried the meat in a little vegetable oil, though bacon grease would've been better. The cookbook worked surprisingly well; it turned out that Colonel White Beard *did* know a thing or two about poultry.

His first attempt at making fried chicken-bat was pretty good, with the chicken coming out showing an 'Uncommon' rarity, but Nacho completely screwed up the biscuits in the oven, round after round. He could only wince and hang his head in shame when the adventurers came in to eat. He loaded them up—and with his newly enhanced skill level, they were getting a full *twenty-five* percent extra added to any stat when they combined his iffy pan-fried meat and his depressing biscuits.

Crave also gave him the noble task of boiling water constantly, and soon, he was going through cords of wood to keep his oven and stove going. The cramped kitchen rapidly grew hotter than the Kansas City Plaza shopping center on a humid August day.

At the end of the long work hours, Nacho moved his chair into the farthest corner and settled as comfortably as he could on the hard wooden seat, trying to sleep, or at least turn off his brain. His worry for Reuben and Brie was driving him nuts. They were still alive, but for how much longer, if he didn't do anything about it?

He'd processed twelve of the chicken-bats, and each had yielded about twenty pounds of meat. At six credits per pound, he'd added one *thousand*, four hundred and forty credits to his stockpile just from prepping. Selling his meals? That brought in an additional six credits per meal for another eighty credits. Most of the meat liquified before he could get around to doing anything with it, but there was always another chicken-bat in the many coops below.

The Chaos Coop truly was a gold mine.

Nacho spent six hundred credits to upgrade his Small Blades ability to the ninth level, making him likely more dangerous than any two other players in the dungeon in terms of sheer deadliness. He was disappointed, but unsurprised, that he was blocked from upgrading to the tenth level until he was a Tier one Common cook; the restriction was a Juxtaposition mechanic that eventually forced players to upgrade—which meant ever more expensive food. Even after raising his Skill, he was still left with over a thousand credits.

Deadly intent glinted in his eyes as he glanced at the leg chain once more. When the time came, he was going to cut some throats, and he had the perfect knives for the job. Then he realized… he still had plenty of credits available to upgrade his cooking Magic. "Why not? If I eat a bunch of my own cooking and then go into battle, I'd have an even larger advantage."

Another six hundred credits took his Skill to level nine. By now, his cooking would give him a forty-five percent boost, and he was still left with four hundred and twenty-three credits to play with. Unsure of what to do next, Nacho forced himself to rest. He was exhausted from the back-to-back Skill usage.

He shifted on his simple wooden chair, made slightly more comfortable by the little cushion, with his feet propped on a nearby shelf. Nacho had to smile. His life hadn't been perfect—far from it—but he'd found the love of friends. The cook kept tossing around the idea of just escaping. He could do it anytime he wanted to, and then he could meet up with his friends and form a guild with the Armor Mountain people—they seemed like good people, especially with the contrast that Crave and his lackeys provided.

He slowly opened his eyes, and the creeping despair was gone.

A flash of blue light made him start. Just as before, a man in a toga and sandals appeared with his arms crossed, grinning. He wasn't there in real life; no, he was *there* in Nacho's gaming vision, like an item in the Store.

Mr. Toga's blue eyes twinkled, and the smile revealed a mischievous dimple in his cheek. "Here you are, back with Richard Crave and the gang. You're not going to *stay* here, right? I mean, if you just follow what you did before, my boon doesn't mean all that much."

Nacho bolted upright as his earlier guess was confirmed. "You're Kronos? You're a Patron?"

The movie-Zeus-look-alike nodded. "That's right. I didn't contact you before, because what was the point? That was all just playtime possibilities. This is a definitely-real type of situation. Which means I'm here to make sure you don't do what you humans do all too often."

"What do we humans do?" Nacho questioned him, unable to mask the slight condescension in his tone.

Kronos casually wandered about the kitchen, glancing here and there, and walking right through tables and shelves. "Oh, you know, fall into a rut and then decorate it instead of getting out and away. A picture here, a throw rug there, 'oh, sweetheart, should we découpage the furniture'?'" Kronos turned and glared at the cook. "The answer is always *no*. Don't découpage anything. Ever."

"Not sure I know what 'découpage' means, but I'll take your word for it. I'm not staying with Crave. I was abducted." Nacho found himself grinning like a fool. It was nice to know that his Patron was his kind of person. He wiggled his foot to make the chain clink. "Do you want to help a guy out? Can you break these chains?"

Kronos frowned as he took in the predicament. "I can't break the chain. Notice I'm in the gaming system, not here in real life. Between you and me, since you're not a Warlock, I shouldn't even be here at all. I just took a moment to sneak in, check on you, make sure you haven't given in to despair."

Willing himself to make the most of this opportunity, Nacho inhaled and released the breath slowly. "I have a ton of questions. Like where Reuben and Brie are. What's the nature of the Juxtaposition? Are you gods, aliens, or just really powerful players that got bored and decided to mess with a weaker world? What's the square root of an impossible number? Who are the CrossHumans? Why all the Earth culture references, since you're clearly not human?"

Kronos dropped his head back and made a very frustrated grunting noise. "Me showing up to check on you is one thing. Me shattering the traditions of the Juxtapositions? Notice the plural, cookie. Juxtaposition*s*, for there are *many*. No, my unorthodox boon has already drawn a ton of attention. It's never been done before, but come on, you know how grueling the game seems. I mean, it is *impossible* for a lot of people, and we have a very specific outcome in mind—survival of the flatulent. Wait. No, your idioms are so... plentiful. Survival of the *fittest*. We need the best and brightest to survive."

Kronos was on the move again, vanishing into the oven and materializing out the other side.

Nacho's eyes followed him around the kitchen. "We need to

survive to win the game, kill the CrossHumans… is this a gambling thing? Am I a prize stallion?"

Kronos spun on a heel, whipping around at an impossible angle. "Yes, you *are* a prize stallion. I basically singled you out, Nacho, but not just you; you and your friends, who are very much alive. I have great expectations for you three, and so far, you've been playing the game perfectly. It's that *Fourtuna* who's getting in my way. He doesn't believe that the *endgame* I have in mind is possible."

"Is he wrong?" Nacho quietly inquired. Even though he did not know what the ultimate goal of his Patron was, it sounded as though everything was in the air, if other Patrons were shocked by the attempt.

"No, you can do it. There are two types of Patrons: those who have hope in their hearts, and those who are greedy brats, milking the system until they squeeze it dry. The latter ought to go down in flames, bright flames, burning out in the rocket's red glare. Or a firework. But I digress… humans have such a variety of stories, songs, poems, video games, and so *many* streaming services." Kronos shook his head in wonder. "What's with that?"

Nacho didn't want to get sidetracked by talking about technology and individualized companies. Kronos seemed to realize his reluctance and stared into his eyes. "It's about time you escaped, my friend. Crave is problematic for many, many reasons. He never told you about his wife, did he?"

"None of us talked about our past." Nacho swallowed his concerns and started to limber up. "There's a reason for that. The past has teeth, and it'll go for the throat every time."

"The future is *far* hungrier. It eats the very seconds of our lives." Kronos laughed as they philosophized about his domain of time. "Get out of here, so you can start your own guild and feed your friends. Also, do something about the Bove? That thing was a bit of fun gone wrong. I'll try to come back, you know, when I'm needed most. There are more than a few of us Patrons in your corner, Eli Naches. Also, you're overworking your biscuit dough. If you'd been born in Mississippi, you would've known that."

Nacho made a face. "Yeah, people in the South do know how to cook. Last question: *please* explain the culture references?"

"The stories of you pesky humans, Earth in particular, make us old weary beings optimistic. If there's one utterly precious commodity in the universe, it's hope." With a wink, Kronos vanished abruptly.

Outside the kitchen, the sound of Hogan's clanking plate mail approaching set Nacho on edge. However strange his conversation with Kronos, there had to be some good information. He'd go over every word eventually, but for now, getting a key to unlock his chains was at the top of his to-do list.

With that goal in mind, the uneasiness at Hogan's impending arrival shifted into excitement and readiness. "Let's see what level nine in small blades looks like up close and personal."

CHAPTER THIRTY-SIX

Hogan walked into the kitchen alone, ready for some breakfast. It was early, but the adrenaline dump from his Patron's visit had ensured that Nacho was wide awake. Sizing up the bruiser, the cook knew he was going to have to play the opportunity smart. Not only was the ex-con in plate mail, but his sword looked like it would only be satisfied if it butchered an entire medieval village.

"Well, tortilla-head, we went out looking for your friends last night, but we ran into that big cow monster again instead. I think it's following you. We couldn't get to them, but maybe the cow thing did. Anyway, I'm ready for breakfast. Get on with it. Crave mentioned something about biscuits?"

"Right." Nacho teetered off his chair. "Anyone else up?"

"Does it matter?" Hogan sneered and slapped the rickety wooden table. "*I'm* here."

Turning to hide his involuntary eye roll, Nacho went over to his fire and threw more wood on it, stoking the flames. The biscuit recipe in his *Aria*—Auntie Brickbuilt's Cast-Iron Skillet Biscuits—called for super cold unsalted butter, buttermilk, flour, baking powder, honey, and salt.

The kitchen had come with an icebox, and Crave had donated huge chunks of ice for the cause. The Store also offered dry ice, which Nacho thought might work better, but it was more expensive, and Crave had decided that he was already spending too much money until he got a large return on his investment.

Nacho measured out the flour, baking powder, and salt into a bowl. He wouldn't miss being chained up, but he *would* miss the kitchen. He was reluctant to leave behind such a prolific number of utensils, including a pastry cutter, which he was going to use in a minute.

Hogan grimaced as the cook got to work. "I know your biscuits are going to taste like raw flour again, and I'm tired of your chicken-bat meat. Can you do Buffalo-style wings for lunch?"

"I *can*, if you want to donate a couple hundred credits to the cause." Nacho started cutting the butter, which started out very cold. He had to work fast to keep it from melting, since it was already approaching sweltering in the kitchen.

Hogan noticed the temperature as well, as he was already sweating in the preheating kitchen. Nacho thought about suggesting the bruiser take off his armor, but he knew that might put Hogan on edge. He didn't *want* to go up against him in that armor. It had to be magical, as shiny and nearly impenetrable as it appeared... but it *was* Tier zero. In Nacho's memory, Hogan had lost the armor when he'd leveled.

The massive fighter sneered as his eyes flashed blue. "I could buy that recipe. I have the credits, but I don't want to. Just cook."

"Let me double check my cookbook. I *might* have a recipe for wings." Nacho paused and thumbed through his cookbook. He knew he had already collected such a recipe, but he had wanted to see if he could manipulate another two hundred credits out of Hogan. No such luck. As for the guy watching him work, Nacho didn't mind the audience, and the longer Hogan stayed, the more he would sweat.

Nacho rapidly added the dry ingredients to the still-cold butter, rolling the pastry cutter's blades through the white powders and the yellow butter until they resembled coarse sand. He made a well in the mixture, poured in the buttermilk, and then added the honey.

"You like this cooking thing?" Hogan didn't wait for an answer, mumbling something and shaking his head before returning to speaking in a normal tone. "You actually had to *choose* this. That's crazy, or is it that you're just a weakling? Us warriors go out and kill, and be all heroic and stuff, and you're here in this kitchen. It's hot, and you're so weak that we were able to just chuck you in chains and make you work. You don't mind the heat?"

"It's hot," Nacho agreed with a hidden smile. He was anything *except* weak.

"What about the other stuff I said? Were you some kind of cook back before the Juxtaposition? You a fry cook at a diner?" Hogan leaned back in the chair at the square table in the middle of the room.

"Nah, just a college student trying to get by." Nacho found a clean space on a cutting board and flattened out his dough to start the process of folding it, which should create the layers biscuits were known for. He had to get the right height going, and he didn't have many chances. The more he worked with the dough, the more the butter would melt, and the tougher the dough would be. Kronos had warned him not to overwork the dough, and when a god-like being provided unsolicited information, it was wise to listen.

Shaking himself from his reverie, he stopped himself from doing just that. He dusted his hands off and pushed circles into the dough using a round cutter, finishing the preparation by coating two cast-iron skillets with a thin layer of chicken-bat fat.

Next came the most important part of his plan.

He had two pans of biscuits. To one, he added his cooking Magic, imbuing it with as much magic as possible. At ninth level, the biscuits glowed a bright gold for a long moment. The other skillet would just contain normal biscuits.

Hogan didn't notice a thing, too distracted by the heat. He stood up and fanned his reddening face. "It's so hot in here, and this is boring. I'll go up top, take a walk… maybe kill someone."

"Hold on." Nacho slid the two skillets into the oven. Auntie Brickbuilt suggested that the biscuits needed to touch each other so they wouldn't expand out over the top of the pan. "Don't you want to know about my life before the Juxtaposition, and why I chose to be a cook?"

Hogan sighed and unclipped the straps holding his breast plate. He didn't take it off, but just that gesture was promising. He sat back down heavily, the chair creaking in protest. "Why not. Tell me."

"I only ever made mac 'n cheese and hot dogs before. Nothing fancy." Nacho took two chicken-bat wings out of the icebox before pulling out his *Aria*. Colonel White Beard's Big Barroom Buffalo Wings recipe called for salt, pepper, garlic powder, onion powder, and baking powder. It was the baking powder that got them crispy. Who knew? He coated the wings with the seasonings, getting ready to dive face first into his work —but he wasn't actually cooking just yet.

He poured a liberal amount of canola oil in two pans. Soon the wings were sizzling, and Hogan adjusted his cuirass again. Sweat dripped down his face. "You must like the heat."

"It is necessary to make things delicious. Just like the system tells us, if we want the future to be delicious, we need to do it ourselves." Nacho used a little pot to melt butter, which didn't take too long, and he added more honey to the melted butter. The day before, he'd found a little brush he could sweep across the top of the biscuits, and he decided to steal that during his escape.

"So what were you before the Juxtaposition? Only a college student? What else did you do? I thought you had a proper story to tell." Hogan sighed angrily as he fanned his flushed face. Then, unironically, he answered his own question for himself. "I was a prison guard. I'm used to dealing with scumbags and dirtbags."

"You *sure* you were a prison guard?" Nacho prodded the overheating man, knowing that getting him angry would only make him hotter. "I heard Whitney saying he thought you might have been an actual prisoner. You know, a convict."

"He *did*, huh? Whitney talking trash about me?" Hogan grunted out bemused laughter. That was an unexpected response. Nacho used tongs to flip the wings, and added his cooking Magic to only one of the sizzling segments. Again, Hogan didn't notice a thing.

Whitney walked into the room, and Nacho was pleased to see he wasn't in his armor, nor did he have his sword. "You guys talking about me?"

"The cook here says that you were talking about me behind my back. What's up with that, Whitney?"

Whitney shrugged and grabbed a chair for himself. "I ain't said nothin'. You say you were a guard, sure, you're a guard. It doesn't matter."

"Everyone else asleep back there?" Hogan appeared to have dropped the issue instantly, forcing Nacho to turn under the pretense of checking the biscuits in order to hide his glower.

"Yeah, except for Suzy. She has guard duty." Whitney sniffed at the tang of buffalo sauce in the air. "Smells good. I could eat. Funny, using my Skills makes me so hungry."

"What are your Skills?" Nacho quizzed as if he didn't know them incredibly intimately.

"I have a special lunge attack," Whitney proudly proclaimed. "I can cut through *anything* when I do this lunge thing. I need some room to do it, and I also have a defensive thing."

"A defensive thing?" Nacho turned a hunk of the meat, keeping his eyes neutrally focused on the stovetop. "That's neat. I'm making wings and biscuits, special order."

"Even though I wanted them for *lunch*." Hogan growled quietly.

Whitney giggled his trademark high-pitched maniac laugh. "Big wings, right there! Those bats have wings, but buffalo wings? More like *steakhouse* wings. Biggest ever."

"Buffalo-style," Nacho stated agreeably, if slightly off-topic. "I'm going to make them extra spicy. I bought a bottle of Frank's Red Hot Sauce."

"I don't like spicy food." Whitney turned sullen instantly, the mark of a person with emotional control issues. "I'll have a biscuit, though."

Nacho felt his pulse quicken. He had expected to just take down Hogan, but it seemed he had to get through Whitney as well. He had already decided that he wasn't going to be spending another night in the Chicken Coop of Chaos. He had to get away. His mind racing, the cook took the pans of fragrant biscuits out of the oven and set them on the counter to cool. He turned and checked the wings, finding that they were cooking up nicely, going crispy and delicious.

Whitney threw an elbow into the seated Hogan. "Why don't you take off that armor? It's hotter than hades in here; I'll help ya."

Nacho hid his smile. Despite the minor unexpected hiccups, things were progressing perfectly. Hogan agreed, stood, and soon was in his undershirt; the stench rolling off of him told anyone with a nose in the vicinity that he hadn't taken a shower in several days. He propped his armor against the wall, next to the decorative skeletons. Nacho had thought of moving them, but after dozens of work hours with no one else to talk to, he'd found himself kind of liking them.

The cook brushed the honey butter mixture across the top of the golden-brown biscuits just out of the oven. He'd used his cooking Magic Skill twice, and he was feeling the hunger and thirst keenly. He'd be able to fix that in a minute, and he found himself grateful, not for the first time, that his class made such a thing possible.

He set the non-magical biscuits on the table, and the two thugs dug into the meal. Nacho didn't bother with the butter for his own meal, instead taking biscuits for himself out of the other pan and wolfing them down, working to keep his face neutral as the system sent him a friendly message.

Cooking Magic detected! Ahh, you're not just cooking, you're cooking with love. Delectable! Those yummy biscuits can increase a single stat boost of 45% of maximum! Which do you want to enhance?

Nacho chose his Fitness, which went from ten to fourteen and a half—he'd eaten a half-portion of biscuits, which had addressed his hunger. By the time he swallowed his last mouthful, the wings were ready. He threw in the hot sauce, melted butter, and some honey into a bowl. He coated the two biggest wings in the bright red sauce and delivered the serving to Hogan.

Neither of them commented on the lack of a System message. Yes, they'd eaten his food the day before, but it was easy to forget such things. It was also early, and Hogan and Whitney weren't the sharpest tools in the shed. Confident that they were occupied with their meals, Nacho went back to his stove and gorged himself on his own wings. The meal was, by far, the most delicious thing he'd made yet; a quick check informed him that they had gotten all the way up to 'Rare' rarity. ;Just goes to show how important a kitchen and proper tools are to my class, abyss it."

He was nervous, and normally he lost his appetite in nerve-wracking situations, but the crispy flesh, the sweet and tangy sauce, and the juicy meat had him chowing down happily, despite the fact that in a few moments he was going to be doing some light kitchen murdering.

Nacho went over his mental plan again, reminding himself that his Small Blades ability added another ten percent of damage on top of his boosted stats. Lastly, when using the HungerCry Knives, he was going to be twice as fast in his attacks, which should enable him to double his enemy-chopping time.

Hogan ate noisily but cleared out enough of his mouth to call out. "Doritos, what did you do before the Juxtaposition? You said you made mac n' cheese and hot dogs. You weren't much of a cook. What were you, then?"

"Gamer. I played a lot of video games." Nacho approached from behind Whitney. He would've rather attacked Hogan first, since the man was the bigger of the goons, but Whitney was right there, fully absorbed in eating a biscuit. He felt a pang of guilt over the waste of some good biscuits, especially after he had stopped overworking the dough.

"But how did you pay your bills?" Hogan's questions were distracted. "Thought you were a student?"

"Nah, didn't really play by the rules... Assassins get a lot of leeway in that regard." Nacho called up Cry, which would work better as a weapon then the Hunger cleaver. He grabbed Whitney by his hair and slammed the knife into his neck.

Hey, Player, it's Active Combat time! Wow, you are a treacherous chef, aren't you? Guy doesn't want to eat your wings, so you stab him in the neck? Good luck with your mellow murder!

Nacho's dagger did a base damage of five Health Points, which wasn't ideal. Happily he'd worked in percentages, but even eighteen percent of five wasn't all that much. With no time to lose, he stabbed the dagger into Whitney's neck again and again, blood flowing like a river.

The System flashed with every strike.

. . .

Damage dealt: 7/30, 14/30, 21/30, 28/30!

Up until now, Nacho had mostly been going up against monsters he could kill with one shot. Whitney was *far* tougher, but he couldn't manage to fight back. Nacho wasn't doing very much damage per strike, but he'd completely surprised the pair of goons. Nacho was able to hit Whitney four times before the guy even *tried* to get to his feet.

As good as the speed was, there was another benefit of using the HungerCry Knives. When he cut an apple, he got fifty percent more yield. While attacking, he was releasing fifty percent more blood. Geysers of gore sprayed Hogan, blinding the big moron.

Whitney flailed, but thanks to the stat boost, Nacho was at least as strong as the guy. He stabbed Whitney a final time.

The System was as gleeful as ever.

Poor little Phillip Whitney! He's dead, but you get 0 credits for the kill.

Nacho couldn't pause to consider anything other than chasing after Hogan, who had wiped his face and was running for his sword.

The man never got there.

The reformed Assassin's increased Fitness allowed him to easily overtake Hogan, and he grabbed the bruiser by his shoulder and slammed the Cry knife into his back twice.

A System message flashed in Nacho's vision.

Damage dealt: 7/30. 14/30.

. . .

Nacho had stabbed people in the back, but not someone as big and as deserving as Hogan. "In this game, I'm not an Assassin. I'm a cook, Hogan... and you're on the menu. I'm going to treat you like the ingredient you are, and use you to whip up a recipe for escape."

Blood gushed out of the wounds, but Nacho wasn't done. He got another shot in before the enraged man turned around and swung at him.

Damage dealt: 21/30.

Hogan's thrown fist cracked into Nacho's face.

Health remaining: 26/30. Sucks to be you! A Fist can deal almost as much damage as your main weapons!

Grunting, Nacho summoned up the Hunger cleaver and swiped into a one-two combo. A cleaver to the arm and a knife in the gut was enough to finish the job.

You murderer! How could you...? Just kidding, nice one! You killed Chad Hogan! He's dead, but you get 0 credits for the kill.

Hogan slipped to the floor and landed on his back, face slapping sideways to the floor. Whitney had somehow stayed in his chair, bleeding over the biscuits and wing meat. What items had been in their Storage Slots burst into existence around them; the only guaranteed proof that someone was truly dead.

. . .

Congratulations, Player! Active Combat is over! It looks like you got punched in the face. Scrumptious scrum!

Nacho waited breathlessly to see if his attack drew any unwanted attention. If Red Suzy Blacke was on duty, she might come running with her bow and fire powers. Once an entire minute passed, and everything remained quiet, he finally felt confident that he would be able to escape after all. A single glance at the items ejected from the dead goons' Storage Slots revealed that there wasn't anything he could use. He wanted to fill his own slots with cooking utensils, including that pastry cutter and another skillet.

The key that he needed hung around Hogan's neck, and he used it to free himself. Standing over the dead man, Nacho considered taking Hogan's armor and sword—both were magical. Instead, he took his pad and pencil and scribbled a note to Crave.

Dear Richard,

Cooking is just the beginning for me. I'm leaving this armor, the sword, and some fresh biscuits as an act of good faith. I was kidnapped, and it was a bad decision on your part. This is the price of your choices; don't rack up more debt. Don't mess with me or my friends, and we'll call our score settled.

Your former cook,
Nacho

He left the note on the armor, then realized he was covered in blood. A moment later, Nacho had bought a new outfit from the Store. After changing and washing his face, he was ready to fly the coop. In a final opportunistic sweep, the reborn killer grabbed a blanket and threw additional supplies—including the pastry cutter—into an empty yellow and red Store box.

The shadows were perfectly placed to allow him to skulk out of the kitchen and into the fresh air. He no longer had his Midnight Blend ability, but he did have some experience getting in and out of places without being seen.

All thanks to Kronos.

After managing to avoid Suzy, he soon emerged up top, standing in the cold light of the new morning, and smiled.

People were dead, he was freezing… but he was free.

CHAPTER THIRTY-SEVEN

Nacho hurried away into the forest and got back on a game trail. Running warmed him up, the blanket felt good across his shoulders, and the world smelled so much better than his... *cooped* up kitchen. He chuckled at his own wit. It had been raining a lot above ground, given how green everything was, and the edge of dampness to the cold air.

Reuben and Brie must've retreated a bit, because they were out of transfer distance once again. Nacho kept checking his Stat Sheet as he made his way north, waiting to see when they came into range once more. He'd need to triangulate their location, but that shouldn't be too difficult. Now that he was away, his mind turned to what he had just done.

Though he hadn't necessarily liked killing Hogan and Whitney, and he wasn't sure what that decision might do to the world, but Crave had two less flunkies. Other henchmen remained, such as Red Suzy Blacke and Rizzo the Dungeon Rat. Would their eventual destinies change, given that everything else had shifted? There would be no way to know.

Still, it was safe to say that Crave and Nacho were now the bitterest of enemies.

Motion caught his eyes, and he dropped into a ready position.

Whuf.

"You again? How do you keep finding me?" Nacho scooped up the green dog, noting that pale green highlights were starting to creep along its darker green flank. "Come on, you can't stay here. Crave will kill you just for whatever scrap of a credit he can earn."

Grasping the wriggling puppy to his chest, Nacho continued his hurried pace along the trail. After checking for the hundredth time, he sighed with relief the instant that his friends were back in range. Moments later, he smelled a fire, so he followed his nose until he spotted Reuben standing next to a tree, wearing his prized leather Helm of Helming. He had equipped his left gauntlet and was holding a bow. He and Brie had evidently cleared away the underbrush near a deadfall of trees, which offered them protection on three sides.

Once Nacho got close, he stepped out onto the trail. "Reuben! It's me, Nacho. Don't shoot!"

"*Nacho?*" Reuben dropped the bow unceremoniously into the dirt as he ran and grabbed his best friend. "Nacho! What the *what?* We thought you might be dead. I said you were still a part of The Dinner Party, so you had to be alive, but Brie wasn't so sure. I told her we had to keep hope alive—and I was right!"

As they approached the deadfall, Brie leapt to her feet, bounding over the fire with a Combat Dash. She smacked into Nacho, hugging both him and Reuben for all she was worth. For the escaped cook, it was heaven. His best-friends-turned-family were still alive, and they were all together again. He guided his friends back to the fire, because the morning was frigid.

Nacho figured they would have some time before Crave came calling. The man was definitely going to come after him, friendly note notwithstanding. He'd poured over a thousand credits into Nacho, and there was no way he wouldn't want him back. Besides, Nacho had killed both Hogan and Whitney, and Crave wasn't the type of guy to forgive and forget. Then again... there *were* a few times that Crave had let things drop because there was no strategic advantage. There was a possibility, however small, that such a response might turn out to be the case this time.

It was hard to tell.

Once they were comfortably seated around the fire, Nacho told them about his adventures and how many credits he had earned, as well as the addition of Colonel White Beard's recipes to his *Aria*.

"Biscuits?" Reuben blinked slowly, a grin forming at the edges of his mouth. "I'm loving this idea of biscuits. Cool dog, by the way. Is it an alien?"

"I mean... I think *we're* the aliens here. As for the biscuits, I'll need a kitchen once we get settled, because cooking in a kitchen is *so* much easier than balancing pans on makeshift rocks over a fire." Nacho pulled a face and looked back forlornly. "I'll miss that kitchen. Where's the Mayor? Taye, Kristie?"

Reuben squeezed his eyes shut. "They survived the cow attack and came south with us, along with a few others, to see if we could free you. Taye is actually a pretty good tracker, and then we used the 'transfer credit' option to determine when we got close. We got separated after that thing came charging through again, and we're not sure what happened to them."

"The cow thing is... a Calamity-class monster, a creature that ranks up faster than anything else around it and goes on massive killing sprees." Nacho explained with great concern, as though merely speaking of it would call the beast to swoop in on them. "It's called *the Bove*."

Brie raised an eyebrow at his dramatic flair. "With 'the Bove' around, I'm pretty sure Mayor Dan took his people back to Armor Mountain to make sure his wife and daughter are okay. We don't know for sure. Reuben and I figured we'd stay behind to run a frontal assault on the dungeon entrance.

Reuben was going to lead the way, and I planned to come in after him, swinging my hammer."

"Risky." Nacho was so glad that, in the end, that hadn't been necessary. "Especially with the number of ranged attackers they have."

Reuben laughed nervously. "We would've learned how powerful the Ring of Cheese turned out to be, wouldn't we?"

"Glad we didn't have to." Brie ended the conversation with a firm hug.

Nacho looked into the faces of his friends. "I say we go to Armor Mountain and try to start a guild. I had a taste of what we might be able to accomplish if we had enough people. I was able to upgrade *two* of my Skills all the way to level nine, and I *still* have seven hundred and seventeen credits left."

Reuben smiled excitedly. "We noticed, and we liked it. We did a little work on our own, while we planned your rescue. We found a few Boarcanotors, big boar things, that we killed. Also took out an entire herd of Wight-Tailed Deer. Got a couple hundred credits ourselves."

"Good job." Nacho felt his brow furrow. "Speaking of monsters, we're going to need to take out the Bove. We've seen what it can do, and it's only going to get more powerful. Sooner is better than later. I'm thinking we might be able to find its lair, since it hit Taye and his family early. We might be able to track it from there."

Brie tilted her head consideringly, placing her big hammer on the ground in front of her. She knocked the handle of her weapon against her knee, thinking. "That might be harder now, with Jimmy dead. It's not that Mayor Dan and Taye blame us for what happened, but they don't exactly *trust* us. The night we met, there was the Bove attack—which killed five of their people—and then raiders came and killed another friend before kidnapping you. Now that you're on Crave's hit list, I'm not sure that Mayor Dan will want us to join them."

Nacho opened his mouth to suggest they sneak back to the Coop of Chaos and wipe out Crave and his party one by one.

He knew their movements well enough to plan a raid... but he stopped before the thought left his lips. He might be able to handle the bloodshed, but would Reuben and Brie? Brie might, but not Reuben. The big guy was as soft as they came. Even more so, he didn't *want* to spend this Juxtaposition murdering people, and certainly not forcing his friends to do the same. He'd already lived that way, and it still weighed heavily on him.

Not this time. Hogan was wrong—being stuck in the kitchen wasn't punishment; it was a gift, when he could *choose* to do it.

Nacho thought about adding a stick to the fire, but they had to get moving north. There was a good chance that Crave would send people out to hunt for them as soon as possible. "Why don't we run back to Armor Mountain and see what Mayor Dan and Taye say when they try my new biscuit recipe? Also, I can cook chicken now! I think I might be able to fry up most any barnyard fowl."

Reuben feigned confusion. "I don't understand. Will your fowl food taste good, somehow?"

Nacho chuckled delightedly as Brie sighed in mock annoyance. "Reuben, you and I are birds of a feather."

"We featherbrains will flock together." Reuben smiled warmly at him. "It rhymes, so it has to be true. Hey... where'd the dog go?"

The group scanned their makeshift clearing for a few moments, but none of them were going to risk themselves searching for an untamable monster. Still, Nacho felt a slight pang of loss when it didn't return. He shook the feeling off, knowing that there was a good chance that it'd find him randomly again, or one of them would die if they went hunting for it now. In any case, he couldn't worry about it.

The other two had stashed Nacho's backpack and gear back at Rocky Top when he'd been taken, so they opted to swing by there first, before hurrying on to Armor Mountain. On the way, they kept their eyes open for deer or any chicken monsters, but it seemed the local fauna had begun to lay low after the numerous Bove sightings. The monster cow liked human meat the most, but anything living could be snacked upon.

It took the trio most of the day, but they reached Rocky Top before the sun went down. Six fresh graves greeted them, marked by sticks lashed together with string to create crosses. Those six deaths were such a waste, though the same could be said about *all* the casualties of the Juxtaposition, which were countless.

Nacho was pleased to retrieve his backpack and supplies, which included a pretty good amount of flour, sugar, salt, pepper, and baking powder. He couldn't transfer everything from his box to his backpack, so he had to get creative, lashing a few things to the outside. On the plus side, he found a pocket that was perfect for his Frank's Red Hot Sauce. It was ironic that in the past, he'd have prioritized magic daggers and poisoned arrows, but now he was more concerned about his ingredients. "What a difference a character class makes."

Since they weren't using their Skills, Nacho pushed them onward at the highest speed he could enforce. He figured Rocky Top was the first place that Crave would check, and he had no idea what kind of lead they had. They should be able to camp somewhere along the game path on their way to Armor Mountain, which was a full day's walk away.

As they moved rapidly through the forest, practically bare of leaves due to the season, they discussed what they could do with their collective nine-hundred and seventeen credits. Nacho wanted to set aside enough credits for an oven and a stove— both were definitely Tier zero class items, so they'd be two hundred credits apiece. Other random kitchen items tallied up to roughly another hundred credits. That still gave them four hundred and seventeen credits to play with, so leveling their abilities was definitely the next step.

He was already ninth level in both Small Blades and cooking Magic, and fifth level in Ingredient Processing. He didn't *need* to upgrade his Ingredient Processing until they came across monsters higher than seventh level, so he pushed his friends to spend the money on themselves instead.

Brie was at second level with her Athletic Endurance, which wasn't that critical, since Nacho could keep her fed. As for Combat Dash and Defensive Whirl, she was level five for both. It was Reuben that truly needed the leveling love. His Marketing Skill was still at level zero, which he didn't like. Healing Hug was at third, and Positive Vibes were at fourth.

Nacho gladly transferred the credits to Reuben, who used the two hundred and eighty credits to boost himself up to fifth level in both his useful Skills. He managed the entire process as they traveled and gave Nacho a glimpse of his updated Stat Sheet.

Reuben Colby
Class: Healer
Level: 0
Experience Points: 100 to Level 1!
Current Credits: 13 (637 total Dinner Party pool)
Build Type: Balanced, Instant

Body:

- *Fitness: 10*
- *Metabolic efficiency: 10*

Mind:

- *Mental energy: 10*
- *Circuit: 10*

Satiation:

- *Hunger: 100*
- *Thirst: 100*

Total Health Points: 30
Bonus Physical Damage: 5%
Health Regen: 10% Health Regen/minute
Total Mana Pool: 25
Bonus Spell Damage: 5%
Mana Pool Regen: 10% Mana Regen/minute

Skill Slots (3/4)

- *Healing Hugs (Active) Level 5: 25 Health Points Restored Upon Hugging*

  Mana Cost = 10%
  Hydration Cost = 5%
  Metabolic Cost = 0%

- *Positive Vibes (Active) Level 5: Weapon blessing: (applies to whole party, lasts 5 minutes) Adds 10% physical damage*

  Mana Cost = 5%
  Hydration Cost = 10%
  Metabolic Cost = 0%

- *Marketing (Active) Level 0: Able to lure creatures to a location. Impacts up to Level:1*

  Mana Cost = 5%
  Hydration Cost = 5%
  Metabolic Cost = 5%

- *Open slot*

Nacho didn't have much experience in sharing Stat Sheets with party members, as he'd rarely been in a party during his time as the Shadow Killer. He did note that they still had six hundred and thirty-seven credits left, but saving them for his eventual kitchen simply didn't make any sense. They had to use every last one of their credits to improve their chances at combat first. Credits were renewable; their lives weren't.

The Bove was going to be a high-level Tier one monster, requiring Brie to do huge lump sums of damage, and that could only be possible if her Skills were at the *peak* of Tier zero. That meant increasing her Combat Dash ability to the max at level nine, giving her an additional eighteen percent increase in her damage.

Alternatively, upping Reuben's Positive Vibes ability would accomplish the same thing, and that could be spread out among multiple people. Checking his math one more time, Nacho made the final choice. They would crank Reuben's ability up to nine. As soon as the upgrade was complete, he realized that it wouldn't be long before they'd have to start leveling their classes. They couldn't get Tier one Skills without being a Tier one player, and that thought was *concerning*. The Dinner Party hadn't even been active a full month in this world yet.

They found a pretty secure place to camp in front of a stand of trees, an alcove made of tightly grown alien-looking climbing vines. Starting a fire, Nacho made his signature pancakes, which he imbued with cooking Magic, since that would help Brie dish out more damage.

After dividing up watches—Nacho was given the last one—they got to sleep most of the night away. Lying next to the fire, back with his friends, he slept well enough to dream.

Too bad that in the Juxtaposition, dreaming could get weird.

CHAPTER THIRTY-EIGHT

Nacho knew he was dreaming, but he couldn't wake himself up. A man in sunglasses stood in the middle of the game trail, dressed in jeans, cowboy boots, and a leather jacket. He wore a long, sheathed katana strapped to his side, and even if Nacho hadn't already known *who* it was, the sunglasses were a dead giveaway to *what* he was. The cook gulped and prayed that the man wouldn't have that particular sword in this version of the Juxtaposition: it was pure evil.

"Arriod. I'm not going to let you destroy my people again." There was no mistaking the identity of the CrossHuman, and the minute Nacho was hit with that realization, he was jolted awake. The night's fire had reduced to a pile of gray ashes next to him. Reuben was awake, packing up his stuff, but Brie wasn't in sight. They'd let him sleep through his watch, which he was both grateful for—as well as a little peeved.

"Where's Brie?" Nacho wanted them all together. His dream of Arriod couldn't be a good thing. He didn't think the CrossHuman could've shown up in the AKC this early in the game, but he could always be wrong. There was a lot about the CrossHumans that people didn't understand.

Reuben frowned at him. "Brie went out hunting. She should be back any minute. Don't worry, she took one of your 'pocket pancakes' with her."

"Ugh, I was just carrying them. That's what everyone is going to call them forever, isn't it?" Nacho ignored the nodding and packed everything he had, then made the Healer start moving; refused to wait for Brie to return. He tracked her down and led her back to the ashes of their fire, sighing a breath of relief when the three of them were back together again. He wasn't going to be able to relax until they reached Armor Mountain. "We *cannot* be separated right now. We have people after us, the Bove is on the loose, and we are *not* safe. We need to stay together and stay sharp."

"I know that you are trying to come from a good place, but we *are* adults," Brie informed him primly, greatly annoyed that her hunt had been interrupted. She strapped on her gear and headed down the trail, taking the lead with her hammer thrust through some straps on her backpack while carrying the bow and arrow. Falling back into their established pattern, Nacho followed her, and Reuben took up the rear guard.

They walked until noon that day without incident. The sun at its peak cast a golden light through the trees as shriveled autumn leaves spun off branches to float to the ground. The dead foliage gave the forest a fragrance as much as the slightly damp dirt under their boots... and also made a crunching sound whenever it was stepped upon.

When someone *crunched* out of the forest in front of them and moved to stand on the game trail, Nacho felt the hair on the back of his head rise. There, standing *right in front of them*, was the figure he'd seen in his dream. Jeans, boots, and leather jacket, every stitch the same. This guy had a leather satchel hanging off his back, and a sword hung at his side that *wasn't* the katana. The cook held up a hand, his mouth dry as he whispered, "Stop, Brie."

It might not be Arriod... but it was. Of *course* it was, even this early in the game. The dream must have come from

Kronos. Arriod moved and Nacho flinched, but the disguised CrossHuman only lifted his hand and waved.

Reuben waved back. "Hey. Nice day for a walk. I'm Reuben."

"Hi, Reuben." The figure's voice was exactly as the former Assassin remembered. Nacho couldn't move, couldn't think; he felt his mind fracture into a million pieces. He thought he'd have months—if not *years*—before they had to deal with the CrossHumans. That still might be the case, but this encounter didn't make it seem likely.

Brie immediately saw the problem, while her amiable fiancé was clueless. She whispered her worry under her breath, keeping her eyes ahead. "Why the sunglasses? They're cheap in the Store, but it's not *that* bright out."

Reuben moved to walk by Nacho, but the cook pulled the big guy back. "Don't. We don't want to mess with that guy. He's not human. That's *Arriod*."

The figure overheard the hushed comment and started. He reached up and touched his sunglasses, "We'll need to have a conversation another time."

He then laughed incredulously and turned on his heel to leave the path—the crunch of the leaves giving away his trajectory. From every indication, he made his way farther west. Soon, the sound of his passing faded away.

Nacho sniffed the air to see if he could smell a portal—they always produced a strong chemical smell, like sulfur mixed with ammonia used for cleaning a slaughterhouse's floor. Light was also involved, and lots of noises; essentially, exactly like anyone might expect of a magical portal to another world. Only, he didn't *think* there was a portal on this side of the AKC. The one existing portal he recalled was by the Muddy River to the east.

"Give me the bow," Nacho ordered quietly. "Be ready. He might not be alone. This close to the start, he might just be acting as a scout. At least… that's what he was last time. As far as we knew, Arriod got his start on this world as a scout, but he was someone incredibly important in his world. At least he didn't have the katana yet."

"This is something you need to explain." Once Brie handed over the bow and the quiver of arrows, she adjusted her helmet and took a fresh grip on her hammer. "What are you not telling us, Nacho?"

"Or *haven't* told us?" Reuben snapped his fingers. "This is about the… CrossHumans, right? You mentioned something about them a while back. Nacho, what's going on?"

"Let's just listen and be ready. Talk when safe." Nacho tried to get his friends to listen as hard as he was. He probably shouldn't have been freaked out, because Arriod couldn't be *that* high of a level yet, not even if he'd gone on a killing spree like Crave had. Still, Arriod eventually became a terror to everyone in the AKC, and his feats had been as legendary as the Bove, though that took place *much* later on.

Had Arriod been on their Starter World all that time? Probably not. Nacho suspected the man typically moved from world to world when things got dire, or when he could cash in on all the credits he gathered from killing people… while taking their bodies back to make sure that his people were well-fed.

No one came at them. If Arriod was traveling with a group of other CrossHumans, they were going about an ambush all wrong. Regardless, Nacho wanted to get to Armor Mountain now more than ever. "Let's move. Keep your eyes and ears open. If we do get attacked by someone in sunglasses, they're not human."

"How do you *know?*" Brie demanded of him in a low tone.

Reuben attempted the answer. "Something with the eyes. Snake eyes? Tell me they're at least *part* snake."

"Close but no cigar." Nacho gripped the bow warily while Brie stood in front of him, and Reuben behind. "There's only one physical difference that we know of: humans have round pupils, and the CrossHumans have pupils in the shape of—you guessed it—a cross. They come from the Cross World, which is their version of our Starter World. You always wondered why it was called the Juxtaposition? Well, this is a fantasy world juxtaposed with the Cross World. Humans versus CrossHumans pitted against each other in a game to the death."

"Let me guess… you can eat the CrossHumans." Brie shook her head at yet another little horror that was playing out in her mind unbidden. "Things get bad here, at least we can go through portals to this other world, hunt them, and eat them instead of humans?"

Nacho laughed darkly at that thought. "Not to paint too rosy a picture for you, but the CrossHumans did most of the hunting. They seem to have a better idea of what's going on than we do. If that joker in the sunglasses is who I think he is… that's *Arriod*, leader of a guild on Cross World that found success with hunting and killing humans in staggering numbers."

"Seems like something you'd warn us about right away," Reuben stated, his tone as close to accusatory as it had ever sounded.

"I didn't say anything because…" The cook winced and forced the words out. "It was why I was killed. I was the sacrificial lamb that allowed two guilds to join. Crave's Final Victory, and a woman named Kala, who created the Gorged Guild. She changed the name of her guild once the food situation became clear. They had to join together because Arriod was doing such a bang-up job with his… hunting. Humanity was already on the edge of extinction. There's a *lot* I haven't been able to tell you. So… *so* many terrible things. I had a good reason. How do you explain to your friends that Humanity as a whole only has a little more than three years left, unless things change *drastically*?"

"You… do your best not to tell them and just try to make life as different as possible." Brie engaged in some uncharacteristic sympathy and attempted to change the subject on his behalf. "Cross-hatched pupils. Hashtag pupils. This is so weird and nerdy."

"Just crosses, *not* pound signs." Nacho rolled his own normal eyes. "Where did that even come from?"

"Portals to another world?" Reuben's laugh was quiet, like

he was afraid to be heard. Both friends were taking Nacho's fear seriously, to his relief. "That's kinda perfect. I mean, we get the fantasy tropes here on Starter World, and that should include portals. I'm so glad I'm getting my money's worth. Did you ever go to the other side, Nacho?"

"No," he admitted easily. "To be honest, I never wanted to. It was pretty clear the CrossHumans might've been cannibals *before* the Juxtaposition. They seemed to have zero problem eating near-CrossHuman flesh. As far as we could ever tell, we're *exactly* the same, except for their pupils."

The Dinner Party got moving in earnest, arriving at Armor Mountain in the late afternoon. They found the entrance to the Deep Buggy Darkness just as they'd left it, sealed up tight.

Nacho briefly considered staying in the antechamber for the night, but he knew they couldn't. Time was short, and he had to warn Mayor Dan's people about the current triplet of threats: Arriod, the Bove, and Crave, eventually known as the ABCs of terror for people living in the AKC.

They trekked their way around to the front of the big slab of limestone on the east side of the mountain, which was where they found a man stationed up top next to a shoddy brick wall. A rope ladder was rolled up next to him.

Nacho waved. "Hey, guard, we're here to see Mayor Dan and Taye. Can you throw down the ladder?"

The guard's face came into view, a middle-aged woman with a nose like a knife blade. Nacho had to do a double take, realizing with a sinking gut that his day of being visited by the past wasn't over. There stood Kala; the same woman who would start the Sunrise Brigade Guild, which would eventually become the Gorged Guild.

Crave might have done the actual work, but it was Kala who had ordered Nacho's death.

CHAPTER THIRTY-NINE

Kala didn't yet have her Death Knight armor, her helmet, or the big black sword, but it was her all right—she had a nose so sharp he could cut his finger on it, and dark hair with a slash of gray down the middle. She'd been some kind of boxer or martial artist before the Juxtaposition, or so the rumors had said. Nacho could believe them, because she looked like she had come out of her crib throwing punches.

The guard didn't lower the ladder, but she did go and get Mayor Dan, and *he* sent the ladder spooling down the cliff-side. Nacho, Reuben, and Brie quickly climbed up, glad to find the little settlement at the top. The rocky campsite was more plateau than mountain, with a wide area free of trees. The peak of the mountain was to the east, a treacherous climb over crumbling layers of limestone. People had thrown up tents here and there, the cheap Store tents that didn't smell right and leaked.

They'd built a straw-and-clay wall on the northern part of the plateau, since the forest sloped downward to ground level. Other adobe walls had been constructed in areas where attackers might be able to climb up. It was a relatively good fortress for having only a week's worth of work put into it, and

Nacho had heard stories of the Armor Mountain colony—stories that ended in tragedy because of the Bove, and then a colony of acid termites, which had blown in on the wind at some point.

Or… had they crawled up from the Deep Buggy Darkness because no one had managed to clear it in time? That was a strong possibility.

Several people were clustered around a central fire surrounded by tents. Mayor Dan led Nacho and his friends over, and they waved when they spotted Taye and Kristie the pink Warlock.

Nacho scanned the clearing to inspect what sort of security was set up and found a guard patrolling the western ridge. Standing up there, the guard would have a clear view of the entire plateau. The southern and western cliffs were basically impassable… unless something had wings. The acid termites had wings, and 'winged and acid-spewing' wasn't a great combination, unless someone liked melting flesh.

"Before you ask, we're not going to leave here to help you fight someone." Mayor Dan firmly crossed his arms, shaking his head and frowning. "We lost a lot of people, Nacho. We're not sure we want the trouble."

"We *don't* want the trouble," Kala confirmed with a mean hiss. Behind her was an older man with the same knife-like nose. That was her father, and Nacho felt a tremor go through him as the older man briefly met his stunned gaze. The cook remembered killing this exact man—the nose had made him stick out among all of the other kills—but he couldn't remember the guy's name. His death was why Kala had insisted on Nacho dying before they joined Crave.

The big woman's frown deepened. "We're only *just* holding on here. If this Crave came after you once, he might come after us to get you again. We don't want any more death."

"It's naïve to think there won't be more death," Brie shot back instantly. As much as Nacho didn't like Kala for good reasons, it seemed Brie had taken an instant dislike to the future Death Knight.

Reuben put up his hands placatingly. Was he using his Marketing Skill? Or was the soft glow on his face from the fire? "Look, here's the thing: Nacho knows more about the Juxtaposition than *anyone*. I won't go into the specifics, but I *can* say if you work with us, we can take care of threats before they happen. If we band together, if we use the guild function, which Nacho understands, we'll all survive."

"How do you know so much?" Kala's eyes flashed with suspicion.

"I received a boon from a Patron: a whole bunch of information packs for free." Nacho didn't mention that he'd talked directly to his Patron just the night before—he hadn't even told Reuben and Brie yet. There was a whole big conversation they needed to have privately first. "Listen, I have an idea of what's coming, and I can assure you that Crave is going to be a problem whether I'm here or not."

No one looked convinced, so he decided to offer some free advice. "Another thing: this mountain is looming over a dungeon, and unless you clear the entire thing, anything that you build here is going to get destroyed by acid termites. Second, there is a competitor race and a win condition for this... this Armageddon. The race is called 'CrossHumans', and there are a whole *load* of other threats you don't know about. But before we try to tackle any other problems, we need to take care of *the Bove*. You've seen what it can do, and it's not going to be getting any weaker. If Taye can help us figure out where it goes, I think I can find its lair. Work with us. Guild up, grind out some credits, and let's go hunting."

Taye kept his gaze on Nacho, unsure of whose side to take. "A boon from a Patron. Like Kristie's magic? But you're not a Warlock."

"Right, you know I'm a Common Cook, a Satiation Player. Believe me, we're rare, but we're *vital* if everyone wants to avoid suffering. That won't be apparent until you hit level ten, also known as Tier one, level zero. That's when everything changes. I'm sure you've seen how expensive food becomes as you advance Tiers? If you join with me, you won't have to pay those unholy prices."

Kala wasn't going to give him a break. "Great, now this guy wants us to listen to him because he's a *cook*. Yeah, let's listen to the *cook* in a world where only fighting is useful. I don't believe this."

Some old guy with a grizzled beard took off his battered old Kansas City Royals hat and smoothed down his thinning hair. He nodded, and Kala saw it. She liked it. Kala was a woman who enjoyed wielding power. How much of this argument was for her to win followers, and how much was to protect their colony?

Taye asked the next logical question. "If you're Tier one, why not keep eating Tier zero food?"

"It doesn't work," Nacho replied instantly, confident in his answer. "Once you level up, you need that Tier's food. You've tasted the food from the Store by now, and you know it's not good. My cooking is… slightly better."

"It's pretty good, at least in comparison." Mayor Dan nodded at a woman who stood close to him. If Nacho had to guess, he figured she was probably the wife the mayor had mentioned. "What do you think, Beck?"

The curvaceous woman with crow's feet and iron gray hair smiled politely at Nacho. "I'd have to taste his pancakes. You said they were a little dry?"

"Dry for now," Reuben quickly amended. "But Nacho is improving all the time, and he has a fabulous new biscuit recipe. Not only is his food better than the Store's, but it can increase your stats. Tasty buffs for those with a discriminating palate!"

"We'd need to read up on what guild rules can do," the mayor's wife announced decisively. "No surprises. We simply can't trust many people in this world."

"A good way to stay alive," Nacho agreed with a solemn nod.

"All that means is that we can't trust *you*." Kala stared daggers at him, and her father joined her. Such a cohesive family.

Reuben stepped between them. "Listen, Kala, human beings are good at two things: adapting to circumstances, and coming together to survive. That's our real magical ability: to tell each other stories that draw us together, because we are *much* stronger together than we are apart. Yes, there will be difficulty, and there will be growing pains, but the more people we gather, the stronger we'll become. We're going to be transparent, and you should read up on guilds, Mrs. Mayor. In the meantime, Nacho can explain the pluses and minuses."

The Healer was amazing at applying the social lubricant, even if Nacho was pretty sure that it was his Marketing Skill in action. If the people were level one, or less, they would be drawn to Reuben, and that definitely seemed to be the case. They were actively listening to him and then staring right at Nacho, as if *he* were the guy who knew everything. In a lot of ways, he was.

Reuben had always been a natural politician, and he liked people. The only thing standing between him and real power was his sweet soul.

Nacho was struck dumb for a second, but he cleared his throat and started clarifying as succinctly as possible. "As with most larger organizations, there are upsides and downsides to guilding up. One minus is a big one: taxes. The biggest one is a Guild Tax, so every time you kill a monster, some of those credits transfer to the guild's coffers. Another drawback is that under the *standard* contract, let me say that again: the *standard* contract... a Guild Master can tell any member to do *anything*, and they are forced to comply. The Guild Master is granted a kind of compulsion magic, which can make them dangerous if you elect the wrong person."

Nacho kept his eyes off Kala. He'd heard horror stories of her rule over the Gorged. This rough and tough woman wasn't going to get any softer the longer she was in the Juxtaposition, that was for sure. The cook idly wondered if Myron was on Armor Mountain at that very moment. Ugh. *Myron.*

Reuben laughed awkwardly. "Okay, so those are terrible. But the *benefits* surely must outweigh the drawbacks?"

The cook nodded, and Reuben breathed a slight sigh of relief. "It's an effective way of making money quickly as a group. Being in a guild gives you bonus credits for killing monsters and clearing dungeons with other guild members. The price for building supplies are also reduced. I see your clay bricks, which are *fine*, but you could afford to instantly buy stone walls, as well as stone houses. We could build a real-life castle up here, and we *should*, even if we kill the Bove."

A few of the players who'd been at the Rocky Top fight shivered at the memories of the Calamity-class monster cow.

"Now, we don't need to have a Guild *Master*. We can always get a non-standard contract with a Guild *Leader*." Nacho kept talking, and people perked up at the new information. "The difference is most noticeable in the restriction that the leader is accountable to the members, and frankly, I think it is a good idea to choose that. I have less information about that style of guild charter, so we should all read it very carefully. Another thing; while this area is defensible, it is lacking in necessities. There's not a natural spring up here, but we might be able to collect rainwater. Also, we might be able to dig a cistern, maybe run pipes? There are pipes available in the Store."

Reuben patiently waited for Nacho to finish rambling, and then he started the hard sell. "See? There are definite benefits. If we gather together early, if we beat other groups to the punch, we can keep each other safe. But we need to do this quickly! If building materials are price-reduced, and if we have a castle, that's going to be *worlds* better than this tent city you guys purchased—I'm sure you noticed the smell of the tents. I'm pretty sure we can buy homes that smell better, at the very least."

"You get used to the smell," the old guy in the Royals cap

scowled, "but it's the *leaking*. The rain nearly washed me out of my own place."

Reuben grinned and pointed at the man. "Stone doesn't leak. We get you all some stone houses, and you'll be set."

There was no chatter or discussion, and the encampment grew strangely quiet for a moment. Neither Kala nor her father was buying it, however. "These people talk about safety and castles and-"

"What we need," Nacho held up a forestalling finger, "is a guildhall. We need a place to keep the charter. If the guildhall is destroyed, the guild is destroyed, and whoever did it will get our combined credits and raw materials. Just think of it as an enhanced game of Capture the Flag, only letting someone else grab your flag means we all die."

Kala slapped Nacho's finger down. "This guy wants to tax us, and he wants to have the power to order us around? There is no *way* that's happening."

Taye's eyes glowed. He was checking the fine print. "He's telling the truth. This is a servitude contract, and once you sign, you sign forever—as long as the guildhall isn't destroyed. This isn't a contract you can opt out of; it's a magical command spell. This is a powerful charm. If he told you to jump off the mountain, you'd have to do it."

"*I* wouldn't do that!" Nacho tried to speak over the hubbub. Mayor Dan was keeping quiet and watching, but his eyes kept going to Taye. He'd clearly only vote if Taye voted for it. His wife was more of a wildcard. Nacho couldn't forget she'd done well in the Evaluation, despite her age and the fact that the last video game she'd played had probably been the free Solitaire on her PC.

"Why wouldn't we elect Reuben as the Guild Master?" Mrs. Mayor wondered loudly.

"Guild *Leader*. Don't go the standard route if Nacho says it's a bad idea," Reuben rumbled with laughter. "You don't want me. You absolutely want the cook. This is Nacho's show; I'm just the clown bumbling around and hugging people—healing them with hugs. I assure you it's perfectly legitimate and not at all creepy."

Another pause greeted the admission, and Mrs. Mayor pointed to their blonde Berserker. "You're awfully quiet, Miss Brie. What do you think about all this?"

Brie shrugged and swiveled her hand back and forth. "You want Nacho. He knows how this works, and we can trust him. He's a good guy, but not *too* good. While I love my Reuben, he's a bit too sweet to be a good leader during the end of the world. Nacho isn't sweet. He's salty, and we'll need that."

Reuben couldn't hide the goofy grin on his face. "She's not wrong. You need someone a bit ruthless. I'm many things, but ruthless is not one of them."

"What would we call the guild?" Taye's eyes were still glowing. He'd found one of the parameters. "Looks like we'd need a name."

Nacho took the query as a good sign. If Taye was considering guilding up, the mayor would fall in line, and then he figured so would the man's wife. Would Kala and her father? What about the old guy in the ragged Royals cap? Knowing Kala from before, Nacho was certain she'd walk away before joining. If she couldn't be in charge, she wanted nothing to do with the entire operation.

He had an idea for a guild name, the Breakfast Buffet, which would be a play on the joke of being The Dinner Party. Luckily for everyone involved, Reuben beat him to the punch. "Nacho's Chips. Because if the Chips are down, you know you're in trouble."

The big guy abruptly guzzled a whole water bottle and ate a bite of pocket pancake. That proved he had been using his Marketing Skill after all, which was pretty expensive, given that it took five percent out of all three pools—Mana, Hunger, and Thirst.

"Can you make nachos?" Taye wondered with a strange glance. "I'm in, based on the *non-standard* contract, if you can make nachos."

"The recipe would be two hundred credits, but we might find a Tier one cookbook that would provide a bunch of recipes. Those cost four hundred. But yes, Taye, as long as I have a recipe, I can make nachos. It might take me a bit to get right. I'm not a very *good* cook yet."

"Great, a cook who isn't very good at cooking." Mrs. Mayor smiled to take the sting out of the words, more warmly than Nacho had expected. "I like his humility—and I like the idea of a guild, especially if we can hold our leader accountable, like you say we can. But we all shouldn't join, not yet. We'll take volunteers, we'll test how it works without the binding parameters, and then we'll make our decision. Nacho, I don't know you, but I do know your friends went after you without a thought for their own safety. If you can have such good friends —especially this Reuben, who is a doll—you must be a good person."

Nacho remembered his parents, his upbringing, some people he'd met in the greater Kansas City area, and he nodded. "Well, ma'am, I hope I'm an okay person, because I've met my fair share of bad."

Kala flung out her hands with a frustrated grunt. "This is *insane*. You're going to trust this *random* person? Why not choose Iron Becky, Mayor Dan, or even *Taye?*"

A grin spread across Brie's face. "*Iron* Becky?"

The older woman kept her face perfectly still. "Hair's silver, and I don't take much guff from anyone. It comes from teaching seventh graders for a bit longer than I should've."

Taye squinted at Kala. "What's wrong with *me?* You said my name like I was the last resort or something. Look, if Nacho has game knowledge, he's the man who should be leading us."

Nacho didn't address Kala or her father, knowing they were lost causes. He addressed the old guy in the Royals cap instead. "Here's the thing: I do have a unique perspective-"

"Leave Old Bill out of this!" Kala utterly lost it. "You can go *unique* yourself in the butt! In the morning, I'm taking whoever doesn't want to serve some nacho-cheese-*tyrant*, and we'll form our own guild!"

"But not here," Iron Becky informed her sternly. "*We* have Armor Mountain."

"For now," Kala growled as she and her father marched away.

"She thinks people would be happy with *her* as a Guild Master?" Mayor Dan shook his head and sighed. "Don't you worry about them. This isn't the first problem we've had with Kala or her dad. She's wanted to run the show for a long time now. You were just the straw that broke the camel's back."

"We should make sure she doesn't start any trouble." Something in Brie's eyes said that she thought using her hammer to solve the solution might be the best way to go. Like Nacho, she had always been salty, and she'd added a bit of pepper since she'd become a Berserker.

"Don't bother," Iron Becky said in a firm voice. "They're not that big of a deal. It's pretty clear who the six people are that will be leaving with Kala."

"Is one of them a short guy, unibrow, likes to play with knives?" Nacho had to know if the Assassin was already active.

Mayor Dan, Iron Becky, and Taye all grunted the same name at the same time. "*Myron.*"

Nacho sighed with satisfaction; these were clearly good people. As to Myron…he knew how to handle that man, especially since the cook had the MurderSong Blades.

CHAPTER FORTY

One hundred and eighty-six were people living on Armor Mountain, which was a good number for a community. All of them were between the ages of sixteen and fifty-five, so The Dinner Party fit right into the younger age bracket. The entire place had fairly naturally separated out by age, so Nacho's people found a little place to set up on the southern side of the encampment with the other early-twenties crowd. They spent twenty total credits on two cheap tents, then got back to planning with the current leaders of the makeshift settlement.

After a total accounting, it was found that the population had a pool of nearly three thousand credits. That had been one of the benefits of not knowing how to access the Store right away: even though they were making money, they couldn't spend it. Mayor Dan and Iron Becky—having done most of the fighting that had been necessary—had a thousand credits between them, a third of the community's total.

The Armor Mountain colony was doing pretty well, thanks to Taye, but Nacho knew that they needed to do better. He and Reuben decided that the quickest way to secure their collective safety would be to load the people up on buffs and send them down into the Deep Buggy Darkness underneath their mountain home. Reuben had wanted to tell the Armor Mountain clan that the trio had already been down in the dungeon, but Nacho and Brie didn't think that was a good idea, at least not until they'd signed the charter.

The Dinner Party continued working with the mayor, his wife, and Taye to hash out the guild charter, but in the end, there was only so much they could change. They couldn't change the Guild Command spell—they had to remove it entirely—but they were able to alter the tax rate and add in conditions allowing people to leave the guild if they were mistreated. There was also an option to select a new guild leader, likewise based on mistreatment, based on a majority vote.

After that point, it was pretty clear that they were going to accept the remaining defaults to the charter, which was what Nacho suggested. The Patrons had for some reason set up the System to ensure people joined together for the common good. So as long as the Guild Master wasn't an evil person, the benefits were clear. Even better when you opted to be a Guild *Leader*, as he had.

Sitting in his tent, wrapped in his sleeping bag, Nacho went over the details of the proposed guild charter with his best friends one last time.

The Pros:

- *10% off buildings and building supplies and specific other Store items.*
- *Gain additional bonus credits on every kill. Based on monster, minimum is 1.*

The Cons:

- *10% tax on any credits gained (sales tax, kills, trading) automatically delivered to the guildhall's coffer.*

- *Fealty to the Guild Leader unless there is a full vote to depose
  —not really a con, but it goes in this column.*

There shouldn't be any big issues with feeding people after they settled the charter. He planned to buy higher rarity ingredients, having considered that might be one of the problems with his cooking—bad quality ingredients. He should've thought of that before, but he'd initially figured 'flour is flour, so why bother getting a better version'?

When they went out to propose the idea to the other people living in the settlement, Kala took off with a half-dozen people, just as she'd promised—which included a daggerless Myron. Nacho figured that when they ran into the Death Knight and her unibrowed assassin again, the Chips guild would have an impressive start to a castle.

Everyone else that remained decided to join the guild, even if a good chunk of them did so reluctantly. Knowing that they would be fed, sheltered, and enabled to grow stronger was enough to make almost anyone join under such favorable terms. With that knowledge, all that was left was to spend a thousand credits to form a guild. Luckily, the purchase included a guildhall.

They wouldn't get such a bargain on buildings ever again.

The Chips planned to designate a mead hall as the guildhall on the plateau; the location seemed to have been made for such a purpose. Inside the dual-purpose building, Nacho would have his kitchen. That would provide a nice camouflage for the Guild's center of power, since the other guildhalls he'd seen— the Final Victory, the Gorged, and a coven of wizards called the Midnight Fist—all had selected medieval throne rooms with the paper copy of the guild charter hanging on the wall surrounded by security.

Nacho's plan was to splatter batter on his charter, then slap it on the wall surrounded by recipes in a similar state, so if anyone *did* manage to storm his walls and capture the guildhall, the invaders would just skip over the charter, never guessing that such an important document would be treated so poorly.

Like always, they had *so* much to buy, but he couldn't get sidetracked. While Nacho missed the sweet setup of the Chicken Coop of Chaos's kitchen, such a luxury had to wait. They needed to build the guildhall first, which would be mostly kitchen, but it would also provide a huge central dining area with a large fireplace. Beyond the building itself, walls were necessary for protecting their mountaintop fortress.

The barrier they had set up currently was impressive, but not completely impregnable. A determined attacker could climb up the western crags or come sneaking up through the northern forest. The south was a sheer wall, while the east sloped down to a cliff only about ten feet high, where they had secured the rope ladder. *That* would be where the Bove would come clambering up, if they didn't take care of the beast sooner rather than later.

Their survival was a race against time. One of their enemies *would* attack them eventually, and if it wasn't Kala's band or the Bove, it would be Crave and Red Suzy Blacke, coming to get revenge.

A terrible irony to Nacho was that Reuben did most of the public relations work, and most people thought *he* should be the Guild Leader. The Healer laughed it off and let them know that he didn't want the job, while Brie was as stand-offish as a secret service agent watching over the president-elect.

Mayor Dan might've been the next logical choice for Guild Leader, but he didn't want the job. For one, he knew how much of a pain in the butt it was to be in charge. For another, his understanding of the gaming system wasn't anywhere *near* sophisticated, and his previous experience would actually serve as a detriment. That left Iron Becky, who understood the Juxta-position better—though not as thoroughly as Taye—who broke out into a sweat at the very idea of taking responsibility for the community.

That ultimately left Nacho, who felt oddly comfortable with the task. Maybe it was because he'd seen Crave rule, and he knew he'd be better than *that*. Crave had done a good—if brutal —job at organizing the dungeoneers of the Final Victory. After all, in the end, the Gorged would've joined Crave's guild, and not the other way around. He was pondering all this when he heard someone scratching on his tent as if trying to knock. "Who is it?"

"Becky," the woman called in her harsh tone. "You don't need to come out. I just wanted to tell you that everyone that's still here has decided to join the Chips. We're on board with paying the thousand credits for the guildhall and charter. Then maybe tomorrow, we can get serious about powering up for the Juxtaposition?"

Nacho wasn't sure what to say. It had all moved so fast. This community was taking a big risk on him and his friends, and he still wasn't all too clear on their motivations. "Why are you guys doing this?"

"That's easy, kid. I wasn't there, but Taye was. He said the minute the Bove attacked on Rocky Top, Reuben and Brie charged that cow monster. Reuben threw himself in front of it, and your girl with the hammer went to work. You impressed Taye, and lord help me, but we've trusted that kid with our lives. Why stop now?"

The woman retreated back into the night, and Nacho stretched out. He felt himself relax in a way he hadn't for a long, long time. Other people were on watch, he was surrounded by a clan who had decided to trust him, and his friends were alive. They were going to make a difference in this iteration of the game, even if he'd spend most of it in the kitchen. Good. Killing people, especially with the HungerCry Knives, was messy and sad.

Creating delicious food was going to be so much more fun.

The next day, after breakfast, Reuben went around telling everyone that they would be setting down the guildhall that day. He included a reminder that they didn't *have* to join, but they *would* have to move their tents. Some people grumbled, while others talked about leaving; but most stayed, at least to witness the spectacle of building the first permanent structure they'd seen in the nearly two weeks they'd been on the Starter World.

Once the tents had been cleared away, what remained was dirt, stone, and old ash-blackened rings of rock marking where the fires had been.

Nacho stood still, trying to picture where the guildhall would be best situated. No one else had offered to donate credits to the cause beyond Mayor Dan and Iron Becky, ironically and unwittingly highlighting the importance of an automatic tax.

He experienced a moment of doubt; how was he going to justify charging his guildmates for the meals he cooked? They were already paying ten percent of their kills to him, and Store meals were cheaper. Nacho shook off the concern; he'd just open his kitchen. People who wanted to pay would pay, and people who wanted to eat from the Store could do so if they wanted.

Of course, he would offer Store prices for anyone who traded in their kills, because he'd get credits from processing the ingredients. He would gladly pay for people to bring him fruits and vegetables, such as a credit an apple or per pound of bulk ingredients like wheat.

Everyone was watching, and Nacho felt a little exposed. He had rolled the sleeves of his shirt up, and it seemed like they were expecting him to say something. At that moment, he knew he couldn't pass the task off to Reuben.

Nacho inhaled shakily. Even though honesty was the best policy—for the most part—he wasn't used to opening up. "I know many of you don't know me, and you think that I'm just some kid with dreams of a kitchen of my own. But I was given a boon by a Patron, which allowed me to learn the rules in a very intimate way before the start of the Juxtaposition. I'm not going to lie to you…"

"We're living life on hard mode."

After taking a few deep, calming breaths and trying to ignore the fact that a hundred people were hanging on his every word, he was able to continue. "I found myself with time to prepare. It's why the three of us have backpacks, sleeping bags, and combat boots. I know how the Juxtaposition works. I know our biggest threats, at least until my information becomes outdated. I'm going to be fair, but my main goal is survival. Food and water are our biggest concerns, without a doubt, and they will become more and more critical as we go. I'm a cook, and I assure you, that will make *all* the difference. Our guild will get big *quick*, once word gets out about what I can do. You people are joining us at the beginning, and we won't forget that you put your faith in us."

"Who is this 'we'?" a voice called out. "You got a piece of cheese in your pocket?"

Nacho gestured at Reuben and Brie. "My friends are the 'we'. Taye, Kristie, Mayor Dan, Iron Becky, and their daughter Colleen are the 'we'. You all are welcome to become the 'we', once we get the guildhall built. I hope you do. Because *we* are going to work to make sure we *win* this game... not just survive."

"Win the game," Reuben chimed in loudly, "and eat like kings while we do it!"

The crowd started murmuring, but Nacho lifted a hand, and they went quiet once more. "Okay, I'm going to buy the charter and the guildhall. Everyone who wants to join will sign up, and then we'll organize strike teams for the dungeon at the base of the mountain—also, I think Taye found another dungeon close by. At this point, if we can earn credits fast, we can get a full wall built, and then we'll focus on helping guild members to level up their Skills. Yes, we prioritize Skills rather than character class. There's a *great* reason for that."

Nacho waved everyone back. "This thing is going to be pretty big, twenty-five feet wide and two hundred feet long, and I'm going to put a big kitchen near the back. The entrance will align with the rope ladder, and we'll eventually have houses, but for now, we can set our tents along the central road. I'll almost always be in the kitchen in the back when you need me. Hold on!"

The System realized what he was doing and hit him with a message.

Wow! Looks like you found enough like-minded people that you want to form a guild! Were you lonely? Well, not anymore! We detect a hundred and eighty-nine souls there. Tell us, Player, would you like to form a guild?
   Yes / No.

Nacho replied in the affirmative. He was then presented with a whole range of hall choices, from a medieval throne room—the same one which had been very popular—to a baroque pink palace with lots of curlicues everywhere, to a Japanese pagoda, or even a Nepalese chhaang hall. The prices were equally varied, but he was forced to go with the cheapest option. They only had a thousand credits, after all, and it hurt to realize that any buildings after the guildhall would cost a credit per square foot for the lowest quality.

As planned, the brand new Guild *Leader* went with the classic Beowulf mead hall, which had a very specific feel to it— rough wood and rougher stone, a big central beam overhead, and massive tables where adventurers could carve their initials into the wood with their trusty pigstickers. Nacho would keep three long tables and benches in the common hall, but he planned to make a kitchen for himself in the west end of the five thousand square feet. For the moment, he didn't have the credits to buy the exact things he wanted—like a stove, an oven, shelves, or countertops.

Undeterred, he quickly sketched out what he wanted to purchase once the credits started pouring in. He'd have to put in an oven and stove later, though he could choose the basic layout as part of the hall's initial purchase. A room-sized icebox was an absolute necessity, as well as lots of shelves and plenty of counter space. He also added a slot that would face the eating hall, so he could slide trays through to feed his hungry customers. There was no need for a cash register, because he would collect credits automatically through the System.

Nacho felt content with the basic layout, though his kitchen and corresponding icebox room would remain empty for the time being.

Old Bill scowled and shouted, "What's he waiting for?"

"He's having to design it," Taye explained with a groan. "I seem to remember people like you always complaining that *my* generation was all about instant gratification…"

Once Nacho was done selecting the building details, the coolest part came next: the structure went into an open slot in his extra-dimensional storage. "Okay, I'll be putting the building down. Everyone take a big step back. More. *More.*"

When he was sure he wasn't going to squash anyone—not that the System would let such an easily-abused option exist— he 'placed' the building, and the entire length of the mead hall appeared in the sky above his hand. The stone, the wood, the big doors held onto the hinges by leather straps, the two stone fireplaces on either end of the length—every detail was clearly defined. It wasn't transparent; it was a fully formed building sprouting from Nacho's hand. He swung it around a little, feeling mightily powerful as people shouted in concern. It was too bad that it couldn't be used as a weapon, or people would absolutely run into battle wielding barns.

It might look solid, but it wasn't. On the ground, green translucent squares appeared to indicate where the building would sit. Only when he set it down would the building become real. Taye let the expletives fly, and both Mayor Dan and Iron Becky shushed him.

Old Bill was quiet, because it wasn't every day a building sprouted from the hand of some guy who had just spent a bundle of credits on a pre-made structure. Ignoring the murmurs and grumbles from the onlookers, Nacho closed one eye and tried to judge the distances involved. "Hey, Reuben, am

I in line with the rope ladder? I want to create a grand avenue to our guildhall. It'll be super impressive with torches and severed heads on pikes for anyone who defies me."

Reuben laughed nervously as many people's eyes snapped to focus intensely on the Healer. "He's kidding, folks. No heads on pikes. He has a slightly dark sense of humor."

Brie got behind him and double-checked his line of sight. "You're good, Nacho."

Out of an abundance of caution, the onlookers took another few steps back. With a final nod of confirmation from Reuben, Nacho gently laid the building down onto the green transparent squares.

Hey, cook, we're not your buddy, and you won't be able to move this big, beautiful guildhall once you set it down, no matter how much your lady friends want to rearrange things. So, last chance: do you want to solidify this structure and get your guild started on a super sugary slope to success?

Yes / No.

"Yep," Nacho confirmed as he chose 'yes'. The entire structure flashed, and then it was suddenly there: a big Viking-inspired hall that would make King Hrothgar jealous. There were four basic entrances—the main doors were at the eastern end, but two side doors existed as well. Nacho planned to designate his own entrance as the one at the rear of the structure, which was near a few elm trees.

He opened the door and walked into the bare kitchen, then continued through into the icebox room. No counters, no shelves. It was kind of disappointing. First things first; they had the guild, but they needed to hit the dungeons hard to afford castle walls, guard towers, and to level up Brie. So far, she was the best warrior on Armor Mountain, and they needed her at her strongest in order to beat the Bove.

The cook left the kitchen through an archway into the main

room, where numerous settlers were already milling about and inspecting the three long tables, the benches, and the two fireplaces on either side of the hall next to the side doors. The wall at the opposite end from the kitchen was dominated by the magnificent double front doors with impressively large iron fittings.

A woman with short blonde hair and a splash of freckles across her nose perked up as she caught sight of Nacho and wandered over to him. Colleen, Mayor Dan's daughter, sighed happily. "We can sleep here! We can have a fire and sleep here. We can feel safe again."

Nacho felt tears sting his eyes at her words. They weren't there yet. He considered how far they had to go. He truly *wanted* these people to feel safe, but to get there, they still had to risk everything, over and over again.

First off, they had a dinosaur-cow to kill.

CHAPTER FORTY-ONE

A week later, Nacho collapsed onto a bench at one of the long tables. He sat hunched over, absolutely assaulting the soup he'd made from some Rock Tarragon Ptarmigan; which a hunting party had found in a field. They weren't nearly as big as the chicken-bats, but each one was still a good-sized bird monster. Three parts comprised this particular monster—rock, tar, and tarragon, the spice.

They had rock-like feathers, they spit tar, and they both smelled and tasted faintly of tarragon. Brie had killed one of the big stony birds, gained the credits, and then received a message that she'd been given a Monster Drop. Item drops were rare. Most of the time a player killed something, all they got was the credits. But every so often, maybe one in a thousand kills, the Patrons would drop a little bonus to keep things fresh.

This was the first time Nacho had *ever* heard of someone getting a recipe as a drop, and it wasn't even his kill. He would've remembered that. Could it be another gift from Kronos? He wasn't sure, but he added it to his *Aria* without delay.

Suffice to say, the soup recipe included the stone feathers of the bird monster along with typical soup stuff—onions, carrots, and celery. It also called for rice, which Nacho had to buy, though rice was as cheap as everything else at Tier zero.

He'd purchased some industrial-sized storage containers to hold the basics, but he longed for a better kitchen daily. For now, he was using the fireplace on the left-hand side of their guild-hall, and he'd bought a grill so he didn't have to use flat rocks as a makeshift surface to heat things.

Brie had brought the Rock Tarragon Ptarmigans from a hunting trip, but mostly, she ran the Deep Buggy Darkness with Reuben, Taye, Iron Becky, and Colleen. Iron Becky was down-right lethal with her elemental magic, while Colleen provided illusions to draw fire away from the actual adventurers. What-ever wasn't tricked by Colleen's illusions would hit Reuben, who could take an oversized load of punishment, thanks to his Ring of Cheese. He was still learning the parameters of the magic item, but that didn't stop him from constantly praising its effec-tiveness.

The mayor simply wasn't very good at combat, so he acted as support staff unless he was forced to use a battle axe. Mostly, he kept the dungeoneering team supplied with enough food and water to replenish them as they used their Skills. The biggest problem with the five of them constantly running the Deep Buggy Darkness was that it was all insects, all the time, and Nacho didn't want to waste money on a recipe book for bugs— even *if* there were several to consider.

Hungry Bob's Bugs N' Things and *Finger Lickin' Florence's Beetle BBQ Bonanza* were two of the more appetizing-sounding selec-tions. If those weren't scrumptious enough, he had the option of *Get a Leg Up: How to Properly Serve Millipedes, Centipedes, and Scor-pions* written by someone named Auntie Mology. Nacho just couldn't make himself excited about eating giant bugs, espe-cially compared to the increasingly popular stone soup, which had become even more of a hit after he had begun to super-charge batches of it with his cooking Magic.

While the dungeoneers were killing a variety of insects—

Gumdrop Grubs, Candylicious Weta Beetles, and Acid Termites, of which the prolific numbers confirmed that this *was* their spawn point, as he'd suspected—the Chips Guild's hunters were still finding and killing more powerful types of deer. Mostly, they brought in Wight-Tails and ghoul deer, but Old Bill had brought in an Elktopus earlier that week.

It was part elk and part octopus; basically a huge deer with tentacles, which Old and Young Bill's hunting party had hacked, arrowed, and speared to death. The beast was a level seven ungulate that had *not* gone down easily. Nacho would've needed a seafood recipe to make the tentacles edible, so he simply tossed them and collected a bundle of credits for venison processing.

Fifty-one people had joined the Chips so far, but everyone else on Armor Mountain was seriously considering it at this point. Waiting for them to decide was extremely frustrating, since practically everyone had given the go-ahead when they were first getting started. There were two people—the Bills— who were the most outspoken of the people dragging their feet, continually pointing out the 'feudal lord' aspects of the charter to anyone who would listen. It had reached the point that Nacho was starting to be annoyed with himself for warning people to watch out for the contracts. No one had explained it to *him* when he had first joined in his vision, and while it hadn't been the best situation, it certainly had gotten him in the door extremely quickly.

Brie didn't want to let anyone sleep in the guildhall if they weren't members, but Reuben took a different tack—the guildhall was an open benefit. Regardless of fealty, the structure was safer, warmer, and more comfortable than sleeping outside. He believed that if people directly experienced one upside of guilding up, they'd be more likely to take part in order to gain the additional benefits. Nacho trusted Reuben and was confident they'd win the rest over soon enough with food, credits, and walls.

He denied himself the luxurious kitchen of his dreams and

stuck to the basics in order to start leveling up other people as fast as they could—focusing most of his efforts on Brie and Reuben. Not because they were his friends, but because Brie was their best chance to dish out epic amounts of damage in the coming fight with the Bove. Reuben would be right behind her, healing her all the way.

Some people intermittently grumbled about the changes, only wanting to increase their levels, until they started to see the results of increasing their Skills. Spells were more potent, swords slew more efficiently, and people were hungrier, bringing them to Nacho, who cooked endlessly to meet the increasing demand. It was an interesting dilemma, as *he* was always hungry as well, but it also made him a better cook. He was constantly eating his own food, trying out different spices, and learning where he overcooked or undercooked something. Practice made *better*, so he was well on his way to being a world-class chef.

The cook continued buying ingredients with increased rarity, since at Tier zero, even Epic flour was only two points instead of one. Once all of his base ingredients were Epic, he confirmed that better ingredients made all the difference. No wonder those chef people spent so much time at organic markets back on Earth!

While his supplies were Epic, his cooking setup was common, *very* common. He constantly needed to remind himself not to splurge on a fancy kitchen until they got their walls built. Those would defend them—at least from Crave, who had been silent for the most part. There had been reports of Red Suzy Blacke running some recon on their location. That wasn't good news, but so far, Crave was likely occupied with building a guild of his own and leveling up his people.

Even so, it was only a matter of time until he'd go out on the conquering trail. Suzy and the people with her were probably just keeping tabs on them in the meantime. Nacho knew they had to get walls up before Crave's people were ready to attack, especially on the northern part of Armor Mountain. At least neither Arriod nor any other CrossHumans had shown up.

The Bove was a more pressing concern for the time being. It had rampaged its way back east on a killing spree, taking out minor settlements by the dozens. Nacho had talked to Taye, and given Nacho's knowledge of the AKC, he was pretty sure the monster cow had made its lair near the big Muddy River to the east. Yes, Muddy River wasn't the most imaginative name, but it was accurate enough.

Nacho mainly used his kitchen area as a bedroom and as a place to process bug corpses. People brought him bug body after bug body, and he'd peel off the carapace, pull off the wings, and then process out the Putrid Mana. It was a relatively easy way of earning bonus credits, so he'd offered a bounty on all monster corpses... no matter what type.

Putrid Mana processing always made him hungry, so here he was, sucking down stone soup with a pancake kicker. He missed the simplicity of cast-iron skillet biscuits. No one else wanted them for every meal, even *if* game logic told them it would be perfectly fine to eat them constantly. Earlier in the week, he'd upgraded his Ingredient Processing ability to level seven, which meant he could process meat up to level nine. For the time being, he wasn't going to put any more points in the Skill. There was no point—they weren't facing any Tier one monsters yet.

Nacho was planning on doing some shopping with Brie and Reuben that afternoon to look over their Skills and spend some of their credits. Right on time, the duo came back and slumped down on either side of him.

Both were covered in bug splatter and looked dog-tired. Brie helped herself to a Colonel White Beard's fried chicken leg, speaking around her mouthful as she munched. "We cleared out another chamber down there, but I'm worried we're going to hit a Tier one monster. We already have one crazy beast-thing to kill, and I don't really want another anytime soon."

Nacho stood up after a short internal struggle. "Let's go check with the mayor on the wall situation."

Reuben laughed wearily. "It's funny that we still call him the mayor."

"I'm starving over here." The Berserker finished off the drumstick and reached for a plate in the center of the table. "I've been Combat Dashing bugs and Defensive Whirling my way all around this joint. The drumstick is a start, but I'm severely down on Hunger points."

Nacho served them some stone soup and pancakes, though these flapjacks were meant to be more savory than sweet—he'd made them thick and doughy. He also quickly warmed up some of the Elktopus meat, and they ate a big meal together, talking and laughing while reviewing their credit situation.

Reuben had been putting credits aside because he was *positive* that every level one player on Armor Mountain had joined their guild because of his Marketing Skill. He'd increased his Marketing mojo to level two, since it had only cost them sixty credits in total. With Positive Vibes, he was maxed out at level nine—no going up without upgrading his class to Tier one, level zero. Over the week, they increased his Healing Hugs to level six, so he was healing everyone back to full health—thirty Health Points for most—with every awkward embrace. Some people had leveled their class and increased their Fitness, subsequently needing to suffer through multiple hugs if they got hurt too badly.

Brie was at level seven for her Dashing and Whirling, while she'd upped her Athletic Endurance to level three. They were each considering buying an additional Skill from the Store eventually, but they wanted to improve the Skills they already had, rather than go shopping for more. Nacho knew that players had to be careful with buying more Skills. It was absolutely necessary to be *sure* it was worth it. It was likewise smart for a player to wait until they got a feel for their character class before committing to a new ability.

Removing a Skill cost one thousand credits, the same amount as buying a guild charter. Buying a *fifth* Skill? Five thousand credits, and another Skill Slot was a non-negotiable prerequisite. That seemed far off, but the more powerful the creatures they killed, the more credits they'd earn. Already, fifty people working together and giving up ten percent had given them enough money to buy some wall lengths at a credit per square foot. If they got all one hundred and eighty-six people to join? The credits would really roll in.

Among the three of them, Nacho and his friends were holding onto six hundred and eighty credits after all their fun in the past week. While sitting at the table, Nacho frowned. "It's three hundred and forty credits to max out Brie's Combat Dash. I think we should do it."

"What about you?" Brie inquired, her soft side peeking through once more as she tried to make sure he was taking care of himself.

Smiling, Nacho collected their bowls and walked to the sink. He'd gotten really good at doing dishes; one of the curses of being a Common cook. "I'm basically maxed out. Let me show you."

Eli 'Nacho' Naches
Skill Slots (3/4)

- *Small Blades (Passive) Level 9: **18**% bonus damage on all knife attacks.*
- *Ingredient Processing (Active) Level 7: Remove Putrid Mana from monsters up to Level **9**.*
- *Cooking Magic (Active) Level 9: cook food that enhances a stat by **45**% of maximum.*
- *Open Slot*

Reuben's and Brie's eyes glowed as they went over his Skills. The Healer blinked the glow away. "I love the fact that Crave spent so many credits on you. We missed you, buddy, but you used the time *well*. Since we're sharing stats, let me show you something."

In seconds, Nacho was reviewing the big guy's Skills.

Reuben Colby
Skill Slots (3/4)

- *Healing Hugs (Active) Level 6:* **30** *Health Points Restored Upon Hugging*
- *Positive Vibes (Active) Level 9: Weapon blessing: (applies to whole party, lasts 5 minutes) Adds* **18**% *physical damage*
- *Marketing (Active) Level 2: Able to lure creatures to a location. Impacts up to Level:* **3**
- *Open slot*

"See that right there? Level *two* Marketing magic is right there," Reuben announced proudly. "Next time we get everyone together, I'm going to convince them that they all need to join our guild. It's going to be awesome!"

"It will be," Nacho agreed with a grimace. "I have no doubt your Marketing Skill is going to pay off, but we have to be utilitarian at this point."

"Which means I'm the vessel we fill for destruction. Stop, not a *word*." Brie finished with a smirk at her groom. "If we have six hundred and eighty credits to spend on me, we can take both my Combat Dash and Defensive Whirl to nine."

"What about your Athletic Endurance?" Reuben wasn't about to let her ignore the discrepancy.

Brie shook her head and answered, "I'm not sure my Athletic Endurance is going to be worth it. We got it wrong. Athletic Endurance doesn't use my full Hunger points; it merely reduces hunger loss *penalties*. I'm at third level, so I'm reducing ten percent by six percent, which is point six. Rounding up, my Combat Dash costs nine percent of my Hunger. It won't be worth upgrading until I get to level eight, which would reduce it by sixteen percent, which would round up to two full percentage points."

"That math *sucks*." Reuben shuddered as he tried to work out exactly what she had said.

Nacho waved his hand to retake their attention. "Let's max

out your combat Skills. You'll have pocket pancakes if you get hungry, so upgrade away!"

Brie stood, closed her eyes, and started spending credits. When she was done, she showed them just the Skills portion of her Stat Sheet.

Brie McCurdy
Skill Slots (3/4)

- *Athletic Endurance (Passive) Level 3: 6% reduction to hunger loss penalties when using physical skills.*
- *Combat Dash (Active) Level 9: 18% Damage on Dash Attacks, 10 meter dash.*
- *Defensive Whirl (Active) Level 9: Spin toward your enemy, auto-blocking up to 5 strikes.*
- *Open Slot*

Brie grinned and held out a double thumbs-up. "Maxed out at Tier zero. I'm curious about Tier one."

"You'll be even more deadly." Reuben wrapped her in an affectionate hug from behind and kissed her ear.

Nacho made a face and left the pair to their canoodling. "I'll go wash those dishes and pretend I didn't see that. Then we'll go talk to the mayor about the walls. I think it can wait, but we'll see what the consensus is."

It turned out that they should have moved sooner.

CHAPTER FORTY-TWO

The Dinner Party left through the main doors and emerged into the bright sunshine. A frosty wind was sweeping in from the north, letting the world know that it would start snowing any day now... and their first winter wasn't going to be fun. At least they had the guildhall. Private dwellings and other buildings would come later, which meant they needed to keep firewood in mind. Nacho shook his head ruefully. "There is always *something* to be done."

Old Bill liked to chop wood, but wasn't the easiest person to get along with. Neither was Young Bill. The two weren't related, but they were practically the father and son of sourness. The Bills were on his mind because they were chatting with Mayor Dan in the middle of Main Street, the avenue of rock lined with tents that connected the guildhall to the eastern guard station. The path culminated at the rope ladder connected to the low adobe wall. At this point in the day, only a few people were in their tents, since most were out either hunting or dungeoneering.

Reuben and Brie stopped to talk with Abby and some of her friends, all guild members, while Nacho continued down Main

Street to where Mayor Dan and the Bills were talking. A snatch of their conversation caught his attention as he approached. Mayor Dan leaned on his battle axe. "But is it *fair* for you to take advantage of the benefits of the guild without being a *member* of the guild?"

Young Bill wore the Elktopus hide over his t-shirt. "We try not to, but we were up here just like you. We shouldn't be forced to join something that came *after* we did."

Old Bill took off his Royals cap and swiped a hand over the wisps of sweaty hair. "We don't know this Nacho guy from Adam. I'm not signing *anything* until we make sure this isn't another Juxtaposition trick. Mayor, you were going to build the walls anyway, so it's not like we're forcing you to do anything, and *you* can't force us."

Nacho approached the three of them carefully and joined the conversation. "You're right. We're *not* forcing you, and we don't want to force you. Now, I figured if you definitely *weren't* going to join the guild, you'd have taken off by now, like Kala."

Old Bill grunted and replaced his cap. "That Kala and her old man had issues, and don't even get me started on that Myron guy—what in the *abyss*?"

A crashing sound interrupted them as trees suddenly toppled and slammed into each other, creating a thunderous reverberation. A demonic *moo~o~o* followed—the angry cry of a Holstein mixed with a Tyrannosaurus Rex.

The Bove had arrived.

It hit the mountain like a meteor and started climbing, the power behind the Bove's hooves cracking the stony face and causing the entire mountain to shudder. Its leathery wings flapped as it clattered up the side of the mountain, lowered its horns, and bashed right through the adobe wall.

The Calamity-class monster was bigger than the last time they'd seen it. Its inner reptilian mouth had busted out through the cow's natural teeth and head, the black and white Holstein hide stretched around the lizard maw. Its horns had also grown thicker, as had its hooves—the keratinous monstrosities had taken on edges like battle axes. Even more horrifying, its back-end snake tail had grown; now the mouth was half as big as the one on its face.

People scattered from their tents; the correct response, given the horrific monster coming for them. The smell it released was even worse: a thousand pounds of cow manure shoved into rotten sausage casings, along with a vague chemical smell, caused by the Putrid Mana leaking from its orifices.

Nacho's heart dropped into his stomach.

In the time it took them to realize what was happening, the Bove had made it to the top of the mountain. The monster lowered its head and charged through tents, which put up no more resistance than wet paper, as it targeted Nacho, Mayor Dan, and the two sour-faced Bills.

Unsurprisingly, the Juxtaposition seemed *thrilled* with the situation.

Hey, Player, welcome to Active Combat! Looks like you're udderly outclassed! Health Regen won't work, and the Store is closed during Active Combat. Here's hoping this is a missed-steak!

Young Bill had the best reflexes of the bunch, and he sprinted away without a sound. Mayor Dan and Old Bill stood still, shocked like deer in front of a runaway concrete mixer. Old Bill was weaponless, but Mayor Dan finally moved to lift the battle axe. Shaking himself from his frozen panic, Dan shoved the older man behind him and bravely raised his weapon.

The cook had his knives, but that was it. He knew it would take a hot minute for his friends to run over. The main problem was that the mayor and Old Bill didn't have a minute, and if Dan tried to use that battle axe against the Bove, he'd only make it angry.

Nacho's extra Small Blades skill wouldn't do much against the Tier one monstrosity, but the HungerCry Knives *could* pierce the Bove's Putrid Mana-reinforced skin, thanks to their special ability to carve meat one Tier higher than his own. He raced across the dirt and stone, tackling Mayor Dan and Old Bill and flinging them to the side as he spun up and over them. He landed just to the side of the Calamity's trajectory with both knives ready. "Come on, Bove. Let's get those wings off you so you can be *ground* beef!"

His shouted challenge drew the Bove's attention, and it abruptly changed course, hooves clattering like tank treads across the stone. It apparently decided not to use its horns, instead opening its big lizard mouth in an attempt to chomp Nacho in half. He got lucky, dodged its bite, and laughed as he twirled his knives. "I've been getting out of practice; let's do this!"

The Bove twisted around, managing to bash Nacho in the head with the side of its horn, and the too-cocky cook went flying across the stones, taking a third of his maximum damage from that grazing blow.

The malevolent cow bellowed cacophonously and rose up on its back legs in an attempt to crush Nacho underneath its front hooves. At that moment, Brie raced forward, full-on glowing from Reuben's Positive Vibes and likely a healthy dose of Nacho's pocket pancakes. Her Splatter Mallet looked like a tiny stick next to the Bove, but she brought it down on one of the Bove's horns... snapping it off and causing reddish-black blood to pour from the small wound left behind.

The Calamity's scarlet eyes flashed in confusion. It had mowed through every party, every settlement, every little collection of frightened people; eating them without any victims managing to deal a single point of damage to it in return. But this time, it had met someone who could make it hurt—even if just a *little*.

Losing a horn drove the Bove to complete bewilderment, and it turned on clattering hooves and fled, clacking all the way to the edge of the mountain. It scampered like a scared heifer toward the ruins of the adobe wall it had demolished and flung itself off the mountainside. Wind gusted under its wings, and the Calamity glided down through the break in the trees left by its destruction on its way up. The frightened bovine hit the ground running, pulling its wings in tight and fleeing for all it was worth.

Nacho burst into laughter at the sheer fact that they had survived. Blood was leaking from a gash on his forehead and slowly drying on his face, and he barely cared. "We broke off one horn, and we'll break off the other. We have it on the run, and now we have some information and a blood trail to follow. Brie... how many Health Points does the Bove have?"

"You're not gonna like this." Brie hefted the hammer on her shoulder. "It has two hundred and twenty-two Health Points. According to the message, I have to do fifteen percent of the total health in a single blow to get past its natural armor, and between my stats, Positive Vibes, and the sandwich I just ate... I just *barely* managed it."

Old Bill was brushing off his jeans, but paused at her explanation. "Wait, what do you mean, 'you ate a sandwich'?"

She explained, without much humor, the benefits of Nacho's cooking. He should've already known about it, or maybe it had been purposeful ignorance, but Old Bill approached Nacho. "Well, kid, you saved my life—you went up against that thing with just a couple kitchen knives despite probably knowing they wouldn't do squat. Fine. I'll join your guild, so long as you stop trying to get yourself killed to make me join you."

Other people had walked up to join in the chatter about the skid marks in the stone from the Bove's deadly hooves. Reuben jumped at the opportunity to command an audience, and Nacho spotted a definite glow about him as he talked.

That was the Marketing ability at work, and it was clear that there was no way any of his listeners were above level three. "People, you've seen us in action. We've talked. We want to build more walls to keep things like the Bove out, and we will do so without or without you. We would prefer to do it *with* you.

This is the last chance to join in as a founder… will you *please* ally with us?"

"Enough already." Young Bill had crept back over after sprinting away, unable to meet anyone's eyes as he raised a hand. "I will."

Several others did as well. Brie's face shone with a proud smile as she gazed at her fiancé. "That Reuben is something else."

"You just love him for his Marketing Skill," Nacho teased her as he wiped away a stream of blood.

"You know better than that." Brie kept on staring at Reuben as he started to sign people up, though she absentmindedly gripped her hammer a little tighter. "Do you know where that thing is going?"

Thanks to Taye, Nacho did. It was going to run back to safety near Muddy River. Luckily, he knew of the only place that could possibly fit such a massive creature. Of course, going in after it had only meant death in the previous version of the game. They had to get to the Bove before it holed up in its lair.

"You know what? I think we might have a chance."

CHAPTER FORTY-THREE

Nacho was itching to leave as soon as possible. It was still afternoon, and ideally, they'd be able to kill the Bove before nightfall. Most of the settlers had already rifled through their ruined tents in an attempt to salvage their gear, and many would be moving into the guildhall now that they were members and felt comfortable doing so.

Brie had scared the Bove, and Nacho *loved* how it had retreated post haste. Even so, the fight had only just started. He made his way to Reuben's side and addressed the murmuring crowd. "Hey, everyone, thanks for joining the Chips—we're glad that we were able to drive off the Bove, but the three of us have to go after it immediately. No one but Brie is going to be able to hurt the thing, and I don't want to risk anyone's lives but our own. We will be back as soon as possible. Can anyone help organize things while we are gone?"

At that moment, Iron Becky and Colleen pushed their way through the crowd to hug Mayor Dan, tears streaming down their faces as they sobbed in horror at nearly losing him. The display brought renewed chattering from the crowd about the attack. Reuben turned to his friend and noticed the dried blood on Nacho's forehead. "Dude, you're hurt? Let me heal you."

"Nah, already done. Health Regen is amazing." Nacho let the big guy hug him anyway, but he was adamant about moving out immediately afterward. "Reuben, we've got to grab our traveling gear and go; we need to strike the Bove as soon as possible. You'll have to tank the damage while Brie slaps around our big beefy friend."

"As long as you provide snacks," Reuben deadpanned as he gave Nacho his full attention. "I am not risking my life without snacks."

"That's a deal." Nacho didn't mention *he* could also hurt the Bove, but the minor damage he could do with the HungerCry knives wasn't going to amount to much. At some point, he would get some armor, but for the time being, he planned to stick to a supporting role. His primary job was to keep his players fed, and that meant he had to be light on his feet.

Mayor Dan was suddenly hugging Nacho, and being hugged so he could be healed was *entirely* different than being hugged gratefully by a Midwestern mayor. The older man teemed with gratitude. "Son, you saved my life. Young Bill, everyone, did you see that? Did you see Nacho risk his life to save me? I'm a *politician*. Most of the time, people would rather see me get *hurt* than step up like this! I knew we put our trust in the right man."

Nacho awkwardly disentangled himself and settled the man back. "Mayor Dan, if I let you die, I'd never hear the end of it. For one thing, your wife would kill me herself. For another? If anything happens to me... you're next in line for Guild Leader."

"Hey!" Reuben complained.

"You don't want the job anyway." Nacho waved his friend away, then turned back to the mayor. "We're going after the cow. While we're gone, you're going to get everyone out of the dungeon—I think Taye and some people are still down there. You've gotta stay on high alert until we're back. We've seen Red

Suzy Blacke lurking around, and it would be just like Crave to come after you while we're busy hunting the monster. You need to protect the guildhall, but each other even more so."

Nacho didn't mention that even if they could kill the Bove, it was pretty much guaranteed that their list of enemies wouldn't grow any shorter. Thankfully, the mayor agreed, and in no time, The Dinner Party was climbing down the repaired rope ladder with their backpacks strapped on tightly. Nacho hadn't acquired his grand traveling kitchen yet, but he did make a point to lash some pots, pans, and a few plastic containers of spices and essentials onto his gear.

They'd come up with a rough sheath for Brie's hammer so she could have easy access while carrying their bow as they hiked in the open, and Nacho began idly thinking they might just have to either invest in an archery Skill for Brie or find an option for a ranged Berserker attack. Brie turned her face slightly so they could hear her from her position at the front of the group. "I would like a Berserker Skill that allows me to do damage without running. I feel lame having to run back and forth while I fight. You're thinking of a ranged weapon, aren't you?"

"I am," Nacho informed her agreeably.

"We could invite Taye into The Dinner Party," Reuben suggested, then nudged Nacho. "Or Colleen; she seems like she'd *really* enjoy getting closer to *one* of us."

Nacho had considered Taye and decided to focus on that portion of the conversation. "If Crave does hit Armor Mountain while we're gone, they'll need Taye. Other than Brie, he's our best Body Player and can do the most damage, especially after we started leveling up his Skills. His Eagle Aim and Fast Quiver are downright impressive once he gets going."

He kept them on the trail of the Bove, which was easy enough to do after finding its wide trail through the downed trees. It was about an hour later when they started encountering the people the Bove had killed, or what remained of them. A boot here. A shirt there. A woman's gnawed-on dress.

Reuben took that one pretty hard. "Is anyone else worried about our little kingdom back on Armor Mountain? We're sure the Bove has gone this way, and it isn't going to try to double back and take them out while we are busy hunting it?"

"It went this way, all right." Brie pointed to a fresh pile of steaming manure that wasn't just thrice-digested grass. Nacho refused to linger on what else might be lurking in that demonic cow patty.

Reuben hurried them past the nauseating mess. "Well, *that* was awful."

"What if we can't get to the Bove before it retreats into its lair?" Brie quietly wondered aloud.

Reuben responded by growling, "We'll kill it in there. We are *not* letting this thing hurt any more people."

It was clear that the affable man was shocked and infuriated at the monster cow's path of destruction. Nacho tried to lighten the mood. "Too true! Because, you know, the more people this thing kills… the fewer customers we'll have."

No one laughed.

They started moving more cautiously as all natural sounds suddenly ended. The birds stopped singing, the skittering of small animals in the undergrowth abruptly cut off, and even the wind died down. They were peering around trying to find the new threat when Nacho sniffed the air and scented a fire in the distance. Moving to the ridgeline, he glimpsed a trail of fire flashing in the southern part of the forest. If there were flaming arrows, then Red Suzy Blacke couldn't be far behind.

Nacho informed his friends about his suspicions, and they kept their eyes open as they raced along through the remains of the day. The trio journeyed fast, keeping an eye out for both Crave's people and the bovine monstrosity. They didn't want to get ambushed again, and the Bove was *unnaturally* fast. Fortunately, Nacho and his friends didn't encounter any more monsters.

It seemed that all the other creatures had scattered in the wake of the first truly terrible monster to terrorize the countryside of the AKC. There would be others, some migrating from other places, burrowing up from the ground, and still more emerging from the darkest depths of the various dungeons around—the deeper the players went, the more Putrid Mana filled the air. Most people in the Juxtaposition thought that the deep denizens started at higher tiers than those monsters closer to the surface, but no one had ever managed to confirm it.

Twilight was setting in when Nacho finally came around to the idea that they were not going to be able to catch up to the Bove before full nightfall. It was equally clear that the beast wouldn't be stopping until it reached his lair. As the sun painted both sky and forest in various shades of red, Nacho stopped his friends and sighed in resignation. "Well, according to Reuben, there's no retreat and no surrender."

"Let's just go a *bit* farther." Reuben pointed to a nearby rise. "Even if we don't find anything, we can camp up there."

By the time they crested the top of the ridge, the stars were already coming out. Nacho, Brie, and Reuben found themselves in the ruins of a settlement, where shredded tents flapped on broken tree branches. The Dinner Party silently agreed to move off the hill and settled on camping near a thicket of bushes growing between a cluster of trees just out of sight of the obliterated encampment.

They cleared away the brush and started a fire, keeping their flank protected. Once the outer coals reached the right temperature, Nacho pulled out his pan and made pancakes for dinner. Truthfully, he couldn't help but be proud of his creation. He'd come a long way since those first few blackened bits of yuck, and Reuben ate half a dozen without needing to stop between every bite and suck down water. They even had plenty of credits available for syrup, and when they were full, Nacho even remembered to tell them about his recent visit from Kronos.

Reuben rumbled with dark humor. "Your pancakes are so much better without the stick pieces, though I *do* miss the blackened crust. Blackened pancakes are like blackened shrimp, right? A delicacy?"

"No." Brie curtly changed subjects. "You actually saw your Patron?"

"I did. In the kitchen of the Chaos Coop, no less. It was… strange. He said it was against the rules to talk to me, and he didn't tell me much, except that there seemed to be two sides among the Patrons—those who seemed to care about humans, and those who didn't. I'm pretty sure Kronos is in our corner, but it's hard to say for sure."

"It's interesting that he's still around." Brie used the side of her fork to scoop every bit of pancake and syrup off her plate. It absorbed her entire focus, like she was performing surgery, and it was only then that Nacho realized how utterly exhausted she was.

"He wanted to make sure I didn't give up on… you know, my life, the game, the whole thing. For a while there, I thought you two were dead." Needing to keep his hands busy, Nacho poured some water into the pan. He had brought a little soap as well, and he idly swished the suds around the pan as it warmed the water. Doing dishes while camping was a pain, but it wasn't impossible.

Reuben raised a hand with a grin. "Not dead! Not even close."

"Let's keep it that way." Nacho hummed softly as he scrubbed. "Losing you two… made me a much worse person."

"Some of the Patrons are good, and some are bad; does it matter which is which?" She stood up abruptly and moved off into the darkness. "I guess we don't have much say, either way. I'll take the first watch. Forget I said anything."

Reuben squinted at her and then at Nacho. "Did you understand what that was all about?"

Nacho took a fork and carefully began scraping off some of the burned-on pancake batter, which had finally pulled loose. "I have no idea, but could it be that Brie talked with a Patron of her own and can't tell us?"

Reuben paused, blinking rapidly as he tried to consider the implications. "If the Patron had given her some kind of boon that only worked if she didn't talk about it? It would make sense, but only in that context. Otherwise, she's always told us everything. Especially me."

Nacho finished cleaning the pan and threw the water into the weeds. "We can't talk about this either, if that's the case. The Patrons listen, and the whole gaming system is aware of us… what we do, what we say. It's how they can tailor those System messages just for us."

They didn't speak again, keeping the fire small, and took their usual turns of sleeping and taking watch. They were up again at first light, following the path of destruction through more trees; Sickamores, elms, and even a few of the Oilbark trees. At one point, they encountered a few Golden-Heart Demon Apples, which were growing more and more violent by the day.

The murderous fruits were akin to the Red Pernicious apples, only these were growing tentacles *and* teeth as they became more and more ripe. Eating the furious fruits was tricky, as they were mean and rotten on the outside, but had a deliciously sweet center. Uniquely, they inherently forced their Putrid Mana to the surface, so even at Tier zero, it was possible to eat their deliciously crisp cores without having to process them. It had taken a couple starving adventurers to brave the teeth and tentacles, but their sacrifice once upon a time had proven valuable to Nacho.

Brie shot a few of the apples with arrows and collected the credits while Nacho processed them. Twenty more credits were quickly available to be used as needed.

They found more destroyed settlements, more bones, more clothes, and a broken spear or two in the wake of the Calamity's devastation. By noon, they reached what *had* to be the entrance to the Bove's lair, which dwarfed everything around it. Numerous trees had been ripped from their roots and stacked in a mish-mash pile fifty feet tall to surround the mouth of the cavern. Everything around the pile of trees had died, and a river a half-mile wide proceeded to chug brown water south to points unknown. That was definitely the Muddy, running north to south.

There had been enough dungeons and monsters to keep the clusters of players localized in the AKC, though every now and again, someone would come from another area to spread stories of post-apocalyptic panic and mayhem from other places as far away as Denver and St. Louis. No one had ever made it from further than that in the three years that Nacho had survived.

The Bove's lair looked like it had been hit by a concussive bomb. Along with the shredded trees, trampled wildlife and discarded bones were amassed in haphazard heaps in the dirt and drying mud. The intermingled trail of mud, slop, and feces led all the way up to a rambling walkway of trees and into the cave itself. Reuben bravely stepped forward, fighting to keep his gaze off his feet. "We're going in there, right?"

"I hate being right. Of *course* this is the Bove's lair." Nacho winced and hesitated, knowing what his friend *wanted* him to say, instead forcing out what he actually thought was the best idea. "It's a bad idea. No one, and I mean *no one*, ever managed to come out of there. We could wait until it comes out again to hunt and get it then."

"Could be days. Could be a week! Do we really want to be gone from Armor Mountain that long?" Reuben shook his head. "The answer is no. We're going in there."

Brie handed the bow and arrow to Nacho. "Yes, we are. I broke off one horn. I'll break off another and shove it down the thing's throat!"

Reuben's mouth dropped open. "Celestials, sweets. That's hardcore."

"That's who I am." Brie tossed her greasy hair, trying to be dramatic.

Meanwhile, Nacho whipped his backpack around and started pulling out treats. "Yes, we're going in there, but first?

Who wants to have leftover pancakes and fried ptarmigan drumsticks?"

"Were they made… with *love*?" Reuben reached for the food without waiting for an answer. They were. Everyone ate heartily, and soon they were buffed to the max and standing in front of the opening, weapons in hand.

They had a demon cow to kill.

CHAPTER FORTY-FOUR

Nacho hauled his pack, full of mostly food and water, while Brie and Reuben hid theirs in the tangle of trees. The cook carried the bow in his left hand and the lantern in his right, allowing them to see a little of the mammoth cave. The smooth stone floor angled downward, but the whole place didn't get any smaller. In fact, it got larger—the Patrons probably wanted to accommodate the size of their wicked beast and accordingly gave it a lot of extra space.

"What's the plan again?" Reuben licked his lips nervously.

"Smash," their resident Berserker replied while tossing the handle of her hammer up and down lightly.

"Let's *adjust* that strategy some." Nacho raised the lantern higher in an effort to see deeper into the natural cavern, but all they got was a refraction from glittering stones in the sides of the wall and rock formations around them. "Brie should go in there, get one big bash in, and then race away. The thing will go for her, but then Reuben can get in the way. It's okay if you take some damage-"

"Easy for you to say," Reuben whined good-naturedly.

"-while Brie races back and hits it again," Nacho finished in spite of the interruption.

Reuben raised his right gauntlet in a fist. "Then let's get smelly. Or should it be 'let's get cheesy'? Opinions on my catchphrase connected to my Ring of Cheese?"

"It can't smell worse than this." Brie wrinkled her nose. She wasn't wrong. The place reeked of manure and the flatulence of a whale decaying from the inside out.

"How about 'I just made this fight ten times cheddar'?" Nacho suggested on his friend's behalf.

"Not bad." Reuben allowed a small smile to peek through as he breathed through his mouth to keep the smell to a minimum. "Too bad we're not getting bonus credits for puns."

Brie shushed them. She had wrapped a pancake and Elktopus slider in a cloth and took a bite to keep her spirits up. It was a testament to her toughness that she could actively eat despite the stink. They moved farther into the massive cavern, cautiously following a smooth floor that sloped downward. Nacho felt tiny, but the lantern revealed occasional deposits of trash and cast-off clothes piled along the edges of the cave.

A strange coincidence was that they started finding Costco shirts everywhere—Nacho recognized the familiar red and blue uniforms. There must've been a Costco nearby when the Juxtaposition happened, and a bunch of the employees likely all appeared together. Maybe they were the Bove's very first victims?

They descended deeper into the cavern, but there was still no sign of the monster. The scent became stifling, and soon they were having to trek around substantial piles of manure. More Costco uniforms cropped up, and the team finally came to part of the cave where vines had descended in thick panels from the ceilings. The vines seemed to have grown through the eye and mouth holes of various skulls, or... were the skulls *part* of the vine? It was hard to tell, but some of the eye sockets glowed with a ghostly blue bioluminescent light and chattered their teeth at Nacho and his friends.

"I thought zombies weren't a thing?" Reuben's eyes were wide as he whispered at Nacho.

"I don't know *what* this is." The skull vines dominated the back of the cave, hanging in a curtain that blocked whatever passage lay beyond. Still no sign of the monster.

Nacho couldn't believe he was standing in the lair. He wasn't sure who had killed the Bove last time, since there had been so many rumors. Some said it was Kala and the Gorged, while others claimed it had been a Necromancer with his army of the dead, and still others said it was the Shadow Killer— Nacho himself—that had slain the beast.

The rumors also claimed that the lair had been full of the osteosynthetic vines—also known as Skullgainvillea—as well as dangerous exploding mushrooms. Both the mushrooms and the vines had made the lair impassable, and it looked like at least one of the rumors was true. That meant that someone *had* come out of the cavern alive at one point, and that fact gave Nacho a faint glimmer of hope.

Reuben surveyed the partition of vines apprehensively. "Undead carnivorous plants. They're like Venus flytraps for humans?"

"I hate waiting." Brie gulped down the last bite of her makeshift slider and let out a frustrated yell. "Bove! Come on out! *Fre~esh* meat!"

A rock-shaking bellow rose from below, and the Bove rushed out of the Skullgainvillea, sending the bones clacking together like nightmarish maracas.

The fight was on.

Hey, Player, aren't you brave, going after the Bove so early on? We don't recommend it, but it's your funeral; let's get to it! People just like you are dying to get into cemeteries! You know the drill! Welcome to Active Combat! No Store and no Health or Mana Regen. Good luck!

. . .

"Gonna give us all some good vibrations!" Reuben hit them with Positive Vibes just as Brie Combat Dashed fearlessly. She struck the Bove as hard as she could with that hammer, but the monster cow had learned that Brie could hurt him. He jerked his big frame to the side, and the hammer cracked onto the stone floor.

Lowing angrily, the beast turned and tried to use its horn to gore her—its bad horn, happily. Not so happily, the horn had broken off at a point, and it was already growing back, adding a girthy thickness around the base and a serrated spear-like protrusion to the front. Brie immediately went into her Defensive Whirl, striking aside the horn attack and spinning away to avoid the hooves as they struck at her.

That attack meant Brie was down twenty-three percent on her Hunger points in the first exchange of the fight. She was too close to the Bove to use her Dash, so she just hammered the weapon with the extra bonus.

"Blast it!" the Berserker screamed. "I dealt no damage! The thing still has two hundred and twenty-two Health!"

She was forced to use her Combat Dash to speed away, but that cost her another nine percent in Metabolic costs, and she'd be down to sixty-eight Hunger points. Reuben ran forward, both gauntlets raised in a boxer's stance. "Time to get *cheesy!*"

The Bove attempted to trample Reuben, but the health tank managed to land a gauntlet on the thing's nose before attempting to dodge the attack. He didn't quite make it and wound up under the hooves of the demon cow. Every time a hoof landed, a glow marked Reuben's body, and the scent of pungent cheese filled the air.

Nacho dropped the lantern and bow, pulling food out of his pack for Brie: she was going to need it, and Reuben would need water if he survived.

The Bove spun to trample Reuben again.

Meanwhile, Brie had skidded to a stop and went dashing back in. She planted the head of her massive hammer solidly into the Bove's shoulder, and it bellowed in agony.

Brie triumphantly proclaimed, "A hundred and eighty-nine health left!"

Reuben rolled out from the hooves and limped away, gasping from exertion and shock. "That should've killed me... holy cow. Pun intended. It did thirty points of damage, but I'm... still here? Not sure how much damage I can absorb, but we'll definitely be going max cheese on this fight."

"You go max cheese every day!" Nacho yelled to his friend, infuriating the creature they were attacking.

The Bove was *not* amused at their banter. It rose up on its back hooves and stretched out its wings, snorting furiously. Brie retreated, then dashed back in and slammed the hammer into its belly. It dropped down, but she whirled the hooves off her head and ran just far enough to whirl back and crack her hammer into its lizard face. A few of the monster's teeth went flying, and she was forced to Combat Dash to escape getting trampled.

Reuben sprinted forward and grabbed the monster's attention with a punch to its bleeding snout. No damage was dealt, but Reuben got a horn in the chest for his trouble. His ring flashed, as did his whole body, and the bleu cheese stink of the ring boiled out from him. It was strong enough to make even the Bove's fiendishly red eyes water, and the thing paused— giving Reuben time to run. The demon bull realized its mistake a second too late and chased after him.

The Healer had absorbed at least forty-five points of damage so far, if not more, and it looked like they were going to find out exactly how much he could take.

Brie ran to Nacho, breathing hard. "My hunger is down to fifteen percent; would be ten percent, except for my endurance. That Bove still has a hundred and twenty-three points. We might need to retreat, because this thing isn't going down, and I'm starving!"

Nacho flipped her another pancake, which wasn't ideal. She grabbed it and started gulping as fast as she could, which led to coughing. She had to wash the quarter portion down with water. Pancakes were not great for combat situations. He needed to work on some sort of gel or combat slime. Even a smoothie would be better.

The Healer was only going to keep the Bove busy for so long, and he *had* to be running out of cheese damage absorption. Just then, he made a mistake. Reuben ran too close to the Skullgainvillea, and the vines swung several chomping skulls at him. He managed to duck them, but the lesson was clear—getting too close to the walls meant getting bitten and tangled.

Reuben escaped the killer carnivorous vines with a mere inch to spare, but that momentary distraction allowed the Bove to grab him in its teeth and chomp down—only to be given another blast of cheesy stink for its efforts. It flung Reuben away in disgust, and he went bouncing across the floor. Each bounce also caused him hurt, and the Bove rushed after the downed man.

Nacho started snapping out orders. "Brie, you have to stop using your Defensive Whirl, just don't get hit! You should be back up to thirty-five Hunger Points, meaning you have three more dashes in you. Hit him hard, then run, but keep the Bove on you. Then you can dash back into him. You might take some damage, but Reuben can heal you."

The Bove trampled Reuben, and this time, he was left bleeding and wounded. The big guy was tough, however, and he got to his feet to wrap his arms around himself. "The ring is out! It can absorb three times my Health Points, which the Patrons decided to tell me *after* the fact. Do we have a plan?"

The demonic bull bellowed and thundered on clacking hooves toward Nacho and Brie. The Berserker didn't answer her fiancé. Still chewing, she sped forward in a blur, swinging her hammer into the face of the Bove hard enough to send more fangs scattering across the floor. At this point, if she kept focusing on the thing's mouth, it would have to *gum* them to death.

Nacho hated that he couldn't do much in the fight—but he could feed Reuben, and he was going to have to play matador with the Bove at least once. Brie tried to run normally and didn't get too far from the Bove before she was slashed in the back with a hoof. She managed to stay on her feet, then turned and hit the monster, but she didn't use her Skill, so the hammer only bounced off.

The demonic bull flung its massive head and bashed Brie to the ground. If she hadn't had her armor on, she'd have been killed by that strike for certain. They were in a bind; Brie could use her Combat Dash two more times, but if Nacho's calculations were correct, they had to hit the Bove three more times—it had at least ninety Health Points left.

"Heal her!" Nacho shouted to Reuben as he ran forward and got the Bove's attention. Staring down a creature that had haunted his dreams for years was no fun, but they were close to putting this thing down. He wouldn't be able to eat it, but all he had to do was survive one attack. The Bove clattered forward on its massive hooves, huffing as it eyed the cook with malice.

Nacho didn't have a magic ring; all he had was his own skin, muscle, and bone. Getting hit by the Bove would be like getting hit by a souped-up monster truck that smelled like a septic tank. He wasn't encumbered by armor, so he easily dove to the side, and the demon cow clattered by. At first, Nacho was relieved, but he'd forgotten about the snake-mouth tail. The reptilian appendage lashed out in passing and ripped into Nacho's leg.

Health remaining: 15/30!

He was flung across the floor and found himself staring up into the Bove's mouth. Saliva dripped onto Nacho's shirt… and Brie came dashing by, driving that hammer into the thing's jaw once again. Bone cracked like a gunshot, and Nacho was surprised that the bull's mouth didn't come unhinged. He rolled away as blood sprayed the floor.

"Fifty-seven points left!" Brie screamed. "I can hit it one more time with Dash, and then I'm out if we don't eat."

Brie led the bull away as Nacho found himself covered by Reuben. It was awkward, but he felt the healing energy repair his leg, and then managed to get to his feet. The Bove let out a bellow, and though it was missing teeth, had a cracked jaw, and was generally in a world of hurt… it had chased Brie down and was about to trample her.

At the very last second, she turned, Defensive Whirled, and the Bove stopped like it had hit a brick wall. All that meat came to a screeching stop, and the Bove went up and over her, only to come crashing down.

With the Bove stunned, The Dinner Party ran for the exit. Nacho managed to snatch up his pack and the lantern, but not the bow. They ran as fast as they could up the slope and out of the cave.

Reuben was slimmer and in far better shape than he'd been when they first started their adventures. He was able to keep up with both Brie and Nacho as they raced out of the cave. They were all bent over, gasping for breath, when an arrow, streaming fire, went zooming past them to clatter onto the stone.

Nacho squinted in the sunlight. Directly in front of them stood Richard Crave and his merry band of cutthroats—with two cutthroats missing. Hogan and Whitney were not in attendance, for obvious reasons. Red Suzy Blacke had another arrow nocked, aimed right at them.

Crave stood with one hand resting on the pommel of his scimitar. The other held the magic black feather. "Well, well, *well*, Nacho. I'm assuming you went after the big cow monster and tried to make hamburger out of him. How did it go?"

Nacho straightened and smiled with a mirth he didn't feel. "How do you like your meat, *Dick*? You seem like a well-done with ketchup kinda guy."

CHAPTER FORTY-FIVE

Crave wiggled his magic sleeping feather at Nacho. "Actually, I like my steak medium-rare."

"We're going to kill them, right?" Rizzo gripped two black short swords. He had probably found them in the deeper levels of the Chaos Coop. "Then we'll go after the dungeon down there. Feels like a big one!"

"Good luck getting by the Skullgainvillea." Nacho swung his backpack around.

Red Suzy Blacke leaned into her bow. "If you pull out anything I don't like, you're dead."

Crave laughed a little. "They're *already* dead. Especially our former cook. We just need for them to tell us what they got for killing the *Bove*, and what they've seen down there, besides Skullgainvillea, whatever that is."

Alongside Crave, Suzy, and Rizzo stood some huge guy in scale mail. Bald, scarred, and sneering, the new goon must've been an Olympic weightlifter back in the day. He had a fluted morning star which leaked magical shadows balanced on one shoulder. A quick glance confirmed that Crave had also picked up a few new spellcasters along the way.

Nacho managed to pull out another Rock Tarragon Ptarmigan drumstick out of his pack. He wiggled it at Crave and the gang. "Just wanting a last meal. It's only a drumstick, not a weapon."

He took a bite and felt the cooking Magic hit him. He wiped his mouth and casually tossed it to Brie, who caught it and started eating ravenously. It seemed Crave, Suzy and Rizzo had forgotten that his food was, in actuality, a weapon. That was easy to believe, since for decades back on Earth, people just ate and didn't worry about magic.

Brie swallowed quickly. It had been a chonky drumstick, an entire half portion. Nacho squinted at Crave. "I'm surprised that you didn't go after Armor Mountain with us gone."

"We thought about it," the Assassin freely admitted. "Nice guildhall. Not much in competition. But I figured we'd get you out here, away from your people, so I can get a bit of revenge on you for killing Hogan and Whitey, collect your credits, and go back to Armor Mountain with some story about how we tried to save you, but you died—and they should join my guild, the Final Victory."

Nacho tilted his head. He heard the distant clomp of a certain demonic bull. "Final Victory? No. I'm thinking *this* is your last hurrah."

"*What?* The cow is still alive!" Suzy let fly an arrow. The assembled spellcasters threw a lightning bolt, a missile of pure destructive magic, and a freezing wind full of icicles in near-simultaneous panic.

Brie whirled out in front of Reuben and Nacho, deflecting the arrow and all three of the magical attacks. The three members of The Dinner Party scattered as the Bove came crashing out into the sunlight. It was leaking blood, had lost a horn and any number of teeth, but it was still hangry and looking for a last meal.

It lunged forward in a rage and grabbed one Mind Player in its teeth, biting the poor guy in half as the snake-tail mouth whipped around and grabbed another. Both mouths were still chewing furiously as it turned and went after the others.

Suzy might've leveled up some, but her fire arrows still weren't powerful enough to pierce the hide of the bull. Mace guy slammed his weapon against the muscled hide of the thing, but again, nothing was happening.

While the Bove swept through Crave and his party, Nacho staggered over to Brie and pulled pancakes out of the side pocket of his pants. Brie made a face. "I'm not exactly excited to be eating *your* pocket pancakes, Nacho! I have trouble eating my own."

"You need the cooking Magic," he insisted as he pushed the food into her hands. Reuben gave her a water bottle to wash the hasty meal down. "Num, num, here comes the airplane."

Screaming rose from the ranks of Crave's new guild, but they were doing a fine job distracting the cow monster. Brie quickly decided that she'd had enough and sped in with her hammer; hitting the monster on a back leg and breaking it with a loud *crack*!

She had plenty of Hunger stored to Combat Dash away from the retaliatory strike. "Down to twenty-four Health! One more shot should do it!"

The demon cow tried to retreat, but it was having difficulty moving its bulk around on a broken leg. Brie had to Defensive Whirl to stop the snake tail from taking a bite out of her and danced nimbly back, her attention laser-focused on the injured beast. The Bove was breathing hard and wallowing desperately, flinging snot and blood with every movement.

It was almost dead.

While Crave's people retreated, the Guild Master himself sprinted at Nacho with his scimitar raised. A look of fury painted his face. The sword arced down... and Reuben stepped forward and caught the blade in his metal-covered fist. "No one talks to the cook, except someone who wants to praise his culinary skills. *I* handle the complaints."

The Healer slammed a gauntlet into Crave's face, snapping

his nose and causing the Assassin to stagger back and wind up on his rear. The big guy must've taken some damage in catching the sword, but the move was worth it, both for protection and style points.

At the same time, Brie used her final Combat Dash and jumped into the air, putting everything she had into one final attack as she dropped the hammer. The Bove's skull shattered, and the beast dropped like a stone. It let out one final grunt and went rigid, finally dead and gone.

Just like that, a huge weight lifted off Nacho's shoulders. They had done it. They had done the *impossible*, and killed the Bove before it got so strong that it was untouchable. They had killed it less than a month into the Juxtaposition, meaning they had just saved tens of thousands of lives.

A tear trickled from his eyes and a wide smile appeared on his face, he was beaming so hard that it made his lips feel like they would tear,

Brie wiped the sweat from her brow, grinning at her team. "I must say, that is so much more satisfying than making a goal in lacrosse."

"You little...!" Crave pulled himself up and swayed in place, holding his nose. "We're not done, Doritos. Not by a long shot."

Nacho decided right then that he wasn't going to let this guy live. While in the Probability Vision, they'd been comrades—if not close friends—he knew, deep-down, Crave wouldn't stop until he got his revenge. He wouldn't get any credits, but he was going to slam his Cry knife into Crave's gizzard and cut the Assassin into bite-sized pieces.

He never had the chance.

Crave flashed forward and brushed Nacho's face with the feather. The cook, full of indignation, had a definite feeling of déjà vu as he pitched forward into unconsciousness onto the gross ground in front of the Bove's lair.

Nacho woke up seconds later on his back with Brie clutching his shirt. "Good. You're awake. We ran Crave off, try and pull yourself together. Until then, I'll make do with another pocket pancake."

After nodding in stunned agreement, Nacho stood up and approached the lifeless Bove, touching the big, knotted muscles of its shoulder. He couldn't help attempting to process out some of the Putrid Mana, but the System laughed at him.

Nice try, buddy, but this is a Level 19 (Tier one Level 9) monster, and you can only do up to Level 9. Better luck next time! Keep eating your vegetables and saying your prayers, and maybe someday you can eat the big beef.

Nacho grinned and shrugged. It had been worth a shot. Staring down at the Bove, he privately mused at how much things had changed. Hogan and Whitney dying, the Bove gone, figuring out food this early... it changed things. His experiences in the Probability Vision meant less and less as reality diverged from his waking dream, but... that was a very good thing.

The cook turned and saw Brie and Reuben holding hands as their Health Regen took care of any lingering wounds.

Yes, things had changed, but he still had his two best friends. In the end, Nacho had the ultimate boon: he knew the game. He'd just have to keep on cooking.

EPILOGUE

Killing the Bove didn't give them many credits—only forty—but the System did give Brie a ten credit bonus for killing something above her Tier, which felt more like a kick in the teeth than a reward after how hard it had been to take out the monster.

Weirdly enough, they'd gone back inside the cave to find more of the skull vines blocking their way—the deadly strands had at *least* quadrupled. Nacho wasn't sure what was going on, but it was definitely suspicious. "Is it just me, or do you guys think the Juxtaposition is hiding something back there?

"You're right, and we abyss-well know it." Brie limbered up, getting her hammer ready for a bit more work. "Come on, guys. I don't know about you, but I'm not about to let some *foliage* stand between me and whatever is past here."

There was something deeply satisfying about watching the Berserker smashing the skull-shaped plants one by one. Each time she landed a hit, it sounded like a baseball bat *cracking* to announce a home run. The plants, being plants, couldn't do much to defend themselves if the players didn't get in range, and soon, the path forward was clear.

Nacho followed behind his friends, holding the lantern… and his breath. For him, this was the start of a new history for this world. They were about to go somewhere no one, as far as he knew, had ever gone before.

As they passed under the pulpy remnants of the Skull-gainvillea, The Dinner Party found a number of red and blue t-shirts with embroidered 'Costco' logos scattered around the muck-smeared cavern floor. Reuben nodded toward the only remnants of the people that had been at work when the apocalypse had hit. "Poor Costco employees. They even *died* in bulk."

They passed uneventfully through the corridor in the back of the cave and followed it down until they came to a part of the ground that began sloping downward, eventually forming a spiral large enough for even the Bove to traverse. At the bottom of the ramp, their lantern gleamed against metal set into the wall in a pattern too regular to be natural, but the surfaces were too filthy for them to make out what it was. They cautiously progressed through another hall and a variety of caves, not finding another monster. Unsurprising, since the Calamity-class monster had claimed this den for its own.

Once they were certain they weren't about to be ambushed, they continued to slog along a long hallway of rough-cut stone, half-submerged in stinking river mud and cow feces. At the end of the hall, two torches flickered on the wall, illuminating doors which seemed likely to be the official entrance to a dungeon. Only… the door panels didn't look right. They weren't medieval portals with ornate iron fittings. Instead, they were metal-framed glass panels slightly apart, with only darkness beyond.

"Wait… I recognize this," Reuben whispered as he squinted at the smeared logo on the doors. "Could it be?"

Nacho slopped forward through the mud and squeezed through the gap in the glass doors, where a set of shelves had fallen over. He reached down and picked up one of the slightly crinkly bags that had fallen, holding it up to the light. "It's… chips. Doritos, Fritos, Ruffles… Earth chips."

"I was right. Look how big this place is..." Reuben was practically *shaking* with delight. "It all makes sense! The clothes, the way the System didn't want us to find this... it's a Costco!"

Nacho looked around the cavernous space and found the logo everywhere. It *still* took a minute for the reality to sink in. He was in a chip aisle, in a Costco, maybe a half-mile under the ground. He'd been that deep before, plenty of times... but not here. Only ever in System-generated dungeons.

"I don't know what this means." The cook turned and gestured around helplessly, even as Brie and Reuben wandered up to him with shining eyes.

"It's simple, isn't it?" Reuben laughed too hard to actually be finding this funny. "Toto, I'm pretty sure we *are* in Kansas!"

"What does this mean for us?" Brie took a more practical route. "If we're *not* in another world, can we find a way to get access to our old technology? Weapons?"

Nacho couldn't answer her. There was too much to process, and he... just wasn't sure. "I guess all we can do is look at the facts? This is a Costco from our world. That means it was either transported here as well, or the Patrons somehow covered the Earth in an extra layer of rock, dirt, and monster junk."

Something bellowed from deeper down the rows of dark shelves, and the Juxtaposition finally decided to chime in.

Greetings, Player!

Welcome to the Bove's Lair Costco and Scary Shelves Dungeon! Looks like you're the first players to find the UnderFun! You earn five thousand *bonus credits! We're keeping an eye on you, Eli 'Nacho' Naches, you and your Chips.*

Note: Finding the UnderFun may or may not have triggered key game scenarios ahead of schedule. You'll know eventually if your little discovery was good, bad, or ineffectual. Such discoveries add spice to life! We hope you savor the new experiences!

. . .

"Yeah..." Nacho backed up, heading toward the door. "We need to leave. If the Bove was just the door guard, what else is in here? Nothing that we can handle yet, that's for sure."

"Wait." Reuben darted past him and scooped up an armful of chip bags. "*Now* we can go."

They had only made it to the ramp when they heard a sound that made Nacho's blood run cold.

Moo~o!

The Dinner Party turned slowly, trying to swallow their fear as they came face to face with a *second* Bove. Their weapons were out, and they were ready to flee... until it lumbered closer. Brie was the first to lower her hammer. "It's just a cow? It's small, maybe a yearling?"

"That thing is *huge*," Nacho warned them, scraping his knives over each other to give them a sharper edge.

"It's just a regular cow. Level one, Tier zero," Reuben pointed out, having been the only one to take the time to actually check the creature. "C'mere, fella. You've been alone, haven't you? Lonely?"

The beefy calf accepted getting a rope tied around its neck and placidly followed the group up the ramp and out of the cave, even though it tossed its head and balked a little before going out into sunlight for what appeared to be the first time in its life.

Nacho watched the creature closely for the entire eight hour trip back to Armor Mountain, but as far as he could tell, it really was just a standard cow. They were met with fanfare upon making it home, even though everyone seemed to be just as concerned with the cow as the cook originally had been when it was hoisted up the side of the sheer cliff with the help of a dozen pulleys.

The entire community lined Main Street as they led their prize down the road. Taye's eyes were shining as he glanced between the gore-encrusted group and the young cow. "Did you really kill the Bove? Is this its calf?"

"It could be? We don't know for sure. Hold on." Nacho

nodded at the questioning glances of the other people. He raised his arm, and the hubbub died down. When it became possible, he shouted for everyone to hear, "The Bove is dead! *We did it!*"

The crowd roared in approval, and The Dinner Party stood a little taller as they soaked in the praise. Nacho took the rope and gestured at the cow. "Join us in a few hours for a feast!"

There was another outburst of applause, though Reuben pouted slightly. "Aww. I thought we'd have a pet."

"No way to keep it without a farmer." Nacho patted his sad friend's arm. "It'll turn into a second Bove if we leave it."

The crowd was breaking up, going about their business, though Taye came for a closer look. "How did you do it? We lost against it with a dozen people and had to run for our lives."

"Crave showed up and accidentally helped us." Brie smirked as she remembered how the fight had ended. "Mostly by being cannon fodder."

"*Entirely* by being cannon fodder," Reuben corrected with a chuckle as he mimed someone panicking and flailing their arms. "'Ahh! How is The Dinner Party so amazing and we're so bad at everything? Run away!'"

"What happened here while we were gone? The place is looking more put together." Nacho's trained eyes were taking in every change, including a rubble pile and a fresh set of mortared bricks. "How many have signed up for the guild?"

Young Bill walked closer at that moment, looking disgusted. "If you must know, we all signed up. Look at your charter, local-tyrant-in-the-making. By the way, I'm not a fan of being called 'Young Bill'. It's insulting. You can call me 'Scrubz' from now on if you want, since I gave in to the peer pressure like all these other scrubz."

"Can do, Scrubz. Is that an upgrade, though? Insulting people, then adopting the name?" Nacho replied in a blasé tone. He turned his eyes from the disgruntled man to the Chips Stat Sheet. He was still new to it, but he managed to find the information he needed.

. . .

Chips Guild Stat Sheet
  Total Guild Credits: 2576 + 1500 contribution from various sources
  Total Number of Members: 189

Guild Leader: Eli 'Nacho' Naches
  Sub-Guild Leader: Daniel Chronour
  First Officer: Reuben Colby
  Current Membership Roster: Daniel Chronour, Rebecca Chronour,
Colleen Chronour, Taye Cunningham, Kristie Ford, Abigail James…

The names went on and on, but Nacho pointed out a startling discrepancy. "What's this extra fifteen hundred credits?"

Mayor Dan patted both Brie and Nacho on the back. "To thank you, a bunch of us wanted the guild to give you something special. Specifically, we want Nacho to have his kitchen. We know it'll be expensive, but you three saved us. Doesn't hurt that your food is the only luxury we have in this place."

Iron Becky nodded in agreement. "Nacho, cooking in the guildhall fireplace can't be comfortable, but we're not sure it's all you need. It's four hundred apiece for the stove and the oven, right?"

Nacho put her mind at ease with a shake of his head. "No, just two hundred each. Thank you-"

"You deserve that, and more," the gray-haired woman interrupted warmly. "Keep the extra. Maybe go for broke and get an *Epic* version? We want you to have the best kitchen possible. Let's go buy it and set it up right now."

"Let me think about what will benefit us the most." As the Guild Leader, Nacho wasn't going to use a single credit more than he truly needed. Every speck of income counted when it came to their survival. But… he was going to grab the oven, the stove, and… maybe also set up counters and shelves?

"I think starting tonight is a great idea, but I'm going to need some privacy as I figure out my kitchen." Nacho grabbed the mayor by the shoulder. "Can I talk to you really quick? I need your help with a… private matter."

Brie looked suspicious, and Reuben reached out for his friend as though he were leaving forever. "Nacho, this is our moment of triumph! We should spend it together. What's going on? Hey! Get back here!"

"Oh, calm down, I'll be back in just a few minutes!" Nacho grumbled at his over-dramatic friend. "Listen, Dan, I'll need a couple hours to butcher this cow, gotta keep it alive as long as possible while I process it, but then can I get your help with…"

———

That evening at sunset, the smell of steak was wafting through the air and creating a mouthwatering aroma. Almost everyone was packed inside the guildhall, waiting for the cook to announce that dinner was ready. When Nacho entered the dining room with the sizzling portions, there was nearly a riot. Luckily, Mayor Dan rose to his feet and shouted everyone down. "Chips! Can I have your attention, please!"

He had the charisma to quiet down the entire crowd, even the Bills, young and old, who scowled at the mayor with sour expressions on their faces: they just wanted to eat in peace. Nacho wondered how much of a problem they were going to be, but then again, having a dissenting opinion drew healthy debate. When too many people agreed on every subject, they tended to form a cult; not a proper society.

Once the room hushed, Mayor Dan cleared his throat. "As everyone knows, we're celebrating the end of the Bove! We also have to celebrate the start of the Chips Guild. We've made more on the dungeon dives in the past few days than we have in the almost two weeks we've been encamped on Armor Mountain. We have Nacho, Reuben, and Brie to thank for that. Stand up, you three!"

Nacho and his friends got together and waved. The room exploded with cheers and clapping—even the Bills and their contrary contingent applauded lightly. The mayor raised his hands, and silence slowly filled the area once more. "Now, many of you don't know this, but Reuben and Brie were set to get married on the day the Juxtaposition started. Rumor has it... Brie still has the dress."

"By the Patrons, we're *not* doing this right now!" She clapped her hands over her bright red face and backed up as though a wave of monsters were closing in on her location.

"Oh, yes we are!" Nacho snickered as he eased away from the table.

Reuben gave Nacho a long look and rapidly deduced Nacho's plan, bursting out with an exultant, "*You* planned this?"

"You know, a lot has changed in the last few weeks. Who knows if people still feel the same way they did at the start of all this...?" Nacho pointed at Brie, and Reuben's eyes snapped over to her searchingly. "Maybe you should ask her again?"

Reuben took off his janky leather helmet and dropped to one knee without another second of hesitation. "My love, I know it's the end of the world, and that the Juxtaposition might have some crazy rules for getting married... but I want to marry you, right here, right now. You still have the dress, and I've been carrying the tux. I'm pretty sure that Nacho and the mayor have located a minister for us."

"They did indeed!" A man rose from the bench and waved. "I'm a certified Kansas wedding officiant, and I'm ready if you two are."

"I will *always* marry you." A glistening tear tracked down Brie's face, and she stepped forward to pull Reuben to his feet. "Always and forever."

In the end, Reuben cleaned up using the water in Nacho's kitchen, while Brie ran off with Iron Becky to get dressed. The Healer gave himself a sponge bath out back, then put on the tux. Nacho helped with the tie, expertly tying a double Windsor knot that his friend would never be able to make himself.

Reuben grinned and pulled his friend into a hug. "Thanks for doing this, man. I appreciate it more than I can say."

Nacho patted his friend's face before pinching his cheek. "The Juxtaposition robbed you of your wedding. Let's steal it right back."

It was a quick ceremony, with Nacho and Reuben standing in front of everyone. Brie came in through the back door in her wedding dress with her hair fixed up, her makeup sparkling in the lantern light. She still held the Splatter Mallet, which somehow seemed to work with the wedding dress.

The classic vows were exchanged, in sickness and health, 'til death do they part.

The 'I dos' were followed by a lingering kiss. Nacho watched that kiss with a full heart. He wasn't sure if Kronos was on his side or not, but he'd been given a gift—not just in his understanding of the Juxtaposition, but in the glimpse of a life without his two best friends. It made being with them even more precious, because he knew what he was without them.

The dinner reception that followed was filled with laughter and cheers of celebration, and Nacho served the meal to everyone without asking for a single credit. The only option on the menu was fresh steak harvested from what Nacho could only assume was offspring of the Bove. He wasn't sure if it was just him, but he felt a deep sense of satisfaction at chowing down on the same type of creature that had haunted his nightmares for years.

The cook perked up as Reuben and Brie came over, finally ready to eat after dancing until the line was gone. Their eyes were sparkling, and the Berserker held out her plate. Nacho waved at the only food option, "For the bride and groom, may I recommend two choice cuts of Grilled Armageddon?"

ABOUT DAKOTA KROUT

Dakota Krout, a heartwarmingly clever author known for weaving fun, punny, and clean humor into his LitRPG fantasy novels, brings joy and laughter to readers through his best-selling series: including Cooking With Disaster, Divine Dungeon, Completionist Chronicles, and Full Murderhobo! His work, celebrated for its wit and charm, earned him a spot as one of Audible's top 5 fantasy picks in 2017, alongside a top 5 bestseller rank that was featured on the New York Times.

Drawing upon his experiences in the Army, Dakota expertly crafts vast, imaginative worlds with intricate systems that captivate and delight. His background in programming and information technology not only infuses his writing with a distinct, logical flair; but also fuels his innovative spirit in managing his publishing company, Mountaindale Press. These unique perspectives shine through in his stories, making him beloved by fans of all ages who seek a wholesome and humorous escape.

Dakota's journey in publishing has been filled with gratefulness, and a deep desire to continue bringing smiles and laughter to his readers. "I hope you Read Every Book With A Smile!" - Dakota Krout

Connect with Dakota:
MountaindalePress.com

Patreon.com/DakotaKrout
Facebook.com/DakotaKrout
Instagram.com/DakotaKrout
Twitter.com/DakotaKrout
Discord.gg/mdp

ABOUT MOUNTAINDALE PRESS

Dakota and Danielle Krout, a husband and wife team, strive to create as well as publish excellent fantasy and science fiction novels. Self-publishing *The Divine Dungeon: Dungeon Born* in 2016 transformed their careers from Dakota's military and programming background and Danielle's Ph.D. in pharmacology to President and CEO, respectively, of a small press. Their goal is to share their success with other authors and provide captivating fiction to readers with the purpose of solidifying Mountaindale Press as the place 'Where Fantasy Transforms Reality.'

Connect with Mountaindale Press:
MountaindalePress.com
Facebook.com/MountaindalePress
Twitter.com/_Mountaindale
Instagram.com/MountaindalePress

MOUNTAINDALE PRESS TITLES

GameLit and LitRPG

The Completionist Chronicles,
Cooking with Disaster,
The Divine Dungeon,
Full Murderhobo, and
Year of the Sword by Dakota Krout

A Touch of Power by Jay Boyce

Red Mage and
Farming Livia by Xander Boyce

Ether Collapse and
Ether Flows by Ryan DeBruyn

Unbound by Nicoli Gonnella

Threads of Fate by Michael Head

Lion's Lineage by Rohan Hublikar and Dakota Krout

Wolfman Warlock by James Hunter and Dakota Krout

Axe Druid,
Mephisto's Magic Online, and
High Table Hijinks by Christopher Johns

Dragon Core Chronicles by Lars Machmüller

Pixel Dust and
Necrotic Apocalypse by David Petrie

Viceroy's Pride and
Tower of Somnus by Cale Plamann

Henchman by Carl Stubblefield

Artorian's Archives by Dennis Vanderkerken and Dakota Krout

Made in the USA
Las Vegas, NV
03 May 2024

89477072R00268